CRUEL ACTS

Jane Casey is no stranger to the crime world. Married to a criminal barrister, she's got the inside track on some of the country's most dangerous offenders, giving her writing an unsettlingly realistic feel.

This authenticity has made her novels international bestsellers and critical successes. They have been nominated for several awards and in 2015 Jane won both the Mary Higgins Clark Award and Irish Crime Novel of the Year for *The Stranger You Know* and *After the Fire*, respectively. She is also an active member of Killer Women, a London-based group of crime writers.

Born in Dublin, Jane now lives in southwest London with her husband and two children.

🐦 @JaneCaseyAuthor

Also by Jane Casey

THE MAEVE KERRIGAN SERIES
The Burning
The Reckoning
The Last Girl
The Stranger You Know
The Kill
After the Fire
Let the Dead Speak

STANDALONE NOVELS
The Missing

CRUEL ACTS

JANE CASEY

HarperCollins*Publishers*

HarperCollins*Publishers* Ltd
1 London Bridge Street,
London SE1 9GF

www.harpercollins.co.uk

First published by HarperCollins*Publishers* 2019
2

A catalogue record for this book is available from the British Library

ISBN: 978-0-00-814903-1 (HB)
ISBN: 978-0-00-814904-8 (TPB)

Typeset in Sabon LT Std by Palimpsest Book Production Ltd,
Falkirk, Stirlingshire

Printed and bound in the UK by
CPI Group (UK) Ltd, Croydon, CR0 4YY

For Sinéad and Liz,
my wise women

The investigator should pursue all reasonable lines of enquiry, whether these point towards or away from the suspect.

Code of Practice for Investigators

1

The house was dark. PC Sandra West stared up at it and sighed. The neighbours had called the police – she checked her watch – getting on for an hour earlier, to complain about the noise. What noise, the operator asked.

Screaming.

An argument?

More than likely. It's not fair, the neighbour had said. Not at two in the morning. But what would you expect from people like that?

People like what?

A check on the address had told Sandra exactly what kind of people they were: argumentative drunks. She'd never been there before but other officers had, often, trying to persuade one or other of them to leave the house, to leave each other alone, for everyone's sake. It was depressing how often she encountered couples who had no business being together but who insisted, through screaming rows and bruises and broken teeth, that they loved each other. Sandra was forty-six, single and likely to remain so, given her job (which was a passion-killer, never mind what they said about uniforms) and her looks (nothing special, her father had told her once). Generally, she didn't mind. It was peaceful being on her own. She could do what she wanted, when she wanted.

Sandra had a look in the boot of the police car and found a stab vest. Slowly, fumbling, she hauled it around her and did it up. It was stiff and awkward, made to fit someone much taller than Sandra. Still, it was in the car for a reason. She walked up the path to the front door. Everything was quiet. Hushed.

Maybe one of them had taken the hint and left before the busies arrived. Sandra shone her torch over the window at the unhelpful curtains, then bent and looked through the letterbox. A dark hallway stretched back to the kitchen door. It was quiet and still.

A screaming argument that ended with everyone tucked up in bed an hour later? Not in Sandra's experience. She planted her feet wide apart, knowing that she had enough bulk in her stab vest and overcoat to intimidate anyone who might need it. Then she rapped on the door with the end of her torch.

'Police. Can you open the door, please?'

Silence.

She knocked again, louder, and checked her watch. God, nights were hard work. It was the boredom that wore you down, that and the creeping exhaustion that was difficult to ignore when you weren't busy. She wasn't usually single-crewed but some of her rota were off sick. She never got sick. It was something she took for granted – the colds and viruses and stomach bugs all passed her by. It made her wonder if everyone else was really sick or if they were faking, and whether she was stupid not to do the same. She tried to suppress a yawn with an effort that made her jaw creak. It was tempting to call it in as an LOB. Sandra smiled to herself. It wasn't what they taught you at Hendon, but every police officer knew what it stood for: Load of Bollocks. Then she could get back into the car and go in search of refs. She hadn't eaten for hours, her stomach hollow from it. Knowing her luck, she'd be about to bite into what passed for dinner and her radio would come to life.

The trouble was, there was a kid in the house. You couldn't just walk away without finding out if the kid was safe. Not when there was a history of domestic violence and social services being involved. Chaotic was the word for it: not enough food in the house, patchy attendance at school, the boy needing clean clothes and haircuts and a good bath. How could you have a kid and not take responsibility for him? OK, Sandra's parents had been short on hugs and they hadn't had a lot of money to spend on her and her brothers, but they'd been reliable and she'd never once gone hungry. Nothing to complain about, even if she had complained at the time.

She bent down again and peered through the letterbox, moving the torch slowly across the narrow field of view this time. It cast stark shadows in the kitchen and across the stairs. But there was something . . . she squinted and changed the angle of the torch, trying to see. There, on the bottom step: light on metal. And again, two steps up. And again, three steps above that.

Knives. Kitchen knives.

They were stuck into the wood of the stairs, point first. All the way up, into the darkness at the top.

Sandra wasn't an imaginative person but she had an overwhelming sense of fear all of a sudden, and she wasn't sure if it was her own or someone else's.

'Hello? Can you hear me? Open the door, please, love. I need to check you're all right.'

Silence.

Oh shit, Sandra thought, but not for her own sake, despite being scared at the thought of what might confront her inside the house. *Oh shit something very bad has happened here. Oh shit we probably can't make this one right. Oh shit we should have come out a lot sooner.*

Oh shit.

3

She got on her radio and asked for back-up.

'With you in two minutes,' the dispatcher said, and Sandra thought about two minutes and how long that might be if you were scared, if you were dying. She'd asked for paramedics too, hoping they'd be needed.

The second police car came with two large constables, one of whom put the door in for her. His colleague went past him at speed, checking the rooms on the ground floor.

'Clear.'

Sandra was halfway up the stairs, listening to her heart and every creak from the bare boards. The torch was slick in her hand.

'Hello? Anyone here?'

The thunder of police boots on the steps behind her drowned out any sounds she might have heard. Bathroom: filthy in the jumping light from her torch, but no one hiding. A bedroom, piled high with rubbish and dirty clothes. No bed, but there was a pile of blankets on the floor, like a nest. A second bedroom was at the front of the house. It was marginally tidier than the other one, mainly because there was almost no furniture in it apart from a mattress on the floor. Shoes were lined up neatly in one corner and a collection of toiletries stood in another.

The woman was lying across the mattress, half hanging off the edge, a filthy blanket draped across her. Her head was thrown back. Dead, Sandra thought hopelessly, and made herself smile at the small boy who crouched beside the body.

'Hello, you. We're the police. Are you all right?'

He was small and dark, his hair hanging over his eyes. He blinked in the light, his eyes darting from her to the officer behind her. He wasn't crying, and that was somehow worse than if he'd been sobbing. Sandra was bad at guessing children's ages but she thought he could be eight or nine.

'What's your name?'

Instead of answering he huddled closer to the woman. He

4

had pulled one bruised arm so it went around him. It reminded Sandra of an orphaned monkey clinging to a cuddly toy.

'Can I come a bit closer? I need to check if this lady is all right.'

No reaction. He was staring past her at the officer behind her. She waved a hand behind her back. *Give me some room.*

'Is this your mummy?' she whispered.

A nod.

'Is your daddy here?'

He mouthed a word. *No.* That was good news, Sandra thought.

'Was he here earlier?'

Another nod.

Sandra inched forward. 'Did you put that blanket over your mummy?'

'Keep her warm.' His voice was hoarse.

'Good lad. Good idea. And you put something under her head.'

'Coat.'

'Brilliant. Can I just check to see if she's all right?' Sandra stretched out a gloved hand and touched the woman's ankle. Her skin was blue in the light of the torch, and even through the latex her skin felt cold.

'He hurt her.'

'Who did, darling? Your dad?'

The boy blinked at her. After a long moment, he shook his head slowly, definitely. It would be someone else's job to find out who had done it, Sandra thought, and was glad it wasn't her responsibility. The closer she got to the woman on the mattress, the more she could see the damage he'd done to her. And the boy had watched the whole thing, she thought.

'All right. We'll help her, shall we?'

His huge, serious eyes were fixed on Sandra's. She wasn't usually sentimental, but a sob swelled up from deep in her

5

chest and burst out of her mouth before she could stop it. She held out her arms. 'Come here, little one.'

He shrank into himself, turning away from her towards his mother. Too much, too soon. She bit her lip. The sound of low voices came from the hall: the paramedics at long last.

'I'm sorry, but you can't stay here. We've got an ambulance for your mummy. We need to let the ambulance men look after her.'

'I want to stay. I want to help.'

'But you can't.'

The boy gave a long, hostile hiss, a sound that made Sandra catch her breath. The paramedics crashed into the room, carrying their equipment, and shoved her out of the way. She leaned against the wall as they bent over the figure on the mattress. It was as if Sandra had come down with a sudden, terrible illness: her stomach churned and there was a foul taste in her mouth. A cramp caught at her guts but she couldn't go, not in the filthy bathroom, not in what was going to be a crime scene. She clenched her teeth and prayed, and eventually the pain slackened. A greasy film of sweat coated her limbs. She lifted a hand to her head and let it fall again. What was wrong with her?

The boy had scrambled back when the paramedics crashed into the room. He crouched in the corner of the room among the shoes, those round solemn eyes taking everything in. Sandra watched him watching the men work on his mother's body, and she shivered without knowing why.

2

It was a day like any other; it was a day like they all were inside. Time pulled that trick of dragging and passing too quickly and all that happened was that he was a day further into forever.

He sat on his own, in silence, because he'd been allocated a cell to himself. It was for his protection and because no one wanted to share with him. He wasn't the only murderer on the wing – far from it – but he was notorious, all the same.

That wasn't why no one wanted to share with him. His health wasn't good, a cough rattling in his chest all night long. That was more of a problem than the killing, he thought. But he'd taken his share of abuse for the murders, all the same. No one liked his kind.

He shifted his weight in the cheap wooden-framed armchair, feeling it creak under him. He had never been a fat man but prison had pared away at his flesh, carving out the shadow of his bones on his face.

The room was fitted out like a cheap hostel – a rickety wardrobe, a small single bed, a desk against the wall. There were limp, yellow curtains at the window. At a glance you might not notice the bars across the same window, or the stainless steel sink, or the toilet that was behind a low partition.

That was one good thing about being on his own. He'd shared cells before, when he was younger. You never got used to the smell of another man's shit. Of all the smells in the prison – and there were many – that was the worst.

He picked up the envelope that he'd left lying on his desk. It was open. A screw would have read it before he ever saw it. That was standard. Small writing, black ink. He wasn't used to seeing it: his name in that writing. He turned it over a couple of times. Nothing important in it or he'd never have seen it. But no one writes a letter without saying *something*, even if they don't mean to say anything at all.

He ripped the envelope getting the letter out of it. The paper was flimsy, the words on the other side bleeding through. He wasn't a great reader at the best of times. His eyes tracked down the centre of the page, the scrawl transforming itself into phrases here and there. *Don't forget we're all trying . . . I know you can . . . easy for me to say . . . coming to see you . . . your appeal . . . lose heart . . . forget what happened . . . start again . . . have hope . . . your son.*

'Fuck you.' It was a whisper, inaudible above the banging and shouting and echoing madness of a prison in the daytime. With a wince, he got to his feet and crossed to the toilet. He stood over it, tearing the letter in half and half again, ripping the paper until it was a handful of confetti. He dropped it into the bowl. He'd imagined the ink would run but it didn't. The paper sat on the surface of the water, the black writing burning itself onto his retinas. He pissed on it in a stop-start trickling stream, annoyed by that as much as the way the paper stuck damply to the sides of the toilet. He flushed, and waited, and grimaced at the scattered, dancing fragments that remained in the water.

He had a whole life sentence stretching ahead of him but that wasn't what made him bitter.

If by some miracle he got out, he would never be free.

3

The lift doors closed and I shut my eyes, then forced them
open again. It took about half a minute to go from the ground
floor to our office: thirty seconds wasn't quite long enough
for a cat nap, even for me. The weight of the box I was
carrying pulled at the muscles in my shoulders and arms but
that was fine; it distracted me from the wholly unpleasant
sensation of mud-soaked boots and trouser legs. I didn't need
to glance in the lift's mirror to see how bedraggled I was after
a long night and a cold morning at a crime scene in a bleak,
muddy yard. I only had to look to my left, where Detective
Constable Georgia Shaw was hunched inside a coat that was
as saturated as mine. Her usually immaculate fair hair hung
around her face in tails. Like me, she was holding a heavy
cardboard box filled with evidence bags and notes.

'We drop this stuff off. We do our paperwork.' I paused to
cough: the chill of the night had sunk into my chest. 'We finish
up and we go home.'

Georgia nodded, not looking at me.

'Nothing else. Home, hot baths, clean clothes, get some
sleep.'

Another nod.

'If anyone manages to track down Mick Forbes and he

gets arrested we'll have to come back to interview him.' Mick Forbes, a scaffolder in his fifties, the chief and only suspect in the murder of his best friend, Sammy Clarke, who had been battered to death in the muddy yard where we'd spent the night.

Georgia sniffed.

'So get some rest while you can.'

'OK.' Her voice was a whisper.

The lift doors opened and I strode out, trying to look as if it was normal for my feet to squelch as I walked through the double-doors into the office. *Head high, Maeve.*

A quick scan of the room was reassuring: a handful of colleagues, mostly concentrating on their work or on the phone. A few raised eyebrows greeted me. An actual laugh came from Liv Bowen, my best friend on the murder investigation team, who bit her lip and dragged her face into a serious expression when I glowered at her. But for a brief moment, I allowed myself to feel relieved. I'd got away with it this time. I'd rush through the paperwork and then escape, unseen by—

DCI Una Burt opened the door of her office. 'Maeve? In here. Now.'

I stopped, caught in the no man's land between her door and my desk. Common sense dictated I should put the box down rather than carrying it into her office, but that meant leaving my evidence unattended. 'Ma'am, I'll be with you in a minute—'

'Right now.' The edge in her voice was serrated with irritation and something more unsettling. The box could come with me, I decided, and trudged through the desks to Burt's office.

My first impression was that it was full of people. My second was that I would rather have been just about anywhere else at that moment, for a number of reasons. The pathologist Dr Early sat in a chair by the desk, tapping her fingers on a cardboard folder that was on her knee. She was young and thin and intense, rarely smiling – which I suppose wasn't all that surprising, given her job. Today she looked grimmer than usual. Standing beside her, to my complete surprise, was a man who was tall, silver-haired and catch-your-breath handsome. My actual boss, although he was currently supposed to be on leave: Superintendent Charles Godley.

'Sir.'

'Maeve.' He smiled at me with genuine warmth as I put the box down at my feet. 'You look as if you had an interesting night.'

'Not the first time she's heard that. But I'll give you this, Kerrigan, you don't usually look as if you spent the night in a sewer.' The inevitable drawl came from the windowsill where a dark-suited man lounged, his arms folded, his legs stretched out in front of him so they took up most of the room. Detective Inspector Josh Derwent, the very person I had been hoping to avoid. I could feel his eyes on me but I wouldn't give him the satisfaction of reacting. Instead I smiled back at Godley.

'It wasn't the most pleasant crime scene, but I'll live. It's good to see you, sir.'

'You too.'

'Are you coming back to us?' I had sounded over-enthusiastic, I thought, and felt the heat rising to my face. Una Burt wouldn't like it if I was too keen to see Godley return. She had only been a caretaker, though, standing in for him while he was away on leave.

'Not quite. Not yet.' The smile faded from his face. 'I'm here for another reason. I've got a job for you.'

'For me?'

'For you and Josh.' Una bustled around to sit behind her desk, pausing until Derwent moved his feet out of her way. She sat down, pulling her chair in and leaning her elbows on the desk – the desk she had inherited from Godley. He was much too polite to react, although I knew he would have

11

recognised it as her marking her territory. Currently, he was a visitor in her office and she wanted him to know it.

'What sort of job?' I asked, wary.

'Leo Stone,' Godley said. 'Our latest miscarriage of justice.'

I frowned, trying to place the name. 'I don't think I know—'

'Yeah, you do.' Derwent's voice was soft. 'The White Knight.'

That sounded more familiar to me. Before I'd run the reference to earth, though, Godley snapped, 'I don't like that name. I don't like glamorising murder. We're not tabloid journalists so there's no need to use their language.'

Derwent shrugged, not noticeably abashed. Before he could say something unforgivable and career-threatening, I spoke up.

'You said a miscarriage of justice.' I didn't know why I was distracting Godley from Derwent. If the situation were reversed he would sit back and enjoy my discomfort. 'What's happened?'

'He was convicted last year, in October. He's been in prison for thirteen months now. One of the jurors in his trial has spent that time writing a book about the experience, and self-published it without running it past a lawyer. In it, he happens to mention how he and another juror looked up Stone on the internet, against the judge's specific instructions, during the trial.' Anger made Godley's voice clipped, the words snapped off at the end. 'They discovered Stone's previous convictions for violence and told all the other jurors about it.'

'I think my favourite line is, "We left the court to discuss the evidence we'd heard, but it was just a pretence. We had already decided he was guilty, because of what we'd found out for ourselves."' Burt leaned back in her chair. 'Exactly what you don't want a jury to say. But instead of making his fortune selling his book, he's earned himself a two-month sentence for contempt of court.'

'So Stone's appealing.' It wasn't a question: there wasn't a defence lawyer in the world who would let an opportunity like that slip through their fingers.

12

'He is. At the end of this week. And the appeal will be granted,' Godley said.

'Right.' Lack of sleep was making my head feel woolly. 'Well, there'll be a retrial. The problem was with the jury, not the evidence.'

'There should be a retrial. But that's the issue I have.' Godley looked at me, his eyes even bluer than I'd remembered. 'What do you know about the case?'

'A little. Not much more than I read in the papers.' I tried to remember the details I'd gleaned. 'They called him the White Knight because he seemed to be rescuing his victims. He kidnapped them and killed them, either immediately or later. By the time we found the bodies they were too decomposed to tell us much about what he'd done.'

He nodded. 'We only found two bodies but we're fairly sure there's at least one more victim. I wouldn't be surprised if there were more out there. He was a nasty piece of work. He was abusive in his relationships, he had convictions for fraud, burglary and theft, and he had a lengthy history of violence towards strangers, as the jury found out.'

'When is he supposed to have started killing?' I asked.

'He got out of prison three years ago after serving five years for burglary. The first murder was a month later – a woman named Sara Grey. It was opportunist. Impulsive. I don't believe he planned it particularly well but it worked so he tried it again.' Godley folded his arms. 'Don't be misled by the nickname. He was a murderer, plain and simple, but they had to try and make him into something more exciting. They twisted the facts because they wanted to sell newspapers, not because it was true. He saw his opportunity to kidnap women and he took advantage of that. Three women disappeared in similar circumstances, but he was only charged with killing Sara Grey and Willa Howard. And he was convicted.'

'OK.' I was trying to read Godley's expression. 'But why

13

does that involve us? It was Paul Whitlock's team who investigated the killings, wasn't it?'

'It was, and he did a good job. But Glen Hanshaw was the pathologist who did the post-mortems.'

'Oh.' I didn't need to say any more. I understood the problem now. Glen Hanshaw had been a good friend of Godley's. He had clung on to his job despite the ravages of cancer, right up to the end. I was starting to see why Godley was so upset.

'There have been two acquittals in murder trials since he died, largely because he wasn't there to defend his findings.'

'And because his findings were shaky,' Dr Early said. She glanced up at Godley, her face set. 'He was a fine pathologist but he started making mistakes in the months before he died and he wouldn't accept that his judgement was impaired.'

'The pain medication affected him,' Godley said. 'He wanted to work – it was the only thing that mattered to him. But he needed to be dosed up to be able to do the job.'

'He should have known better than to persevere. It was self-indulgent.' It was professionalism that made Dr Early sound so severe. I knew she had done her utmost to help and support Dr Hanshaw, and that she had mourned him as a mentor, if not a friend. Glen Hanshaw had been a short-tempered misogynist and I'd never really understood Godley's fondness for him.

Now the superintendent sighed. 'Whether he should have been working or not, he's become a target for defence lawyers. If he was involved in a case, you can expect the evidence he gathered to be challenged. And in the case of Leo Stone, the defence team are going to be looking for anything they can throw at the new jury to distract them from Stone's guilt.'

'The trouble with retrials,' Derwent said, 'is that they've heard all the best lines already. If you go back with exactly the same case and run it the same way, the defence know what to expect.'

'Which is where you come in,' Godley said. 'I want to put a stop to the attacks on Glen's reputation and his work. Dr Early has agreed to review his cases going back to before his diagnosis, and specifically his work on Leo Stone's prosecution. In the meantime, I don't want any cases to collapse purely because of his involvement. His reputation matters, and not just because he's not here to defend himself. If all his decision-making is called into question we are going to see a torrent of appeals, especially from prisoners with whole-life tariffs.'

'The worst of the worst,' Una Burt said. 'And they have nothing better to do than look for grounds to appeal. They're in for life; they don't have anything to lose.'

Godley turned to me. 'Maeve, I want you and Josh to look at the case against Stone. Start from scratch: witnesses, families, the works. I'll arrange a meeting with Paul Whitlock.'

'He's going to be pleased,' Derwent observed. 'Nothing like having another team come and take over your case.'

'He'll be professional about it,' Godley said sharply. 'He'll understand why I don't want to take any chances. Whitlock's priority, and mine, is making sure that the right man is in prison for the murders of Sara Grey and Willa Howard. If that man is Leo Stone, I want him off the streets and behind bars.'

'So don't wind them up, Josh.' Una Burt leaned all the way back in her chair, acting casual although her eyes were bright.

Derwent looked hurt. 'Why single me out?'

'Because I trust Maeve to behave herself.' *And I don't trust you.* She didn't need to say it out loud. I suppressed a wince. Burt didn't like Derwent, but I was the one who'd suffer for it.

'Josh, I want you working on this case because I know you'll do a good job. But Una is right. This is a high-profile investigation and you will be under scrutiny. It's worth bearing that in mind from the start.' There it was: the smooth diplomacy

I'd missed so much from Godley. Derwent subsided, placated, and yet, from the satisfied expression on her face, Una Burt seemed to feel as if she'd won too. I had missed Godley more than I realised.

'Can Georgia finish up on your case from last night?' Burt asked me.

'She should be able to handle it. We don't have anyone in custody yet.'

'I'll get someone to take over as OIC.' Burt squinted through the window that gave her a view of the office. 'Chris Pettifer doesn't look too busy.'

I didn't want her to get someone else to take over – it was *my* case after all – but I knew that it was pointless to protest when DCI Burt had made up her mind. I made my face blank and nodded when Burt told me to brief Pettifer on the case before I went home.

'You can take the files on the Stone case. Get your head around it before tomorrow.'

Or I could sleep, I thought, since I hadn't for twenty-four hours. I could have a long bath and a decent meal and sleep.

'Fine,' I said.

Derwent stood up and stretched. 'That's useful. You do the reading, Kerrigan, and you can give me the highlights tomorrow.'

'Why can't you read up on it yourself?' The question slipped out before I thought about whether it was appropriate for me, a detective sergeant, to ask a detective inspector why he wasn't doing his job.

'I'm busy,' Derwent said coldly.

'Right,' I said under my breath, and bent down to pick up the box at my feet. Godley opened the door for me. Because I was tired and not really paying attention I started to move towards it at the precise moment when Derwent was walking past, and collided with him. I stepped back, horrified. He looked down at his shirtfront where a long black streak of mud had suddenly appeared on the immaculate white cotton.

'Kerrigan.'

'It was an accident,' I said quickly.

He gave me the kind of look that he usually reserved for child-killers at the very least, and for a beat I held my breath. Then he lifted the box out of my hands as if it weighed nothing and walked away.

'I can manage,' I said to his retreating back, futilely.

'Thank you, Maeve,' Una Burt said from behind her desk, and I remembered where I was, and left her to her discussions with Godley and the pathologist.

4

Derwent was always a fast mover. By the time I made it out of Una Burt's office, he was already on the other side of the room, well out of reach. He set the box down beside Pettifer's desk with a remark that made the big DS throw his head back and laugh. I started towards them – it was still my case to hand over, I thought with a shiver of irritation – and checked myself as Georgia stepped into my path. She had found a hairbrush and cleaned herself up a bit. She'd managed to find the time to reapply her mascara, I noted.

'What was that about?' She nodded towards the office behind me. 'Is that Superintendent Godley?'

'Yeah.' Of course Georgia would have spotted him. She had an extraordinary instinct for career advancement.

'What's he doing here?'

'He had a job for me.'

'Can I help?'

I raised my eyebrows. 'You don't even know what it is.'

'So?' Georgia's blue eyes were unblinking. I could see it from her point of view: a chance to impress the boss before he came back to the team. Get a head start. Make progress.

'I'm not in charge of this one.'

'Who is? DI Derwent?' She swung round, looking for him.

'You're going to be working with Pettifer on the Clarke case,' I said firmly. 'Once that's out of the way, we might be able to use you. But at the moment—'

She pulled a face, obviously annoyed. 'Pettifer can finish the Clarke case on his own.'

'He could, but he isn't going to.' I stared her down for a long moment, daring her to take it further, and in the end she broke first.

'So what's the case?'

'Reinvestigating—' I broke off to cough. 'Reinvestigating the Leo Stone case.'

'The White Knight? Wow. I would love to work on that.'

'Noted.' There was nothing to encourage her in my tone of voice.

'Why did Superintendent Godley want you to work on it?' Her eyes were narrow.

Derwent leaned in between us. 'Because he has a soft spot for Kerrigan.' Georgia laughed.

'Because he thinks I'll do a good job,' I said stiffly.

'Of course you will.' Derwent patted my arm.

Instead of arguing the point I walked away from both of them to talk to Pettifer myself. Georgia could try to convince Derwent to let her work on it too. If he wanted her, he'd include her in spite of my objections. If he didn't want her help, nothing I could say would persuade him. Either way, I didn't need to hang around.

He caught up with me in the kitchen where I was waiting for the kettle to boil.

'What's up with you?'

'Nothing.' I coughed again. Shit, I didn't want to be ill. 'I'm tired. I'm cold. I want to go home.'

'*My* home.'

'I'm renting it. That means it's my home. Temporarily, anyway.' I still wasn't used to living in a space that I associated so completely with Derwent. For instance, I'd discovered there was no bleach strong enough to take away the mental image of him lounging in the bath.

'As long as you're looking after it.'

'Yeah, I don't want to piss off the landlord.'

'Oh, you've done that already. Look at me.'

I did, reluctantly. He was holding the sides of his jacket open so I could see the muddy mark that ran across his chest. Not just the shirt: the tie too. 'I said I was sorry.'

'No, you said it was an accident.'

'Well, it was.' I took a deep breath. 'But I'm sorry.'

'Finally. You're forgetting your manners.'

'Speaking of which, I could manage the box by myself. You didn't even ask before you took it.'

His eyebrows went up. 'Don't try to pretend that's why you're in a mood.'

'I'm not in a mood.' I turned and leaned against the kitchen counter, gripping it for courage. 'I am very annoyed that you decided to stir up trouble by hinting that Godley wanted me to work on this case for any other reason than that he thinks I'm a good detective. You of all people know how unfair it is to suggest he puts professional opportunities my way for personal reasons.'

Derwent gave me his stoniest look. 'That's not what I did.'

'Isn't it?'

'No.'

'Saying he had a soft spot for me?'

'It's banter.'

'It needs to stop. It's not a joke. Someone like Georgia who doesn't know any better will take it seriously, and I've had enough of it. You know it's not true and you know there are a lot of people who'd like to believe that it is.'

'You can't live your life worrying about what other people think.'

'Spoken like someone who doesn't ever have to worry about it.'

20

'*You* don't have to. That's my point. You're choosing to care.' He shrugged. 'These people aren't worth getting upset about. If they want to think the worst of you, they will, whether I say anything or not.'

'Maybe, but you don't have to throw fuel on the fire.' Frustration was a knot in my stomach. It was impossible to explain how I felt to Derwent, and he didn't have the imagination to put himself in my shoes. The gulf between his life and mine was unbridgeable. 'You have no idea what it's like to have to prove yourself over and over again,' I said at last.

He rolled his eyes. 'I have a fair idea.'

'Because I've told you before. And yet, here we are, having the same conversation all over again.' I turned away from him and squashed the teabag against the side of the mug, viciously. When I flicked the teabag at the bin I had the very small satisfaction that it went in first try.

'I'll keep it in mind,' Derwent said at last. He almost sounded sincere. He would never admit he had been wrong, though, and nor would he apologise.

'Thanks for being so understanding.' I poured the milk into my tea and watched little white specks bob to the surface. 'Oh, for *fuck's* sake, who puts gone-off milk back in the fridge?'

'Poor Kerrigan. It's not your day,' Derwent said, and left, whistling as he went.

I leaned against the wall, defeated. I was tired and cold and fed up. All I'd wanted was a hot bath, a good meal and an early night. Instead I had nothing to look forward to but a long evening on my own, reading about someone else's investigation and some very dead women. Not my day, not my week, not my year.

5

I had read the files and looked at the photographs until my eyes burned; I had watched the CCTV that the first investigation had painstakingly located and analysed. I knew the circumstances of Sara Grey's disappearance inside out. Still, as Derwent drove down the Westway, I felt my pulse getting faster. Sara Grey. Victim one, chronologically.

'Bloemfontein Road is coming up on the left. Not this one, the one after.'

Derwent slowed to make the turn.

'This was where the tyre gave up.'

'Puncture?'

I nodded. 'They never worked out where she picked up the nail. There was nothing forensically interesting about it. Probably bad luck rather than Leo Stone's planning. We have CCTV of her here, turning into Bloemfontein Road.'

'Tell me about her.'

'Sara Grey was twenty-nine at the time of her disappearance. She was engaged to Tom Mitchell, who was the same age as her. She was a primary school teacher; he had his own property development company.'

'Did they ever check to see if he had employed Leo Stone?'

'I didn't see anything about it in the files.' I scrawled a

22

note to myself to look into it. 'He was in Latvia on a stag weekend when it happened. Otherwise he'd have been suspect number one.'

'Being out of the country doesn't let him off the hook as far as I'm concerned. It's a bit too convenient.'

'Poor guy. If he'd been in the UK you'd be even more convinced he was involved.'

'It's always the husband. Or the fiancé. Or the boyfriend. Or the ex.'

'Not this time. The original investigation focused on Tom, though, before her disappearance was linked to the others. They were looking for money worries or secret affairs or any kind of motive. They didn't find anything.'

Derwent grunted, not convinced.

I leafed through my notes. 'There was nothing to say Sara was being stalked – no concerns for her safety, no threats. On the day she disappeared no one was following her – at least as far as the investigators could determine.'

Derwent had slowed down to a crawl, creeping down Bloemfontein Road. 'So what happened then?'

'She parked just where that Volvo is. It was eleven at night but it was a Saturday, a summer night. There was a lot of traffic on the main road and there were people around. It was a warm evening – there'd been thunderstorms earlier but it was clearing up. When she got out of her car, she was seven hundred and eighty yards away from her home at 37 Haddaway Road.'

Today the light was flat, the clouds brooding over our heads. It was hard to imagine the street wrapped in the dark heat of a humid summer night.

Derwent pulled in a few cars ahead of the Volvo and parked. 'Then what?'

'Then she sent a text message to her fiancé telling him what had happened.' I flipped to the relevant page and read it out. 'Flat tyre!!! I don't know what to do.'

'The poor bloke was in Latvia. How was he supposed to come to the rescue?'

'She probably just wanted to tell someone what had happened.'

'No, she wanted to make him feel guilty for being off on a stag weekend instead of here.'

I raised my eyebrows at him. 'That's a very jaundiced view, even for you.'

'She was high maintenance. I have limited patience for that.'

Melissa, Derwent's girlfriend, was not the sort of person who would be low maintenance. If it had been anyone else I might have said as much, but Derwent had made it clear time and time again that while my personal life was endlessly entertaining, his was not available for discussion. Beside me, Derwent drummed his fingers on the steering wheel, as if he knew what I was thinking. 'Then what happened?'

'He replied: "Oh shit. Where r u? How bad is it? Driveable?" Obviously it wasn't. She checked their AA membership and discovered it had lapsed so she decided to walk home. She sent him a message to that effect at 23.15.' I showed Derwent the relevant page.

I can't drive it. Left the car on Bloem Rd and I'm walking home. You can sort it out when you get back tomorrow. ☺ <3 <3

Derwent grimaced. 'Something for him to look forward to.'

'He replied, "Typical! Call me when you get in."' I flipped the page. 'According to this, "No further calls were made or received from Miss Grey's phone and no further messages were sent by her. Mr Mitchell did not hear from his fiancée again after the message sent at 23.14. Cell site analysis revealed the phone remained switched on for a further twenty minutes, at which point it was powered down. Mr Mitchell informed

24

police that it was highly unusual for Miss Grey to turn her phone off."'

Derwent peered out of the car. 'It looks like a safe enough area.'

'It is. And they'd lived here for a year. She knew exactly where she was and she knew the quickest way home was going to be on foot.'

'She should have been safe here.' After a moment, he focused on me again. 'So what route did she take?'

'We don't know.' I pulled out a map I'd printed off. 'This is Haddaway Road where she was heading. The direct route is along this road here, Haigh Road, leading into Radcliffe Road.'

'Any reason to think she didn't go that way?'

'A bit of her mobile phone handset was found on Radcliffe Road in a hedge.'

'OK. Sounds promising.'

I flattened the map out and pointed to a star I'd drawn. 'It was here. Quite a long way from the path. I wonder if it was thrown out of a moving vehicle.'

'What makes you say that?'

'This sighting of a couple arguing.' I leafed through the file and pulled out the witness statement. 'The witness was a Mrs Hamilton. She lives on Cordray Road, here.' I showed him where it was on the map. 'She was driving home and happened to glance along a side street in this area – she couldn't be specific about which street it was but it was somewhere off Simpson Road.'

Simpson Road was about a quarter of a mile south of Haigh Road. 'That's way off the route she should have been taking,' Derwent said.

'Exactly. It was around the right time though. The investigators spent a lot of time trying to get Mrs Hamilton to remember anything else but she wasn't a great witness, reading between the lines. She got more and more confused and in

25

the end she said she couldn't be sure of anything she'd told them. She withdrew her statement.'

Derwent groaned. 'Good work, lads.'

'It was a dark night, she was driving, she glanced down a side street and sort of saw two people who might have been arguing. It wasn't going to make or break the case even if she remembered every detail.'

'What did she say about the man?'

'Nothing. He was standing behind a white van. She didn't see more than the back of his head.'

'Leo Stone's pretty distinctive. He's tall, for one thing. She'd have noticed that, surely.'

'She said not. All she could say was that he was taller than the woman.'

'How tall was Sara Grey?'

'Five two.'

'Right, so my nan would be taller than her.'

'Yeah. It wasn't altogether helpful testimony. Wrong place, right time, few details.' I tapped my pen on the map. 'The van, though.'

'I like the van.'

'We all like the van. It's one of the only points of comparison we've got, apart from where the body ended up and how it was left, and that's Dr Hanshaw's territory.' I didn't need to say the rest because Derwent knew as well as I did that if that was called into question, we could lose Sara Grey altogether. The pathologist's evidence was a big part of what had put Leo Stone behind bars. Without it, he could walk for good.

Derwent opened his door. 'Let's follow her route. Work out the timings. What time did Mrs Hamilton see the arguing couple?'

'Half past eleven.'

'So how long did she have to get there?'

'Fifteen minutes or so.'

26

He looked me up and down. 'Your legs are about twice as long as Sara Grey's. You'll have to take baby steps.'

Even with Derwent slowing me down ('Oi, giraffe, put the brakes on') it was possible to walk as far as Simpson Road in fifteen minutes. The area was middle-class, quiet, the houses well kept. It had been two and a half years since Sara Grey disappeared and there was no point in looking for evidence but I imagined her walking home, moving fast, her head down, and I wondered how she could have ended up so far off course. For once, Derwent was thinking the same as me.

'Why would you go this way?' He pulled the map out of my hand and studied it, frowning. 'If we assume Mrs H was right about what she saw.'

'These are busier roads than the direct route. Maybe she wanted to stay where there were more people around. Alternatively, something was making her uneasy. If someone was following her, she might have taken a different route home, trying to shake them off.'

'Wouldn't she have wanted to go straight home? Get indoors where she was safe?'

'Not if she was concerned about them knowing where she lived. She'd never feel safe again if she led them to her door, even if she made it inside without coming to grief.'

Derwent shook his head and walked away.

'What?'

'Just . . .' He swung back to face me. 'What a way to live, that's all. Working out what risks to take. Who to trust. Walking fifteen minutes out of your way to give yourself a better chance of making it home in one piece.'

'That's life, isn't it? What's the alternative? Staying at home?'

'Maybe.'

'You're not serious.' I folded my arms. 'If anyone should stay at home, it's men. They're the ones who cause most of the trouble.'

'Like that's going to happen.'

'Well, women shouldn't have to hide away either.'

'It's for your own good.'

'You have to live,' I said quietly. 'You look over your shoulder. You check who else is in your train carriage. It's second nature – like looking both ways when you cross the road.'

'I don't always look both ways.'

'I know.' I had hauled him back onto the pavement out of harm's way more than once. 'I can't decide if it's male privilege in action or reckless stupidity.'

'Bit of both.'

I started walking back towards the car. 'Let's assume for a minute that Leo is our killer. What was he doing here? He doesn't seem to have any connection with the area. He didn't grow up here. He never lived here. So why go hunting here?'

'Good point.' Derwent looked around. 'This is the sort of area you'd only visit if you had a reason to. What are we close to? Westfield?'

We weren't too far from the giant shopping centre that was one of the main attractions of west London. 'I don't know if Stone is a big shopper. Hammersmith Hospital is the other side of the Westway. And so is HMP Wormwood Scrubs.'

'Did he ever do time there?'

'I don't know. I'll check. And I'll check if he visited anyone there.'

'You think he didn't act alone?'

'It's one possibility,' I said. 'At the moment, I don't feel as if I know anything about him.'

'Maybe he followed her off the Westway. If he saw the flat tyre he'd have known she was in trouble. Offer to help – Bob's your uncle.'

'They checked the CCTV and didn't see it. The only person who saw a van was Mrs Hamilton.'

'And she didn't get the VRN.'

'What do you think?'

28

Derwent sighed. 'All this time in the job and I've never had a single witness with a photographic memory.'

'Me neither.'

'They must exist.'

'They're too busy passing exams and winning pub quizzes to be witnesses.' I thought for a second. 'He had the van. Where was he working when this murder took place?'

'You should find out.'

'I should, and I will.'

Derwent stopped beside the car and stretched. 'So this is the last place anyone saw her alive. When did they find her body?'

'A long time later. She disappeared on the twelfth of July 2014, and her body was found in December. And the only reason it was discovered was because Willa Howard's body was dumped in the same nature reserve. A visitor to the reserve found Willa, and then DCI Whitlock's team searched the rest of the area. They were the ones who located Sara's remains. That's when it became clear that Leo Stone was responsible for Sara's death as well as Willa's.'

His forehead crinkled as he considered it. 'Even though there's basically nothing in the way of physical evidence or eyewitness testimony.'

'Leo has always sworn blind he had nothing to do with Sara Grey's disappearance.'

'He would.'

'He convinced her parents he was innocent.'

Derwent shook his head. 'Then they're as gullible as their daughter was.'

6

'So, three months on from Sara Grey's disappearance, he's on the hunt again. And he finds Willa Howard slap bang in the middle of Bloomsbury.'

'Before that, there was Rachel Healy.'

Derwent frowned. 'He was never charged with her murder.'

'Because they never found the body.'

'Is that the only reason?'

'Not entirely,' I said. 'When they searched Stone's house they found blood under the floorboards, but it was degraded. They couldn't get a full DNA profile, but what they found didn't match Willa Howard or Sara Grey. They checked it against the DNA of missing women from the greater London area over a five-year period and the most similar one was Rachel Healy. She disappeared three weeks before Willa Howard and hasn't been seen since.'

'And the blood was the only thing that connected her with Stone?'

'Yeah.'

'Let's stick with Willa and Sara for now, since he was charged with their murders.'

'What about Rachel?' I had read about her last of all, the previous night when I was yawning and desperate for sleep;

it hadn't taken long and it had woken me right up. Of all of Stone's possible victims, she had received the least attention. No body, no evidence, no leads. A dead end.

'If we have time, we can talk about her. But there are probably good reasons why they left her out of the original case. Three weeks before Willa Howard doesn't leave much of an interval. Sara Grey was three months before that.'

'It's not scientific. They don't mark murder opportunities on their calendars,' I snapped.

'That's not what the profilers say.'

'And you have so much time for what profilers say.'

He grinned at me. 'It's science. They're basically infallible.'

I rolled my eyes, knowing full well that he thought the opposite of what he was saying. 'Look, what are the chances the blood *doesn't* belong to her? She fits the profile of the other victims, and the way she disappeared—'

'Noted,' Derwent said, in a way that meant *I don't care*. 'Back to Willa.'

'Willa is the reason they found Stone in the first place. Say what you want about the original investigation but DCI Whitlock did a good job with Willa. She went missing on the thirty-first of October – Halloween. The last time anyone saw her was in the Haldane, a pub about five minutes' walk from here.'

We were parked in Corona Mews, a narrow cobblestoned lane with three-storey mews houses on either side. Some of the buildings were businesses, the shutters pulled back on the ground-floor spaces that the private homes used as garages. It was an expensive little enclave, despite its faintly bohemian air, and it was quiet. This was the secret hinterland of Bloomsbury, part of a warren of close-set streets that were invisible from the busy thoroughfares that bordered the area, funnelling traffic north to King's Cross and south to Holborn.

'So what are we doing here?'

'Willa's disappearance was out of character – she didn't

31

turn up at a family event the following day, her phone was off, she'd just broken up with her boyfriend. The local CID started looking for her straight away. She hadn't used her Oyster card on any of the local buses or the underground and they didn't pick her up on CCTV. She was very striking – she was tall, with long fair hair that she wore loose, and she had been distressed when she left the Haldane because of the argument she'd had with her boyfriend. It was Halloween. There were lots of people wandering around, but no one remembered seeing her.'

Derwent was listening intently. 'He must have picked her up near the pub.'

'That was the theory. They canvassed the area, looking for anything unusual, and they found Miss Middleton.'

'Who is Miss Middleton?'

'She is the resident of number 32, Corona Mews, and she does not like visitors.'

On cue the front door of number 32 opened and a narrow face appeared. 'You can't park there.'

Derwent slid down his window. 'Police.'

'Am I supposed to be impressed?' She made little shooing motions. 'Go on. Hop it. This isn't a car park.'

'Miss Middleton?' I leaned across so she could see me. 'We wanted to talk to you about Willa Howard.'

'What, again?' She was a foxy little woman with wiry dyed-red hair and sharp brown eyes. I guessed she was eighty but she was spry with it. 'I thought I was done with all of that.'

'Not yet, I'm afraid.'

Derwent got out of the car and she stared up at him, hostility warming into something more like appreciation. 'Well.'

'May we come in? I promise to wipe my feet.'

'You'd better.' She gave a short cackle. 'Got to put me face on, since I've got visitors. Make your own way up.'

For a pensioner, she had a fine turn of speed, and by the time I shut my door she had disappeared.

32

'I know I'm going to regret this,' Derwent said.

'Once we're finished here we can go to the pub.'

'But we're on duty.'

'I'll buy you a lemonade.' I peered up the stairs. 'Can't keep a lady waiting, sir. You'd better go first.'

Viv Middleton was waiting for us in her sitting room, enthroned on a reclining armchair that faced an enormous flat-screen television. She had applied dark lipstick with more speed than accuracy. The place was spotlessly clean and sparsely furnished – a sideboard, a small cupboard, a single upright chair to one side of the recliner with a library book on it. It looked as if it had been decorated last in the early 1980s. Two big windows overlooked the street and from the recliner, Viv would have had a perfect view.

'You can take the chair if you want,' she said to Derwent. I got, 'You'll have to stand.'

'Don't worry,' Derwent said, adopting his usual pose with his feet planted far apart. 'I've been in the car all day. I need to stretch my legs.'

'Ooh, well don't let me stop you.' She cackled happily. For once, Derwent looked embarrassed. He folded his arms and stared at the floor.

'Miss Middleton, you were a key witness. What can you tell us about the van you saw?' I asked.

'It was parked outside my house for two weeks, on and off. He'd come early in the morning and go late at night. Too quick for me, even though I was watching for him. I left notes on it, you know. Telling him he couldn't leave the van there. And I made a note of the registration number. Complained to the council a few times but they're useless.'

'So you never saw the driver,' I checked.

'Not Stone. No. I saw him in court. Horrible-looking man. Give me the shivers. You could see he was a killer.'

'Did you see anyone else near the van? Or driving it?'

She shook her head. 'I only ever saw him driving away. I'd

hear the door go and look down but he parked the wrong way for me to see who was driving. He'd get here early in the morning and I don't do mornings.'

'What was he doing here? Was there any building work going on in the street?' I asked.

'There's always someone doing building work. Listen to that.' She held up a hand and I heard the distant whine of an electric drill.

'And none of your neighbours saw him?'

She snorted. 'They don't notice anything. Half of them are rented out – what's it called – holiday stays type of thing. The other half are too far up themselves to notice a van unless it's blocking their Ferrari or Jaguar.' She dragged out the syllables of the car names, rolling her eyes for comic effect.

'Not like you,' Derwent said. 'How come you live here?'

'I spent sixty years working for a lovely man, an American. I was his housekeeper. He was rich as you like but he didn't get on with his family because he was gay, you see, and they couldn't accept that. He left me this place for the rest of my life. His family want to get me out but there's nothing they can do. I'll be carried out of here.' She grinned, showing off false teeth as white and regular as piano keys. 'All I need is someone to look after me now. What is it they call them?'

'A carer?' Derwent suggested.

'No, that's not it.' The grin widened. 'A toy boy, that's the one.'

Miss Middleton gave us special permission to leave our car parked in front of her house while we walked down the narrow cobbled streets to the Haldane pub.

'How did they link the van to Leo Stone?' Derwent asked.

'The registered owner was traced to a Travellers' site in Hertfordshire. He said he'd sold it to a man he knew as Lee. Lee had promised to register it as his, but he hadn't completed the paperwork. He didn't know where Lee lived but he had a mobile phone number for him.'

'Lee being Leo?'

'Lee being Leo. They found him in Dagenham, in a house that belonged to his aunt – she died a few years ago and left it to him.'

He'd been watching television and drinking cheap lager at eleven in the morning, almost four weeks after the disappearance of Willa Howard.

'When they searched the house they found a room with a new hasp and padlock. He said there was no key and they never found the key in the house or garden, but when they cut the padlock off they found this.' I handed Derwent a spiral-bound album of photographs and he flicked through it: the front of the small, post-war house – three windows and a door, like something drawn by a child. The hall, a narrow and dim space with old-fashioned wallpaper. A dirty kitchen. An untidy sitting room, the surfaces covered in dented cans and takeaway containers. A pile of clothes in the corner of the room. A blanket thrown over the end of the sofa. The door behind the sofa. The padlock. The room behind it: a cheap bedframe with broken slats fanning out underneath it. A new mattress on the bed, still covered in protective plastic. No furniture, except for a large steel storage cupboard in the corner of the room. Derwent paused.

'And this is significant, I take it.'

'Turned out to be. It was second-hand, bought through a local buying-and-selling group and collected from outside the seller's home while they were at work. The buyer paid cash. It was designed to contain hazardous materials. It even had an integral sump in case of any spillages.'

'Useful.'

'Very.'

It was empty, the inside spotless except for a wisp of plastic.

35

'They didn't work out exactly where the plastic came from but it's the type decorators use for protective sheeting when they're painting a room. There's no record of Leo buying anything like that but he was in and out of building sites. He could have nicked it.'

The next picture was a close-up of the plastic. Derwent pointed at a smudge. 'Is that blood?'

'A tiny amount of it, and it belonged to Willa Howard.'

'Well, there you go.' Derwent snapped the book shut and gave it back to me. 'That's him done and dusted.'

'When they were searching the house they took up the floorboards in that room and found Rachel Healy's blood.'

'Or someone else's.'

'It could have been someone else's. But how likely is that?'

Derwent raised an eyebrow. 'That he killed someone else or that Rachel's blood was a partial match?'

'The blood matching.'

'Partially.'

'Yeah.'

'I don't know,' I admitted. 'I'm not a blood expert.'

'He wasn't charged with her murder. There has to be a good reason for that.' Derwent checked his watch. 'Pub?'

'Pub.'

We walked in silence down the cobbled streets. I was thinking about Willa Howard running to her doom, blinded by tears and anger, and about Rachel Healy and why I couldn't forget about her. Derwent, from his expression, could have been thinking about anything at all.

'This is the pub.' I pointed. It was a square, squat building on a corner site, a survivor from the 1930s with the original bar and a certain hipster cachet as a result.

'Looks nice.'

'It looks like the sort of place that has no CCTV, which is in fact the case.'

'Typical.'

36

'Indeed.' I stopped. 'Let's go back to Willa's disappearance. You have to imagine it's Halloween.'

'Yeah. Busy night.'

'And it's unusually warm – twenty-four degrees. The streets on either side of the pub were full of drinkers standing around making noise.'

'Potential witnesses, though.'

'They saw nothing. I've got to hand it to Whitlock here. His team tracked down a lot of the customers from the pub and looked at their photographs and video footage from their phones. It was a big night, lots of people wearing costumes, lots of moving and still images.'

'Which showed what?'

'Willa Howard sitting at the bar beside her on-and-off boyfriend, Jeremy Indolf. They were having a drink together to discuss their relationship.' I looked up from my notes. 'He was seeing someone else and Willa wasn't happy about it.'

'Fair enough.'

'He made her cry. She gave as good as she got though. The bar staff all remembered her because she was so feisty. She was calling him every name under the sun. None of the bar staff wanted to go near that end of the bar, but they had to because Jeremy kept ordering drinks. Eventually she picked up his drink and poured it into his lap, then stormed out. And disappeared off the face of the earth.'

'The boyfriend has to have been a suspect.'

'He was, but they ruled him out pretty quickly. He co-operated fully with the investigation. According to him and the staff, he stayed here for another hour, drinking and trying to chat up other women.'

Derwent snorted. 'He couldn't manage two. What was he going to do with a third?'

'Jeremy is nothing if not ambitious. Anyway, he didn't do anything to Willa and he didn't call anyone or send any messages asking someone else to harm her. What he did do was drink. By the time he left, he was barely able to walk. We have CCTV of him heading towards Russell Square underground and weaving across the pavement. An hour after she left the pub, Willa was long gone, but no one saw where she went and she didn't appear on any CCTV footage that the original investigation recovered. There was nothing to say where she had gone.'

'They were bloody lucky to get the VRN for the van.'

'And to find "Lee". And to discover a trace of Willa's DNA in a cupboard in his house. Don't get me wrong, they put in a lot of legwork to find the van, but if that bit of plastic hadn't been recovered from the cupboard, we'd be no further on.'

'Every investigation needs some luck.' Derwent looked hopefully at the bar. 'You said you'd buy me a drink.'

'If we can talk about Rachel Healy.'

'There's always a catch with you, isn't there?'

'I like to get my money's worth,' I allowed.

'Come on, then.' He didn't sound as if he minded too much; maybe Rachel had been playing on his mind too. He held the door open for me and I walked in, feeling the shiver of recognition: the bar, the green-painted walls, the worn and faded floorboards – I had seen it all in the files.

Willa had seen it all the day her life spun out of her control, when the biggest problem she had was an unfaithful boyfriend. If she'd met her boyfriend somewhere else, or if he hadn't been cheating on her, or if she'd argued with him earlier in the evening . . . but she hadn't.

Wrong place, wrong time.

38

7

It was the middle of the day so the bar was quiet except for some mellow swing music and the barman's girlfriend talking him through her plans for a weekend away. We sat in a corner, knee to knee, leaning across the table like lovers so no one could overhear our conversation.

'Rachel Healy.' I held up her photograph. It was a formal portrait taken when she started working at an estate agents, Gallagher Kemp. She looked groomed, her fair hair glossy and smooth, her make-up professionally discreet. Her smile was warm, though, and the gap between her front teeth enhanced her beauty instead of detracting from it.

'Pretty girl,' Derwent observed.

'Woman,' I said automatically. 'And yes. She was stunning.'

'Wouldn't go that far.'

I placed the photograph on the table with exaggerated care because I really wanted to smack him with it. He drank some lemonade and only the tell-tale deepening of the creases at his eyes gave away that he was smiling against the rim of the glass.

'She disappeared nineteen days before Willa Howard. She worked late that night.' I took a map out of the file and put it between us. I had drawn a star on the Chelsea office of Gallagher Kemp estate agents. 'It was a Monday in October and they weren't too busy but she'd been away on holiday and she needed to catch up. Gallagher Kemp do commercial property at a very high level, according to their website. If you have a company of five hundred people to rehouse in the City, they're a good place to start.'

'When you say she was working late—'

'She was in the office, not showing any premises to prospective renters, so that's not how she met her killer. Her boss was also working late – his name is James Gallagher. He said they left together. He gave her a lift and she asked him to drop her off in King's Cross, although she lived in Tufnell Park. He left her near the station and drove home – he lives in Islington – and she went on her way, and no one ever saw her again. She never made it back to her flat. Ordinarily she got the Northern Line but she didn't use her Oyster card or bank card and as with Willa there was no sign of her on CCTV.'

'Who reported her missing?'

'Her flatmates. They got the brush-off from their local police station – you know the drill.'

'She's a grown woman and not vulnerable and there's no reason to be concerned for her safety yet.'

'That's the one. No one took it seriously until the following day when she didn't turn up for work and didn't call in either. Someone rang her flatmates and they said she hadn't come home. James Gallagher kicked up a bit of a fuss at the local police station, which helped set the wheels in motion.'

'Decent of him,' Derwent observed.

'He was the last person to see her. I'd imagine he was quite keen to find her, because otherwise he could have been a suspect.'

'That or he felt guilty about leaving her somewhere that turned out to be dangerous.' Derwent frowned. 'But we don't know that Leo Stone was the specific trouble she encountered.'

'There's the blood under the floorboards.'

'Which is not an exact match.'

'No,' I admitted. 'It could have been hers but equally it could not have been.'

'That's the trouble with DNA. On the one hand, it's pointing us at Rachel Healy. On the other hand, that blood could belong to someone else. It's not enough to get a conviction as it is. We'd have been better off in the old days when it was blood type only. Juries want a hundred per cent certainty these days. Close isn't good enough.' Derwent flipped a beer mat off the edge of the table and caught it as it spun around in the air. 'Then there's the point that her body was never recovered from the nature reserve where the other two victims ended up.' Flip. Spin.

'Nope. I think every inch of it was searched, too. Whitlock didn't want to miss something obvious.'

'So what do you think about the blood?'

'I think we should assume it was Rachel's.'

'Why?'

'Because assuming it isn't won't get us any further and we haven't identified any other women he might have attacked. Our best chance is to be positive about connecting Rachel Healy to Leo Stone and work to that end.'

'This is a man who kills without spilling blood, though. The only blood we found from the other victims was a speck on some plastic. He's incredibly disciplined about it. You've seen the pictures – the room was spotless. So you have to believe he took Rachel to his house and for some unknown reason killed her in a messy and uncontrolled way, and that he was sufficiently excited by that to go back and take another woman off the street nineteen days later.'

'Maybe it went wrong.'

'Maybe it was nothing to do with him,' Derwent countered, and my throat tightened with irritation.

'Well, the blood had to come from *someone*. Even if it wasn't Rachel Healy, and I think it was, someone died violently in that room and bled through the floorboards. How does that fit in with your incredibly disciplined killer?' My voice was a shade too loud and Derwent grinned.

'Shh. You'll scare the barman.'

'He's not listening.' I leaned sideways to check, all the same. His girlfriend was still talking, although she had moved on to the tattoo she was planning to get and where it should go.

I took a grip on my temper and returned to Derwent. 'If it wasn't her blood, where did Rachel Healy go?'

'Someone else killed her. A boyfriend. An ex. A stalker. I don't know.' Derwent tapped the beer mat against the edge of the table. 'It's more of a stretch to believe it was Stone than that someone else wanted her dead. Two women a week die at the hands of partners or ex-partners. Did we look at her boyfriends?'

'I don't know. I assume so – at least before Whitlock got involved. There was a whole month where nothing much happened on the investigation, remember.'

'That won't have helped.'

'No. No one helped Rachel, alive or dead.'

Derwent leaned back, watching me with that close attention I slightly feared. 'Don't get hung up on her.'

'What's that supposed to mean?'

'You need to keep some perspective on it. She's been missing for years. Your chances of finding her at all are slim, let alone making a case that Leo Stone killed her. If she's dead, it doesn't matter to her.'

'She has a family. Friends.'

'And you can't bring her back for them.'

I looked away instead of at his face. I didn't want to admit that he was right, but I knew he was. The CD changed to piano music, cool notes drifting through the dusty air like snowflakes. The barman dropped the cloth he had been using to polish glasses and leaned across the counter, drawing his girlfriend's face towards him so he could kiss her. She held on to his wrists and closed her eyes and I found I was holding my breath . . .

'You're quiet.'

I came back down to earth with a bump. It was just as well Derwent had his back to the bar because he would probably have heckled, or at the very least criticised the barman's technique. 'It's this case. It looks solid from a distance but it all falls apart when you poke it.'

'Don't tell me you're having doubts about Stone.'

I shook my head. 'It's too much of a coincidence to think his van was here and Willa's blood was in his house by chance. But Miss Middleton never saw Leo Stone at the van. No one did. They didn't trace a building company that was using him around here. According to him he'd been off work for a month because of back pain and Miss Middleton got the VRN wrong when she wrote it down.'

'Back pain my arse. His van was here. He was hunting in this area. It's perfect. No CCTV. No nosy neighbours. Plenty of footfall from the pubs, people coming home late. Easy access to main routes out of the city centre.'

'That's a good point. We're not far from Euston and King's Cross. The Euston Road is the A501 and if you stay on it and keep heading west, it turns into the Westway.'

'See? It all fits. He was using that as his main route through the city and dropping off it anywhere that seemed quiet and residential. This is exactly the sort of place where no one is going to notice you hanging around. You heard what Miss Middleton said about the area. It's a backwater between busy areas. It's not unusual to have strangers passing through, or hanging around for a few days at a time. No one is going to look twice at a man in a white van unless they're an elderly lady with nothing better to do.' Derwent drained the last of the liquid in his glass and burped. 'Come on. Back to the car. It's time to go and talk to Dr Early about body dumps and decomp.'

'I can hardly wait.'

8

Derwent breezed into Dr Early's office. 'Knock knock, Doc. What have we got?'

She looked up from her paperwork. The desk was, as usual, piled high with folders. Some of them had slid sideways, spilling their contents: forms, lab results, photographs . . . I had trained myself to look anywhere but at the pathologist's desk. It was all right if you were prepared for what you might have to look at, but a glance could be scarring. Once seen, some horrors couldn't be unseen. 'Too much work and not enough hours in the day.'

'Same,' I said. 'Is this a bad time?'

'Not if you're here to talk about Leo Stone.' She stood up and with unerring confidence hooked a file out from the middle of the cascade of papers on her desk. There was a system to the chaos. 'I've set things up in the meeting room next door.'

We followed her obediently, in my case wondering what she meant by *things* and suspecting I wasn't going to like whatever it was. I was much too experienced now to be worried about fainting or vomiting at a grisly post-mortem, but I couldn't claim to take every detail in my stride.

'Here we are.' The room was dim, the blinds closed. Dr Early tutted impatiently as she adjusted them, turning the slats so we could see the images on two large noticeboards that filled one end of the room. As light flooded in, the shadowy pictures leapt into focus. 'I've done one side for Sara Grey and the other for Willa Howard. You wanted a quick catch-up, I take it?'

'Ideally.' Derwent's attention was on the noticeboards. He strolled down to look closer, his hands in his pockets, but the way he stood – his absolute focus – told me he was concentrating on what was in front of him, and that he was by no means as casual about it as he pretended to be.

'I've pulled this together from the files and the evidence that was presented at trial. I'm going to explain all of this to you as I would explain it to a jury, so if I use too much jargon, feel free to stop me and ask any questions you might have. Also, some of this isn't my speciality. If you really want the details on this, you need a forensic entomologist.'

'You'll do for now,' Derwent said, and Dr Early ran the end of her pen along a series of photographs that filled the top left corner of Sara Grey's noticeboard.

'This is the body where it was discovered in the nature reserve. It was actually the second one that was located, I believe, but she died first so I'm going to start with her.'

The photographs were taken from every possible angle and all showed the same thing: the skeletonised remains of a human being who had been left to disintegrate on open ground. The grass was trampled in front of the body but it had grown up to a height of four or five feet around her, and through her. There was something almost beautiful about the grass, the tiny wildflowers, the leaves and the bones, especially in the close-up images where it was possible to forget that these were the mortal remains of pretty, shy Sara Grey, whose face smiled back at me from the centre of her board.

'I went and had a look at the dump sites to see if there was anything I needed to know about the locations – if they were especially wet, for instance, that would affect what we found.' She pointed to a large sheet of paper that stretched between the two boards. It was covered with inscrutable marks and shapes. 'This is my best artwork, so be kind.'

'It's lovely,' Derwent said kindly. 'What is it?'

'A map of the site.' She sounded a touch defensive. 'I know it's hard to follow but it makes sense to me. Sara was dumped here. She wasn't dressed or wrapped in anything and no attempt was made to cover her or Willa.' Dr Early indicated a roughly oblong squiggle on the map. 'This is a rectangular building around a hundred metres away from where the body was left. It's a bird-watching hide, which is significant because pedestrians aren't allowed in *this* area of grassland' – her pen traced a triangle in front of the hide – 'in case it disturbs ground-nesting birds. The path runs on the other side of the building, here. It's this line of dots.'

'How accessible is the area?' I asked.

'The car park isn't far away at all – a couple of hundred metres the other side of those trees.' The trees were a row of asterisks that ran behind the grassland where the body had lain. 'This nature reserve doesn't have a permanent guard in residence. There's nothing to steal, for one thing. There are gates and fences, but it's not what you'd call secure. They also issue permits for night visitors from time to time, so no one would think it was strange to see a car or a van in the car park outside the usual opening hours.'

'Do they keep a register of visitors?' I asked, and Dr Early looked surprised.

'I didn't ask.'

'Never mind, you're doing well,' Derwent said with a glower in my direction. She wasn't a police officer, after all; I couldn't expect her to think like one. 'Keep going.'

'The site he picked was far enough from the hide that no one there would notice any smells or unusual insect activity in this area – from a hundred metres away, you might see a larger number of flies than you'd expect or even a larger number of scavenging birds and butterflies and moths than would be typical for this area, but you wouldn't connect any of those things with a corpse unless you were looking for one which, of course, we always are so for us it would be obvious but for your average layperson none of that would ring a bell.' She ground to a halt, a little out of breath.

'Right,' Derwent said. 'Of course.'

'And the other thing about picking a reserve where there's birdwatching is that they don't allow . . .' She looked from me to Derwent expectantly. I got it first.

'Dogs.'

'Exactly. It was a brilliant place to choose. No dogs allowed, so no dogs sniffing out the bodies until long after nature had done a huge amount of work in removing the soft tissue, the muscle, the skin. All we really have to go on are the bones at that stage, and bones are extremely useful but they don't tell you the full story. For instance, if she had soft-tissue injuries, we're not going to know what they were. The soft tissue goes with the first wave of insect activity – the blowflies and the greenbottles and the flesh flies. Female blowflies can sniff out a dead body within minutes. They don't have strong mouthparts so they can't tunnel into the body. They lay their eggs anywhere that's easily accessible – injuries, eyes, mouths, nostrils—'

'I get the picture,' Derwent said quickly.

'Right, right. It's all so clever, that's all. Nature tidying up after itself. The insects help decomposition along, and they do it in a way that's completely predictable, which is particularly helpful for us.' She clicked her pen. 'But I'm getting ahead of myself. I was talking about injuries and how we can't prove what killed Sara Grey.'

'What? Not at all?' Derwent sounded disconcerted.

'We can't prove it. We can suggest certain things, and rule other things out. Like, for instance, there's the fact that Dr Hanshaw didn't find any broken bones when he examined her. We didn't recover all the bones, but that's not unusual in a case where a body has been left in the open. Being buried tends to hold things together a lot more.'

My eyes flicked to the images of Sara Grey's skull pillowed in the grass. 'Aren't those skull fractures?'

Dr Early's eyes gleamed. 'I was hoping one of you would notice. Yes, look at this image of the head. You can see quite clearly that there has been significant damage to her skull.'

The head was tipped back, the neck at an awkward angle, the chin pointing to the sky. Leathery remnants of muscle and skin coated the bone in places but I could see missing teeth and a couple of wavy cracks that ran from the eye socket up towards the crown of the head.

'Here's a better image of the top of her head – see the way the fractures waver across the bone?'

We nodded.

'That's a sign that she was already dead when the injuries happened. A post-mortem fracture has these crumbly edges – it's like snapping a biscuit in two. You won't get a clean line. If you're alive, the break will be straight because the bone has more give in it. Think of snapping a piece of chocolate. You get a straight edge.'

'I'd rather not think about food in this context,' Derwent said. 'If you don't mind.'

'Really?' Dr Early looked surprised. 'I always think the biscuit and chocolate analogy works for juries. Everyone can visualise it.'

'It's very helpful,' I said and she beamed.

'The other thing is the colour of the break. See how it's lighter than the rest of the bone? Definitely post-mortem. What I can't tell you is how she acquired the injuries. It could have been accidental. Dead bodies are really hard to manipulate – dead weight is a bugger to move around, no matter how strong you are or how small the victim is. So he could have dropped her a few times or whacked her into a doorway without meaning to hurt her.'

48

'When he was finished with her he didn't care any more,' I said, and something in my voice made Derwent turn to look at me with a raised eyebrow. Dr Early didn't seem to notice.

'Probably not. She became a problem. Something to be dumped, not cherished.'

'Cherished is an odd word to use. He killed her,' Derwent said.

'Mm, but how he killed her is the point. No nicks or marks on the bones, so almost certainly not stabbing – she had no defence wounds on the bones we recovered from her hands and arms either. Her hyoid bone is intact, which strongly suggests she wasn't strangled. I think she was asphyxiated. It doesn't take long to starve the brain of oxygen and achieve loss of consciousness so she would have had minimal opportunity to fight back and harm herself. I think he smothered her not long after he kidnapped her.'

The muscle was flickering in Derwent's jaw. 'Where's the fun in that?'

'That's not a question I can answer,' Dr Early said seriously. 'But I think it's worth looking at Willa Howard in more detail.'

I had been strenuously avoiding looking at Willa Howard in any detail at all. There was something more unsettling about the images of her, probably because she was more recognisably herself than her sister in death. The flesh had melted away from her body but there was still skin on her bones, and much of her hair had survived, spread out around her in straw-like profusion. She was lying on her front with her head turned to one side, her hands by her sides, palm up.

'Willa was over here.' Dr Early pointed to another squiggle on the map, further away from the hide. 'When you visit the site you'll see why she was found first – the body was in the lee of a fallen tree. A visitor to the site decided the tree would make a great vantage point for a picture, even though it was off the path. He stumbled over her.'

'Jesus,' Derwent muttered.

'It must have been quite a shock,' Dr Early agreed. 'Luckily for him she was quite advanced in decomposition. The worst part – from the point of view of smell and maggots and so forth – is between four and twenty days after death. The gases build up inside the body. Once the abdominal wall is breached the body deflates and starts to dry out and most of the insect activity is from beetles, mites – that kind of thing. She was well into this stage when she was found in the first week of December, which was some five weeks after she disappeared.'

'So you think she was killed straight away as well.'

'It seems possible. But unlike Sara, she did have some injuries we can see. This is an X-ray of her skull – see the missing tooth at the front, here? That was broken off around the time of her death. The root is still there.'

'Sara was missing teeth too,' I pointed out.

'Yes, but we recovered them. They became dislodged from the jaw after the gum deteriorated, once there was nothing holding them in place. Willa's was snapped off and we didn't find the tooth.'

'It doesn't rule out asphyxiation, does it?'

'Not at all. We don't know what method he employed but he may have needed to use more force on Willa. She was a little taller and heavier than Sara.'

'And she was angry. She'd been drinking and arguing with her boyfriend.' I could imagine her, her body humming with adrenalin and fear, lashing out at Leo Stone because how *dare* he attack her . . .

'There was the blood on the plastic in the cupboard,' Derwent said. 'That had to come from somewhere.'

'Probably this injury, or a nosebleed. Something like that. Unfortunately we did lose a certain amount of detail to decomposition before she was found.' Dr Early peered at the X-ray as if it would reveal something new to her. 'There are three things, really, that I wanted to draw to your attention. One: Dr Hanshaw also concluded that the women were asphyxiated and there's nothing to contradict his assertion. As I said, without being able to see the physical manifestations of asphyxia – the pinpoint haemorrhages and so forth – it's a case of excluding other modes of death. We are left with asphyxia as the most likely method of murder, as it's relatively non-violent.'

'Unless he poisoned them,' Derwent said.

'I know you're joking but we did test for poisons. We tested their bone marrow and their hair, and it's the hair that's the second thing I want to talk about.'

'What about it?'

'Look at the condition of Willa Howard's hair compared to how it was in life.'

'Being dead isn't great for your looks, as I understand it,' Derwent said.

'No, but it doesn't change the consistency of your hair so quickly,' Dr Early countered.

Willa's hair had been long, smooth and thick. Every witness in the bar had commented on it. I frowned at the dry, frizzed-out thatch that covered her scalp. It was orange-tinged and it had snapped off in several places, leaving the ends uneven. 'It looks as if it was bleached.'

'That's exactly what happened. She was soaked in bleach. I'd guess her entire body was immersed in bleach at least once if not more.'

'To eradicate evidence?'

'Maybe. Or to try to slow decomposition. The third thing about these bodies is the most interesting, at least to me. The women seem to have died relatively quickly after they were kidnapped, but they weren't dumped in the nature reserve for a significant period of time after their deaths.'

'How significant are we talking?' Derwent asked.

'Weeks. Maybe more in the case of Sara Grey. And I know that because of the insect activity I mentioned earlier. Dr Hanshaw got a forensic entomologist to sample insect life from the bodies and from the area around the bodies. It's a reliable way of calculating how long the corpses had been there and what condition they were in when they arrived. What she found was a very small number of the insect first responders – the blowflies, the greenbottles, the flesh flies and so forth. There were plenty of beetles and mites who target fly larvae though – every decaying corpse is also an insect crime scene, I always say – so they *had* been present at one time, but the larvae hadn't matured through their three stages to burrow into the ground and become pupae – or if they had, it was somewhere else and they were left behind when the bodies were moved.'

'What does that mean?' Derwent asked.

'It means he kept the bodies until they weren't usable any more,' I said.

'That's my interpretation.' Dr Early looked from me to Derwent, eyes bright. 'The trouble with necrophilia is that it's so *messy*.'

I shuddered. 'Doesn't bear thinking about.'

'Toughen up, Kerrigan,' Derwent snapped. 'You do need to think about it, because we need to work out where he kept the bodies between the cupboard in his house and when he dumped them here. Not in Dagenham – there wasn't a trace of post-mortem body fluids from either Willa Howard or Sara Grey, and from what you're saying, Doc, there would have been a lot.'

'Absolutely. The body's own enzymes begin to liquefy the internal organs even without the help of insects. You can slow the process by keeping a body cold, but unless you find some way of mummifying them, you're going to find they deteriorate.'

'And there's no evidence he tried to do that,' I checked.

'None at all. Unfortunately there isn't much evidence of what he did, either. By keeping them until they had completed putrefaction he reduced the chances of anyone literally sniffing them out at the dump sites and he destroyed a lot of the forensic evidence we might have recovered otherwise.'

'It was all so well planned, wasn't it?' I said. 'We only found Willa Howard by chance, and that led us to Sara Grey. Leo Stone doesn't strike me as a particularly deep thinker but he managed to kidnap women, keep them for as long as he liked, move them without being spotted and then dispose of them effectively.'

'He's spent years in prison. He probably spent the whole time planning what he was going to do when he got out.' Derwent's mouth twitched. 'He had all the luck until he got arrested. You've got to think it's our turn to be lucky now.'

9

Of course, luck wasn't with us the next day either. The judges' decision was a foregone conclusion, and everyone knew it, but the tension in the air was as thick as the mist that pressed against the small high windows. The lights were on, the old pearly shades casting a soft glow that fell on the walls of law books, the high wooden bench where three judges sat, sombre in their full wigs and gowns, and on their clerk who was busy with paperwork, his pen racing across the page. It fell on the attentive barristers at their desks in front of the packed benches of the public gallery. It fell on the tiny dock with its over-arching iron bars that separated the prisoner from the rest of us who sat in the courtroom. We were free and he was not.

Not yet.

I sat in the last row of the public benches. Despite its importance, the Court of Appeal was held in a small room, and it was packed. The court reporters were choosy about which cases they covered but this one was a guaranteed front-page splash. A murderer was always news. A murderer of women was even better, especially if the women were beautiful, especially if they had everything to live for, especially if they met a horrible end at the hands of a perverted stranger. But best of all was a gruesome series of murders combined with a miscarriage of justice. That was a story that had everything.

I looked at the man in the dock. Leo Stone, the man who had been haunting my thoughts, a nightmare made flesh. His eyes were closed, his face pale and impassive, his hair dark and greased back from a low forehead. He was tall but gaunt; his skin fell in loose folds from his prominent cheekbones and sagged from his jawline. Often, prisoners didn't come to the Court of Appeal. It was quicker and cheaper to make them attend by video link, but on this occasion, I could understand why he had wanted to be present. I knew better than to think murderers always looked like what they were but something about Stone's physical presence chilled me. The words and images from the files I'd read battered the inside of my skull along with a single word: *evil*.

'If he's stuck for cash he can always write the Leo Stone diet book,' Derwent muttered, leaning over so his elbow pressed against my side painfully. 'There isn't a spare ounce on him.'

'Not the time or the place,' I hissed. 'And give me some room.'

Derwent shrugged and folded his arms across his chest, making himself even broader. His knees moved an inch or two further apart, which I wouldn't have thought possible. I shifted to my right, trying to put some space between his thigh and mine, and collided with my neighbour on the other side.

'Sorry.'

Godley nodded, preoccupied. Unlike me, he was concentrating on the judge's speech and sat statue-still. Beyond him sat DCI Paul Whitlock, who was in his late fifties. I'd met him before the hearing started, in the echoing, cathedral-like main hall of the Royal Courts of Justice. He had given me a quick, bruising handshake, without a smile. He had retired after Leo Stone's conviction, before the crowning achievement of his career had turned into a messy disaster, and he lived on the Kent coast now. I assumed he spent most of his life out of doors because his skin was like old leather. Under his tan, he looked drawn and tired. What we were watching was the dismantling of a case he had built, painfully and in the full glare of public scrutiny. I could imagine how he was feeling.

The words fell from the bench like wood shavings, dry and dusty, delivered in a refined Anglo-Indian accent.

'It is one of the abiding principles of the British legal system that a jury trial must be fair. A jury must be impartial. They must base their opinions on the words of counsel, on the evidence they hear and on the judge's guidance. It is abundantly clear that in this case the jury did not do their duty. Rather, they chose to ignore all instructions and plunged into a world of speculation and ill-informed comment, aided by the media's distorting lens. The duty of a jury is a sacred one. A defendant is entitled to expect that a jury will conduct themselves fairly. Otherwise justice cannot be done. And it has not been done in this case. The appeal is granted. I order that the prisoner, Leo Stone, be returned to prison and a further application be made to the Crown Court for bail pending a retrial.'

A murmur ran through the courtroom. In the dock, Leo Stone opened his eyes for the first time, staring about him as if he had just woken up. His eyes were dark, the pupils invisible. One of the officers with him took his arm, but gently.

'Come on.'

Stone didn't move. His eyes scanned the public gallery, row by row, until they stopped. For a moment I thought he was looking straight at me. Then the man in front of me raised a hand to shoulder height: a salute that received an answering nod from the prisoner. Only then did Stone turn, dropping his head and rounding his shoulders as he trudged down the steps to the cells below the courtrooms, where he would wait for a transfer to prison. Freedom was within his grasp but it wasn't his quite yet.

The judges rose and filed out through a door behind them, and as the door closed the barristers abandoned their respectful demeanour instantly. The juniors gathered up their papers and legal reference books, moving with the speed born of long experience in the Crown Court, where the next case followed on the heels of the first. The opposing silks leaned towards one another as they tucked pens into pockets and settled their gowns on their shoulders more firmly, laughing as if they had been working together rather than competing for the judges' favour. The journalists had slid out of the benches at the earliest opportunity, scattering down the long, tiled corridor to find a quiet nook where they could call their newsrooms.

On my right, Godley sighed. 'Well. That's that.'

'Nothing else they could do.' Whitlock stood up. 'Frustrating, though. In some ways it feels worse than if we'd lost the first trial. I took a lot of satisfaction out of locking Stone up. It made me feel the world was a safer place for him being behind bars.'

'We'll put him back there for you. Fucking juries.' Derwent eased his hips forward, slouching. It wasn't actually possible to lounge on the high-backed wooden benches but he gave it his best shot.

Harry Hollingwood QC paused at the end of our bench. 'Quick chat before I go back to chambers?'

'Of course.' Godley got up, energised. I made to follow him and Paul Whitlock, but hung back to let someone pass through the heavy doors before me. He hesitated for a beat, looking at me and I returned the scrutiny: dark hair, dark eyes, heavy eyebrows, a slight frame. The man who had been in front of me in the hearing, who had waved at Leo Stone.

'Come on.' The man behind him nudged him. He was a head taller and correspondingly broad, his shoulders straining against the fine fabric of his three-piece pinstripe suit. It was exquisitely fitted, I noted, just as I noted that he was strikingly handsome and roughly my age. He had a full beard, which

57

ordinarily did nothing for me, but he made it look good. He stared at me briefly, assessing me in much the same way that I was eyeing him, but whether he was impressed or not I couldn't tell.

The first man mumbled something and pushed the door open. I followed them out and stopped, watching them walk away down the corridor, one looking dazed and hurrying to keep up with the other's long stride.

'Not what you'd expect.' Paul Whitlock nodded in their direction. 'Considering.'

'Who are they?'

'Chap with dark hair is Kelly Lambert.'

I shook my head, not recognising the name.

'Leo Stone's son.'

'His *son*?'

'Long lost. Stone never married his mother – it was a casual relationship. They were both young when Kelly was born – early twenties, they would have been. Stone's forty-eight now, though he looks older than me. Kelly's mum died when he was young and he was taken into care. He had no contact with his dad for a long time, but Stone was in and out of prison so it was probably for the best. He wouldn't have been a good influence, put it that way.'

'How come they got back in touch?'

Whitlock shrugged. 'Lambert found him when he was in prison in 2013. Started visiting him. When Stone came out, Lambert helped him get his life back on track. Lambert's a carpenter. He got his dad some labouring work on building sites. Nothing skilled, but enough that he had a bit of cash. He wanted to keep him out of trouble, he said.'

'That worked well.'

Whitlock gave a short laugh. 'You said it.'

'Did you look at him as a suspect?' Derwent asked.

'He had solid alibis for all the disappearances.' Whitlock shook his head. 'Kelly's an argument for the care system.

Whoever looked after him, they did a decent job. He seems to be the kind of chap who sees the good in everyone. Either that or he doesn't want to believe that half his DNA is from a murdering shit. He's been campaigning to get his dad released. Absolutely refuses to believe his dad could have done anything like that to those women, even though Stone had a history of violence towards his mum before they split up. Stone was a suspect in her death but they never made it stick.'

'It's a big jump from domestic abuse and burglary to murdering strangers,' I said, as neutrally as I could. Whitlock bristled all the same.

'It's a good case. It's solid. Stone got lucky on a technicality. There'll be another trial and this time he'll go away forever.'

And I'll be proved right. He didn't need to say it. I didn't blame him for minding, in fact.

'Who was the other guy with Kelly Lambert?' Derwent asked, saving me the trouble.

'That's Stone's solicitor, Seth Taylor.' Whitlock grimaced. 'Clever guy. Arrogant, though. He's made his reputation off how he handled Stone's case. They didn't give us an inch, all the way through.'

'I wouldn't have thought he had much material to work with,' Derwent said. 'It was pretty cut and dried, as I understood it.'

'It didn't seem that way once the defence got to grips with the evidence.' Whitlock shook his head. 'Tell you what, if I ever get in trouble with the law, I'm calling Taylor. He's all charm on the outside but if you challenge him, you'd better come prepared for a fight.'

'DI Derwent is always prepared for a fight.' I said it for the pleasure of making Derwent scowl.

'I'm looking forward to seeing his face when Stone gets convicted again.'

I looked around, checking for eavesdroppers, and noticed

a young woman in dark tights and a bulky coat. She was sitting in one of the alcoves outside the court, apparently concentrating on her phone.

'We should take this somewhere else,' I said quietly. Derwent, naturally, ignored me.

'Jesus, I feel sorry for Lambert but he's out of his tiny mind if he thinks his dad is innocent. I've never seen a more obvious psycho. He needs locking up again, as soon as we can possibly manage it. If we can get him put inside for anything at all, we should.'

'We can't harass him,' I said.

'I'm prepared to risk upsetting him if it means no one else dies,' Derwent snapped.

'Harry's waiting,' Godley said, with maximum disapproval, and on this occasion even Derwent took the hint.

10

The café in the Royal Courts of Justice was at the back of the ground floor, in an old courtroom that had been refitted with cheap tables and chairs. It was crowded with that peculiar mix of people that frequented the RCJ: the tax cases, the personal injury suits, the police officers and criminals and their families and the lawyers, all pretending to ignore one another. Hollingwood had found a table on the other side of the room. His junior, Kit Harries, waved at me energetically from the queue.

'Coffee? Your usual?' The barrister's voice carried easily over the noise in the café. I gave him the thumbs up rather than trying to answer.

'Do you know him?' Derwent was beside me all of a sudden.

'Kit? Yeah, he's a nice guy. I've worked with him a few times.'

'He looks better with his wig on.'

The barrister had a lot of very fine straw-coloured hair and a round face, and his wig had made him sweat so his hair was plastered to his head. As usual, Derwent wasn't kind but he was right.

'He's a lovely person and he's married, so be nice.'

'I'm always nice.'

'Not in a way that's noticeable to the casual observer.'

Derwent moved away from me, grinning to himself. As if to prove me wrong, he went across to the queue to help Kit with the drinks. I followed Godley and Whitlock to the table, not without some misgivings. Derwent would take the opportunity to talk to Kit about me, unsupervised, and I liked Kit but he wasn't the most discreet person I'd ever encountered. I couldn't think of anything I needed to hide, specifically, but then again I couldn't think of anything I'd like Derwent to find out about me. He knew too much already.

Without his wig and gown, Harry Hollingwood looked different too. His grey hair was swept back from a high square forehead and brushed against his collar at the back. He was compact, fit, fiftyish and he looked good-humoured, despite the loss in court. His small brown eyes were shrewd and full of life.

'Sit down, sit down. I thought we should have a little post-mortem before we all went home.'

'It was the result we expected,' Whitlock said, which was his way of reassuring the lawyer that he didn't blame him.

'Couldn't have gone any other way. The point is that we've got to prepare ourselves for a retrial.'

'How soon can we expect the retrial?'

'Soon,' Hollingwood said. 'He'll be in the Crown Court tomorrow to be formally released from prison. How long do you want him out?'

'Not long.'

'Well, then. We'll seek an early trial date. In the circumstances, we should get it. But that obviously means you have less time to conduct your reinvestigation. A month or two.'

'We'll manage,' Godley said, with a confidence that I didn't feel. 'Have you met Maeve Kerrigan? She's one of my best detectives.'

Hollingwood nodded to me. 'Kit speaks very highly of you.'

'I've always enjoyed working with him.' I hoped I sounded

like a tough and experienced detective sergeant, even if I was flustered to the point of blushing by what Godley had said.

'I should say that the previous investigation was excellent.' Hollingwood turned to Whitlock. 'We were very happy with the evidence as it was gathered and presented to us. I am simply conscious of the fact that time has passed and the defence has had an opportunity to revisit the case they ran. We want to be prepared for them to take issue with anything that was awkward for them in the previous hearing. We'll be disclosing anything new that you find out, of course, but with any luck it will be unanswerable.'

There was a brief hiatus while Derwent and Kit returned with the coffee. Kit had the expression of a man who had gone through a car wash in a convertible with the roof down. Derwent was at his most bland. He smiled at me as he sat down: never a good sign.

'What was the defence?' I asked quickly. 'I read the files the other day and it seemed there wasn't much room for doubt.'

'There's always room for doubt in a defence case,' Hollingwood said. 'They don't have to prove he didn't do it. They only need to confuse the jury. The idea is to reinterpret the evidence so the Crown's account of what happened seems open to debate.'

'He had a really good brief,' Kit contributed. 'One of those guys who does a closing argument that makes the jury fall in love with him a little bit. Make 'em laugh, make 'em cry.'

'I don't see where the doubt comes in,' I said. 'Stone was sitting in the house when they went there to ask him about the van. There was forensic evidence of Willa Howard having been in the room behind him.'

'No,' Kit said, grinning. 'That was the mistake we'd made, according to his brief. There was forensic evidence in the *cupboard* in the room behind him. The defence alleged he'd found it dumped on a street corner and thought it would be useful. The defence said that someone else had used it to imprison Willa Howard before or after her death, and that Stone had unwittingly brought it into his home.'

'And locked it in a room? And hid the key so we never found it?'

'They said that Stone was worried about being burgled. He was obsessed with security.'

'Yeah, funny how serial killers like their privacy.' Derwent shook his head. 'Surely there's no way the jury would have fallen for it.'

'You don't need to convince all twelve of them. You can get a mistrial if you confuse three of them beyond the point where they know black from white.' Hollingwood leaned back in his chair, amused rather than upset by it. 'The prosecution has to play it dead straight – no showboating, no dramatics, just concentrate on the facts. The defence can do what they like.'

'And as for being convincing, they won over more people than you'd think. Journalists, campaigners . . . and Sara Grey's family.' Whitlock's voice dropped at the end of the sentence, and I realised with a mild sense of shock that he was angry. 'I need to warn you about that. You're going to have to handle them with care. They turned against the police during the initial investigation into Sara's disappearance. My understanding is that the local CID didn't impress them and stepped on a few toes. The fiancé was out of the country when it happened, but the detectives had their concerns about him. That bothered the family, who felt they were wasting time instead of locating her. Then they took offence at some of the questions that we had to ask. Sara's body was well away from where we found Willa Howard. It was the cadaver dog that found her, not us. And there were differences in how the bodies were positioned. We didn't want to assume they were both left there by the same killer. Dr Hanshaw was confident that both women had died in the same way, but by the time

64

we found them, they had been left to nature for some time. The remains were skeletonised. He wasn't able to specify a definite cause of death for either of them. Now, of course, the question is whether he missed something.'

Beside me, Godley was absolutely still. He wouldn't give away how much he minded Glen Hanshaw's reputation being questioned, but his very silence was loaded with emotion, I thought.

'The Greys believe that we've never found Sara's killer – that she wasn't killed by the same person who killed Willa Howard, and that person was definitely not Leo Stone. They've bought into a conspiracy theory that we're deliberately trying to mislead them. They don't trust us, but they trust Stone and his son. Kelly Lambert made friends with them – can you believe that?'

'Is that why they don't want to believe Stone was Sara's killer?' I asked.

'That and the lack of forensic evidence. They don't think she would have stopped to talk to him that night. She was quiet – a bit shy. Timid. She wouldn't have argued with a guy like Stone. She'd have crossed the street to avoid him.'

'If he let her do that.'

'Then there's the fact that there was no trace of her in Stone's house or his van.' Whitlock sighed. 'I wish we'd connected the two cases earlier, but we didn't. I wish I'd been able to investigate Sara Grey's disappearance. It bothered me that they hadn't taken it seriously enough. They could have put more resources into it. Then again, we knew Willa Howard was missing almost as soon as she disappeared – within twelve hours. It was a densely populated area with a lot of footfall, even at that time of night. Halloween jogged people's memories too.'

'You did a remarkable job to track down the van.' Godley leaned forward, holding Whitlock's gaze with that intensity that made you feel you could walk through fire for him, that you wouldn't mind dying for him . . . 'Without the van, we would probably never have made a connection between the missing women and Stone, even if we'd found the bodies. The van broke the case.'

Whitlock ducked his head. 'We did all right. I had a good team. I may be wrong but I don't think there's much new ground to explore when it comes to Willa Howard's death.'

Except how she died, and where, and when. I thought of Dr Early revisiting the files, the photographs. 'How do the Howards feel about this?'

'They think Stone is guilty. It's easier for them than the Greys, I think, because they didn't believe a word of the story about him finding the cupboard in the street. There's the van in the right area and the blood – that's enough for them. They fell out quite badly with the Greys over it, which was a shame. Nice people.'

'Are they the kind of nice people who would mind if we apply to exhume their daughter's body?' Derwent, blunt as ever.

Whitlock winced. 'Depends on how you approach it.'

'With great sensitivity,' Godley said, and I wondered if he'd forgotten how Derwent preferred to work. I had a question to ask myself.

'Tell me about Rachel Healy.'

'A dead end.' Whitlock's face had hardened, stubbornness making it into a thing of angles. There was something in Whitlock's voice that sounded final, as if the subject was irrelevant and therefore the discussion was at an end.

'She went missing not long before Willa Howard.'

'We concluded the disappearance was too close to Willa for it to be connected. He took one in July and one in October, not two. That's the sort of thing a killer does when they're losing control – when they're running out of time. Stone had no idea we were going to knock on his door, and he didn't take a fourth woman after Willa Howard, though we didn't catch up with him for a few weeks.'

66

'Maybe something went wrong,' I said. 'Maybe it wasn't a satisfying murder as far as he was concerned.'

'We did look for her. We never found the body. The conclusion we reached was that she was never in Stone's house or his van. The blood from under the floorboards wasn't conclusive. It sent us on a wild goose chase. We were under pressure to clear up as many disappearances and murders as possible and Rachel Healy got lumped in with the other two.'

'There was a reason the CPS didn't charge him with her kidnap and murder,' Hollingwood said. He was watching me, his face open and friendly. I knew when I was being placated and it prickled along my nerves. 'I didn't want Rachel Healy on the indictment. The evidence that he was involved in her disappearance was circumstantial at best. The forensics were the weakest part of our case. I was of the opinion that including her and introducing the idea that a third woman had died in that room – whether it was Rachel Healy or not – could only damage us. It would have provided an opportunity to the defence to muddy the waters. We had no body. We were asking the jury to take too many leaps of faith – that she was dead, that Stone had been involved, that her body had been left somewhere other than the area where the other two women were found, for a reason we didn't know. Too many questions there, don't you think?'

'Questions that deserve an answer,' I said.

'We did our best.' Whitlock, bristling.

Derwent got there before I could. 'No one's saying you didn't. There's a reason she's on this case.'

She being me. I opened my mouth to change the subject before he said anything else, but he steamed on.

'Kerrigan can charm the birds from the trees and find things you never knew were missing. If there's a way to trace Rachel Healy and tie her murder into this case, Kerrigan will find it. Once she's decided she's going to do something, she doesn't give up.' Derwent paused for a beat. 'It makes her bloody irritating to work with, obviously, but she's right about this one.'

'Thanks,' I said, and he grinned at me. A ripple of amusement ran around the table, a welcome break in the tension. I waited until they'd stopped laughing.

'Anything on Rachel Healy will be new to the defence. If Stone killed her, he thinks he got away with it. At the moment we don't even know where she was before she disappeared. It's not going to be easy to make enquiries after so many years, but it's surprising what people can remember when you ask.'

'All this time and not a sign of her body. I really wanted to find her.' Whitlock grimaced. 'I dream about her sometimes. Gets under your skin, you know.'

I did know, all too well.

'We'll look after her,' Derwent said to Whitlock. 'We won't let you down.'

The retired policeman nodded and attempted to smile. It flickered across his face uncertainly, like a lightbulb about to blow.

11

'The rural dream. You can keep it,' Derwent said. 'Why would anyone want to live here?'

'Grammar schools. Commutable distance from London. Local amenities. Decent lifestyle.'

'Yeah, but apart from that.'

'I don't think we're seeing it at its best.'

We were driving out of London towards Aylesbury, a medium-sized market town where Sara Grey had grown up. Her parents still lived there, outside the town. It was a cold day, the sky the colour of steel, and the fields were boggy from heavy rain the night before. Crows hunched in the branches of trees and along fences like witches' familiars, their rasping call echoing across the countryside.

I went back to the opinion column I was reading out from my phone.

'"In the era of social media, when everyone has access to the internet all the time, is it even possible to have a fair trial by jury? A case such as that of Leo Stone is the ideal test: a horrific series of headline-grabbing crimes, a suspect who seems to fit the image of a ruthless killer, grieving families and photogenic victims, and an unregulated internet full of rumours. If it's a crime to be unattractive, then the prisons should be overflowing. Leo Stone was on trial for murder but he was judged on his past and his appearance. That's not justice – it's prejudice."'

I paused expectantly, and was not disappointed.

'What fucking horseshit.' Derwent glowered at a driver who was failing to give way to him.

'There's more.'

'Of course there is.'

'"What must Leo Stone's lawyers have thought when they read juror Stan Maxwell's self-published account of the trial? They must have been pleased that they had grounds for an appeal, but I think they must have been horrified too. How easily a man can lose his freedom and his reputation. By his own account, Maxwell and his fellow jurors read the rumours that spread, unchecked, across the internet. They searched for the secrets of Leo Stone's life: the missing pieces of the puzzle that they weren't supposed to know. They cheated the system. They cheated Leo Stone. They cheated justice. This is how easy it is to lock up an innocent man: a few un-flattering pictures, a few stories that float without attribution or evidence to tether them to the facts of the case, a few arrogant and prejudiced jurors with smartphones."'

Derwent grunted. 'Well, he's not wrong there. Nice of him to mention the dead women too.'

I checked. 'He didn't.'

'I know,' he said patiently. 'That was my point.'

'Wait for the next bit.'

'Go on.'

'"But even if they had confined themselves to looking at the evidence, there's no reason to believe the jury would have been able to make a fair decision. Two murder appeals have been successful already this year because of the revelation that the Home Office pathologist Dr Glen Hanshaw failed to uphold the highest standards of his profession in the months before his death, through ill health and arrogance.

Hanshaw is dead and gone. His legacy is a black mark on the legal system that nothing can erase.'"

'Fuck's sake.'

'Don't crash the car.' I put a hand on the dashboard to brace myself as Derwent swerved impatiently around a cyclist.

'That makes it sound as if poor old Hanshaw was deliberately trying to trick people. He was doing his best.'

'Which wasn't good enough.'

Derwent shifted in his seat, irritated. 'He could have done with more oversight but he wasn't that sort of person. There was no one around to tell him he wasn't coping. At least, no one he trusted. No one he'd listen to.'

'If that ever happens to you, I promise I'll tell you to quit.'

'If I'm dying and I still want to go to work every day, you have my permission to shoot me.' He glanced sideways at me. 'This is why you need to start looking for a new bloke.'

'Sorry, what?'

'You'll end up like Glen Hanshaw if you don't. You have nothing in your life but work.'

'Excuse *me*—'

Derwent held up a hand. 'Save the outrage. Tell me, when was the last time you went out? Not on a date. Just out.'

I opened my mouth to tell him it was none of his business and shut it again.

'Ages, is it? Months? Last year some time?'

'I don't remember.'

He whistled. 'Worse than I thought.'

'I've been busy. I've been working a lot.'

'Pulling double shifts. You must be raking in the overtime.'

There it was: a door offering me a way out. I could explain myself by telling Derwent I was just saving up for a deposit so I could buy my own flat and stop paying him rent.

The trouble was, it was a lie.

Worse than that, it was a lie he would spot in a heartbeat.

'I might be a bit lonely.'

71

Another glance, this time unexpectedly gentle. I had to look away at the passing streetscape before I could go on. 'It's so much easier when you're in a relationship. You wake up on a day off and you go and do something. No planning. No *fuss*.' I swallowed. 'Everyone I know seems to be getting married, or they're just married, or they've just had a baby. None of my friends are ever at a loose end. They have their own lives – it's not their fault that I don't.'

'What about Liv?'

'She's having IVF.'

'Seriously?'

'Don't say anything. She and her girlfriend want to have a baby. They've picked a donor but it hasn't happened yet.'

'I was about to volunteer,' Derwent said, and I laughed before I could stop myself. There was a chance – a small one – that he was actually serious.

'Listen, Kerrigan, you've been under a cloud since that two-timing shitweasel dumped you and went off to play happy families with his new bird. You've got to get your head straight.'

'That two-timing shitweasel', otherwise known as the love of my life, Rob Langton. Derwent wasn't his biggest fan. 'Thanks for the advice.'

'You're not getting any younger, you know. If you want to have kids, you need to meet someone in the next year.'

'I'm not *that* old.' Outrage made my voice squeaky.

'Your clock is ticking, whether you can hear it or not. Think about it. You meet someone. Then you've got to spend a year or so getting to know them. Then you'll want to get married because your parents would shit a brick if you had a child out of wedlock. That'll take another year to organise. And then you'll be cleaned out financially. You won't want to take maternity leave until you've built up a bit of cash. Call it another year. Then you can't assume you'll get pregnant straight away. All the time your fertility is declining. Sad, really.'

'You seem to have given this a lot of thought.' My voice was so cold it could have flash-frozen a side of beef. Derwent wasn't noticeably affected.

'It's just common sense, isn't it, but you don't seem to have any.'

'I know you've embraced domesticity—'

'This has nothing to do with me.'

'You're so right. So why are we talking about it?' I waggled my phone at him. 'Do you want to hear the end of this or not?'

'Give it to me. I can take it.'

'"After his successful appeal yesterday, Leo Stone deserves an apology from all of us. The Metropolitan Police, too, must bear responsibility for this miscarriage of justice. The CPS is insisting there must be a retrial, wasting more time and money. An innocent man must suffer because they can't bear to admit they made a mistake. Sara Grey's family have campaigned for Leo Stone's release from prison. They, like me, believe Leo Stone is innocent of these murders. He is a victim of this crime, like the two women he was alleged to have killed. If the Home Secretary has any sense she will discourage the CPS from pursuing him any further so the Met can reopen the case and, this time, bring the real killer to justice."'

'Who wrote this?'

'A journalist named Christopher Fallon.' I showed Derwent the byline photograph, knowing it would irritate him further.

'State of him. Pencil-necked twerp, telling me I can't do my job. Listen, Christopher, if I want your opinion I'll come round to your house and beat it out of you.'

'He'd be shaking in his shoes if he could hear you.'

Derwent glowered at me instead. 'You don't think that sort of piece affects public opinion?'

'A tiny number of people will read it.'

'The victims' families will read it.'

'True. But they don't love us anyway.'

73

Derwent didn't reply, because it was true. That was one very good reason why we had decided to do places before people.

I concentrated on the directions DCI Whitlock had given us, aware that if Derwent took a wrong turning it would be my fault. The roads got narrower as we came closer to the Greys' home, and Derwent slowed down. The slackening speed of the car seemed to mirror my reluctance to get there.

'They're angry. Very angry. They won't trust you and they definitely won't help you,' Whitlock had warned us. I liked to make my own mistakes, instead of inheriting the results of other people's poor judgement.

'That's it up there.' I pointed to the right, where a white, thatched building stood in a gravelled yard. It was a barn conversion, half-timbered and sagging under its heavy roof. It appeared ancient but well looked after.

'Big, isn't it?'

'They're well off. She's a retired GP and he was a management consultant.' I hesitated, waiting for him to turn the car through the gate. 'Remember what the boss said. We need to be on our best behaviour.'

'I know you're not implying I would do anything else.'

'I wouldn't dare.'

Derwent parked beside a battered Volvo and a newish BMW. 'Let's see those convent manners, Kerrigan. I'm counting on you to charm them.'

Charm was not going to be enough, I thought, on edge as Derwent rang the doorbell.

The car had been loud on the gravel, so they had known we were outside. Even so, it took a long time for anyone to come to the door. When it opened, an elderly man stood in front of us. He was leaning on a stick.

'Mr Grey?'

A nod.

I introduced myself and Derwent. 'Thank you for agreeing to speak with us.'

'We had no choice.' He stepped back and disappeared into the house, leaving us to shut the door and follow him into a huge double-height room with a brick fireplace at one end and a kitchen at the other. A slim, pale woman sat on one sofa, her face tight with tension. Mrs Grey, I guessed, and corrected myself: *Dr* Grey. She stood up as we approached, but her eyes followed her husband, not us. He had a dragging walk, one foot sliding along the ground as he moved.

A second man stood by the fireplace, his hands in the pockets of immaculately pressed chinos. He had the ruddy complexion of a man who spends a lot of time on golf courses, and his hair was slicked back from his forehead. I knew before he spoke that he was going to have the sort of plummy voice that made my hackles rise.

'Hi. Tom Mitchell.' He leaned across and shook hands with Derwent, sketching a wave in my direction. 'I was Sara's fiancé at the time of her disappearance.'

'Please tell us' – Mr Grey sat down with a grunt of effort – 'what exactly this charade is supposed to achieve? You're investigating Sara's murder all over again so you can prove that Leo Stone did it.'

'We're examining every aspect of the previous investigation to make sure we haven't overlooked any details,' Derwent said.

'And if you have?'

'Then we'll advise the CPS accordingly.'

'What a waste of everyone's time,' Mr Grey spat. 'An exercise in reinforcing a set of errors that should never have been made. A cover-up for your friends, so no one realises they framed an innocent man.'

'There was a considerable amount of evidence that suggested Mr Stone was your daughter's killer,' I said tentatively.

'That's what you wanted everyone to believe.'

'The fact is that no one knows who took my daughter.' Dr Grey's voice was low and precise. 'No one ever traced the person who killed her. I'm absolutely sure of that. We're asked to believe that Leo killed her purely because her body was left in the same area as Willa Howard. Well, I'm sorry. It isn't convincing to me and I don't think it would have convinced the jury if they hadn't broken the law to find out more about Leo.'

Leo. 'Are you in contact with Mr Stone?'

'Not directly. We get messages from him.'

'Written messages?'

'No. His son Kelly is in touch with us. He passes on communications from Leo.'

'What sort of communications?' Derwent asked and Dr Grey glanced at him before she answered.

'He's very grateful to us for our campaigning on his behalf. I always say it's in our interests as well. We want Sara's *real* killer to be located and punished. He shows tremendous empathy to us in our difficulties. Kelly, too. He's quite remarkable.' Dr Grey took out a handkerchief and pressed it under her eyes. 'They want us to get justice for Sara's sake, not just because Leo is incarcerated. I can't *believe* that after all this, you're pursuing him *again.*'

'What would you prefer us to do?' Derwent asked.

'Find the real killer, of course.' She flung out a hand in irritation. 'Your stupid colleagues wasted *weeks* bothering Tom and his friends, even though he wasn't in the country when poor Sara disappeared. He couldn't have been involved and we said so. But they didn't listen. They were utterly determined to make him into a killer. They wanted to turn us against him but we didn't listen, did we, Tom?'

'No. And I was very grateful.' Tom looked from me to Derwent and back again. 'I'm not going to tell you how to do your job but I can save you a lot of time if you're drawing up a list of suspects. I wasn't involved.'

'Thank you, sir.' Derwent's voice carried the slightest overtone of I'll-be-the-judge-of-that.

'The fact is,' Dr Grey said again, 'your colleagues struck lucky when they found Sara's body. They saw an opportunity to make Leo take responsibility for Sara's death as well as the other girl's. Far easier than looking for a second killer.'

'But the two bodies were left in much the same way,' I began.

'A dead body is a dead body, especially if it's left outside. There was nothing left of her. She was *eaten*, Detective. Animals took her flesh. Her face. Her hands. She was utterly decomposed. Have you read the pathologist's report?'

'I've spoken with the pathologist who is working on this case now.' In the face of Dr Grey's anger I felt like a badly prepared student. I should have read Dr Hanshaw's report as well as talking to Dr Early.

'They didn't even find all her bones. The small ones disappear. They were missing twenty-three bones – vertebrae, toes, fingers. Bones that I *made*.' She stopped, choking with emotion, the mother in her elbowing aside the rational scientist who believed in facts above all. 'I blame them for not finding Sara's killer. I don't think the original investigation was adequate in any way. I do not believe that Leo was involved in the slightest, with either murder. I will not help you to lock him up again.'

'That's not our aim.' I really hoped Derwent wouldn't contradict me. 'Our intention is to review the evidence and make sure the correct person is prosecuted for murder. If the evidence leads us towards Mr Stone, we'll know that the original investigation was sound. If it leads us away from him, please believe me, we'll follow the facts. We don't want an innocent man to be behind bars. We want justice for your daughter too, and we'll work as hard as we can to get it.'

'I gather from DCI Whitlock that Sara's possessions are here,' Derwent slid into the quiet aftermath of a speech that I was both proud and embarrassed to have made. 'Is it possible for us to look at them?'

'I suppose so,' Dr Grey said heavily.

'I'll show you.' Tom Mitchell started towards the stairs that led up to an upper floor. He moved quickly, full of nervous energy. I caught a flash of gold from his left hand as I followed him: a wedding ring. 'It's all boxed up, I'm afraid. But the police went through everything. They couldn't find anything in Sara's life that would have made someone want to harm her.'

He led us into a room that should have been a bedroom but it had no furniture in it. Boxes piled on top of boxes filled the space instead. The room smelled musty and he pushed open the window.

'She'd moved out, you see. There was nothing here. All her things were in our flat. I kept everything for a long time. I didn't want to clear Sara out of my life, I suppose. But in the end I had to. She wasn't coming back. Barbara – that's Dr Grey – didn't want to unpack it so it ended up here.' He stood in the middle of the room and looked around, his posture somehow conveying bafflement and longstanding grief. 'Not much, is there? Not for a whole life.'

I felt unexpectedly sorry for him, and angry with myself for my reverse snobbishness. Bad things could happen to wealthy, privileged men who wore Ralph Lauren cashmere jumpers and inherited signet rings, the crest softened and blurred by time. Life wasn't easy for anyone who mourned, whether they were rich or poor.

'What do you think happened to her?' I asked, taking advantage of the fact that the door was closed.

'She was in the wrong place at the wrong time.' He rubbed his head with his left hand and winced. 'I keep forgetting I've got a ring on this hand and end up battering myself.'

'Recent addition?' Derwent asked.

'I got married a couple of months ago.'

'Congratulations.'

'I felt weird about it. The Greys said they understood, but—'

he broke off. 'Oh, you know. It shouldn't have been this way. It should have been Sara.'

'Is that how you felt?'

'A bit.' He looked miserable. 'A lot. I couldn't stop thinking about her.'

'What does your missus make of that?' Derwent asked, and I was glad he had, because I was wondering the same thing.

'She understands of course.' He held himself stiffly, guarded now. 'She was one of Sara's best friends. It helps that she knew her so well. We talk about Sara a lot. She misses her too.'

'I'm sure she does,' I said.

'Vanessa was supposed to be our bridesmaid.' Tom sighed. 'I'm lucky to have her.'

We got back into the car after a long and thoroughly unhelpful search through Sara Grey's possessions – the clothes, the photographs, the school reports and letters, and books she had loved. The Greys had sent us on our way without warmth, just as angry as they had been when we arrived, despite my best efforts.

Derwent drove out through the gate with a sigh of relief.

'They really don't want Leo to be guilty, do they?'

'Nope.'

'They must see something in him that I don't.'

'The son has obviously worked hard on them. Plus the original investigation burned through any goodwill there might have been towards us by focusing on Tom.' I shook my head. 'Maybe it's just that they don't feel any better for having Leo locked up. It hasn't brought their daughter back. If he's the wrong man, they can keep looking for justice.'

Derwent nodded. 'So how long would you give Tom Mitchell's new marriage?'

'Months.'

'Weeks, I'd say.'

'Days.'

'It's over already.'

'It never started,' I said soberly. 'He's not over Sara yet. Maybe he'll never get over her.'

'Poor bloke,' Derwent said, as if he meant it.

12

On a fine day, St Leonards-on-Sea would have been a nice place to visit. The shingle beach was long and empty, the rain sweeping across it like a curtain as the tide came in. The waves were noisier than the cars that swished along the promenade that ran between the beach and the tall Regency terraces that defined the area. They had been built for a wealthy town that had never quite materialised, though the houses had been grand enough, with elegant columns and graceful porticoes. Most of them were now divided into flats, including the Howards' home. They occupied the bottom two floors of a white-painted house that looked out to sea.

'It's an upside-down house. We use the downstairs rooms as bedrooms and upstairs is our sitting room.' Mrs Howard hauled herself up the stairs ahead of us, wheezing. 'It's the views, you see. I like to look out to sea. Always interesting. Always inspiring.'

The sitting room ran across the front of the house, with three tall windows framing the view. The walls were lined with landscape paintings that had an abstract quality: saffron yellow sand, teal-coloured sea, squared-off purple hills, white cliffs, scarlet sunsets. An easel stood in front of one window with a half-finished painting leaning on it. Mrs Howard cast it a longing look before she sat down.

'Thank you for taking the time to talk to us,' I said.

'No, no. It's a pleasure. Anyone who can help us is welcome.' She was a round woman with a sweet face that was made for smiling. There was something dead in her eyes, though, a dullness that I'd seen many times before. 'My husband isn't here. He didn't want to be.'

'I can understand it must be upsetting to talk about Willa.' It was that sympathy for the bereaved that always redeemed Derwent in my eyes: he really meant it.

Mrs Howard raised her hands and let them fall into her lap, a helpless gesture. 'It's upsetting whether we talk about her or not.'

'Do you understand what's happened with the appeal and why it was successful?' I asked. 'It doesn't mean that the courts are convinced Mr Stone is innocent. Nor does our investigation.'

'No, I understand that. DCI Whitlock rang me himself to explain it to me. Such a nice man.'

'Yes, he is.'

'He worked so hard on the investigation. They all did.'

'We may not be able to do much more than they did, but we're going to do our best,' I promised. 'We're determined to put together the strongest case we can for the retrial.'

'You can't find evidence that isn't there.' Mrs Howard sounded wistful, not angry. 'He did such a clever job.'

I thought for a moment that she was still talking about DCI Whitlock, until she went on. 'I truly think he's an evil person, you know. Evil. That's the only word. The way he took those women. The way he kept them. That awful metal box where he hid them.' She gave a tiny sigh. 'We knew from the moment she disappeared that she was gone. At least, I did. I never had any hope that we'd see her again.'

'Why was that?'

'She would never have gone off without contacting me. She wasn't that sort of person. We were very close. She told me everything – all about Jeremy, her boyfriend. She told me about everyone in her life. We spoke every day, often more than once. I would have known if she needed me. I would have sensed it. All I could feel was an absence.'

I was trying to imagine a situation where I would willingly tell my mother even half of the things that went on in my life. Derwent took over.

'I know you'll have answered these questions before, but was Willa worried about anything? Was anyone bothering her?'

'She was very angry with Jeremy.' Mrs Howard shook her head. 'She spent far too long with him. He was never going to grow up. We could see that, even if she couldn't. He was a weak person. Immature.'

'Was there anyone else of significance in Willa's life?'

'No. No one. She couldn't seem to get over Jeremy. I mean, the waste of it. She was a gorgeous girl – talented, creative, kind . . . she deserved so much more. She would have been a wonderful mother. And I know Jeremy wasn't directly responsible for her death but it was his idea to meet in that horrible pub. Have you been in it?'

We nodded.

'I wanted to be in the last place where Willa was. Stupid, really, to think she might be hanging around there. She was happiest here, by the sea, so if her spirit is anywhere, it's here.' Mrs Howard sniffed, her eyes brimming. 'It smelled horrible. Stale beer. Cheap air freshener. I sat on the stool where she'd sat, looking at the last things she saw. Maybe someone was watching her while she was in the pub. She had such glorious hair – like a cloak. I always thought she was pure pre-Raphaelite.'

I could see what Mrs Howard meant. Willa had had a heavy kind of beauty – a strong jaw and straight eyebrows – and her hair had hung down to the small of her back.

'The barman was nice. He gave me a drink on the house. Gin and tonic. Mother's ruin.' Mrs Howard began to sob, looking from Derwent to me like a child. 'That's all I could think. Mother's ruin.'

I put down my clipboard and went to sit beside her, putting my arm around her shoulders. Derwent leaned forward, his face stern.

'Mrs Howard, what happened to Willa was horrendous. You deserve answers and we'll try to get them for you, I promise.'

'I thought it was all over. I thought he was behind bars and we could move on, whatever that means, because it's not as if I can forget, is it? But then he got out again. Willa's brother is getting married next month – his girlfriend is pregnant, in fact, so we're going to be grandparents. The circle of life, starting again. It was a comfort to me to think of it. But now Stone is out and I know he's out and I have to think about him all over again.' She took a few heaving breaths, getting her emotions under control. 'It was bad enough when he sent the letters.'

'What letters?'

'From prison.' She sniffed. 'On her birthday. And at Christmas. As if he had the right to contact us.'

'What did he say?' Derwent asked, but she shook her head.

'I'm not prepared to repeat his words.'

'Mrs Howard—'

'Oh, you can read them yourselves. I've got them. It's not that I don't want you to see them. I just don't want to think about them. Or him.' She looked across the room in the direction of a vast Victorian bureau.

'Are they in there?' I asked.

'In the top drawer. There's a folder of them. It should be on top.' She stood up, energised. 'I'm going to go and tidy myself up and make a cup of tea for us. I don't want to be in the room when you read them. I don't even want to see them. But you take your time.'

84

She bustled out of the room and I waited until I heard water running in the kitchen next door before I stood up and slid the drawer open. A plastic folder lay on top of the papers in the drawer, as Mrs Howard had promised. 'Got them.'

'Over here.' Derwent was clearing a space on a coffee table that had been stacked with art books and gallery catalogues.

I shook the contents of the folder out and Derwent arranged the letters in order of date, using the end of his pen rather than touching them with his hands, as was his habit. The letters were written on cheap, flimsy paper in black pencil. Stone's writing was large and irregular and it was hard to read them.

'This is the first one.'

'That's right after he was convicted,' I said, checking the date.

Dear Mr and Mrs Howard.

I am very sorry for your trubbel. I know you loved your littel girl. She was so prety and good.

I saw you crying when the jury come back. It was as espected. I am use to prison but I supose it is all new to you.

If I cud of said the truth at the trial I wud of.

Why did you call her Willa is what I want to know.

Please write back.

Leo Stone
HMP WINLOW

'Imagine getting that in the post unexpectedly.' Derwent shook his head, disgusted. 'He shouldn't have been allowed to write to them. How did he get the address?'

'No idea.' I was reading the next one.

Dear Mr and Mrs Howard.

No letter from you but I want to wish you a happy xmas enyway. It will be hard for you. Al the days are the same here but theres carols and speshel diner on xmas day.

Do you have a xmas tree I wunder. Did you buy a pressunt for Willa she cant open it enyway.

They say kids are a blesing I think they brake your hart

Please write back

Leo Stone
HMP WINLOW

'He drew holly on it.' I pushed it away. 'He was winding them up, wasn't he?'

'Bastard,' Derwent said softly, reading the third letter.

Dear Mr and Mrs Howard.

It will be your littel girls birthday soon. Shes the same age as my son Kel. He told me.

If he trys to tawk to you dont lissen. He is a wierd kid. Hes tryne to get me out but I dont think he will have to much luck there I am in here for the long hall wich I am sure is a good thing you may think but theres reasons for wats hapened if I cd tell you.

It is lonly in prison I think aboutt Willa alot. All her luvly hair was runed wen they found her such a pitty.

LEO

'Is that the last one?'

'One more.' Derwent sounded as nauseated as I felt. He pushed it across the table to me.

Dear Mr and Mrs Howard.

Do you think aboutt Willa cos I do.

Do you have eny pix of her as Id like one. Not dead but normal smiling.

She was a silly bitsh to get herself killed tho wen you think aboutt it. You should of told her not to tawk to strangers or didnt she lissen.

Ill write agen soon. Write back to me please

Leo

'No wonder Mrs Howard didn't want to read them again.' I shuffled them back into the folder and fastened it so Leo Stone's words were sealed away. 'What an absolute shit.'

'What did he think he was going to achieve?' Derwent rubbed his jaw, the faint dry rasp of stubble just audible from where I knelt beside him.

'What did the Greys say? He was full of empathy for them.' I waggled the folder. 'That's not the impression he gives here. Quite the opposite.'

'Everything comes via Kelly, doesn't it? Kelly may be making him sound nicer than he really is.'

'Do we need to take the letters away?'

'I think so.' He dropped his voice. 'For her sake, we should.'

'Tea!' Mrs Howard pushed the door open with a rattling tray. I went to help her, shoving the folder at Derwent so he could hide it. Her eyes were red, up close, and her face was swollen but she smiled at me. 'Thank you. So kind.'

We let her fuss over us, choosing biscuits from the plate she offered, making conversation about St Leonards-on-Sea and the house and her art. Eventually, reluctantly, Derwent put his mug on the table.

'Mrs Howard, I need to ask about the letters. Did they come from the prison?'

87

'No. They were postmarked in London. I didn't keep the envelopes. I didn't really want to keep the letters themselves but Graham insisted that we should because he said they might be important.' She shoved her hands between her knees and squeezed them. 'And – and, well, it was sort of a link with Willa. I didn't want him to talk about her but he was the last person who saw her. I thought – if I could bear it – maybe he would talk to us about her. He would tell us how he caught her. What he did to kill her. What he did afterwards.'

'Mrs Howard,' Derwent began, but she cut him off.

'The thing is, we don't *know*. I imagine things. I can't help it. He never said anything about what happened to her. We don't know if she died then and there, when he grabbed her, or if he kept her alive for a time. We don't know if she suffered, you see. I say I know she died very shortly afterwards but I don't *know* that. Only he knows and he won't tell anyone the truth.' She swallowed convulsively. 'I know he's playing games with us. I know he enjoys it. I know writing these letters was the only way he had any power over us when he was in prison. That was why he wrote – to taint Christmas and her birthday. To remind us that he had taken her away.'

'Mrs Howard,' Derwent said again. 'It's all right.'

'No, it isn't. I'm sorry, Inspector, it isn't. It's never going to be all right again.'

'I appreciate that, but—'

'The worst thing,' Mrs Howard said, as if he hadn't spoken, 'is that I'm so ashamed of myself. I wanted to write back to him. I wanted to engage with him. I wanted to make him *like* us. I can never, ever forgive him for taking my daughter but I would have pretended I had forgiven him, if he would only tell us what happened to her.' She bit her lip, hard. 'I can't bear him. I can't bear that he's out. What he said in the last letter – of course we told her not to talk to strangers. She was such a lovely person, though. She wouldn't have wanted to offend anyone. He played on that, I know he did.'

88

'Did you write back to him?' I asked.

'No. Graham made me promise not to. I agreed.' She looked away, her eyes filling again. 'I thought he was in prison forever. I thought there would be time to persuade Graham we should respond. I thought we might gain his trust. And now he's out.'

'Temporarily. He won't be out for long.' Derwent stood up, towering over her, his face a scowl. For once it felt protective rather than threatening. The thought crossed my mind that if I was ever in trouble it would be Derwent I'd call. You'd want him on your side.

You certainly didn't want him on anyone else's side.

'Are you in touch with any of the other victims' families?' I asked as we followed her back down the narrow stairs to the front door.

'No. I know they thought there might have been a third girl, but they weren't sure. I don't know anything about her. And the Greys – well, we don't speak any more. For some reason they've decided to believe he didn't hurt their daughter. I don't understand it.'

'Grief affects people in different ways.'

She looked at me sadly. 'I know that, dear. Graham and I might as well be living on different planets. He's so busy all the time now. He's never here. He barely sleeps. He volunteers a lot. Throws himself into things. He needs to be around people, whereas I find socialising very difficult. I'd rather be alone with my thoughts.'

'It takes time.'

'So they say.' With an effort she dragged the heavy front door open and stood back to let us out. 'I used to paint people, you know. Portraits. I can't do it now. I tried, but when I look at their faces I don't really see them. I only see Willa.'

13

'Well? What have you found out?' Una Burt had been watching for our return to the office like a shark lurking offshore, waiting for unwary swimmers. I was getting tired of being ambushed.

'Not much.'

Derwent shot me a curious look as he took off his jacket and hung it on the back of his chair: it wasn't like me to sound negative even if that was how I felt. 'We've visited the locations where the women disappeared and spoke to Dr Early to discuss the pathology. We've also met all of the victims' families to introduce ourselves.'

Burt sniffed. 'You could have done that with a few phone calls.'

'I thought it was important to meet them face to face. And it was.' Derwent came around his desk, getting closer to the chief inspector. Invading personal space: step one in Derwent's method of dealing with criticism. Una Burt was quite used to it and stood her ground.

'What do you think you found out?'

'That we can't depend on the Greys for any help unless we find them a new suspect.' Derwent seemed to be concentrating on rolling his shirtsleeves up, one fold every sentence. 'That

Leo Stone sends messages to the Greys via his son. That he sent letters to the Howards. That Stone is a sadistic bully, whatever else he is. Oh, and that Rachel Healy's family hasn't had any communications from Stone.'

'But the other two have. Interesting.'

'I don't think that means we should leave Rachel Healy out of the investigation,' I began, and got a glower from Derwent.

'We talked about this in the car.'

'Yes, and I disagreed with you. I'm still disagreeing with you.'

Derwent turned back to Una Burt. 'We're not sure the Healy case connects.'

'I am.'

He went on as if I hadn't spoken. 'Aside from the forensics, which are frankly questionable, we've got nothing on her. She walked out of her office and no one ever saw her again – so far, so similar to the other two. But I don't think she's one of his victims. It was too close to Willa Howard's disappearance. A three-month gap between Sara Grey and Rachel Healy, and then a couple of weeks between that and Willa Howard going missing, and then nothing. That's not a pattern I recognise.'

'We don't know enough about Rachel Healy's disappearance to say either way.' My throat hurt from talking: it was what I had been doing all day, with Derwent and with Rachel Healy's sister, Zoe Fell, who had opened the door of her Herne Hill home with a baby on her hip and a scowl on her pretty face. I played it back in my mind, trying to work out why it had gone so badly.

'You want to see me about Rachel? I wonder why. No one's been interested up to now.' She stepped back to let us in. 'And take off your shoes, please. Bertie's started crawling and I can't keep hoovering the carpet.'

There would be no tea and biscuits here, I'd thought, pulling off my shoes and following her through to a small sitting room full of baby toys. She put the baby down and he immediately began to crawl towards the door. Derwent shut the door.

'Sorry, buddy. Trapped.'

Bertie made a sound like a pigeon cooing and sat back on his bottom to consider his options, favouring his mother with a huge, dribbling smile.

'He's a gorgeous baby,' I said.

'Thanks.' She was staring at him, not me. She was very like her sister, I thought, but older, thinner, as hollow-eyed as mothers of babies tended to be. 'What do you want?'

'You may have seen that Leo Stone was successful in appealing his conviction this week.'

'No. I didn't see anything. I don't watch the news. What has that got to do with us?'

'As you know, there was some evidence that he may have been involved in Rachel's disappearance but we don't feel it was fully explored previously. We're taking over the investigation and looking at all the evidence again.'

She took a deep breath and let it out slowly. 'Too little, too late.'

'I appreciate it may seem that way,' I said, wishing I was somewhere else. 'But we are taking a fresh approach. We aren't going to give up on finding out what happened to Rachel.'

'Were you close to your sister?' Derwent held out a toy to Bertie, who didn't take it.

'Put that down, please. Leave him alone.' Zoe snatched the baby up and sat with him on her lap, holding him for comfort as much as anything. 'Look, Rachel had her own life and I had mine. I was working in a very demanding job and I didn't see a lot of her. The last time I saw her was about three weeks before she disappeared.'

'How did she seem? Was she worried about anything?'

'She was happy. I'm not just saying that because I want a happy memory of the last time I saw her. She was glowing. I thought she'd found a new boyfriend but she said she hadn't.

92

Then she said I wouldn't approve of what she'd been doing, which worried me, quite frankly.' Zoe sighed. 'We didn't have a normal sibling relationship. I was more like a mother to her. Our parents died in a car accident when we were in our teens. I had to take over from them when I was nineteen and Rachel was thirteen. It put a strain on our relationship.'

'So maybe she wouldn't have confided in you if something was bothering her.'

'Maybe not.' She shook her head. 'But I'd have known if she was upset about something and she wasn't. The opposite. As I said, she was happy.'

'Tell me about her previous boyfriends,' I prompted.

'She wasn't the sort of person who liked being tied down. She was casual about relationships. A free spirit. She dated a lot, I know that, but I don't think she was serious about anyone. She had a boyfriend at university. I doubt they were still in touch. The last time she mentioned him was to say he'd got married and had a baby, which was absolutely not what Rachel wanted.' Zoe bit her lip, lost in her own thoughts. That suited me fine since every word she'd said had hit home for me. *Imagine finding out your ex-boyfriend had got married and had a baby. How would that make you feel?* The words echoed through my mind in Derwent's voice and when I risked a look in his direction he was staring at me meaningfully.

I cleared my throat. 'What was his name?'

'Mike Brendon. He was nice. A real gentle giant. She broke his heart.' Zoe shivered. 'He was better off without her. He said as much to me the last time I saw him.'

'Which was when?' Derwent asked.

'Oh – their graduation, I think. Years ago.' She looked at Derwent then. 'You can't possibly think Mike had anything to do with it.'

'It's worth checking every line of enquiry.'

She laughed, a jarring sound. 'They could have done that first time round, couldn't they? It would have saved you the trouble.'

Derwent didn't take the bait; he wasn't there for an argument. 'So that relationship was over by the time she left university. Was there anyone else in her life?'

'I mean, one or two people.'

'People?'

Zoe caught the sense of Derwent's question. 'Men. She was straight, Inspector.'

'If she was seeing a woman,' I began tentatively, 'would she assume you would disapprove of it?'

'Are you suggesting I'm homophobic? Because I am not.'

'No, not at all. I'm just trying to work out what Rachel might have wanted to keep from you.'

'Anything. Nothing. She was always like that, growing up. Pointless secrets, all the time, for the pleasure of telling me I didn't know something about her.'

'OK. Do you know the names of the men she was seeing?'

'I never met any of them. One was a colleague. Dan, I think. But that fizzled out during the summer before she died.'

'Whose idea was it to break up?'

'Oh, gosh, I don't know. It was mutual, I think. No one was heartbroken. Rach certainly wasn't and Dan, whoever he was, kept working in the same office so it can't have been that bad. But you should talk to her colleagues if you want to know what was going on. They saw a lot more of her than I did.'

'She was an estate agent, wasn't she?'

'Commercial property.' The baby was beginning to complain, arching his back and wriggling. She set him down on the floor again. He made a beeline for Derwent's feet and began to haul himself up by the creases in Derwent's suit trousers, until he was standing with two dimpled pink paws braced on Derwent's knees. He beamed at Derwent, who grinned back, not seeming to mind the snail-trail of saliva the baby was smearing on his trousers.

'Look at that. Gold-medal standing up. You know what you're doing, don't you?'

Zoe's voice was cutting. 'Forgive me for saying so, but I don't think the same is true of you. You don't seem to have any idea what you're doing here.'

'We're really here to reassure you that Rachel hasn't fallen off our radar. In fact, finding out what happened to her is a priority for us,' I said.

'I wish I thought that was true.'

'What sort of a person was Rachel?' I asked.

'She was fun. She was light-hearted. Kind. Impulsive. Easy-going. Easily led. She was a bit immature.' Zoe Fell's chin began to tremble uncontrollably. 'I loved her so much. She was my entire family. She was all I had.'

Una Burt listened to our account of the meeting with a frown on her face. 'It sounds as if Rachel was doing something she shouldn't have been doing. Sleeping with the wrong person could have got her killed.'

'That's my take on it too.' Derwent sounded faintly disappointed to agree with Una Burt about anything. 'She's a distraction from the real investigation.'

'What if her private life has nothing to do with her disappearance? What if she isn't a distraction? You can't discount the blood as if it wasn't important,' I said.

'The blood told us nothing. It could have been a match for Rachel or thousands of other people.' Derwent turned his aggression on me this time, and I knew I was standing in for Una Burt but I didn't like it. 'It wasn't a match, or at least we couldn't prove it was a match, which amounts to the same thing. We don't have a body. And there wasn't more than a speck of blood in the house from Willa Howard. There was nothing at all from Sara Grey. Do me a favour, explain why the whole room would be saturated in Rachel Healy's blood if she died the same way as the other two.'

'I don't know,' I said stiffly. 'But I don't know it rules her out either. And neither do you. Plus, the blood came from somewhere. Something bad happened in that room to someone.'

'It doesn't seem as if you're on the same page.' Una Burt looked from me to Derwent and back again, a tiny smile curving the corners of her mouth. 'How unusual. You usually work so well together.'

'It's not a problem,' I said, sensing danger.

'But it could be.' She folded her arms, the smile widening a fraction further. 'Let's not waste your energy in bickering. Josh, you can concentrate on the two known victims. Maeve, feel free to pursue the Rachel Healy angle.'

'That's not necessary.' Derwent's voice was flat. He knew, as did I, that Una Burt's intention was to play us off against each other, as if we needed competition to work hard.

'You can have Liv Bowen. And Maeve, let me know if you need any support. I'm sure I can find someone to help you. Georgia, maybe.'

'Look, I don't think there's any need—' I started to say, but Burt held up her hand.

'You'll be more productive this way. You don't have time to waste arguing with one another.'

She turned and walked back into her office, closing the door behind her with a certain finality. I looked at Derwent, who was chewing his bottom lip thoughtfully.

'Well done.'

He looked wounded. 'What? What did I do?'

'You didn't back me up.'

'How can I back you up? I don't agree with you.'

The two of us stared at each other for a beat. Derwent looked away first, retreating behind his desk. He sat down to concentrate on some paperwork, which was an absolute give-away that he was more agitated than he seemed. Paperwork usually only happened with a gun to his head.

I sat down at my own desk and began reading through the file on Rachel again. I would speak to her colleagues and her flatmates, I decided, just to rule out any personal issues that might have resulted in her death. And if I was right, and Leo Stone had taken her, I'd need to work out how to investigate that. CCTV was out: it would be long gone at this stage. Time would have blunted the memory of the best witnesses, assuming I could find them. If she had been snatched off the street, I would never know how, unless Stone himself confessed. I wasn't ready to try interviewing him yet. I needed to know a lot more about Rachel Healy's disappearance before I showed my hand.

Anyway, he was a past master at no-comment interviews. Between his experience and his shit-hot lawyer's instincts, I would get nowhere.

So I needed to find her.

An hour slipped by as I stared at maps, calculating distances and marking possibilities. What I needed was a geographical profiler, someone who specialised in interpreting an offender's movements. People leaned towards the familiar, the places close at hand, especially when they were under pressure. The more they tried to seem random, the more they gave them-selves away. If I believed that Leo Stone was responsible for Rachel Healy's disappearance, I should be able to prove it, to Derwent and to anyone else.

'Are you OK?'

I looked up, my concentration evaporating. Derwent was standing beside my desk. *Speak of the devil.* 'Why?'

'Tough day.'

'Yeah.' I tapped the end of my pen on the map. 'Are you worried about this case?'

He looked as if the idea had never occurred to him. 'No.'

'All these people are depending on us. You keep saying we'll put him behind bars again but the more I look at this case, the more I think we were lucky to get a conviction first time round.'

Derwent's jaw tightened, which was a sure sign that he was

losing his temper. 'What am I supposed to say to them, Kerrigan? "Sorry, we might have lost our shot at this but at least he spent a year inside and hey, if we wait long enough he might kill someone else so we can get him for that."'

'I'm not criticising you.'

'Funny, it sounds as if you are.'

'No, I know you're saying what they need to hear. And we need them to trust us. I'd say the same myself. I just don't know if I believe it.'

'You can't let yourself think that way. It's not going to be easy to go back through someone else's investigation but at least there are leads to follow. We're not starting from scratch.'

'We are when it comes to Rachel Healy. No one seems to have spent any time on her.'

'All right. Someone dropped the ball. You're going to pick it up.' His face softened. 'You put yourself through it, don't you?'

'I want to do right by her.'

'You will.' He hesitated, then burst out with, 'For what it's worth, I don't want to work with Liv on this.'

'She'll work hard for you.'

'I know, but I want you.'

I stared up at him, lost for words. He didn't wait for me to find any. With a brisk nod, he slung his jacket over his shoulder and left for the day.

14

As befitted a commercial property specialist, the Chelsea offices of Gallagher Kemp were housed in a prime bit of London real estate. It was a small white-painted building, with lavishly ornate detailing and high arched roof-lights that suggested someone had abandoned a giant birdcage on the corner of the street. It stood at an angle to the road, a sign that it had been there for longer than the rest of the buildings around it. London was peppered with little survivors like it: structures that had ducked changing fashions and aerial bombardment and predatory developers until they achieved listed status. It was more successful as a piece of architectural history than an office, I thought, sitting in a draughty reception area that had been carved out of a grander hall. Still, I could see how multimillionaires would feel at ease with the stained-glass windows, the marble floor, the classic Scandinavian furniture, the ice-blonde receptionist, the cut-glass decanter and tumblers on her desk, and the owners' Aston Martin and Jaguar parked on the street outside.

'How many people work here?' I asked the blonde, who took a long time to come up with the answer: eight employees, including her, and the two owners.

'So it's quite a small operation.'

'We keep it small. Company policy.' A man came through the door behind the reception desk at speed, his hand outstretched. 'James Gallagher.'

'DS Maeve Kerrigan.' I stood up to shake the proffered hand, more amused than anything that he gave me a very obvious once-over from head to feet. He was thin, snapping with energy and a polished kind of charm. He wore his thick greying hair on the long side, his shirt open at the neck, and his suit so fitted that I could see the muscles move in his thighs when he walked. Not actually handsome or particularly tall, he moved with the confidence of a man who was both, and he almost carried it off. He was fifty, I knew, because I had looked him up, but he could certainly have passed for younger.

'Come through to my office.'

I followed him, glancing into high-ceilinged rooms with large desks where younger colleagues murmured into telephones.

'Is being quiet company policy too?'

He grinned at me as he sat down behind his desk. 'It is indeed. Amazing how much noise a room full of estate agents can make unless you persuade them to mutter. Please, sit. Can I get you something? Water? Tea?'

I shook my head. 'I'm fine.'

Perhaps judging that he had spent enough time on being charming, he let his face become serious. 'You're here about Rachel, I understand.'

'That's right.'

He leaned forward, his hands clasped loosely on the blotter in front of him. 'Why now? It's been three years. More.'

'We're looking into Rachel's case again because it may be connected to another case that is currently under investigation.'

'What does that mean?' The way he asked it wasn't quite rude but it wasn't far off it. I replied in the same way so he would understand that in this conversation, we were equals.

100

'Exactly what I said. There's a possibility that it's connected to another murder investigation but equally it might not be. I'm looking at all the evidence again to see if we can rule her in or out.'

'And you've started here.'

'You're not the first person I've interviewed,' I said, 'but you do have the distinction of being the last person who saw Rachel alive.'

'Apart from her killer.'

'Obviously.'

There was no outward sign of tension in him: he was a very good poker player, I guessed. The only tell was that his eyes were fixed on mine. That was as much of a giveaway as someone not being able to look me in the eye, did he but know it.

The door behind me opened. Gallagher looked up. 'Ah, Per.' To me, he said, 'This is Per Kemp, my partner.'

I turned to see a tanned, tall man with fair hair and green eyes leaning against the door frame. He had a dazzling smile and similar taste in clothes to his colleague, although he looked less self-conscious, less abrasive.

'They told me a police officer was here. I thought we'd been found out.'

'Let's not make any jokes, Per. The police aren't famous for having a sense of humour.'

'Not about missing women,' I said coolly, and the smile evaporated from Kemp's face.

'Ah, Rachel. That's why you're here.'

'Tell me about her. What was she like?'

It was Gallagher who answered. 'She was my employee for two years. She was very good at her job and I promoted her twice. You can look at her records – we've got them some-where. She got on well with her colleagues.' He shrugged. 'I'm sure Per would agree with me, though he has less to do with the day-to-day running of the agency.'

'I remember her very well. She was extremely attractive.' Per sat down in the other chair, drawing it forward so he was closer to me.

From the other side of the desk, I sensed the faintest hint of unease. Gallagher fiddled with his pen for a moment, then burst out with, 'Per, there's really no need for you to be here.'

'If I can help, though.'

'But you can't. You didn't have anything to do with her.'

Kemp blinked at his partner. 'You want me to go.'

'I don't need an audience for this discussion. You didn't work with Rachel and Sergeant Kerrigan here wants to talk to me about her projects and so forth.'

Kemp looked at me. 'So, should I go?'

'That's up to you.'

'The thing is,' he said slowly, folding his arms and leaning back in his chair, 'I'm interested in what you have to say, James.'

'Per,' Gallagher snapped. 'Not now.'

There was a moment of absolute stillness as the two men glared at one another. Then Kemp laughed, showing off those white teeth again. 'I'll see you later, miss. I'm sorry I can't help with your questions.'

'If you think of anything—'

'I'll give him your details,' Gallagher said firmly. Kemp sauntered to the door, taking his time. His partner waited until the door was shut before he relaxed, his shoulders dropping at least two inches.

'What was Rachel working on when she disappeared?'

'Yes, of course. Sorry. I got sidetracked.' There was a faint sheen of sweat on his forehead, I noticed. 'She wasn't dealing with anything particularly difficult or complicated. I think she'd just been away on holiday, so really she was getting back into the swing of things.'

'But she was working late.'

'Yes. I try to discourage it. I don't want the staff trying

to outdo one another by staying later and later. Also, I like to have the place to myself to get things done. Nothing but interruptions during the day. I love it when the phone is off and the emails dry up around six o'clock and you can actually concentrate. What I don't want is a lot of younger staff hanging around, and they know that.'

'But Rachel was still here.'

'Yes. She was.' He smiled. 'I'm not all that much of a tyrant. I do get ignored from time to time. And it was a one-off, so I wasn't inclined to send her home. I didn't stay all that late myself and she left at the same time as me.'

'Could she have been waiting to meet someone?'

He leaned back in his chair. 'I don't know. Possibly? She lost me as soon as she decently could, I can tell you that much. I gave her a lift but she asked me to let her out near King's Cross.'

'Where, exactly?' Even after so long, you never knew when an eyewitness would surface with a story about a pretty girl and a white van . . .

'I don't know. Somewhere I could stop, so not the main road. It's an area I drive through often but I don't know it well. Some side street or other.' He ran a finger over his upper lip casually, though I knew he was trying to sweep the sweat away before I noticed it. *Too late.*

'Did she ask to get out all of a sudden or was it her intention to stop there?'

'I don't recall. She must have asked me to drop her off at some stage. I don't remember it being dramatic.'

'And how did she seem?'

He shrugged. 'Just like herself. She was tanned, from her holiday, and I suppose I teased her about it.' He saw my face change. 'No, no, nothing inappropriate. We joked around quite a bit. Give and take, you know. We had a good working relationship.'

I noted the stress on the second-last word, as I was

meant to. I also noticed that he had talked exclusively about work, and not about her as a person, although I'd left my questions open.

'Were you in a relationship at the time of Miss Healy's disappearance?'

'I was recently divorced and very happy to be.'

'You'll appreciate I have to ask this, Mr Gallagher – did you and Miss Healy have a personal relationship?'

His face had reddened. 'I like to keep these things separate. Do you sleep with your boss?'

'No.' Pride made me add, 'And I don't sleep with lower-ranked officers either.'

'Of course. Sorry. I shouldn't have said that.'

'Is it company policy to discourage the staff from romantic involvement?'

'I don't discourage it. I don't encourage it.'

'To your knowledge, was Ms Healy involved with anyone else in the office?'

'You probably need to talk to Dan.'

'Who is Dan?'

'Dan Forbes-Stanton. He's one of my more experienced agents. He's been with me for nine years.'

'Why should I speak to him?'

'Whatever I told you would be gossip. You're better off going straight to the source.'

It was a non-answer and we both knew it. I wanted to know as much as possible before interviewing Dan Forbes-Stanton and Gallagher was giving me nothing. I snapped my notebook shut and regarded him stonily.

He shifted in his chair. 'You're quite intimidating, aren't you?'

'Only if you have some reason to feel intimidated.'

'I don't. I don't. Talking to the police makes me feel nervous. I can't help it. You must run across this all the time.'

I had no intention of making him feel better. Instead I put

104

a business card on his blotter, just in front of his manicured fingertips. 'If you think of anything else I might need to know, get in touch.'

I had formed an opinion of Dan Forbes-Stanton on the basis of his name and his job before I met him, despite all my experience. I expected to see someone both foppish and privileged, someone who would look down on me for my public-service job and my accent. In fact, Forbes-Stanton was slightly built and nicely spoken rather than posh. He was brown-haired and languid, his hazel eyes tired, his general demeanour that of someone perpetually on the verge of yawning. There was, perversely, something appealing about his reserve. It was impossible to imagine him indulging in smooth sales patter or making the effort to dissemble. He would be honest, I felt, no matter how hard that might be.

'You want to talk to me about Rachel.' He folded himself into the chair opposite mine and crossed his legs.

'They told you why I was here.'

'I guessed. I'm one of her ex-boyfriends. The case is unsolved. I knew someone would ask me about it again one of these days.'

'Do you know why I'm asking you about her now?'

A shrug. 'New evidence?'

'Not exactly. A possible link with another case.'

'Oh, right.' He settled himself in his chair again, trying to get comfortable. 'I was hoping you'd found something. I'd like to see someone locked up for harming her.'

'Is that what you think happened?'

'Of course.' He looked mildly disappointed by how stupid my question was. 'She didn't just walk out of here one day and decide to keep walking. She was happy. She had no reason to drop everything and run away. I knew straight away that something terrible must have happened to her.'

'Tell me about your relationship.'

'It was brief. A matter of months. Neither of us planned it. I would never have thought she would be interested in someone like me, and maybe it surprised her too. We got on so well, that was the thing. I made her laugh. We started going out as friends, that summer – lots of long evenings sitting around in beer gardens or walking by the river during our lunch hour. Picnics, open-air concerts on Hampstead Heath. London is pretty special in the summer, when you're not on the Tube. One night we had champagne cocktails in my back garden and ended up in bed. And that was it.'

'But it didn't work out.'

'She was too good for me and I never got over it. I couldn't seem to stop apologising and trying to please her, and that wasn't what she wanted. *I* wasn't what she wanted, after all, and she was very nice about telling me so when she realised. She didn't string me along. She tried to make it work, but there was no chance.'

'What did she want?'

He hesitated for the first time, doubt clouding his expression. 'I've never talked to anyone about this. It can't go any further.'

'It depends on what you tell me. If it's not relevant to the case then I promise it won't go any further. If it is important, it might help to catch her killer and I can't make any promises about keeping your confidence.'

'I understand.' He sat for a minute, considering whether he could trust me, and I felt the frustration knotting my joints. I had been honest with him and I hoped I wouldn't have cause to regret it.

'She wanted to be hurt.'

'Hurt?' I repeated.

'That was what she enjoyed. In bed,' he clarified. 'She wanted me to hurt her.'

'When you say hurt—' I began and he interrupted.

'I don't know the full extent of what she wanted or what

she was prepared to do. More than playing around. I've had a lot of girlfriends and I've done my fair share of experimenting with a bit of light bondage, spanking – you know, the fun stuff. She wanted to do things I didn't consider to be part of a normal sex life. It wasn't something I could do or would do.' He swallowed. 'I don't want to demean the women I sleep with, or hurt them. She wanted that. She wanted to be controlled.'

'When did she tell you this?'

'After we'd been going out for about two months. As relationships go, it was casual – we hadn't made an announcement or anything, but everyone in the office knew we were seeing one another. I thought we were happy together but she was holding this back.'

'How did it come up?'

His eyes darkened. 'She came over one weekend – it was hot, I remember. Humid. Airless. It was almost unbearable in my flat. There was a fly buzzing and buzzing at the window the whole time we were talking, and I couldn't stop thinking about it. Anyway, she cried. She told me she had to tell me the truth but she knew it wouldn't be what I wanted to hear. And then she asked me to hold a pillow over her face while we were fucking and punch her through it so I didn't bruise her enough for it to show.'

I was fairly good at keeping my face impassive but that made me blink. Dan nodded, as if to say: *Yes, I know.*

'It was horrific. I couldn't bring myself to look at her. She was bitterly ashamed of herself. She was trying to change, she said, but it was like an addiction. She wasn't ready to stop yet and she wouldn't stop for me. I wasn't *enough* for her.'

'You sound upset, even now,' I said quietly.

'I am. I was at the time, because I didn't want to lose her, but then after she disappeared . . .' He trailed off, staring into the middle distance. 'I wished things had been different.'

'Why didn't you tell the police all of this at the time?'

'They were digging through her private life. They had her phone, her computer, her diary if she wrote one. I couldn't tell them anything apart from the fact that she liked to be hurt. That wouldn't give them a suspect, would it?'

I tried very hard not to sound annoyed when I answered. 'It might have given them somewhere to start looking for a suspect.'

Forbes-Stanton looked upset. 'I assumed if I told the police, everyone would find out about it, and would judge her. They'd think differently of her. She was so ashamed of it. But I wondered afterwards – if I had tried to give her what she wanted, would she still be alive? If I had met her halfway? I don't know. I felt guilty. I felt she was doing something unsafe before she died and that was how she ended up in trouble.'

'What sort of thing?'

'Meeting someone who would do the things she wanted, and more. She could have got out of her depth very quickly. It wasn't just the punching. She liked being choked, you see, and smothered until she passed out. Hurt. Really hurt. I've always thought it was likely to have been an accident more than murder. Someone went too far and Rachel – Rachel just didn't make it.'

15

It made my life a lot easier that Rachel Healy's flatmates still lived in the same house in Tufnell Park. I had expected that they would be surprised to hear the investigation was ongoing; I hadn't expected that they would be so eager to meet me. Both of them were standing in the bay window watching for me when I got there in the early afternoon. They had taken the afternoon off work, Jenny Palmer explained to me breathlessly as she ushered me into the sitting room, because both of them wanted to be there to see me and talk about Rachel.

'We still miss her.' Katy Lunn was standing by the fireplace holding her elbows, slim and tall in a narrow shift dress. She had fair hair and intensely blue eyes. Self-contained was the word that occurred to me, looking at her: she was as poised and dignified as Jenny was bubbly. The two flatmates made quite a contrast to one another and I wondered if Rachel had been the link between them – if she had made their friendship make sense.

'We haven't rented out her room since she disappeared. I know that probably sounds weird but we could afford to keep it empty and it felt wrong to shove someone else in there in her place,' Jenny said.

'Are Rachel's things still here?' I asked, my interest sharpening.

'Her sister came and cleared away most of it a year after she disappeared. We'd have kept it but I think Zoe wanted to get rid of everything. We still have some bits and pieces that belonged to her.' She looked up at the bookshelves in an unfocused way, and I suppressed a sigh. Of course there wouldn't be much to see. And no matter how shoddy the original investigation might have been, I knew they had taken anything that might have told us where she'd gone or who she had been with. There was something about seeing people's belongings that helped me to understand who they had been, though, and I regretted it.

Jenny sat down on the very edge of the sofa. She was slight, with shoulder-length dark hair and freckles. She wore a red jumper, a pink cord skirt, teal-coloured tights and silver ankle boots, a look that shouldn't have worked but somehow did. She worked for a fashion company, I knew. Dressing like that was as much part of her job as Katy's severe dress was required for her solicitor's firm. I wore a uniform of practical trouser suits for my own job, suits that looked formal enough to reassure grieving relatives but that fitted under a forensic suit when they were required to. Clothes were armour, and camouflage, and I knew better than to think they told me anything reliable about the women in front of me.

'Why are you here now?' Katy asked, and I explained, as I had at Rachel's work. I watched them frown as they thought about what I'd said. They were protective of her, I could tell, and wary of me.

'I know you had a difficult experience with the police before, when you tried to report Rachel missing.'

'They didn't listen to us. It took us a ridiculous amount of time to persuade them to take us seriously.'

'Jenny.' It wasn't quite a reproof from the taller woman but it was enough to make Jenny blush. She looked at me, her expression defiant.

'I wasn't going to say anything about it but you mentioned

110

it yourself. We just felt – we still feel – if they'd only listened to us in the first place we would know what happened to Rachel.'

'There was quite a delay before they started investigating her disappearance,' Katy explained. 'And then they told us it was connected with Leo Stone and the murders he committed, but they couldn't prove that, so Rachel was never mentioned during his trial.'

'You felt she was forgotten,' I said. 'I felt the same way, looking at the file.'

It was as if a long-held tension immediately slackened in both of them. Katy crossed the room and sat down next to her friend. 'What do you want to know?'

'I want to know as much as I can about what was going on in Rachel's life when she disappeared.'

'But if she was one of Leo Stone's victims, that was bad luck, wasn't it?' Jenny tilted her head sideways, puzzled. 'That wouldn't have anything to do with Rachel, apart from her being in the wrong place at the wrong time.'

'Possibly,' I said. 'But I think there have been too many assumptions made about what happened to Rachel. I want to start right at the beginning again. I've spoken to her colleagues and her sister already, but I think you would know her better than anyone.'

'Did you talk to Dan?' Katy's face was severe, unreadable. 'Yes.'

'You know they had a relationship.'

'I gather it was quite brief.' I didn't want to lead them; the impression I'd formed of Dan Forbes-Stanton might have been wrong, after all.

'They were together for a couple of months.'

'Dan was lovely,' Jenny said. She sounded wistful. 'We liked him a lot.'

'Do you know why they broke up?'

The two women didn't look at one another but I had a

strong sense of a silent conversation going on between them nonetheless.

'Rachel wouldn't talk to us about it,' Katy said finally. 'She said he wasn't right for her and that was all she'd say.'

'He was too nice, that was the trouble.'

'Did she tell you that?'

Jenny shook her head. 'That was what I thought. He made her laugh, he made her happy – but that wasn't what she wanted in the end. She liked a bit more excitement. A bit more *drama*.'

'So where was she looking for drama?'

'We don't know,' Katy said. 'But she was hiding something.'

'What makes you say that?'

'She was being secretive about where she went and who she was with. Even when she was seeing Dan, there were nights she didn't come home until three or four in the morning and she wasn't with him.'

'Are you sure?'

'Certain.'

I believed her. Katy didn't strike me as the kind of person who would say something unless they meant it.

'She definitely had somewhere else to be.' Jenny bit her lip. 'Dan called me once to check on her, because she'd told him she was going home with a headache. She wasn't here. I covered for her – I said she was asleep.'

'Did you get the feeling he was checking up on her? That he wanted to control her?'

'No. Not at all.' Jenny looked shocked. 'He wasn't like that – not possessive or anything. He was pretty chilled out. He was just being sweet.'

'Do you have any idea where Rachel went when she wasn't here or with Dan?'

'She didn't tell us anything.' Katy hesitated. 'But I think she was sleeping with someone else.'

Jenny nodded. 'She'd become really secretive. Her phone

was going constantly with messages and calls. She spent a fortune on clothes, too. Her room was full of shopping bags but I never saw her wear much of it. She saved the new clothes for her mystery nights out.'

'So she was seeing someone else. She and Dan weren't particularly serious about one another, from what he said. She was young. It's not all that unusual, is it, for there to be a bit of an overlap between one relationship and another?'

'No.' Again, I sensed the hesitation in Katy's voice. This time, she and Jenny looked at one another for a moment before she went on. 'The thing was, she wouldn't talk to us about it. She wouldn't admit there was anything going on.'

'There was one time I heard her come in,' Jenny said. 'It must have been four in the morning. It was light and the birds were singing. I was still half asleep but I thought she was crying and I got up to see if she was OK. She was in the bathroom. She'd left the door open – I mean, she wasn't expecting anyone else to be up so she wasn't thinking about privacy.'

'The bathroom door is noisy, too. She wouldn't have wanted to shut it in case it woke us up,' Katy interjected.

'What did you see?'

'She was looking at herself in the mirror – twisting around to look at her back. I only saw the reflection for a second because as soon as she saw me she covered herself up again. Her back—' Jenny broke off to gather herself, her composure slipping. 'Her back was covered in marks. Raised welts, all the way across it. It looked as if she'd been whipped.'

That fitted in with what Dan had told me.

'Did she seem upset?'

'Only that I'd seen it. She asked me not to say anything to Katy.'

'And she didn't,' Katy said. 'Not until Rachel disappeared.'

'Did you mention it to the police during the original investigation?'

'I did say something about it but I didn't go into much

detail.' Jenny's shoulders slumped a little. 'It felt wrong to talk about her with strangers.'

'Anyway, that happened months before she went missing. We assumed it wasn't relevant. It wasn't as if the police needed any more distractions,' Katy said icily. 'They could barely cope with the basic idea she'd disappeared.'

'When did you see her in the bathroom?'

'It was July.' And Rachel had gone missing in the middle of October. A long enough gap that you could discount it, especially if you thought she had been the victim of a serial killer who targeted women at random.

'Was that the only thing that made you concerned?'

'It was the main thing,' Katy said.

'There was something weird about how she was acting,' Jenny said. 'She was really happy and up most of the time. She was always the first person to suggest going out or throwing a party or rearranging the furniture. She had loads of energy and she made life fun for everyone else. But at the same time, she wasn't sleeping at all.'

'She smoked and I'd smell it during the night,' Katy said. 'She drank a lot. She barely ate.'

'She was living on coffee and cereal bars, wasn't she? It was only when we made her sit down and eat a proper meal that she ate much at all.'

'Was she anorexic?'

'No.' Jenny sounded definite. 'I work in fashion. Believe me, if she'd had an eating disorder I'd have known about it. I think she was depressed and trying to hide it from the rest of us. She couldn't be bothered to cook for herself. Dan was so good for her. She seemed normal when she was with him. It was when she was on her own that things got dark.'

'You were good friends. Close.' The two women nodded. 'It sounds as if she was quite hard work, though. Didn't you find it frustrating that she was keeping secrets, that she was out at strange times of day? Didn't you ever talk to her about it?'

114

'We thought she'd confide in us when she was ready.' Katy looked at me steadily. 'We were her friends. More than friends – we were her family. We loved her unconditionally. She was going through a difficult time but we didn't judge her for that. We were just hoping things would go back to how they were before.'

'What was she like before?' I asked the question because I really wanted to get a sense of Rachel Healy as a person, but also because I wanted to let Jenny and Katy tell me about her. They had given me their time and it seemed like the least I could do to give them mine. They talked as the light faded outside, as the radiators creaked with the effort of heating the high-ceilinged room and the wind whistled through the gaps around the front door, as commuters began to return to the quiet streets, trudging home laden with bags of food and the newspapers they'd half-read on their journey home. They talked of the time before Rachel disappeared, of how they had met – Katy and Rachel at university, Jenny a year later when a previous flat-sharing arrangement came to an end. Someone had told her about two girls looking for a third, Jenny said. A phone number with no name attached to it and a vague idea of where the flat was. She'd called from her mobile, standing outside the travel agency where she was miserably working, the traffic so loud on High Holborn that she could barely hear Rachel at the other end of the line so that she wasn't even sure of their names when she went to meet them.

'But as soon as I got here, it was fine.'

'We knew immediately she'd fit in,' Katy said.

'I moved in the following week and I settled in straight away.'

'It felt as if she'd been here forever.' Katy cradled the mug of tea she'd made, and flashed a smile at her friend. 'We couldn't believe how lucky we'd been.'

'*I* couldn't believe how lucky *I'd* been.' Jenny laughed, her eyes shining as she turned to me. 'We just knew we'd be friends for life.'

For life. The memory of why I was here settled down over the pair of them like a blanket, draping around them in folds of grief and bafflement. I had lost them again, the distance between my chair and the sofa stretching to infinity, the two of them isolated from me by sorrow. *Come back to me,* I thought, and changed tack.

'Tell me about the summer before Rachel disappeared. What do you remember?'

'I remember everything,' Katy said. 'Everything.'

It had been one of *those* summers – day after day of warm weather, work as a passing irrelevance, long lazy evenings in tiny gardens as blue smoke spiralled up from citronella candles and everything seemed hilarious. As they talked, their words pushed the winter evening away and replaced it with that twenty-something world of few responsibilities, late nights, sausages charred to black and split along their length, the sweet, bitter taste of gin cocktails, crying in the bathroom over a stupid argument, huddling up on the sofa to watch TV as a summer storm dumped a month of rain on London in one evening, secrets blossoming in silences, the hard tap of heels on wooden floors, sunburn and freckles, dishes piled in the sink, a smudge of blood on the bath, a mouse flitting around in the kitchen late at night, fat pink peonies shedding petals across the living room in the breeze from an open window, a careless elbow pushing a glass off a table to shatter into hundreds of tiny splinters that caught the light weeks later, months, even now . . . It had seemed to them as if it was going to last forever – as if they would live forever.

When I went and stood alone in Rachel's bare, echoing room, I could almost hear her voice in my mind. It ran on and on, saying everything and nothing about what had happened to her before and after she died.

16

The office was empty, bluish-grey morning light casting gloomy shadows across the deserted desks. I switched on all the lights, not in the mood for November's dreariness, and plunged into Rachel Healy's phone records. It was the sort of deep dive into boring data that required absolute concentration, which was why I was at work an hour before anyone else. I knew the first investigation had tried and failed to locate Rachel's phone. In one of those fluke incidents that curse an already difficult investigation, it had been stolen from a café table the day before she disappeared. The replacement handset had arrived two days after the last time anyone had seen her, so for the crucial period when she went missing she had no phone at all. The original investigators had, however, secured the records from the phone company, so we knew who she had called and who had called her up to the point where the phone was stolen. DCI Whitlock's team had gone through them a second time when they made the connection to Leo Stone, so mine was the third attempt to glean something useful from the reams and reams of calls and messages that she'd sent and received in the months before she disappeared.

I sat and concentrated as the office slowly filled up around me, so absorbed that I was oblivious to my colleagues' comings and goings. What started out as boring and painstaking work became more and more intriguing the longer I looked at the records. It wasn't so much what I found that interested me as what wasn't there at all.

'*Maeve.*' From Una Burt's tone of voice it wasn't the first time she'd said my name.

'Sorry.' I blinked up at her. 'I was miles away.'

'Well, if you wouldn't mind coming back, I'd like a word with you in my office.'

I stood up and indulged myself with some truly elaborate silent swearing. Looking across to Burt's office, I could see Godley with his back to me, his hands in his pockets as he stared out of the window. Derwent was pacing back and forth, wound up like a toy soldier. In spite of my early start, once again I had the distinct feeling that I was arriving late to the party.

'—and I can't believe that you of all people would think this was a good idea.' Derwent turned to stride back the other way and saw me in the doorway. His voice was flat when he said, 'She's here.'

Thanks for the big welcome. 'What's going on?'

'Shut the door and sit down.' Una Burt settled herself into the chair behind the desk. Godley turned and gave me a distracted smile as I did as I was told, feeling more and more unsure of myself. Derwent flung himself into the other chair in front of Burt's desk, leaning forward with his elbows on his knees so he was altogether too close to me.

'The thing to remember is that you can say no.'

'*Josh*, that's not helpful,' Una Burt snapped.

'Well, it's true.' He kept his eyes on my face. 'If I know Kerrigan, she'll want to say yes, but we all know it's a bad idea.'

'What is?' I looked to Godley, since he seemed to be the person most likely to answer me directly.

'Leo Stone has requested a meeting with the officers investigating this case.'

'What? Why?'

'Your guess is as good as mine.' Godley frowned. 'It's going to be because he wants to get the measure of us. Possibly it's because he wants to put us off.'

'It's an opportunity,' Una Burt said. 'We couldn't drag him in for an interview but you're going to get a chance to listen to him talk about what he did.'

'I am?' I looked back to Godley. 'Why me?'

'He asked for you. By name.' Derwent leaned back in his chair and rubbed his lower lip with his index finger as he watched my reaction. I didn't exactly manage to look impassive.

'What? Why? How did he know who I am?'

'I imagine the Greys talked to him. They're his chums, aren't they?'

'But what about you? You were there too.'

Derwent shrugged. 'Leo likes young women.'

'With that in mind, I'm going to get Georgia to join you for this little interview.' Burt raised her eyebrows. 'Assuming you're prepared to meet him, that is.'

I hesitated for a beat, mostly because I was trying to think of a way to ask for Georgia to stay out of it. Godley read it as reluctance. 'I don't want to put you under too much pressure to say yes, but I'd like Stone to trust you. We don't know if we'll need to interview him formally at some stage. I'd like him to feel he knows us.'

'You want to use her as bait, you mean.'

'That's not fair, Josh.' Godley rarely lost his temper but when he did, you couldn't miss it: the skin on his face seemed to shrink against his bones, hollowing out his cheeks. He glared at Derwent who gave him the same look straight back again.

'I'm going to do it. I want to do anything I can to help the investigation.' I was thinking of Rachel Healy, as I had been for days. 'If he trusts me, he might talk to me. He might tell me where Rachel's body is. That would mean a lot to her sister and her friends.'

119

'Fucking marvellous.' Derwent got up, shoving his chair back, and slammed the door on his way out of the office.

'Dear, dear. He really doesn't like being left out, does he?' Una Burt smiled at me.

'I'm not sure that's why he's upset.' Godley crossed the room to sit down where Derwent had been. The tight look had left his face now that he had got his way. 'He's concerned about you. But Maeve, you do understand that we don't want you to put yourself at any risk. It's going to happen here, in an interview room, because I want it to be recorded.'

'What about somewhere more informal? I could see if the video interview suite is available.' Una Burt already had her hand on the phone.

Godley shook his head. 'I'd rather not.'

'I feel the same way.' I really didn't want to be in a room with Leo Stone without a barrier between us, even if that barrier was nothing more than a table. The thought of him lounging on a sofa was not appealing.

'He's not going to be on his own with you at any point, though I don't think he would try anything. His solicitor is coming with him, and you'll have Georgia.'

'What do you want me to do?'

'I want you to get the measure of him. You're a good judge of character. Tell me if you think he could have done the things we're accusing him of doing.'

'Do you have any doubt that he's guilty?' I asked, surprised.

'There's always room for doubt. You've got to go where the evidence takes you, and that's what Pete Whitlock did. But that doesn't mean you can't question it.'

'Right.' I sounded a lot more confident than I was.

'Remember, he requested this meeting. He wants to find out something from us or he wouldn't be here. Try to keep the conversation general, if you can. Don't give away too much about the investigation. We'll disclose any new evidence at the proper time, before the retrial.'

Una Burt snorted. 'What new evidence? As far as I can see they're just going over old ground at the moment.'

'Well, it got him convicted once,' I said steadily.

'He's coming here at eleven.' She glanced at her watch. 'You've got forty-five minutes to prepare.'

Forty-five minutes was about forty-three minutes more than I needed or wanted. I spent most of them in the bathroom, not quite hiding from Derwent. I knew he was furious about more than being left out – he was as over-protective of me as a clucky hen – but being excluded wouldn't help his mood. I also knew that if he really wanted to find me, he'd walk into the ladies' room without a second thought. In fact, when the door banged I expected it to be him.

'So this is where you are. I was looking for you.' Georgia dumped her make-up bag on the counter and stared at me. 'Are you OK?'

'Never better.'

'You look pale.'

'I'm always pale.'

'That'll be your Irish heritage.'

'I think you'll find Irish people are a bit more diverse than that.'

'You know what I mean.' She lost interest in me, staring at herself in the mirror. Her hair was immaculate, her suit impeccable. She touched the pearls in her ears, checking that they were secure, and leaned in to run her little finger under her eyes.

'It's an interview, not a beauty contest,' I said.

'I know.' She unzipped the make-up bag and took out her mascara. 'Still, no point in looking like you've been dragged through a hedge backwards if you don't have to.'

Unlike me.

After a moment, she pushed the make-up bag towards me. 'Help yourself.'

121

'Thanks.' Which meant no thanks. I slid it back along the counter.

Georgia gave the tiniest shrug possible and started to draw the brush through her eyelashes, her mouth hanging open like a blow-up doll's. I made sure my hair was as tidy as I could make it and left Georgia to it, amused rather than annoyed by her. If only she knew that a convent-school education had left me just about immune to bitchiness . . .

'What are you smiling about?' Derwent fell into step beside me. He had been waiting outside the door.

'Nothing whatsoever. Any advice?'

'Don't do it. Say you've changed your mind.'

'Apart from that.'

He caught me by the arm and swung me around to face him, dropping his voice so no one could hear us. 'What have you got to prove?'

'Nothing.'

'Exactly. So you don't need to do this.'

'It's a conversation,' I said gently. 'It's not even a proper interview. I might as well find out what he wants.'

'You shouldn't go anywhere near him. They're putting you in there to be a target for him and you should say no.'

'Oh, calm down. He'll be on the other side of a table and I've got Georgia to distract him.'

'It's not that he'll try to jump you, darling. He'll make it his business to tear your reputation apart and that's worse.'

I wrenched my arm out of his grasp and put my hand in the centre of his chest, pushing him a couple of steps back out of my personal space. 'Look, there's no way I'm dropping out of this. For one thing, I want a closer look at his hot solicitor.'

'You've got to be joking.'

'What? I'm single. You said yourself I needed to meet someone.' I blinked, all innocence. 'Wish me luck.'

'Kerrigan. I'm serious. Come on. Don't make me beg.'

'It wouldn't do any good,' I said, and left him standing in the corridor, his hands on his hips, the picture of frustration.

Georgia caught up with me outside the interview room, favouring Godley with a smile shiny with lip gloss. He nodded to her but I could tell he wasn't really seeing her. His focus was all on the man on the other side of the wall.

'Remember, don't give too much away,' Una Burt said.

'Got it.'

'We'll be watching you on the video link.'

'Great.' It really wasn't. I didn't want to think about being watched – about being judged for how I was performing. But I had to look as if I didn't mind. I checked that Georgia was ready, and opened the door.

The two men were sitting down at the table already. One – the solicitor – jumped to his feet as soon as the door opened. Leo Stone stayed where he was, his elbows braced on the table. He looked up at me with those dark, fathomless eyes and I managed not to flinch.

'Excuse me for not getting up. It's my knees, you see.'

'Don't worry.' I shook hands with him because it seemed like the right thing to do, in the circumstances. His hands were huge and his palm was slightly clammy – but would I have noticed it if I wasn't busy thinking about the women he'd killed? While I was puzzling that out I shook hands with the solicitor who was more handsome than I'd remembered. The beard was quite a look, along with the three-piece suit and immaculate shoes. He looked like a quintessential Victorian gentleman and absolutely up to date, all at the same time. Today the suit was a plain dark-blue number, but again it was cut to emphasise the breadth of his shoulders.

'Seth Taylor.'

'Maeve Kerrigan. Detective Sergeant Kerrigan.' Stress made me flustered, my thoughts scattering like startled birds. *Get a grip.*

While Georgia introduced herself with maximum composure and charm, I sat down opposite Stone. He was looking straight at me, his eyes fixed on mine.

Bait, Derwent had said, and I had chosen to believe Godley instead.

'Mr Stone, I want to be absolutely clear with you that this meeting is at your request. It's not a formal interview and you're not under caution at the moment.'

'My client understands that.' Taylor glanced at Leo, who was still staring at me. 'I've advised against this meeting, in fact.'

'I wanted it. I wanted to see you, Miss Kerrigan.' His voice was as harsh as two rocks sliding over one another.

'Why was that?'

'I saw you at court the day of the appeal. I wanted a closer look. You're trying to lock me up again so I'm entitled to know what you're like.'

I would have sworn he had looked nowhere except at his son that day.

'I hear you asked for me by name. How did you know it?'

'You've been talking to people. My friends. Stirring them up against me. I know how it works. You can't admit you made a mistake when you put poor old Leo in prison so you've got to make sure I go back there.' His teeth were terrible, greying and coated with brownish plaque. His breath was rank.

'Mr Stone, we're simply reviewing the evidence in preparation for your retrial.'

'Hounding me.'

'Not at all. A retrial was the recommendation from the appeal court. But as Mr Taylor will have told you, the rules of disclosure are very clear. If we find evidence that exonerates you, we will share it with your lawyers. You are entitled to a fair and just trial and that's exactly what you'll get.'

'I'm an innocent man and I've been locked up for life already, my darling. I know there's no such thing as a fair trial.'

'You're not locked up now.'

'No. I'm not.' He smiled and I wished he hadn't. 'Got lucky there, didn't I?'

'It's in everyone's interests for you to get a fair trial, Mr Stone. I promise you, we'll do our best in that regard.'

'You're too pretty to be a copper, you know that.'

I thought he was talking to Georgia at first but he was still staring at me. It caught me off guard, as it was meant to – not because I was flattered but because I knew it was a comment designed to undermine me. This whole interview was dedicated to the same purpose. I looked down at my notes, then up at Seth Taylor. *Keep your client under control.*

He shrugged. *What can I do?*

'Mr Stone—'

He passed one hand over the other and a tiny paper flower appeared on his palm. He held it out to me until it became obvious I was never going to take it. He folded it into a ball and made it disappear, favouring me with the grin again.

'Mr Stone.'

'Do you think I did it? Me, with my bad knees? You should have heard the prosecutor at my first trial. I overpowered them. I carried them into my van. I carried them half a mile through a fucking nature reserve to dump their bodies where they wouldn't be discovered. Me.' He jabbed himself in the chest. 'I've got a bad heart too, love. I'm a big man but I'm not what you'd call able.'

'Leo,' Taylor said urgently. 'I warned you.' To me, he said, 'You can't ask him any questions about any of that.'

I held back the question I wanted to ask, which was how he had been working on building sites carrying heavy loads if he was so incapacitated. Instead I smiled. 'It's not up to me to say what Mr Stone's physical capabilities might have been. I'm sure someone else will go into that.'

'I wasn't up to it,' Stone said. 'You have to believe me. And mentally. I'm not clever enough for that.' Intelligence glittered in his black eyes. He reminded me of a great shabby shark.

'There's clever and clever, Mr Stone. There's book clever, like Mr Taylor here. Then there's your kind of clever.' I tucked my pen into my notebook and closed it. 'You've got common sense.'

'I do.'

'I gather from the Greys that you're full of understanding.'

'Is that what they said?'

'It is. But that's not what I saw in the letters you sent to the Howards.'

The smile dropped off his face. Seth Taylor looked from me to his client, alert. He didn't know about the letters, I thought, and filed it away to think about the implications later.

'Ah.' Recovering his composure, Leo Stone sucked in his lower lip and pulled a face. 'Thought I'd drop them a line. Reach out to them. You know how it is.'

'Indeed I do.' I rested my chin on my hand. 'But you never wrote to Rachel Healy's sister. Now why was that?'

'I don't think you should answer that,' Taylor said.

'I'll tell you this.' Stone leaned across the table. 'I'd love to see you with your hair down, Miss Kerrigan. I bet you're different when you're not in a suit, all butter-wouldn't-melt. I'm going to think about that tonight.'

'How flattering.' I looked to Taylor. 'I think we're finished here, unless you have any other questions.'

'No. I think that's covered it.'

'Someone will show you out.' I got up and walked to the door, not hurrying even though I could feel Stone's eyes on me.

Bait.

I hated it when Derwent was right.

17

It was dark again before I left the office, the whole brief winter's day consumed by Leo Stone one way or another. I watched the video of our meeting twice: once for Stone's body language and once for what he'd said. The second time I noticed Georgia fidgeting, crossing her legs and flicking her hair. The two men on the other side of the table were totally focused on me, which made sense because I was leading the conversation. It took a special kind of ego to mind, I mused, when a man who was probably the vicious killer of at least two women didn't pay you enough attention. And it took a particular wilful blindness to mistake aggression for attraction. But that was Georgia. It explained why she had spent the rest of the day glowering in my general direction and snapping at the slightest provocation. I found it intensely boring that she had set herself up as my competition purely because I was one step further up the ladder than she was, and because I had earned the kind of access to senior officers that she thought should be hers for the asking.

Rain had been forecast and rain was falling when I stepped out into the narrow Westminster side street. It was an undramatic kind of rain, the sort you can ignore if your journey is short but not if you have a long walk to the right underground station and particularly not if you have the kind of hair that responds to moisture by losing the run of itself completely. I was digging in my bag for my umbrella when I became aware of a figure coming towards me. I turned to face the threat head on, my throat tightening, my stomach dropping with fear even though I knew it wouldn't show on my face.

'Hi – sorry, I didn't mean to startle you. Could I – could I have a word?' He had been standing outside for a long time, from the way the water ran off the folds of his leather jacket. His hair stood up in spikes.

'Mr Lambert?'

'Kelly.' He shoved something in his pocket and held out a wet hand for me to shake. It was calloused, the skin rough against mine. He was pale in the glare of the streetlights. 'Sorry for bothering you. I didn't know any other way to contact you.'

'Why would you need to?'

'You saw my dad today. He came to see you. Seth told me.'

'That's right. At his request, not mine.'

Kelly shifted from foot to foot. 'Can I ask you about it? About him?'

'I can't really—'

'I know, I know. It's an active investigation. I don't want to know anything about that.'

'What, then?'

'Look, I'd really like to talk to you. Informally, I mean. Maybe there's a pub around here where I could buy you a drink?'

I was about to say no and he must have sensed it.

'What about a coffee? Just a quick coffee. I bet there's somewhere near here we could sit down for a few minutes. I promise, it won't take long. And maybe it will help your investigation.'

'How?'

'I don't know. Maybe it won't.' An awkward smile. 'I'm trying to think of something to persuade you.'

128

'What do you want, Mr Lambert?'

'I don't know him.' He winced. 'That sounds so stupid, but it's true. I want to ask you what you made of him. I want to know – well, I want to know if I'm wasting my time on him.'

I remembered what Whitlock had said about the long years where they hadn't been in contact and how their relationship, such as it was, had been because of Kelly's efforts. I knew Kelly Lambert was in his mid-twenties but he looked younger – boyish and vulnerable.

And none of that should have mattered to me. Yet I found myself saying, 'We could get a coffee.'

'That would be amazing.'

'Well, you waited a long time.'

He grinned. 'I didn't like to say that in case you thought I was whining.'

'How long were you standing around out here?'

'Couple of hours.'

'You should have come inside and asked for me.' I put up my umbrella and held it so he could duck underneath it. He was shorter than me, which wasn't all that unusual but there were men who minded it, a lot. He didn't seem to care, trotting along beside me as we headed down the nearest side street. 'I didn't want to make it official. If that doesn't cause you any problems, that is. I don't want you to get in trouble.'

'I'll survive,' I said, even as I was trying to think of somewhere we could go that no one from work would pass on the way home.

It was a small and bleak outpost of a coffee chain that I chose in the end, because it was surrounded by other, nicer places. The coffee (which I bought) tasted bitter but Kelly sipped it uncomplainingly. Despite the determinedly moody lighting I could see him better now. His eyes were dark like his father's but that was where the resemblance ended: there was nothing like the knowing malice I'd seen in Stone's face. He wasn't handsome, at least to my eyes – the balance

129

was off between his wide, high forehead and a narrow jaw that was dark with stubble. Still, there was something appealing about him. Curiosity had made me agree to the coffee but I would never have considered it if he had been less diffident or more demanding, I knew.

'I can't tell you anything about the investigation.'

'I know, I know. Seth warned me not to ask you anything.'

'He did, did he?'

'He's Leo's lawyer.'

'I know who you mean,' I said. 'I'm just surprised that he knew you were planning to speak to me.'

'I checked with him first.' He looked down at his coffee. 'He said you'd say no, so it didn't matter.'

'Well, maybe I should have.' I glanced behind me as the door opened on a gust of damp wind, but it was no one I knew.

'I really, really appreciate this.' He put out a hand and let it hover above my sleeve, not quite touching me. 'Please don't leave.'

'I wasn't going to.'

'I wasn't sure. Sorry.' He ducked his head, embarrassed again. 'It's weird sitting here with you. You want to lock my father up and I want to keep him out of prison.'

'I want to make sure that the person who murdered several innocent young women goes to prison. If that's your father, then yes, I am determined to put him behind bars for life.'

'But it might not be.' He looked up at me, eyes wide. 'You're saying it might not be.'

'Don't read too much into that,' I cautioned. 'I'm keeping an open mind but that means nothing except that I'm trained to look at all the lines of enquiry. We're looking at all the evidence, not focusing on the bits that incriminate your father.' *And they're weak enough so far*, I didn't add, but I thought it.

'Look, I know Leo isn't going to win any Dad of the Year competitions. I know he was involved in criminal activities of one sort or another for most of his adult life. And when he wasn't, it was because he was banged up.'

'He probably didn't stop just because he was inside,' I said, amused. 'You'd be surprised what goes on in prisons.'

'Leo's told me some stories.' He gulped coffee. 'I don't know how I would cope, being locked up. I don't think I could stand it. I like my freedom. I've never even had a boss. I work for myself.'

'I hear you're a carpenter.'

'I do custom stuff for a couple of builders and interior designers. Once you've got the reputation you're never short of work. I make my own furniture too.'

'Where do you do that?'

'I've got a little workshop.' He shrank in his seat, staring over my shoulder.

'What is it?'

'I thought I saw someone looking in at us. Someone from your office.'

'What did they look like?'

'Tall bloke. Big. Dark hair. You were sitting with him at the appeal.'

Fuck. Of course it was Derwent. By a super-human effort I didn't look round. 'Is he still there?'

'N-no. I don't think so.' Kelly peered at the door, his face strained and pale. His coffee cup clattered as he set it back on the saucer. 'Do you want to leave?'

'Are you sure it was him?' Clutching at straws. Derwent had left the office ten minutes before me and that meant nothing: he had a nose for trouble, and specifically getting me in it.

'I can't be absolutely sure. It looked like him.' Kelly chewed his lip. 'If you get hassle over this—'

'Don't worry. I can handle him,' I lied. 'Tell me about your father. How did you find him?'

'My foster parents kept in touch with him over the years.

131

Not a lot – he sent them a card now and then, at Christmas. If he was in prison there was nothing in it. If he was out, there'd be a fiver. He never sent anything for my birthday. I don't think he knows when it is.' Lambert spoke without self-pity. If it had hurt him, that was in the past.

'Why did you want to contact him? He was in prison for GBH, wasn't he? Did you know that?'

'Yeah, I did.' Lambert shrugged. 'I know it's bad but I just thought, well, that's part of who he is but it's not the whole story. And it wasn't.'

'Was he glad to hear from you?'

'No.' He laughed at that. 'He was definitely not keen to see me. I had to apply to visit him and he said no the first few times.'

'But you kept trying.'

'You know my real mum died when I was a kid.'

'I had heard something about that.'

'They weren't together. It was never going to be Leo who looked after me. I don't mind that he didn't step up, you know. It would have been hard, living with him. My mum and dad – my foster parents – they were really good to me. I had a decent life with them. They fostered a few of us. Lots of kids running around in the countryside. Running wild, mainly. I don't remember all that much about how it was before – with my real mum – but it was rough. She didn't cope too well. She drank too much and—' He broke off, shaking his head. 'I feel sorry for her.'

'Life is hard for some people.'

'Yeah. That's definitely true. I don't think she had much luck, put it that way. In retrospect, her dying was the best thing that could have happened to me.' He smiled, but it was tinged with bitterness. 'Talk about survivor's guilt.'

'I can't imagine how hard it was for you.'

'It wasn't that bad. I didn't think about it a lot. I was busy. I was behind at school because I hadn't really gone much

132

before I was fostered. And then I started to learn woodwork and it was like someone put the lights on. It made me so happy, making something beautiful out of nothing much.'

'It must be a great feeling. You're lucky you can make a living doing something that makes you happy.' Whatever that was like. I loved my job but there were days when all we seemed to achieve was increasing the sum of human misery, spreading the consequences of misguided acts to the partners, the sisters and brothers, the sons and daughters and parents of those we locked up. Lady Justice cut with a sharp and careless sword. 'So what made you want to find your father?'

He ran a hand over his head. 'I don't know. I suppose I felt there was something missing. I wanted to see if there was good in Leo, you know? If someone was kind to him, like people were kind to me, if that would help.'

'And did it?'

'I thought it was working. He came out of prison and I got him set up in the house – cleaned the place up for him, bought him a microwave. I asked a couple of mates to give him a bit of work here and there. I couldn't afford to support him but I wanted to give him a chance. He was lucky to have somewhere to live. It's not that easy to find a flat for an ex-con – a lot of landlords won't rent to them. I didn't want him in a hostel or on the streets or he'd be back in prison inside the year. I thought if he was away from his old life he might be able to start again. I mean, it worked for me. But then again, I was just a kid.' His whole face was crinkled with sincerity and I felt sorry for him, for his naivety in the face of his father's darkness. It was a good thing he'd grown up far from Leo Stone's influence, to flourish in a good-hearted, simple way. I knew DCI Whitlock had liked him and I did too.

Lambert was following his own train of thought. 'I suppose it was my fault, really, wasn't it? If he'd been around other people more he'd have had alibis for when the women disappeared.'

'I don't think you should take responsibility for anything that's happened.' *Especially not if your father is a sociopathic monster.* 'You can't second-guess what you did. You acted for the best, as far as you could. You couldn't tell what the consequences would be.'

'Do you think he did it?' There it was, the open appeal. There was a vulnerability to Kelly Lambert that he didn't seem to be able to hide, as if he didn't realise that in the real world you couldn't assume everyone was trustworthy or that they had your best interests at heart.

'I can't talk to you about the case.'

'Please. I need to know. I don't think the evidence is convincing but then I don't want it to be.' He gulped, fighting his emotions. 'I would go to the end of the world for Leo if he's innocent. But if he's mugging me off—'

'That's not something I can say, either way.'

'Look, drop the police officer thing for a moment and talk to me like a human. Please.' He leaned towards me, his hands locked together, his eyes on my face. 'What sort of impression did he make on you?'

'I wouldn't go to the end of the world for him, Kelly. But I'm not related to him.' *Thank God.*

'He doesn't make a good first impression.'

I was fairly sure it would make no difference if I was allowed a second, third or fifteenth impression of Leo Stone.

A phone purred into life and I checked mine, remembering with a start that I had Derwent to worry about, if it had been him outside the door . . .

'Hey.' Kelly held up a finger to me as he listened to his phone. *Hold on.* 'Yes. Yes, she's here.'

And I really shouldn't be. I started gathering my things, preparing to make an exit. Kelly held out the phone to me.

'He wants a word with you.'

'Who does?'

'Seth.'

134

Not Leo Stone. The relief was enough to make me take the phone even though I couldn't imagine what Taylor would want with me. I carried the phone and my belongings out to the relative quiet of the street.

'Yes?'

'DS Kerrigan. I misjudged you. I wasn't expecting you to agree to talk to Kelly.' Away from the intensity of his stare I was able to concentrate on his voice, which was low and pleasant.

'He was persuasive.'

'Kelly's a nice guy.'

'That's what I thought.'

'Find out anything useful?'

'You never know.'

'That's cagey.'

'Don't take it personally.'

'I won't.'

I was quite enjoying sparring with him. 'Can I ask you a question?'

'Of course.'

'Why did Mr Stone want to meet with me?'

'His life is in your hands. He was curious.'

'About me.'

'About the whole process. About whatever it is that you're doing.'

'He knows what we're doing. We're preparing for his retrial. You should be able to brief him on what that entails.'

'He wanted to hear it from you. I think he thought he might be able to intimidate you, if I'm honest. I did try to discourage him.'

'Not hard enough.'

'Leo goes his own way. I just go along for the ride.'

'I really doubt that.'

He laughed and I grinned to myself. The café door shut and I looked up to see Kelly Lambert, his hands in his pockets.

'I'd better go.'

'See you soon, Sergeant Kerrigan.'

I gave the phone back to Kelly. 'Thanks.'

'No problem.' He had some trouble wedging it back into the pocket of his leather jacket and stopped to investigate. 'Oh, I'd forgotten that was in there.'

That was a knife, a small one with a fat handle designed to fit in the user's palm and a slender two-inch blade. It appeared in his hand like a magic trick. As a rule I didn't like being around people with quick hands who carried cutting tools. I must have looked shocked because he paled.

'Oh shit, it's not illegal to carry it, is it?'

'No. Not unless you're intending to hurt someone with it.'

'I wouldn't get very far, I don't think.' He dug in his other pocket. 'I was working on this while I was waiting for you. Here. You can keep it. The wood is walnut.'

It was a small owl, the features suggested rather than heavily carved. Lambert's talent was evident in the way he'd worked with the grain of the wood, turning the natural shading into wings and a stippled chest that might as well have been feathers.

'It's beautiful.'

'It's what I do,' he said simply.

I thought about saying I couldn't take it, but I didn't want to seem ungrateful. Besides, it hardly counted as a bribe. 'If you're sure you don't want it.'

'I make thousands of things like that, for fun. I like giving them away.'

'I'll look after it.'

Kelly smiled, pleased, and sketched a salute before he turned away. I wondered if he'd got what he wanted from me, all the same. I wondered if I'd ever know what it was Leo Stone had been searching for.

I kept my fingers curled around the comforting weight of the owl, all the way home.

18

It was dark.

She had gone blind.

No, it was dark. There was a faint blue tone to the darkness, high up on the left. She strained her eyes to see it, to make sense of it.

It refused to become familiar.

Nor did she recognise the smell of the place: her nose full of cold, dusty, green air that was outside her experience. Nothing she could place. It smelled like a cellar, or an abandoned building – dank.

So, conclusion: she was somewhere she had never been before.

Except, that wasn't a conclusion. That was only the start of it. There was the banging headache behind her eyes, and the dry mouth, and the raw feeling on her elbows and knees where the skin was grazed. Her hands felt bruised too, her fingers stiff as she traced a circle around herself on the ground, feeling rough wood, a splinter catching in her skin before she could pull her hand away.

The ache around her left ankle took some time to rise to the top of her list of discomforts but it got there eventually. She ran a hand down her leg and encountered something metal that was wrapped around her. A chain, with quite small links. A chain that was knotted somehow, and connected to something further away, so she couldn't – she jerked her leg – *free* herself or move away because – another jerk – she was *trapped*.

That made no sense at all.

She pulled her hands back into her body and shut her eyes, as if withdrawing from the strange new world where she found herself would make it, in turn, recede.

Because she should have been at home, she thought.

She had been *going* home, she was sure of it.

She could have sworn she had walked through the door. But that could have been another time.

And this was not her home, nor anywhere like it.

Stubbornly, her mind refused to tell her what had happened. There was a fog in her brain, an impenetrable cloud that she was afraid to try to breach. Hidden in it was a world of terror, she suspected, and she wasn't ready yet to confront it.

She could only barely cope with here and now.

She put out her left hand this time and touched something hard almost immediately: smooth plastic. A bucket, she realised after exploring it further, flipping the handle so it fell against the rim. The sound was so domestic, so safe, that she did it again. Beside that, she found a plastic container like a milk bottle. Liquid inside it swished when she tipped it. She spun the lid off and sniffed: no odour at all.

Water.

She drank some before she thought about whether that was wise or not. Persephone in Hades, eating pomegranate seeds, imprisoning herself for six months. How much time would a few gulps of water cost her?

More importantly, how long would the container have to last her?

The bucket.

The water.

The chain.

Fear was creeping around the edges of her mind. She leaned forward, patting the ground, until she found a third container. This was full of rectangular packets of something hard but brittle: muesli bars, she discovered, the kind you could eat instead of breakfast if you were running late and didn't care too much about them tasting like old cardboard.

There were a lot of them, she realised, pawing through the container.

How many muesli bars could one woman eat?

Especially if she only had one bottle of water?

It was like a stupid YouTube challenge, like something her Year Nine class would want to try.

It was *ridiculous*.

The smile stayed on her face until she reached beyond the water container and found another. And another. And another.

As far as she could reach, there was water.

Someone intended her to stay wherever she was for a long time.

On her own.

Trapped.

The first scream surprised even her. It tore out of her throat almost before she had formed the desire to unleash it.

She screamed until her throat was raw, but no one answered her.

No one came.

There was no one to hear her.

Somehow, that was the worst thing of all.

19

Tessa Marsh's disappearance didn't come to us straight away; nothing ever did. It went through the usual channels, the pass-the-parcel of a resource-intensive investigation. It went from the local Response team to the local CID, where an astute inspector looked at Tessa and saw a missing person who had more in common with Leo Stone's supposed victims than with the usual female mispers who crossed her desk.

And Leo Stone had been out of prison for a week by now.

Worth a try, the inspector must have thought, and passed it on up the line until it reached DCI Burt, fifteen hours after Tessa's boyfriend Paul Bliss called the police non-emergency number to say she wasn't at home and she wasn't answering her phone.

'There is absolutely nothing to say this connects with Leo Stone.' Derwent was chewing gum, the short, angry movements of his jaw reflecting his feelings. I was driving, because putting him in charge of a half-ton of fast-moving metal seemed like a bad idea. Fast-moving was a distant dream at that precise moment. We were stalled in heavy traffic, creeping forward an inch or two at a time, and it was hard not to see it as a metaphor for the case. The lack of progress, on both counts, was irritating both of us, but Derwent was the only one shouting about it. 'This is a standard misper, nothing more.'

'She's the right age. The right class. The right kind of woman.'

He shot me a look. 'Devil's advocate. You don't think that Stone did this any more than I do.'

'I'm keeping an open mind.'

'No, you're not.'

'Look, there is a chance that this was Stone's handiwork. He's living in a hostel in Streatham, which isn't common knowledge. Tessa Marsh lives in Streatham.'

'Right. He was in the area. Him and a hundred thousand other people. It must have been him.'

'He's looking at going back to prison for the rest of his life. Maybe he wanted one last fling. Maybe he saw her and he couldn't resist it. Maybe he's the kind of killer who gets a thrill from taking a victim from under our noses. They do exist, you know.'

'We should have had him under surveillance.'

'Too expensive.'

'I know. Too many man hours. And it would have been pointless because he didn't do this.' Derwent punctuated the last four words by slapping the dashboard, something I found intensely irritating. 'But it would have been an easy way to make sure he wasn't accused of every murder and missing person in London while he's out on bail.'

'The media are going to love this.'

'Especially if they get a whiff that Stone might be a suspect.'

I nodded. 'But they would have been all over it anyway. A young teacher – a pretty blonde teacher at that – who works in a crappy state school because she believes in doing good. She's exactly the sort of person who makes an appealing victim. A headline-grabber.'

'She's exactly the sort of person who should never be a victim.' Derwent tapped his fingers on the window, glowering out at the man in the car next to us.

'What is it?' I asked.

'Phone.'

I edged forward a little so we were a couple of feet in front of the other car, in the driver's line of sight. Derwent slid down the window and stuck his hand out. He tapped his fingers against his thumb quickly – *yap yap yap* – pointed at the phone and pointed down. There was something in the way he did it that stated – more clearly than any uniform or badge – *I am a police officer and you are going to do what you're told.* In the mirror I could see the driver panic and drop the phone without even hanging up.

'That's better.' Derwent gave him another glare before he slid the window back up.

'For someone who never worked Traffic it comes naturally to you,' I observed.

'I'd have loved it. Fast cars, telling dickheads what's what, taking shitty, unsafe vehicles off the road . . .' He sounded genuinely wistful.

'Well, your career isn't over. You could end up in Traffic. The car takes the strain so it wouldn't be an issue that you're not as quick as you used to be.'

He turned around fully in his seat to face me, his shoulders up around his ears. 'Excuse me?'

'At your age, you know. You can't expect to outrun the teenagers now. But I bet you could drive at them.'

I could tell Derwent was wrestling with his desire to tell me he was fitter than he'd ever been, that his current stats for a 10k were impressive at any age and that he had a new personal best for a half-marathon, set in October. He settled for: 'Kerrigan.'

'Yes, sir?'

'Shut up.'

I hid a smile as the lights ahead turned green, at long last, and we accelerated away from the petrified driver and the hellish traffic snarl-up that had been hindering our journey to a different kind of misery.

Smiles were thin on the ground for the rest of the day. Up until now, we had been operating on the leisurely timetable set by the court; a retrial couldn't take place for two months if not three, we had been informed, and even that depended on the listings officer at the Old Bailey and whether he had a six-week slot available. There was urgency in confirming that Leo Stone was the right man in the dock, and in uncovering any new evidence we could, but the pressure came from DCI Burt and Superintendent Godley.

Looking for a missing woman was a different proposition.

Especially when you walked into her neat, well-kept house and suddenly admitted to yourself that this was a real human being, a person with dreams and aspirations and a fondness for the colour blue and size six feet and a raincoat covered in daisies, rather than a nuisance passed from one part of the Met to another until someone got stuck with investigating her mysterious absence. The atmosphere in the house was dense with grief and I could taste tension in the air as soon as I walked inside. It reeked like old iron.

'Thanks for coming.' The local DI was a small, boyish woman with greying hair cropped very short. Judy Ownes had very sharp eyes and a no-nonsense manner.

'Who's here?' I could see a press of bodies in the kitchen, through the frosted glass door, and there was a jumble of shoes by the door.

'Family. Her parents, her boyfriend – he lives here. Her boyfriend's best mate. My FLO.'

An FLO was a family liaison officer, charged with being the point of contact and reassurance for the family. It was a bruising, demanding job, and an emotionally draining one. I had done it a few times and I hoped never to do it again.

The DI was in her socks and I took the hint to take my own boots off. I set them neatly beside a pair of ancient trainers that had been kicked off and left how they'd fallen. Habit made me look at the soles before I put the shoes side by side: criss-cross hatching, a crack across one heel. Beside them, a regrettable pair of scuffed suede boots, size ten, heels worn down at the back. Next to them, neat navy leather loafers with insoles, the kind worn by efficient middle-aged women: spotted grips on the sole, wear on the toes. Brown leather lace-ups seemed like the male equivalent of the navy loafers – practical shoes for practical people. They were ridged for extra grip and looked indestructible. His and hers running shoes came next, covered in cracking mud, well worn: Tessa's and her boyfriend's, I guessed. Wellies, again two pairs, one size six and one size eleven. The size elevens were clotted with mud. Then flat ankle boots, as neat and understated as my own: they would belong to DI Ownes, I knew, just as I knew the heavy brogues next to them were the FLO's footwear.

'What happened?' Derwent asked as I straightened up.

'What do you already know?' DI Ownes wasn't going to waste any words she didn't have to.

'Tessa Marsh is twenty-seven and teaches at a local comprehensive,' I said. 'She's fair-haired, pretty, financially secure, mentally stable, has no known reason to run away and this disappearance is completely out of character.'

DI Ownes' eyes crinkled briefly in approval. 'Those are the basics. She was at school yesterday morning when she started feeling unwell. She had an upset stomach. She rang her boyfriend to tell him she thought she had food poisoning. He told her to go home. She decided she was well enough to drive herself, although her colleagues wanted to call her a taxi. The school is a mile and a half from here and she would usually get there on foot or by bike. Yesterday, she had the car.'

'Where's the car now?' Derwent asked.

'Parked on the opposite side of the road. It's that blue Renault. She shares it with her boyfriend.'

'Does she usually park there?' The driveway was empty.

DI Ownes smiled thinly. 'No, she does not. She parks on the drive, as a rule.'

'And he didn't move it.'

'He says not. He says it was on the other side of the road when he came home.'

I turned to look at the coat rack. 'Did she make it into the house?'

DI Ownes shook her head. 'She always wore a duffel coat to school and it's not hanging up, or anywhere else in the house. We haven't been able to locate it. The car keys were in the driver's footwell along with her phone. The car was unlocked.'

Derwent revolved on the spot. 'No sign of a struggle as far as I can see.'

'No. If something violent happened it was outside the house. We haven't found any blood – anything at all, really.'

Like the other women, she had disappeared into thin air. The thought made me shiver. From the grim expression on Derwent's face, he was thinking the same thing.

And if it was Stone who'd taken her, she didn't have long to live.

'The only reason we're here is because our boss is concerned this might be Leo Stone's handiwork. If we can rule him out, we're gone.' There was a challenge in the way Derwent said it and I saw DI Ownes' reaction: a lowering of her eyelids by a couple of millimetres to hide her thoughts. You didn't get to be a detective inspector by giving away your emotions to just anyone. A man might have taken the bait Derwent was dangling, but Ownes was too good for that, too schooled in guarding her reactions, too wary to get into a fight with a police officer who was an unknown quantity.

'If you can get us any further towards finding Tessa Marsh it will have been worth the price of the petrol to bring you down here.'

Derwent nodded. 'Tell us about the boyfriend.'

'Paul. He's the same age as Tessa – twenty-seven. They've been together for five years.'

'Is he upset?' I asked. What I meant was, *Is he upset enough?*

'He's in a state. And her parents aren't helping to calm him down.'

'Do they blame him?' Derwent asked. 'Any history of trouble between the two of them?'

'They're ready to blame just about anyone. And no, no history of violence. They're a dream couple, Tessa and Paul. Lots of friends, good social life, healthy lifestyle . . .' Ownes shrugged. 'Normal.'

'And she didn't have any enemies. And no one could have wished her harm.'

'Basically, no.' DI Ownes looked from me to Derwent. 'We're at a very early stage with this investigation. It may be that you'll turn something up. I'm very concerned for Tessa's safety, though.'

'Let's have a word with this boyfriend, then.' Derwent raised his eyebrows at me while pointing at the kitchen door. *You, in there.* 'I'll just . . . run over a few details with Inspector Ownes.'

Thanks a lot, boss, I thought, and headed for the kitchen with minimal enthusiasm.

Desperate people have the same look, no matter who they are. At the sound of the door opening, every head in the kitchen turned to me. One belonged to the FLO, who was the sort of unflappable motherly woman you wanted in a crisis. The other four pairs of eyes were wide with the fear that I might know the worst news of all.

'I'm DS Maeve Kerrigan. I'm going to be working on finding Tessa, but I don't know anything new yet, I'm afraid.'

Something like a sigh passed through the room, though I couldn't tell where it originated. Disappointment and relief, I thought. They were on the knife-edge of not knowing, that painful, intolerable border between hope and absolute despair.

'Which one of you is Paul?'

One of the two younger men by the back door raised his hand. He had the blank expression of someone who is beyond expressing their emotions, but I didn't miss the tremor in his fingers. He seemed very young to me, from his desperately tight jeans to the carefully tended quiff on his head.

'I know you've already spoken to other officers but it would be very helpful if I could speak to you again.'

'I don't know how it will help. He doesn't know anything.' The speaker had to be Tessa's mother. She was neat in a cashmere cardigan, frilled shirt and pleated slacks. She was scrubbing the work surface although it looked clean enough to me. The smell of bleach caught in the back of my throat.

'I'm doing my best, Mrs Marsh.' There was a whiny tone to Paul's voice that would have annoyed me in just about any circumstances, and it made Tessa's mother snort. She threw the sponge into the sink and turned to face me.

'He spoke to her at eleven yesterday morning. She wasn't feeling well. She was being sick. He told her to go home, to rest. She rang me to let me know she was sick. I think she was hoping I might come and look after her.' Mrs Marsh's eyes filled with tears. 'But we were in London for the day, meeting friends. I got her message when I came home, and the next message on the phone was from *him* to say she was missing.' She gave Paul Bliss a venomous look.

'Helen,' Mr Marsh said, or tried to. He didn't actually make a noise. He was thin and stooped, tidy in navy cords and a fisherman's sweater. Thick, magnifying lenses in heavy-rimmed glasses distorted his appearance, dominating his narrow face. His mouth hung open, as if he had forgotten to close it after his attempt to utter his wife's name.

'Hey, Mrs Marsh, I don't think it's fair to blame Paul.' The other young man was tall, with sleepy eyes. He was wearing an anorak with the word 'DELIVERATION' across the chest and down the sleeves. It was a takeaway delivery service; I'd

147

used them myself, many times. I guessed he was either on his way back from work or on his way there. He patted the air ineffectually. 'You need to calm down.'

'This is my mate, Ollie Jones,' Paul explained for my benefit. 'He's just come round for support.'

'Hand-holding.' Ollie was nodding.

'Well, I'm afraid you're going to have to manage to talk to us without Ollie's help.' I didn't smile to soften the blow. I wanted Paul Bliss off balance, unsure of himself, panicked.

'Finally, someone who's prepared to ask Paul proper questions.' Mrs Marsh took a crumpled tissue out of her sleeve and blew her nose noisily. 'Everyone is so busy worrying about his feelings when my daughter is missing.'

'Helen.' Mr Marsh had mustered more volume this time, rather regrettably. His wife turned on him.

'Don't Helen me! She *called* me and I wasn't *there*. I was having lunch with *your* boring friends when she *needed* me. I'll never forgive you for this, Ken. Never.' She wheeled around. 'And as for you, Paul, you were never good enough for Tessa. I never liked you.'

'Now, now,' said the FLO, moving between them with a deceptive lack of hurry. She flashed a look at me: *Get him out of here*. Paul Bliss seemed to have frozen, a rabbit in the headlights of the speeding car that was Mrs Marsh's temper. I crossed the kitchen and took his arm, physically dragging him out of the room. He didn't put up a fight, letting me manoeuvre him through the doorway and the hall as if he was a child. I tried not to judge people by my own standards – everyone reacted to a crisis differently – but there was no reason for Bliss to be so *pathetic* . . .

However, away from his girlfriend's mother, in the carefully designed sitting room, he seemed more confident, less strained. He sat in the middle of a burnt orange sofa, one arm thrown along the back of it as I introduced him to Derwent. It was a 1950s house and they had chosen appropriate furniture – so much so that it felt like a stage set. A little angular coffee table stood in front of the sofa, a battered rosewood cabinet filled an alcove by the fireplace and a sunburst mirror hung on the navy blue wall behind Bliss.

'How did Tessa get food poisoning?' It wasn't the question he had been expecting me to ask first, and I saw him adjust to it with an effort.

'We had a curry last night. She had prawns.'

'And you didn't.'

'I don't eat shellfish.'

'Food poisoning generally kicks in quickly.' Derwent was in the corner of the room, browsing a bookcase, apparently distracted by their collection of travel guides and plays and the full set of Harry Potter books. 'She'd have been throwing up all night if it was the prawns.'

'I don't know about that. I don't think she was feeling great but I slept through it if she was sick.'

'Why wouldn't she have stayed at home if she was feeling ill?'

Bliss shrugged. 'She's a teacher. Dedicated. She'd have to be literally dying before she'd call in sick and let her kids down.'

'What does she teach?' I asked.

'History and drama.' Bliss half-smiled. 'I call her my little drama queen. She always wanted to be famous.' All at once his face crumpled with tears that were as sudden and copious as a summer shower. 'Not like this. Not at all like this.'

He meant the cameras that were trained on the house from further down the road. The television had been on in the sitting room when we went in there, tuned to a rolling news channel that was intermittently featuring footage from outside. Not for the first time I had the sense that reality had folded in on itself.

On the sofa, Bliss recovered enough to tell us he was a musician and he'd been recording that day – 'livening up the background of someone else's track'. He didn't know where Tessa was or who might have taken her. He had come back to the house at half past five and wondered about where Tessa was.

'I thought she'd taken the car. I know it's hard to believe but I didn't even notice it across the road. I wasn't expecting to see it there. I didn't look. And it was dark, so . . .' He trailed off, uncertain. In fact, it didn't surprise me that he hadn't seen the car. It wasn't in its usual space and neither was Tessa: they were both gone as far as he knew. I'd known people to block out much more obvious signs of trouble because they had assumed there was an innocent explanation.

'When do you think she went missing?'

Bliss answered readily enough, reeling off the details. 'She left school at twenty past eleven. She should have been back here by a quarter to twelve at the latest. I rang her at one and there was no reply, so I think she was already gone by then.'

'But you didn't get worried until later,' Derwent said.

'No, I was worried straight away when she didn't pick up her phone.' Bliss was looking wary.

'But you didn't call us for eight hours after that. You came home and she was gone and you did what?'

'Tidied up. Put on some washing. Watched some TV.' The whiny tone was back. 'I thought she was with her mum. She always goes running to her mum with problems.'

'Not you?' Derwent folded his arms. 'Why's that, then?'

'I don't know.'

'Not a very good boyfriend, are you?'

A flash of anger twisted Bliss's face. 'No, Tessa loves me. We've been talking about getting married.'

'Talking about it.'

'Yeah. She wanted to get married. Start a family.'

'How did you feel about that?' I asked. 'You're a bit young for all that, aren't you?'

'Not really.' He gave me a curious look that reminded me

150

my time frame for settling down wasn't quite the same as everyone else's.

'So what's stopping you?' Derwent asked.

'Money, mainly. It costs a fortune to get married, if you want to do it properly. And Tessa wants to do it properly.' For an instant the horror of it showed on his face: she was gone and he didn't know where or when he might see her again.

We took him back through every detail of his girlfriend's life that week, that month, what had happened in the previous twenty-four hours, how he felt, what he thought, what he feared. We got him to repeat what he'd told us before, listening for the variations, the places where he faltered.

'Well?' DI Ownes stuck her head into the sitting room after Bliss had gone back to the kitchen.

'His story's consistent.' Derwent shrugged. 'That's about all I can say.'

'If he's right about when Tessa disappeared, we don't need to be here,' I said.

DI Ownes frowned. 'Why's that?'

'For most of the time period where Tessa could have disappeared, Stone has an alibi.'

'How do you know? Have you asked him already?'

'I don't have to,' I said reluctantly. 'I'm his alibi. He was with me.'

20

'I think there are enough similarities between this disappearance and the others to justify searching Leo Stone's current residence. In fact, I think we'd be negligent not to.' Una Burt flipped a folder shut and sat back in her chair, eyebrows raised to invite me to reply.

'He has an alibi. It makes us look as if we're fixated on Leo Stone rather than investigating Tessa's disappearance properly. It looks as if we're more worried about what the media will say than with doing our jobs.' I hadn't taken the time to remove my coat before I marched into the office and the heating was making me feel faint, but I stood my ground. Derwent stood beside me, a silent presence. I couldn't tell if he agreed with me or not.

'I would never ask you to do something to satisfy the media,' Godley said, not quite sounding hurt but not far off it. 'I think this is an important element of the investigation, whether it rules Stone in or out.'

'He was here, in this office. He wasn't anywhere near Streatham.' My shirt was sticking to my arms and my back; I couldn't take my coat off now even if I wanted to.

'He could have been there later in the day,' Una Burt said. 'He could have gone from here with the specific intention of kidnapping Tessa, knowing that his interview would provide him with an alibi. We don't know if he had identified her as a possible target already or if it was a case of their paths crossing accidentally. I don't see how he could have engineered her food poisoning or how he might have known she was leaving work early, so I'm inclined to think he came across her by chance, but that doesn't mean he wasn't looking for someone to take.'

'We know he's intelligent. We know he's good at planning. We know he's intensely manipulative,' Godley said. 'One of the things we don't know is why he requested a meeting with you, Maeve. What if he was planning to commit another murder and he wanted you to have to stand up for him, though you're supposed to be locking him up?'

'You know he'd enjoy that,' Una Burt said shortly. 'I watched the recording of your interview with him. He likes irony. He feeds on it.'

'All of those things are true but that still doesn't mean he could be sitting here in Westminster in an interview room with me and simultaneously kidnapping Tessa Marsh from outside her house.' I couldn't quite believe I needed to say this to two senior officers who had far more experience than I did.

And then the third senior officer in the room spoke. 'That's assuming she was kidnapped from outside the house.'

I turned to glare at Derwent. 'Why would you think anything else? You saw the house. It was immaculate. There was no sign of a struggle.'

'It was tidy, but they kept it that way. Upstairs was the same – everything in its place. The boyfriend spent some time in the house before he reported Tessa missing. He could have cleared away anything suspicious, couldn't he, without realising what he was doing.'

I thought about it. 'He said he tidied up and did some washing.'

'So he didn't know that was significant, and neither do we. But the more you think about it, the more you can see it, am I right?'

'Her phone and her keys were in the car and the car was in the wrong place. The car was the last place we know she was.' I was determined to cling to the facts rather than allow myself to be swept up in the others' determined effort to drag Stone into this.

'If you're going to kidnap someone and you've got an alibi for a different time, you're going to do your level best to make it look as if the kidnap took place when you weren't able to do it, aren't you?' Derwent circled me, getting closer. 'He moved the car, he left the phone in it, he dumped her keys, he took her coat when he took her. As far as we're concerned, he's moved her back outside the house. Turned the clock back. Bought himself a few hours. Easy.'

'Risky,' I countered. 'Risky as hell.'

'You're talking about someone who persuaded at least two women to give up their freedom first and then their lives and no one saw a thing. No one saw him take the women and they didn't see when he dumped their bodies. I think risk is what he lives for.' Derwent spun his car keys on his finger and raised his eyebrows at Una Burt. 'So can we tear his home apart?'

'Organise the search warrant. We'll execute the search tomorrow morning.' Burt started shuffling her papers and Godley took out his phone, frowning at the screen: the meeting was over.

I had lost.

And I had lost the coin toss that determined which of us was going to confront Seth Taylor with the warrant so we could get into his client's flat. On the whole I was rather glad that Derwent had won. It meant he was safely on the other side of the car park, talking animatedly to Kev Cox, our crime scene manager, while I dealt with the lawyer. I preferred

Derwent to be a long way away, especially where Seth Taylor was concerned. I wasn't afraid they would fight, alpha males out to prove who was faster and stronger and better, although that was a possibility. I was petrified that Derwent would let it slip that I'd said Taylor was attractive. Let it slip? He would take great pleasure in telling him I fancied him. That had been an unwise confidence, even if it had been worth it to see the look of sheer disgust on Derwent's face.

On the other hand, an angry Seth Taylor was a very different animal from the businesslike, astute, self-contained lawyer I'd encountered previously.

'It couldn't have been him. You know that as well as I do. You're wasting your time.' Summoned in a hurry to the hostel where Leo Stone was living in the run-up to his retrial, Taylor had come as he was rather than delay his arrival by buttoning himself into another three-piece suit. A jumper and jeans made him look less like a GQ model and more like a normal person. His hair was dishevelled, probably because he kept running a hand through it from sheer frustration with me. It wasn't only his appearance that had changed, I thought; he had dropped the professional detachment. Unfortunately, in its place had come a temper so fiery I could have sworn it was raising the air temperature between us by a few degrees.

I concentrated on working my fingers into blue latex gloves, looking down rather than into his narrowed eyes. 'You know it's not my decision.'

'I know you can add up just as well as I can. You were in the fucking room with him when this poor woman disappeared. How was he supposed to be involved? Bilocation?'

'Swearing at me isn't going to achieve anything.' I stepped sideways and Taylor did the same, blocking my path. 'Oh, come on. Let me through.'

'No way.'

'I have a warrant to execute. This search is a formality, not an outrage.'

'It's harassment.'

'It's designed to rule your client out so we can leave him well alone and concentrate on finding Tessa Marsh. And you know that as well as I do, so I don't know why you're getting so angry about it.'

He looked past me at the forensic van that was parked outside the hostel, beside our car and the marked car that was our back-up. 'You haven't exactly done this the subtle way, have you? I know that's deliberate. The press are going to be all over this and you're making sure they get to hear about it while there are some exciting visuals to record. Leo's going to be a target for them, again, and his chances of getting a fair trial will be even slimmer second time round. It makes the Met look good, I get that, but it's absolutely against my client's interests. And you have the nerve to say you don't know why I'm angry?'

'We've got two uniformed officers here in case there's any trouble from other hostel residents who aren't keen on having the police in their building. Kev Cox is here in case we find something, because this is a live investigation and we need a fast response to any evidence we collect. As for the search, I don't have a lot of discretion in this matter. I did, in fact, try to persuade my boss that it wasn't worth our time or the disruption this search would cause Mr Stone. I've made all the same arguments you're making to me, and I got nowhere, and I'm afraid you're not going to get anywhere either.'

'This is ridiculous.'

'Look, you know it's going to happen. The longer you make me hang around out here, the more likely it is that the press will turn up and record every little detail of this search. You don't want footage on the news of me carrying evidence bags out of your client's home and I don't want it either.'

Taylor stood with his arms folded, chewing his lower lip. 'Leo isn't going to be happy with me.'

'Leo has nothing to worry about. Assuming he didn't kidnap her, obviously.'

'He couldn't have.'

'So it seems, but you never know. He likes tricks, doesn't he? Illusions. Sleight of hand. Making Tessa Marsh disappear would be quite the stunt.'

'You're going to get my client convicted of murder because he's fond of tricks. Perfect.'

'No. I'm going to get him convicted of murder if he did it.' I held Taylor's gaze this time until he looked away, and I knew I'd won.

'All right. I'll allow this on one condition. I'm coming in with you.'

'It's not up to you whether I do this or not. I have a warrant,' I said. 'But you are very welcome to come and watch as long as you don't obstruct the search in any way.'

'And Leo?'

'He can watch too.'

This time, Taylor let me walk past him, into the hallway of the hostel where Leo Stone had landed this time. It wasn't typical of the usual places where recently released prisoners ended up. Stone had converted to Catholicism in prison, apparently, which entitled him to a place at this privately run institution in a dilapidated but once grand house. The building was divided into twelve self-contained flats and run by a lay brother who shuffled out from behind his desk to greet me. He wore a long habit and sandals, a uniform I strongly suspected was self-designed.

'Welcome to Daniel of Padua House. I'm Brother Mark.' Brother Mark had the haunted eyes and bony joints of an El Greco portrait. His dark hair stood out at odd angles as if he cut it himself without the benefit of a mirror.

'The blessings of Christ on you and your endeavours,' he murmured when I had explained who I was. 'And of course the poor missing lady is in our prayers, but I hope and believe that you won't find anything to do with her in this house, where of course Leo is a welcome guest, a part of our little family under the care of God the Father and the Blessed Virgin who keeps us in her heart.'

'Thank you,' I said, familiar from an early age with the pious run-on sentences of religious people who are used to being listened to. 'Which room is it?'

'Leo is in flat twelve. The top floor,' he added, inevitably.

'How many floors are there?'

'It's a matter of some eighty steps. Closer to God is what I always tell myself when I have to go up there.' He smiled. 'Not that it helps.'

'I'll manage.'

'I'll come with you.' He patted the pockets of his habit. 'I think it's best.'

'There's no need.'

'We have a full house at the moment. Some of our residents aren't too fond of the police.' Brother Mark flashed me another preoccupied smile. 'I'd like to be there to reassure them.'

It was a long trudge to the top floor, all the same, especially when Derwent and Seth Taylor were on my heels. Brother Mark set a smart pace, the folds of his habit swinging hypnotically in front of my eyes. It was too long since I had been for a run, I thought, as the lactic acid burned in my legs and my breathing deepened. I needed to look after myself better.

That or I needed to find suspects who lived on the ground floor.

On the third floor a door opened as Brother Mark passed it. Light from inside the flat fell on my face like a slap and I screwed up my eyes against it. A small man stood there, grey-haired and stooped.

'It's all right, John. They're not here for you.' Brother Mark sounded firm but matter-of-fact. 'Go back inside.'

'What . . .'

'John.' Brother Mark moved closer to him, dropping his voice. 'They're here to speak to Leo.'

John shrank, visibly terrified. He mumbled something, looking away from Brother Mark towards me. His eyes were huge, his face drained of colour.

'That's right. Close your door, now. It doesn't concern you.' Brother Mark waited until the door had closed, hiding John from view. He turned to me. 'As I said, some of the residents will find this difficult.'

I followed him up the next flight of stairs which smelled, depressingly, of mince, thinking that John hadn't looked scared until Brother Mark had mentioned Leo's name, and if I had to guess I'd have said the police didn't frighten him anything like as much as his fellow-resident.

At last we made the turn to the last flight of stairs. I stopped at the top to let the others catch up, but also to get my breath back. Brother Mark stood to one side of me, his hands folded in front of him, in an attitude of patience. Not just an El Greco; an El Greco *saint*.

Derwent reached me first and was irritatingly unruffled. 'Looking good, Kerrigan.'

'At all times.' I tried to inhale through my nose instead of panting. 'Are you ready?'

'At all times.'

I gave him a look and he grinned at me, his teeth very white in the dim stairwell. Behind him, Seth Taylor stopped a couple of steps from the top. His gaze tracked from me to Derwent, a frown tugging his eyebrows together.

I rapped on the door and it opened before I'd let my hand drop to my side, as if Stone had been waiting.

He was all in black, as before, but his eyes were red with tiredness. His feet were bare, the toenails broken and yellowed. 'You made it up the stairs, then.'

'Just about,' I said. 'Were you expecting us?'

'I've been watching the news. I had a feeling you'd come calling.'

'Leo, I expect you to cooperate with these good people who

are here on important business.' There was something bossy and paternal about the way Brother Mark spoke to the residents, I thought, and it would have annoyed the hell out of me.

Leo Stone stood back. 'Welcome home. Wipe your feet on the way in, won't you.'

'Do any tidying before we got here? Throw anything out?' Derwent's voice had an edge to it and I remembered that this was the first time he'd met Stone in person. Elaborate introductions seemed unnecessary.

'A milk carton, I think. It's in the bin if you want it.'

'I'll have a look. And I'll have a look everywhere else you might have left something.'

'I bet you will. Might as well waste your time that way as any other. You get paid anyway, don't you?'

'That's right,' Derwent said, shouldering past Brother Mark and stopping right in front of Stone. 'We get paid to annoy you. I, for one, would do it for free.'

'Go on. Get on with it. You won't find anything.' The black eyes returned to mine. 'You can do the bedroom, love. It's a long time since I've had anything as fit as you in there.'

'I'll start in the kitchen,' I said to Derwent.

'I'll do the bedroom. And you' – he pointed at Stone – 'you keep quiet and let us do our search. The sooner we're finished the sooner we can leave you in peace. Unless, of course, we find something.'

'Unless you do. But you won't. And if you plant something, my lawyer will spot it.'

'I'm shaking in my shoes, mate.' Derwent disappeared into the flat's small bedroom, satisfied with having got the last word, and I moved into the kitchen before Stone could think up anything else to detain me.

It was a small flat, minimally furnished, and Stone hadn't acquired much in the way of belongings since his release from prison, so in some respects it was an easy search. From the

160

contents of the cupboards and fridge, he was living on sand-wiches and toast. The kitchen itself was tiny, with cheap units and appliances, but it was clean. I checked the underside of every drawer, the back of every cupboard, the oven and the inside of the toaster.

'Very thorough,' Taylor commented from the doorway as I stood on a chair to check the top of the wall units.

'That's the job.'

'And you like it.'

'Searching?'

'Being a police officer.'

I jumped down. 'Yeah. It's fine. Look, I don't mean to be rude but I'm working. I don't have time for small talk.'

Taylor didn't seem to be affronted. He looked at me for a moment that was long enough to make me feel on edge, then nodded and turned away.

What was that about?

I went back to the search, aware that my cheeks were warm. There was something about the lawyer that intrigued me – his intelligence, maybe, and his focus on his job. The temper that he'd unleashed in the car park hinted at a fiery nature he kept well under wraps. There was more to him than met the eye, and what met the eye was pleasing enough on its own. And I liked the way he moved, I thought, which was when Derwent appeared in the doorway.

'What's wrong with you?'

'Nothing.'

'Then why are you looking like that?'

'Like what?' I stuck my head under the sink so I didn't have to look at Derwent, and when I resurfaced he had moved on.

'Do you want to do the bathroom or the living room?'

'How bad is the bathroom?'

'I've seen worse,' Derwent said carefully.

'That means very little.'

161

'Yeah. Well, it's a small room. It won't take you long.'

'I thought you were giving me a choice,' I protested.

'I changed my mind.' He disappeared into the living room. I headed for the bathroom, steeling myself, sidestepping Leo Stone in the hallway. There was a whiff of cigarette smoke from him, although no smoking signs hung on the wall of every room.

'Do you smoke here, Leo?'

'Nope. Not allowed.'

'You mean you go down all those steps every time you want a fag?'

'And back up again. Cancels out the damage, doesn't it?'

'If you say so. But I thought you said you had trouble with your knees.'

He hesitated for a fraction of a second, trying to work out which lie to save. 'Needs must.'

I stepped into the bathroom. It was a sliver of a room, with just enough space for a short bath with a shower over it, a malodorous toilet and a sink coated in shaved-off bristles. I shut the door and locked it so I could wrinkle my nose unobserved. Did he smoke in here with the shower running to hide the smell? Or did he have somewhere else to go? I didn't believe for a moment that he would go to the trouble of walking up and down the stairs every time, knees or no knees.

Searching the bathroom didn't take long at all: the panels were loose around the bath but it was easy to see there was nothing underneath it, and the cistern was exactly as it should have been. A small shelf held Stone's few toiletries – there wasn't a medicine cupboard to look through. I turned my attention to the window, which was set into a sloping ceiling. I pushed it open and climbed up onto the loo seat, hoping it would hold my weight. Braced in the window frame, I could see that Stone didn't have much of a view: a gully between two angles of the rooftop. A collection of cigarette ends had piled up at one end of the gully, where a misplaced slate meant the water hadn't quite drained away. There was something sticking out of the gutter in the middle of the cigarette butts, something that I couldn't readily identify.

I swung my leg over to brace my right foot on the edge of the sink, grabbed the edge of the window and levered myself out. There was an unpleasant moment when I thought I might get stuck and have to call for help, but I wriggled awkwardly and passed the point of no return. The gully was flat, about two feet wide, and the rooftops on either side hid me from view. I crouched and pawed through the detritus: leaves, the cigarette ends, a sweet wrapper and the item that had caught my attention in the first place. It was wedged upside down and covered in mud. I eased it out and turned it the right way up.

A wooden wolf.

I turned it around in my hand, examining it. I was no expert, but it looked to me as if it was Kelly Lambert's handiwork. The grain of the wood ran up the back of the carving, for all the world like hackles. The ears of the wolf were pointed forward, alert. It was beautifully carved, alive in my hand, the wood pale against the blue glove I wore.

I could imagine Stone shying it away in a fit of temper, although his son had carved it for him. Maybe *because* his son had carved it for him.

I placed it in an evidence bag and climbed back through the window, dropping to the floor with a thud that made Derwent frown at me when I reappeared. He had found nothing at all.

'I told you,' Stone croaked, his lawyer a shadowy figure behind him.

'Yeah, you did.' Derwent went past him, dipping a little too close to Brother Mark so he had to press himself against the wall. From his expression he had never seen anything like Derwent before and slightly regretted the experience.

The sound of loud whistling floated back up the stairs, because Derwent was always at his most obnoxious when he was happy or frustrated. I made to follow him and Stone put out a hand.

'Do you know anything about Daniel of Padua?'

'No.'

'He's a patron saint of prisoners. Obviously,' Stone added with a black-toothed grin. 'You'd want someone who cared about prisoners to lend their name to this place, wouldn't you? He was a Jew.'

'Presumably not all his life, given that he's a Catholic saint.'

'No, not all his life. He converted to Christianity, like me, and got martyred for it.' Leo paused to pull a fine fibre off the surface of his tongue. He examined it critically before he blew it away. I managed not to flinch, even though his breath moved my hair. 'Do you know how they killed him?'

'I'd never heard of him five minutes ago, Mr Stone. Of course I don't know how he died.'

The grin again. 'You're funny, aren't you? A funny girl.' He leaned towards me. 'They nailed him to a table, funny girl, and watched him bleed to death. Got any jokes to make about that?'

I shook my head and Leo Stone leaned back against the wall with a satisfied sigh.

'Didn't think so.'

21

When a storm is coming it announces itself far in advance: a weight on the back of your neck, a change in the light, a hum in the air that's not quite audible but still denser than silence. There was no storm in the weather forecast but I was uneasy as I left Daniel of Padua House, aware of the cameras on the other side of the road that were filming my every move. My phone started to ring as I got into the car, Una Burt's name flashing up on the screen. I answered it on speakerphone, on the assumption that Derwent would need to know about whatever was bothering her.

'Boss.'

'You need to get back to the office straight away.' No preamble, Burt at her most brusque. I looked at Derwent who shrugged at me: *no idea.*

'Why? What's happened?'

'Someone tipped off the crime correspondent for the *Daily Messenger* and they're running a two-page spread tomorrow on the investigation into Tessa Marsh's disappearance, including the information that Leo Stone is a suspect.'

'Well, we knew that was coming.'

'They've found out that you met with him. There are pictures,' she added.

'Pictures? Of what?'

'Did you meet Leo Stone's son?'

I closed my eyes. *Fuck.* 'Not officially.'

'What does that mean?'

'I had a conversation with him.'

'It looks like more than a conversation.'

'You did *what*?' Derwent was staring at me.

I shook my head at him. *Not now.* To Burt, I said, 'It was a casual chat, nothing more.'

'As I said, that's not how it looks.'

A slow burn of anger rolled up from my stomach and fanned out across my chest. 'Well, how does it look?'

'More than friendly.'

'It was a short conversation over coffee two days ago and I haven't spoken to him since.'

'Come and tell me about it in person.' *Click.* Una Burt was a great believer in face-to-face communication, which was, at times, wildly inconvenient. We had already wasted the morning searching Leo Stone's new home. Now, instead of hunting for the missing woman, I was going to waste more time tangled up with Leo Stone and his son. And in the meantime the clock was ticking for Tessa.

'If Stone took her, she's dead already.' Derwent had been following my train of thought.

'And if he didn't take her?'

'Then we're not going to be the ones who find her anyway. Someone else will. You don't need to worry about Tessa. From what Una says, you need to worry about yourself.'

'It's nothing.'

'Kerrigan, what have you done?'

I glowered at him as I started the car. 'You know what the papers are like. There's no real news on the case so they start shuffling the facts and pictures around to make a story. Any story.'

'They have to take the pictures in the first place. How come you met up with Stone's son? What's his name again?'

'Kelly Lambert. He came to the office the other day – the day his dad came in for that interview. Kelly wanted—' I broke off. What had he wanted? To make sure I wasn't unfair to his father. To make sure he wasn't misguided to believe in him. 'He wanted to talk to me. I didn't think there was any harm in a short conversation.'

'Was that it? A short conversation? How did they make that into a two-page story?'

'I don't know,' I said, and although Derwent waited to see if I would explain myself further, I stayed silent all the way back to the office.

As we walked into the building, a slight dark-haired figure sprang up from beside the reception desk: Liv.

'What have you been doing?'

'Long story,' I said. 'What's up?'

'Sara Grey and Willa Howard's parents are here.'

'Together?' Derwent and I said it at the same time.

'Separate rooms. We worked out quite quickly it wasn't a good idea to put them together. Burt wanted me to tell you to come up the back stairs.'

'What do they want?'

'Your head on a plate, I should think.' Derwent steered me towards the stairs. 'The papers will have been in touch with them, looking for a quote. They'll know all about your little rendezvous.'

'Stop making it sound seedy,' I said, my voice sharp.

'You see, you wouldn't be so defensive if you were really sure of yourself.'

I would have dearly liked to walk away from Derwent and his provoking, overbearing conversational style. But he was right behind me, all the way into Una Burt's office, where an A3 printout lay across her desk.

'Is this it? Did they send it over?'

A nod from Burt. Her expression was absolutely un-readable; it could have been disapproval or amusement that made her mouth turn down at the corners. 'They want a quote from us. They've left a space for it.'

'Oh.' Derwent, over my shoulder. 'That looks dodgy as hell.'

The first picture had been taken through the coffee shop door: I was leaning forward while Kelly talked animatedly, reaching out to touch my arm. Second picture: outside, on the wet street. Our hands were touching. I was smiling while Kelly looked serious. Third picture: me looking down at something while Kelly leaned towards me, his mouth a little open.

'Did he kiss you or does it just look that way?'

'Of course he didn't kiss me.' I tore myself away from the paper – God, I hadn't even read the captions yet – to glare at Derwent. 'It was the end of our conversation.'

'What was going on here?' Liv pointed at the first picture.

'I was putting my bag down – that's why I'm leaning forward. I think we were talking about the weather or something.'

'And this one?'

'He gave me something. A wooden owl.' I looked at Una Burt. 'He had it in his pocket. He makes them all the time. I found a similar carving in Leo's place today.'

'Why did he give it to you?'

'Because I liked it and he was finished with it. It wasn't a *bribe*.'

'In fairness to the *Daily Messenger*, they don't say it was.' Derwent was grinning. 'It's a love token, according to them.'

'Bollocks. There was absolutely nothing romantic about our discussion. It was helpful to me to know more about Leo Stone and it reassured Kelly to talk to me about his dad. That was it. He wasn't remotely interested in me, and I certainly wasn't keen on him.'

'Picky. Just because he's shorter than you.'

I turned on Derwent. 'Look, do you have anything helpful to contribute or are you here to enjoy yourself?'

'Bit of both.' To Una Burt, he said, 'What do the families want?'

'They want her off the case.'

'That's ridiculous,' I said. 'They're overreacting.'

'The story they're writing suggests that you might be on Leo's side – especially since you're providing him with an alibi for the disappearance of Tessa Marsh.'

'How do they know that?'

'Someone well-informed leaked it, along with the pictures.'

'Who would do that?'

'Someone who wants to cause trouble for you, I imagine.' Una was not going to be drawn into speculation. I had the impression she didn't really care who was responsible. 'They want a quote from you about your meeting with Stone. They want you to confirm he was here at the time Tessa Marsh disappeared.'

'I can't confirm that,' I said icily, 'because we don't know when she disappeared.' A thought pushed its way to the front of my mind: it would suit Seth Taylor to get Stone's alibi into the media at the earliest possible opportunity. He had known where Kelly was going. He had called and found out I had agreed to the meeting. But I had chosen the venue, and Kelly couldn't have told him where we were while I sat there, could he?

Unless Taylor had followed us.

Unless the phone call had been designed to draw me outside so the pictures could be taken. Kelly Lambert had drawn my attention to someone outside the café, making me look around. Could that have been deliberate? Or—

'Surely the Greys are here to lend Kerrigan their support.' Derwent settled himself on the windowsill, his preferred spot. 'They're life members of the Leo Stone fan club.'

'Oh no, the article also suggests that Stone is only a suspect because Maeve wants an excuse to see Kelly Lambert. She's smitten with the handsome campaigner. I'm quoting, obviously,' Burt said to me, seeing the expression on my face.

169

'So the Greys are pissed off because I'm bothering Leo and Kelly, and the Howards are furious because I'm on Leo's side now.' I threw my hands in the air, frustrated. 'I can't win.'

'You have managed to make them agree on something, which is no mean feat.' Liv patted my arm soothingly. 'Don't worry about it, Maeve. No one will remember this story after tomorrow. It's no big deal dressed up as a scandal. The outrage is completely fake.'

'The families are genuine, though.' I was skimming through the article. The journalist had managed to suggest that where she was being vague, it was just that she was holding back information she couldn't share. There was a real skill to writing about nothing and making it look significant. Even I was almost convinced. 'Ouch, the quote from Mrs Howard hurts.'

'What did she say?' Derwent asked.

'That she and her husband can't trust the police any more.'

'Yes, she did say that. She said the same thing to me.' Burt wedged herself onto the edge of her desk, tucking one leg behind the other. 'Now, listen, Maeve. This is why you're here. Not to explain yourself – I'm sure you had your reasons for meeting with Kelly Lambert. You need to repair the damage that meeting has done. We need the families to be on our side, not cosying up with Leo Stone or the media. The less faith they have in us, the more difficult it makes our job.'

'So what do you want me to do?'

'You have to talk to them, in person, right now.'

'And say what?'

'That you're sorry to have upset them. That you acted alone, without the advice or guidance of your senior officers. That they need to trust the rest of us even if they don't trust you, so everyone else can move on with the case. And you need to tell them that you're not going to be working on any high-profile aspects of this case any longer.'

'I'm not?'

'You can't. You're part of the story now. You're a focus for the media. The *Messenger* are better at scandal than factual reporting but all the other papers will follow their lead.' Burt shook her head at me. 'If you had any sense, Maeve, you'd agree with me.'

'Does Superintendent Godley know about this?'

'The article?'

'The fact that your solution is to have me stop working on the case.'

Burt looked down and brushed an invisible piece of fluff off her knee. 'It's for the best. And I'm sure there are ways you can support the lead investigators.'

'But does Godley know about it?'

'Yes, he does.' She looked up at me again and with a shock I realised that what I could see in her eyes wasn't guilt, or embarrassment at going behind Godley's back. It was pity, for me. Godley wasn't there because he didn't want to be the one to carry out the execution, but it was happening on his orders. I looked at Liv, who was nibbling the edge of her thumbnail, and then, reluctantly, at Derwent. He was sitting on the windowsill as if he was carved from stone, his arms folded, his face blank.

'It doesn't seem as if I have much choice.'

'No, you don't,' Burt said firmly. 'But it's the best thing for the case.'

'What about Tessa Marsh?'

'That investigation is proceeding. I'm in touch with the SIO and I can let you know if there are any significant developments. From your investigations I think we can be fairly sure Mr Stone wasn't involved anyway, so you don't need to worry about it.'

It was getting increasingly difficult to talk around the lump that was wedged in my throat. 'And Rachel Healy?'

Burt blinked, caught off guard. Everyone forgot Rachel Healy. 'I'm not sure what's going on there, to be honest with you. Her family haven't complained. I don't know if the *Messenger* tried to contact her next-of-kin, though.'

I thought of Rachel's sister and her plump baby and the exhaustion that had slowed her movements and put an edge in her voice. She was probably too harassed to answer her phone to an unknown number.

'Can I keep working on Rachel, then?'

'It's another dead end.' Burt's voice was surprisingly gentle.

'Then it doesn't matter if I pursue it.'

'I've got more important things you could do.'

I stood up, shoving the chair back. 'No one is interested in finding out what happened to Rachel except me. No one is prepared to spend any time at all on her, though she's entitled to as much care and hard work as any of these women.'

'There isn't a strong connection between her and the others.'

'That's because we haven't made one.' My voice was rising in pitch and volume. 'You can't write her off just because we haven't bothered to make her part of this case.'

'I understand you want to be involved somehow in getting Stone back behind bars, but—'

'It's not because of Stone. It's got nothing to do with him. I don't care about him. I don't know if he *did* kill them. I'm glad I'm not going to be on the jury because I'm not sure I'd convict on the strength of the evidence we've got so far.'

'That's enough,' Burt snapped, dropping the sympathetic head tilt and the sugary manner. 'You don't need to make a scene.'

'This isn't making a scene. If I was doing that, believe me, you'd know it. I'm pointing out that Rachel is a deserving victim and we shouldn't ignore her.' I took a deep breath, rinsing the emotion out of my next words so that I sounded more like a hard-headed police officer and less like a bleeding heart. 'I know she's not an important part of the case. She's not key to the prosecution. I would have thought that you might let me investigate her death for the very reason that she's peripheral to the enquiry at the moment.'

'It's a waste of your time and your skill as an investigator.'

In spite of myself, I smiled. 'Look, ma'am, if you were that impressed with my skill as an investigator, you'd be fighting for me to stay on this case instead of telling me to quit. If I'm disposable, let me work on Rachel Healy and I'll say whatever you want me to say to the Greys and the Howards.'

Which was how, ten minutes later, I found myself standing outside a room that contained both of the families, brought together at the last possible moment.

'Don't take too long about this. They're probably at each other's throats already.' Burt opened the door and marched through it before I could respond, followed by Liv. That left me on my own in the corridor with Derwent, who was draped against a wall as if standing up all by himself was too much hassle. I raised my eyebrows at him.

'Well?'

'Well what?'

'You've been very silent, that's all. It's not like you. I was wondering what you were thinking.'

'You should apologise.'

'To whom?'

'Everyone. The families. The boss. Me.' He wasn't smiling.

'Why should I? I haven't done anything wrong.'

'Debatable. You should still apologise just to get back on the case.'

'You wouldn't.'

'I wouldn't have let myself get into that position in the first place.'

'I've seen you in much more compromising positions than that,' I said, which was accurate but unwise. Derwent glowered at me and peeled himself off the wall to hold the door open.

'Get on with it.'

22

When I walked into the meeting room I saw that someone had put the Greys on one side of the big table in the centre of the room, and the Howards on the other. I understood the impulse to keep them apart but it made for a confrontational atmosphere. Una Burt stood at the back of the room, flanked by Liv and, to my surprise, Georgia Shaw. Georgia was looking straight ahead of her, as if her mind was elsewhere, and didn't appear to notice that Derwent and I had entered the room. *Up to something*, I thought.

'Mr Howard.' I went to shake hands with the round, red-faced man sitting beside Mrs Howard. 'We haven't met.'

'My wife told me about you.' He looked at her, uncertain, waiting for a cue for how to react. Mrs Howard was staring at the table. Her face was flushed and I could tell she was upset.

Derwent leaned past me to introduce himself to Mr Howard as I had. He rested a hand on Mrs Howard's shoulder.

'How are you?'

'I've been better.' She dragged her eyes up because she was fundamentally too nice a person to ignore him. I saw her soften at whatever she could read in his face and in spite of myself I was impressed. God, he was good at dealing with people when he wanted to be.

The next moment, he spoiled it all with a nod across the table. 'Mr and Mrs Grey.'

'It's *Doctor* Grey.' Her mouth was a line. Her husband shook his head and folded his arms, the body language clear.

Una Burt gave me a meaningful look and I cleared my throat.

'Dr Grey, Mr Grey, Mr and Mrs Howard, I understand you were upset by the article that the *Daily Messenger* are planning to publish tomorrow, about a meeting I had with Kelly Lambert.'

'I'm not upset by the *article*. I'm upset by the fact that you thought it was appropriate to have a secret liaison with Kelly.' Dr Grey's voice was pure acid.

'I absolutely wouldn't describe it as a secret liaison. It was a brief conversation. We talked about his father.'

'The thing about Kelly,' Mr Grey said heavily, 'is that he's a decent chap. He didn't get the best start in life but he's done his best with what he had. He's not worldly. He wouldn't see anything wrong with talking to you, but it's inappropriate.'

'In what way?'

'It's vile.' Dr Grey's voice was harsh. 'You want Leo to go back to prison and you'll do whatever it takes to put him there, including cosying up to his son, and in the meantime the person who killed my daughter is walking around *laughing* at you, and at us.'

The pain on her face made me catch my breath. No wonder she hated us. 'I think it's important that you should realise Mr Lambert contacted me informally, as he'll confirm if you ask him. This wasn't an official interview and it wasn't something I planned. It was a quick coffee.'

'We've seen the photographs. You look very happy to be there. Of course, he's handsome.' Dr Grey's face was tight and all of a sudden I understood that she was, if not in love with Kelly Lambert, desperately attracted to him. Beside her, her husband scratched his head, oblivious. A shower of dandruff drifted down, dusting his shoulder. Kelly was sweet, earnest, talented and full of youthful energy. The contrast with Dr Grey's husband couldn't have been starker.

'I have no romantic interest in Kelly Lambert,' I said calmly, as if it was an acceptable suggestion for her to have made. 'I don't imagine you read the *Daily Messenger* very often, but this is how they fill their pages. They have constructed a story around some misleading pictures. There was nothing inappropriate about our meeting. It was a conversation about Mr Lambert's relationship with his father.'

'Why meet with him at all?' The question came from Mrs Howard. 'I trusted you. I thought you were on our side.'

'Mrs Howard, you have to understand that I'm not on anyone's side – if I was, I wouldn't be doing my job. My job is to find out as much as I can about what happened to your daughters, and to investigate the case to the best of my abilities. I've tried very hard to keep an open mind.' I turned to the Greys. 'I haven't assumed that Mr Stone is guilty.'

Mrs Howard gave a soft wail of protest.

'But I haven't assumed he's innocent either,' I continued. 'I hadn't planned to talk to Kelly Lambert, but when he asked me to sit down with him, I agreed. It was an opportunity for me to understand his father a little better. Anything that gives me an insight into Leo Stone helps me to do my job. The article in the newspaper might not acknowledge it, but that's what I was doing – my job.'

'Then why are you being taken off the case?' That question came from Mr Grey. His red-rimmed eyes were suspicious.

Because DCI Burt wouldn't back me up, if you must know. 'I'm working on a different aspect of the case. I'll still be involved.'

'I don't want that.' It was Mrs Howard who spoke. My stomach lurched with unease and disappointment; I had liked her, a lot, and I'd wanted to help her. How had I managed to do the exact opposite? 'You know what he did to us. I told you what he was like and I thought you believed me. Then I see that was an act. You tricked us. Mr Lambert probably thinks you believe him. I don't know, maybe you do.'

'Mrs Howard—'

'You're obsessed with Leo. Why can't you see he had nothing to do with our daughters' deaths?' Dr Grey had gone white with anger. She was staring across the table at Mrs Howard. 'You keep putting pressure on the police to concentrate on him because he fits your idea of what a killer should be. Just because he doesn't have a lot of education and he looks a bit different.'

'He *is* the real killer. You've allowed yourselves to be taken in by him and his conman son.' Mrs Howard's voice was rising.

'I resent the implications of that! He had nothing to do with Sara's death. There's no evidence at all to suggest he was involved.'

'Her body was dumped beside Willa's. How could that be a coincidence?' Mr Howard snapped. He put a hand on his wife's arm. 'Don't engage with her, love. She's a lost cause. She doesn't want to believe he did it.'

'Leo had an explanation for the blood in his house from your daughter. One tiny speck of blood shouldn't be enough to condemn a man for all time. You're the ones who don't want to believe he's innocent.'

'He taunted us.' Mr Howard stood up, his chair tipping so Derwent had to catch it before it fell. 'He wanted us to suffer, more than we had already. He wasn't satisfied with taking our daughter – he had to taint our memory of her.'

'Absolute nonsense,' Dr Grey retorted. 'Leo would never do such a thing.'

'Please, please.' Una Burt stepped forward, flapping her hands ineffectually. 'This isn't helping anyone.'

'Forgive me if I don't feel you can help either.' Dr Grey turned on her. 'I haven't seen much in the way of new ideas from this investigation. What exactly are you planning to do differently this time round?'

'Well, I—'

'Doctor Grey, I'm Georgia Shaw,' Georgia said smoothly, stepping forward with a low-wattage version of her smile that was respectful but warm. She looked and sounded polished and the impression she gave was that she was deeply competent. 'I'm going to be taking over from DS Kerrigan, working with Inspector Derwent.' A meaningful glance for him: nothing for me. I might as well have been a pot plant for all the attention she paid me.

'Why haven't you been involved from the start?' Mr Howard looked to Una Burt.

Caught off guard she coughed, then mumbled, 'I think a fresh pair of eyes may help at this stage.'

'I'm so honoured to be replacing Maeve,' Georgia cooed. 'I hope I'll manage to persuade you that we are really conscious of how difficult this has been for you – all of you. Your welfare is as important to us as making sure the right person goes to prison.' She put a hand on her chest, her expression earnest. 'We all know DS Kerrigan crossed a line. Even she admitted it.'

I remembered doing no such thing, but Georgia was still talking.

'I promise, I won't let that happen from now on. Your daughters feel like friends to me – I think we would have been friends, if we'd known each other.'

Mrs Howard was nodding, her eyes brimming with unshed tears.

Georgia was winding up for the big finish. 'I want to assure you – all of you' – a quick look around the room, making eye contact with all of the bereaved parents in turn – 'I want to make sure they get the justice they deserve.'

Pride is one route to perfect posture if you don't have time for yoga. I walked out of the meeting room with my head held high, even though I knew my flushed cheeks told the truth about how I was feeling. I was halfway down the corridor when the sound of quick footsteps made me turn, sharply, to see Liv running after me.

'What do you want?'

'To see if you're OK.'

I almost laughed. 'Not really.'

'I'm not surprised.'

'Did you *hear* her?'

'Hold on. Not here.' Liv looked back down the corridor warily, then took hold of my arm and steered me into the kitchen, shutting the door that was usually wedged open in defiance of fire regulations.

'Who let her take over the meeting? She acted as if she was in charge and Burt let her get away with it. And then the way she talked! "I'm so honoured to be replacing Maeve." That *cow*.' I paced up and down the narrow kitchen as Liv pressed herself against the sink, trying to stay out of my way. 'I knew Georgia was ambitious but I didn't realise she was that keen to step into my shoes.'

'I think everyone else knew it a while ago.'

'Really?' I stopped pacing. 'I thought I was imagining things.'

'For someone who's generally quite perceptive, you're terrible at knowing how people feel about you.'

'I don't think that's fair.'

'Georgia has seen you as a threat and a challenge since day one.'

'But I've been nice to her.'

'Have you?' Liv's voice was carefully neutral.

'Yes. I have.' I sounded defensive, even to myself. 'She could have been kicked off the team for what happened in the summer. She fucked up and she knew it, but I stood up for her. It would have been a lot easier to agree that it was all her fault and let her take the blame.'

'So she owes you for that. Maybe she resents it.' Liv shrugged. 'Or maybe she knows you don't like her.'

179

'What's to like? She's a backstabbing, two-faced—'

'Shhh.' Liv was practically wringing her hands. 'I don't know how soundproof this room is. You don't want her to hear.'

'I don't care if she does.'

'You should.'

I went back to pacing. 'She's so good at sucking up to people. Everyone in that room was taken in.'

'Not everyone.'

'The Greys were. The Howards were. Burt was purring.'

'Only because she needs them to cooperate with us and Georgia was very persuasive. I'm not surprised Burt was impressed.'

'Did she impress you?'

'No, of course not.' But Liv looked away from me as she said it, and the way she spoke was a shade too casual to be honest.

'Knock knock.' Derwent pushed the door open. 'What's going on? Making me a cuppa?'

'Obviously not. Why would I? You're more than capable of making it yourself.'

'I need to check something,' Liv said vaguely, and slid out of the room.

'Shut the door,' I snapped.

Derwent was the last person to take an order from me, but he did as I asked and then leaned against it. His hands were in his pockets, the corners of his mouth turning up from some private amusement. 'Well?'

'Did you take the pictures that are going to be in the *Messenger*?'

Whatever he'd been expecting, it wasn't that. The smile evaporated. 'What? No. Of course not.'

'Kelly thought he saw you when we were in the café. He thought you were watching us.'

All the warmth had disappeared from his expression. 'I

wasn't aware you'd met up with him until an hour or so ago. If I had known you were with him, I would have intervened.'

'I didn't do anything wrong.'

'The kindest possible interpretation of what you did is that you were unwise.'

'That's absolute bollocks and you know it.' I glared. 'It's not like you to be taken in by a hack.'

'Oh, I don't think what was in the newspaper was true. The pictures were certainly misleading. But you shouldn't have been there in the first place.'

'It was an ordinary conversation. There was nothing underhand about it. And there was no reason anyone should have been interested. Whoever took the pictures must have known very well they would cause problems for me.'

'And you think I took them? Why would I want to cause problems for you?' Anger was still uppermost but I could see hurt pulling at the corners of Derwent's eyes, and hear it in his tone.

'You wanted me to stay away from Stone. Now you've made sure I have to.'

'You honestly think I would threaten your career and embarrass you for that.'

'I think you'd do just about anything to get your own way. And even if you didn't, you're glad this has happened.'

'Is that so?' He said it softly and that made it more menacing than if he'd shouted at me.

'You were furious that I met with Leo Stone. You tried to persuade me to say no and I wouldn't. I stood up to you and you didn't like it because you hate losing. And now I'm learning my lesson.'

He was silent for a moment. Then, 'I see.'

I narrowed my eyes, trying to guess the significance of what he said from the way he'd said it: there was something about him that suggested what I'd said went much further than I'd intended. 'What do you see?'

181

Derwent shook his head; all his defences were up. 'You can try to pin this on me if you like, but it's not about who took the pictures. It's about who had the bad judgement to be in the pictures in the first place. No one forced you to take Kelly out for a chat. You did that all by yourself.' He opened the door and turned for his parting shot. 'So if it didn't work out the way you wanted, you only have yourself to blame.'

23

'I knew that something was wrong straight away. I mean, I just knew.' Paul Bliss stopped talking to rub his eyes with the heel of his hand, and a fusillade of camera clicks filled the silence. Hundreds of flashes bleached the colour out of his face. The shot was tight, so my television screen was filled with Bliss's face and the forest of microphones on the table in front of him. I could see his fingers trembling, though I was watching it from my sofa in my pyjamas rather than standing in the room with him. I would have been there if things had worked out differently. Instead I was watching a live feed, transmitted directly from the police station to the endlessly demanding 24-hour rolling news channels.

'I tried to pretend that everything was normal when I came home and she wasn't there. I – I wanted to believe that she was going to walk in the door any minute. Part of me still wants to think that might happen.'

Behind him, a large poster of Tessa Marsh smiled down on the assembled media. Bliss would be allowed to make his statement without facing questions from the journalists, but they would be desperate to ask when exactly he had decided to call us in, and why he was so sure Tessa hadn't walked out on him, and who did he think might be responsible. This was a chance for the general public to hear his voice and see his agony, so they might rack their brains one more time and locate the stray fact, the missing memory that could solve the case and return Tessa to her family.

'Tessa, if you're watching this—' His voice broke, horribly, and his face began to quiver. I felt myself tense up, willing him to finish his statement before he collapsed. 'If you're watching, please come home. We're all desperate to see you. We miss you and love you. For the sake of your parents, your friends and for me, please make contact and reassure us that you're OK.' He took a long, quivery breath, and sniffed loudly. 'I have to ask that, even though I know you'd let us know if you could. Whoever has Tessa, please, please, I'm begging you. Let her go.'

The last word disappeared as he dropped his head onto his folded arms and gave in to despair, his shoulders shaking. Gone was the cocky musician I'd met two days before. As the hours passed, Paul Bliss had let go of his vanity, his self-confidence and his belief that Tessa was going to come back to him unharmed. What I saw on the television was a man who was in hell.

A hand appeared in the corner of the screen and held on to Bliss's arm. The cameraman adjusted his focus so I could see Mr Marsh, Tessa's father. He looked withered, desiccated by the horror he was enduring. His eyes were dry behind his spectacles. The emotions were there, but held back because of the convention that men didn't cry. Paul Bliss, brought up in a different era, leaned on Mr Marsh's shoulder and howled. It was a sound that made the hairs stand up on the back of my neck. Someone came and helped him to his feet, and he stumbled away. Mr Marsh followed, his shoulders hunched up protectively around his ears – a shy man, hating the spotlight.

DI Ownes stepped into view, looking just as tough and competent on television as she had in real life.

'You've heard there from Tessa Marsh's boyfriend, Paul Bliss. This is an active investigation, ladies and gentlemen, and there may be developments sooner rather than later. I will issue regular statements when there is anything I can tell you about the case. Please don't approach witnesses or my officers as they will not be able to talk to you and you'll simply hold up the investigation. Thank you.'

She stood up and I switched the television off as a babble of questions broke out; she wouldn't answer them and I knew why. There were no new developments. Paul Bliss had been marched out to face the nation's media to generate news where there was none. *Still missing* got you no headlines unless you could offer a new angle.

I sat and thought about Paul Bliss, about whether he had revealed more than he'd intended to. A cocky killer might agree to make a statement, assuming they could act well enough to fool everyone who watched them. Then again, they might feel they couldn't refuse the opportunity to speak, in case it made them look suspicious. Bliss had abandoned himself to his emotions in a way that made me feel he'd really meant what he was saying. Idly, I wondered if Tom Mitchell had made an appeal for Sara Grey's safe return, and if he had wept on camera. I would have looked it up if I'd still been working on the case. I picked up my phone and started to write a text about it, but then deleted it instead of sending it. Derwent didn't need my advice about that or anything else. A person with bad judgement didn't tell a senior officer what to do, did they?

And anyway, it wasn't my job any more, just as it wasn't my job to find Tessa Marsh. I looked up at the picture I had propped on the mantelpiece, at Rachel Healy's composed, charming smile. It was still my responsibility to try to find her.

So there was no point in sitting around feeling sorry for myself. I levered myself off the sofa and went to get dressed in jeans and a heavy jumper. Where I was going, I wouldn't need to wear a suit.

It wasn't actually raining when I parked at Long Valley Nature Reserve, but the memory of rain still hung in the air and every breeze shook loose a cascade of droplets from the trees. I pulled my hood up and zipped my coat, checking the car park from habit. Two cars were parked near the entrance and I didn't recognise either of them. Almost without thinking I made a mental note of their registration numbers and the make and model. One, a Vauxhall Astra, had a bright pink princess sunshade on the side window and the back seat was littered with toys. The other car was an ancient Volvo that sat low on its wheels. Rust had eaten along the driver's door, fringing it with a rough brown frill. RSPB stickers covered the back of the car and a National Trust sticker skewed at an odd angle on the front windscreen.

And that was it for the other visitors. Otherwise, the reserve was deserted. I shouldn't have been surprised. Late November was probably a bad time to birdwatch and the light was dreadful, the sun muffled in heavy grey clouds. The air was raw. It would rain again soon, I thought, and I shivered as I crunched along the path to a hut by the gate. A man was leaning in the doorway, peering at me through the gloom. He had to be the Volvo's owner: he was resplendent in an ancient Barbour, a holey jumper, cords and wellies even more battered than the ones I wore. From a distance, he could have been just past retirement age but a second look persuaded me he was closer to eighty.

He greeted me with a raised hand. 'Lovely day for it.'

'Other people don't seem to think so.' I pushed back my hood and smiled at him. 'Have you been here all day? You must be freezing.'

'The reserve is only open from ten to half past two at this time of year, and I've got a little heater in here. And a cup of

186

tea, as you can see.' It was steaming on a shelf by his elbow. I tried not to look at it with too much longing in case he took it as a hint. 'Are you here to walk around? I've got a map and there's a lovely loop you can do – well, not so lovely in the rain but it's really quite charming on a nice day.'

'How far is it?'

'Three miles or thereabouts. You're probably quite fast at walking but the terrain is difficult in places. And do remember that you'll only have an hour or so. I don't want to lock you in.'

'That would be awful.' I looked around. 'How would I get out if that did happen?'

'Well, of course I would wait for you.' He beamed. Gallantry was going to get between me and finding out what I wanted to know. I swallowed my irritation and smiled back.

'Say someone came here when the gate was closed. Would they be able to get in? Is there a fence?'

'No, no. Not all the way round. There's a hedge but it's quite easy to push through it. And there are gates here and there, and they're not locked. I'm afraid, you know, we can't afford to have a proper fence and the local teenagers do use the reserve when it's supposed to be closed.'

'Teenagers would get through a proper fence if they really wanted to. Do you keep a register of visitors to the reserve? Record the number plates – that kind of thing?'

'Why do you ask, my dear?'

I held up my ID with some reluctance, knowing that it would change the tone of the conversation from friendly to official. The elderly man peered at it and then raised his eyebrows.

'Oh dear. I knew I'd get found out one of these days. All those unpaid parking tickets are catching up with me.'

I grinned in spite of myself. 'I'm not here for you.'

'Why then? The murders?' He said it in a matter-of-fact way, I was relieved to note.

'I'm supposed to be finding a third missing woman.' Or a fourth, if Tessa Marsh had been really unlucky, it occurred to me.

'They did look very thoroughly after the first poor girl was discovered.'

'I know. I just wanted to have a look for myself.'

'I quite understand. No, we don't keep a register of visitors. We don't get so many, though, Most of the volunteers are a bit past it but I think we would have noticed someone carrying a body into the reserve. Assuming they came through the gate, that is.'

'I'm sure you would.'

'It was a dreadful thing to do – leaving those girls here.' He looked truly fierce, bright eyes shining with anger under bristling white eyebrows. 'It spoils it for the children, you see. We used to have school trips here and lots of people came to walk with the little ones. It was safe, here. Away from all the hustle and bustle. And now they don't come any more. I can't blame them, really, but it's a shame.'

It was quiet, I'd noticed already, the valley offering shelter from the suburban sprawl that hemmed it in.

'For their sake, though, I'm glad he put them here.' The man looked down the path, his face softening. 'It's a beautiful place. They could be at peace here, for a while. I'd like to be scattered here, when my time comes. It's a comforting thought that I might get to hang around here after I'm supposed to be gone.'

It might have sounded ghoulish but I spent a lot of time around death and I knew what he meant.

He stood holding the map he had planned to give me. 'Would you like this? Would it help?'

'It absolutely would.' I would have taken it even if I'd had a large-scale ordnance survey map instead of Dr Early's shaky sketch. 'Thank you, Mr—'

'Walter. Just Walter.'

'Thanks, Walter. I'll try not to take too long.'

'I'll wait for you.'

I felt obscurely comforted as I headed off down the path, knowing Walter was watching me go. Someone knew where I was. I didn't often feel lonely when I was alone, especially at work, but something about the circumstances made me miss company. Derwent complaining about the weather would have been better than the sound of my own footsteps and my breath and my heart beating faster as the path snaked over a hill. But I didn't want to think about Derwent.

A thin, high sound made me stop in my tracks: keening. The purest kind of misery. It hung over a rumbling noise that I couldn't place for a moment. I worked out what it was a second before the buggy rounded the corner of the path. The woman pushing the buggy looked exhausted, her coat flattened against her body with rainwater.

'Almost there,' she said to the baby, whose wails got a fraction louder. 'Come on, Lily. Give me a break.'

'She doesn't sound too happy.'

'She's not. Teething. She hasn't slept for two days.' The mother stopped and rubbed a hand over her face. 'I'm exhausted. If she doesn't sleep tonight I'm going to go mad.'

I had no advice to offer her so I settled for a sympathetic smile. I watched her push the buggy away, thinking about Rachel Healy's sister and babies and how Liv didn't know what she was letting herself in for, if she did manage to have a baby, and that we would lose her from the team. It would be impossible to be a murder detective with a small baby, whatever about when they were older. The men managed it, I thought with a surge of outrage that cooled off to the blank realisation that Rob – *my* Rob – would be becoming a father any day now. I had seen a picture of him with his pregnant fiancée four months earlier, and managed not to think about it much until now, in this cold and deserted nature reserve, I couldn't think about anything else.

A baby.

Rob's baby.

If it had been mine, I would be scared but excited. I would be—

I cut myself off from a line of thought that could only hurt, scowling down at the map. I needed to be on the other side of the trees on my right. *Concentrate, Maeve.*

I was ruthlessly efficient as I located Sara Grey's dump site and then Willa Howard's, noting the tree and the landmarks Dr Early had mentioned. If I hadn't had her map there would have been nothing to indicate that this was where the two women had been. There was no sign of anything else suspicious – no hint that Rachel Healy might be nearby. They had looked for her with dogs and search equipment and I was unlikely to stumble upon her by chance, I told myself. It was ridiculous to feel disappointed.

Walter's map suggested there were a few buildings on the nature reserve – a hut at the opposite end of the valley and two birdwatchers' hides. It was too late to make it to the hut that day but it was marked as out of use anyway, a biro-inked star scrawled on the map. I would check with Walter whether 'out of use' meant securely locked up. In the meantime, I walked across to the nearer hide for a closer look at the low building, my boots catching in the long, limp grass that was sodden with rain. It was empty and cold, the window unglazed so there was nothing between you, the birdwatcher, and your beloved birds. There was a door at either end and a bench in the middle so you could sit down while peering out at the beauties of nature, but otherwise it was distinctly lacking in amenities. I looked out at the grassland where Sara had slowly disintegrated, hidden from view.

Why here?

It wasn't all that close to Leo Stone's home. There were many places to leave a body between his house and the nature reserve – any number of rivers, lakes, canals, forests, pits, ditches, waste ground, derelict buildings . . . What was the significance of Long Valley?

If I hadn't chosen to leave by the second door instead of the one I'd used to go into the hide, I would have missed it. An amateurish mural decorated that end of the hide – a faded scene with stiff, stunted trees, bulky owls staring out of the branches, spindly swallows pinned in the sky and mice creeping up ears of grass and ladybirds and spiders and butterflies and a garish woodpecker twice the size of the fox that lurked in the shadows, its face watchful.

The fox was good. Whoever had painted it had caught something of the animal – the blend of wariness and boldness and stiff-legged readiness to sprint. The colours were flat and the paint was starting to peel away; on closer inspection it wasn't as accomplished as I'd thought. It was a child's attempt at a fox, I reminded myself, playing my torch over it. It made me think of something, though.

It was late. I needed to go. Walter would be waiting.

I stayed where I was, staring at the fox. What was it – the eyes? The tilt of the head? The set of the ears?

They had signed it: a long list of contributors in straggling, pockmarked paint. Thurrold School's best artists. I ran my torch down the list, knowing what I would find before I got to the name I was expecting to see.

Kelly Lambert, aged 11.

He had painted his name with care, forming the letters beautifully, just as he had painted the fox with as much skill as he could muster.

Whitlock had checked Kelly's alibis for the disappearances, and I couldn't believe he'd have made a mistake. But as far as I knew from the files, no one had made a connection between Kelly Lambert and Long Valley Nature Reserve before now.

Charming, good-natured Kelly, waiting in the rain for me, carving figures with the knife that was practically a part of him.

Do you think he did it?

Not because he was worried about his father's freedom. Because he was worried we were looking for another suspect.

Or maybe Kelly was as innocent as he seemed and this was Leo's way of tainting a childhood memory that mattered to his son.

I stood in the dank, draughty hide and I felt a chill that had nothing to do with the temperature.

24

Tessa Marsh huddled under a filthy blanket, her hands in her armpits to keep them warm, and tried to work out how long she had been trapped. The darkness made it hard to keep track, and she hadn't been hungry since she woke up – sleepy, yes, definitely. She had been so sleepy she assumed the water was spiked with something. It wasn't normal to sleep so much.

But then, nothing was normal.

Whatever the reason, she couldn't work out how many meals she might have missed, or how many days and nights might have passed in the endless darkness.

That left the bucket. She had used the bucket four times, and cried every time. It was horrible. Demeaning. *Dirty*.

It stank.

She stank.

'If you're keeping me here to have your wicked way with me, I'm going to need a bath first.' She called it into the silence, as if he could hear. Maybe he was listening.

Maybe he was watching her. A night-vision camera would work and she'd never know it was there. She stared blindly around her, searching for a giveaway red light or some kind of reflection, imagining herself in blank-eyed awkwardness on a green-lit screen while someone watched her, laughing himself sick at how ridiculous she looked.

If he was watching, he had seen her try to unknot the chain, the first time she tried.

Now she kept the blanket over her legs, hiding her hands from view as they worked on it.

The chain was keeping her calm.

The chain was keeping her sane.

The chain was her one and only chance.

No one had come, since she had been in the hut. No one had walked nearby. All she had heard was the wind whining through gaps in the walls, and the rain rattling on the roof, and trees creaking like ships on the high seas.

And she had heard her own voice.

She went through phases of calling. Shouting.

Screaming.

Sometimes she thought about Paul. She thought about her parents. Her friends. They would be devastated, she knew. They would be desperate to find her. The police would be looking.

Someone might stumble across her, especially if she made a noise, so she made a noise as much as she could, tapping an empty water container against a full one in time to songs she hummed to herself. She couldn't imagine where she might be that no one would come near – farmland? Woods? But people were everywhere.

Someone would come.

Most of the time she stayed quiet. She slept. She warmed her hands. She worked on the chain.

She slept again, and when she woke up, nothing had changed. But Tessa wasn't stupid. She'd thought about it and she knew that she couldn't stay there forever. She was trapped for a reason. Someone wanted her to be in the hut, but alive. Even though they'd left plenty of supplies, she would run out of food eventually.

So someone had to come.

And when they came, she wanted to be ready for them.

Under the blanket, Tessa reached down to her ankle and began to tease the narrow links over one another, working slowly and steadily. It took a long time. That was all right.

She had nothing else to do.

25

At first glance, there was no way into the house where Leo Stone had lived for a time – where Willa Howard's blood was found on a wisp of plastic, in a cupboard, in a locked room. Someone from the council, the police, or another branch of officialdom had arranged for metal screens to be nailed across the windows and the front door. It was enough to stop squatters from trying their luck, but not enough to prevent the graffiti artists from venting their feelings. *Murdarer* straggled across the door, sprayed on in blood-red paint that had seeped into the brickwork where they had gone over the edge of the metal sheeting. I wondered what the neighbours made of it. The house on the left looked empty, the windows grey with dust and the walls bare. I wouldn't have wanted to live next to Leo Stone either.

I made my way down the side of the house to a narrow iron gate. The local police station held a key for the padlock and had been more than happy to let me take it, once I explained who I was and what business I had with the house. They had checked my credentials carefully.

'Sorry,' the civilian receptionist had said, handing me back my ID having phoned Una Burt. 'We get so many journalists these days. They'll say anything to get into the house.'

I would have said almost anything if it meant I *didn't* have to go inside the house. I had called Una Burt and told her what I'd found at the nature reserve.

'We hadn't made that connection before.' It wasn't quite a question.

'No,' I said. 'Not as far as I know.'

'We'll look into it.' A pause. 'Well done.'

'I thought I could—' But she was gone.

So, I was still exiled from the main investigation.

I was at Leo Stone's house from a sense of duty and a nagging feeling that someone had missed something. DCI Whitlock had searched the house, just as he'd scoured the nature reserve, but he hadn't picked up on the significance of the mural. I knew objectively that he would have done a good job at the house but I couldn't take it on trust.

The gate opened with a shriek of metal, dragging on the concrete path. I shut it and locked it behind me. The last thing I wanted was to have an unexpected visitor join me in Leo Stone's den. I was nervous enough already. It was almost dark, the short day drizzling towards a cold, miserable evening, and I wanted more than anything to go home. Not to Derwent's flat – that wasn't home. It was a stopgap, nothing more. I wanted to go home to my parents, to be fed and scolded and loved. The women who had apparently died in Leo Stone's grim little house had been daughters, like me. They had been loved, like me. They had been taken away from their parents, their homes, and their futures at a stranger's whim, for his passing gratification. Alive, they had meant nothing to him. Dead, they had satisfied some desire I couldn't understand. So I wanted to go home and allow myself to be loved instead of thinking the uneasy thoughts that were hunting through my mind.

The side door was locked and an additional bolt had been screwed into the wood; it too was padlocked into place. I sorted through the keys and, with some difficulty, managed

197

to unlock the door. It had swelled in the rain, or from lack of use, and I had to shove it hard a few times until it gave way. I rubbed my shoulder ruefully, wishing I had Derwent with me for the muscle alone, and sidled through the gap into the kitchen.

I had seen the house in photographs already. They had done a good job of recording the place and the life Leo Stone had led there. My imagination replaced the dirty dishes in the sink, the rotting fruit in a bowl, the dirt on the floor and the grease drips on the cooker. Someone – Kelly? – had cleaned it since then, wiping down all the surfaces, emptying the cupboards. The doors hung open, revealing bare shelves in the light of my torch. Even the pictures were gone from the walls, a few dusty rectangles like ghosts of what had been there: the calendar, the clock, the picture of horses in a field. The room smelled of plaster-dust and dead air.

I walked through to the front of the house, to the icy living room where Leo had been drinking when the police knocked on his door. The metal screens on the windows shut out what little light was left in the day and I wished the electricity was still on in the house. My torch was powerful but it only showed me a dizzy fraction of the room at a time. The sofa had left a tidemark along the wall where decades of greasy heads had rested. A broken stand was all that was left of the television. The carpet was worn and it wasn't my imagination that the soles of my boots stuck to it. I caught a flicker of movement out of the corner of my eye and almost screamed before I recognised what it was: a mouse running along the skirting board past a closed door. It shot into the hall. I followed it and took a quick look at what was upstairs: dark, empty rooms, musty air, a chipped sink in one bedroom with a dripping tap that had left a brown stain on the porcelain. The bathroom was clean, at least, but that didn't make it pleasant. I dragged myself back downstairs, knowing there was one last room to look at: the door I had ignored in the living room, because I was aware of what lay behind it.

The door wasn't locked. I swallowed hard and pushed it open, misjudging how much force I needed. It swung back against the wall with a bang that echoed through the empty house. The room was dark and it looked very different from the crime scene pictures. I took a moment to orientate myself: that was the window, coated with black paint. That was where the bed had been, and the cupboard. There was the stain, where the floorboards had been removed. It was larger than I'd thought: the blood had spread over a wide area, I saw. Rachel Healy's blood, or someone else's. The whole room had been cleaned and cleaned again, and then forensic teams had taken away everything they could for further examination, and then Kelly or someone else had cleaned what was left. I couldn't smell blood in the air. That was my imagination.

But my imagination told me the room stank of death, and I believed it. I thought of the places Rachel Healy had lived – the rooms where she had worked and laughed and slept. If I was right, this was the place she had died.

The darkness seemed to press against my back, trailing icy fingers along my bones. I turned, the torch stabbing into the room, and there was no one there but my heart was slow to get the message. It thudded painfully in my chest, which was doubly annoying when I was trying to listen for any sound that might alert me to a threat. Somewhere nearby, a dog gave two high, sharp barks and my nerve broke completely. I backed away, leaving the door hanging open, and hurried through the chilly hall to let myself out of the side door. The evidence of what had happened was gone, I told myself. I couldn't get a conviction based on a bad feeling. Standing around in the house communing with the spirits of dead women was ghoulish rather than useful. Besides, it was a quick way to get pneumonia.

I was trying every key the local police had given me to find the one that locked the side door, swearing to cheer myself up, when a voice said, 'Hello.' Surprise made my head snap up as I turned and I mistimed it, colliding with the wall with blinding force. I put a hand to my forehead, convinced it was bleeding, and blurted out one last, 'Jesus *Christ*.'

'Oh dear. I'm so sorry. Did I give you a fright?' She was peering over the fence that divided Leo Stone's house from the one next door. She had to be seventy and looked about as threatening as a fluffy slipper: dyed straight black hair, thick glasses on a chain, a purple raincoat. 'Do the police know you're here, dear? Because I don't think anyone should be going into that house unless the police know about it.'

'I am the police,' I said, which was the best I could manage at that moment.

'Are you? Because I'm going to need to see your identification.' Her voice quavered a little and I realised she was scared. 'That's what the police told me to do.'

'Very wise.' I handed it across the fence and occupied myself with the door while she peered at the card.

'This is you, is it?'

I grinned at her. 'My own mother wouldn't recognise me from that picture. But if you want to check my driver's licence, it's a better one.'

'Thank you.' She spent a good long time looking at the licence, and back at me, while I tried to look pleasant and unthreatening. 'Yes, I see. Well, I'm sorry for disturbing you.'

'It's fine.' I took my wallet back. 'You must have had a lot of strange people hanging around in the last couple of years, since Mr Stone was arrested.'

'Oh, yes, dear. It's been awful. And they're so *rude*.'

'Probably because they know you're right and they shouldn't be here.'

'Well, yes. They assume they have a right to poke around here, you know. It's public interest, they say. Well, it's my

200

home and I don't want people peering through windows and knocking on doors to ask me what I knew about what was going on.'

'I completely understand,' I said, as if my next question hadn't been going to be about what she'd seen when Leo Stone was in residence. 'It must be very annoying.'

'It is. People writing books. Foreign journalists, too. I don't see why someone in Denmark or France should be interested in what happened here. Or didn't happen.'

'What do you think happened?'

'Me? I couldn't say. Wouldn't like to speculate.' Behind her glasses her eyes were sharp.

'I bet the police talked to you already.'

'Well, you'd think so, wouldn't you.'

'They haven't?'

'I made a statement over the phone. Saying I hadn't seen anything, you know, because I hadn't. Mind you, I was away when it all kicked off. In Australia.' She drew out the last word, her voice full of longing. 'My daughter's out there, you see. She had me out to stay with her. I was away for six months, April to October. By the time I came back he was on trial, wasn't he? So I ran into all the journalists and whatnot, but the police were finished. Which is why I was surprised to find you here.'

I pulled out my notebook. 'Could I take your name?'

'Jill Ross. Mrs Jill Ross.'

'Were you aware of anything strange going on in this house before Leo Stone was arrested?'

'No. Nothing. I'd have done something about it if I had. Called the cops, you know. But there was no reason to be worried. I was glad to see the house occupied again. Not that I knew *him*, you know. I didn't see *him*. I'd have a chat with the son, you know, in the garden or whatever. Over the fence. He was all right. Loved the sound of his own voice a bit too much, if you ask me, but he was friendly.'

'He's a very outgoing person,' I said, and she sniffed.

'So what are you doing here? Checking up on the place?'

'A bit of that.'

'He's out, isn't he? Leo?'

'For the moment.'

She cackled, and I reflected that a modern-day witch probably would wear purple anoraks rather than black cloaks. 'You don't like that, do you? Him being out?'

'Have you seen him since he was released?'

'No. No one's been round here. You're the first one I've seen in ages.' A scrabbling sound made her break off, looking down. 'Benson. Stop it.'

A muffled bark answered her. It was Benson, I guessed, that I'd heard barking earlier.

'What kind of dog is he?'

'Little terrier, he is. There's a bit of pug in him and a bit of a few other things. He's my pride and joy and a pain in the arse.' She called the last few words after him as, with a skittering of claws, he rattled along the fence into her back garden.

'I bet he's good company.'

'Oh, he is. He has to listen to me yapping all the time. That's why I can't really complain about him barking. The neighbours do, obviously.'

Somewhere in the garden Benson gave vent to a growl that ended in a yelp.

'Leave it! He's gone after something. A rat, probably.' Mrs Ross sighed. 'Hope he doesn't try to bring it in, that's all. Here, don't go through the fence, you little bastard.'

Her answer was a scuffle as Benson did exactly that, wriggling through to the garden on my side to bark in joyful freedom.

'He knows I can't come after him, you see.' She held on to the top of the fence, straining to see. 'I thought I'd blocked up all the loose planks but he digs his way through. Determined,

202

he is.' She peered into the garden, genuinely anxious. 'You can't see him, can you?'

'I'll have a look.' I pulled my torch out of my pocket again and made my way down the side of the house to be confronted with a sea of mud and weeds and a shed right at the back. It was covered from the ground to the roof with spindly bindweed, like something from a grotesque fairy tale. The whole garden had been dug up, I remembered, when they were looking for Rachel. There had been shrubs and even a tree at one stage. Now, like the house, it was bare.

Bright lights snapped on in the garden next door.

'I thought that might help.' Mrs Ross appeared over the fence. 'Can you see him?'

'No.' I crouched, probing the shadows with my torch. The glare of the outdoor lights had done for my night vision. I could hear the dog sniffing around somewhere nearby, but I couldn't see him. 'I think he might be behind the shed.'

'That's where he likes to go. There must be a rats' nest there. Horrible things.'

I really wished I was still wearing my wellies. Gingerly, I picked my way down the garden, sliding in the soft ground.

'They made a right mess of this, didn't they? What were they looking for? Bodies?'

'Evidence,' I said over my shoulder, taking a long stride to reach a concrete paving slab that seemed to offer a safe place to stand.

'And they didn't find any.'

'They found enough.'

'Can't have, or you wouldn't be here.'

It was a fair point. 'I wanted to see it for myself.' Another step landed me on the end of a plank. I edged along it, knowing that if I slipped in either direction I would be up to the ankle in soft, sucking mud.

'I can see him. Benson. Benson, come out of there.'

203

She was looking down the side of the shed. I reached the filthy concrete plinth that extended from under it and bent to look. A small black rump was visible, the tail wagging from ten to two at a high speed.

'Benson.' I clicked my fingers. 'Hey, Benson.'

'He won't come to you, dear. You'll have to grab him.'

There were brambles with sharp, curving thorns between me and the dog. I absolutely did not want to reach through them to grab him. One of us or both of us would end up with severe lacerations.

'*Benson.*'

The rump disappeared and I heard excited snuffling from behind the shed, going away from me. *For fuck's sake . . .*

'Go round the other side,' the witch commanded, elbows on the fence, thoroughly enjoying herself. 'You'll never be able to get him from where you are. He's been a little devil since they moved the shed.'

'Since who moved the shed? The police?' I was half-listening to her, half-concentrating on Benson. I crept around to the other side of the shed and peered down it. He was coming towards me, his attention all on the weeds that sprouted from under the concrete plinth.

'Oh no. No, it was Leo and his son who moved it. It used to be over the other side of the garden.' She pointed at a pile of pavers, neatly stacked by the investigators who had levered them up. 'No, this was never over here. Well, it couldn't be, could it?'

'Why not?' She had my full attention now.

'Because what's under it is the old septic tank, from before these houses were on the mains sewage. Not what people expect, nowadays, but when we moved in all of the houses had their own tank, and you had to leave access to it so they could pump it out when it was full.' She cackled. 'Lovely job, that was. The smell was something you'd never forget. You young people won't remember that. And going outside to use the toilet. If you had to go, you went, but you didn't hang around.'

I lunged and got hold of Benson's collar, drawing him towards me as he tried to nip my hand. He weighed very little I discovered when I was able to grab him with both hands and carry his small, wriggling body over to his owner.

'Sorry, did you say this was built on a septic tank?'

'Somewhere under all that concrete, yes.' She kissed the dog on the mouth, making little noises that I tried to ignore. 'But the police would have known that. Someone must have told them.'

'When was the shed moved?'

'A while ago. Before I went away, in January or February. Freezing cold, it was. Made me wonder why Leo was out there in the garden. He wasn't what you'd call a keen gardener, as a rule.'

'And you didn't mention this in your statement?'

'Never occurred to me, to be honest.' She kissed the dog on the top of his head. 'I'm not the sort to gossip, am I?'

26

'Police are conducting a large excavation in the garden of a house in Dagenham in East London. A police spokesman refused to comment on reasons for the excavation, although the house was at one time the home of Leo Stone. Mr Stone is awaiting a retrial for the kidnap and murder of two women in 2013. He was released on appeal last month. And now to sport and it's going to be a busy weekend—'

Liv turned off the car radio and pointed across me. 'There's a space.'

'I like your optimism.' I set about fitting the car into it, despite the fact it was barely big enough for us and hemmed in by other vehicles. In other circumstances I wouldn't have dreamed of parking there but spaces were hard to come by behind the police cordon. The larger the cordon, the more police that were needed to keep it secure, so the street was cluttered with transport vans as well as the Forensic Science Service's vehicles. The press were a solid mass along the barriers that had gone up overnight, before anyone outside the police had an inkling we would be digging in Leo Stone's garden again. It hadn't taken long for the word to get out. Hundreds of lenses were trained on the scene, recording the nothing-much that was going on outside the house. All the action was in the garden behind it. There was very little we could do about the helicopters that took turns to circle overhead, filming the white-suited forensic officers padding back and forth from the tented area that covered the shed. But I knew they would need images for their reports – something to run while the journalist's voice-over gave viewers the scant details we'd allowed them to know.

The reports might have been restrained but the journalists weren't. I got out of the car to a barrage of shouted questions and camera flashes. I went around to the other side, where Liv was, so I could put on my wellies unobserved.

'Does this have anything to do with Tessa Marsh's disappearance?'

'Are you looking for a body?'

Liv rolled her eyes as the reporters yelled and I grinned at her, despite the grim reason for us being at the house in the first place. You had to find reasons to laugh or you'd never make it through the day.

'Is Tessa Marsh buried in the garden?'

'Have her family been informed?'

The only thing to do was ignore them; I couldn't tell them anything useful. They had to ask, I understood that. I hoped, all the same, that Tessa Marsh's family had been well briefed by now. They would be jumping on every rumour, every suggestion, hoping for good news, fearing the worst.

'Look what you did,' Liv said, as we headed for Leo Stone's house. 'This was a perfectly normal suburban street before you called in the diggers.'

'Perfectly normal is pushing it. You haven't met the neighbours yet.' I showed my ID to the officer who was keeping the scene log and led the way down the side of the house.

'Jesus, it looks like the Somme.' Liv stopped to survey it. 'Did we do this?'

'Not recently. I don't think it ever recovered from the last search.'

207

'How come they didn't know about the septic tank?'

'The neighbour I met was away and all the other residents arrived too recently to know about the septic tanks. It's buried under a few feet of concrete so the cadaver dogs didn't sniff it out during the last search. Or they did and the handlers assumed it was a false positive. The dogs aren't infallible.'

'And neither are we.' Liv shivered. 'When do you think they'll break through the concrete?'

'A while, I should think. Sounds as if they're still dismantling the shed.' I could hear sawing coming from under the canvas tent that covered the entire area. The forensic search team had been on site since seven o'clock and it was getting on for nine. Kev Cox, the crime scene manager, would be taking his time. You couldn't hurry him; even begging didn't work. So the shed would be reduced to its individual parts, which would be numbered and listed on a plan, on the off-chance that they ever needed to reconstruct it. Then they would bring in the equipment to break up the concrete slab. Only then would Kev turn his attention to what lay beneath it. His team would have special scanning equipment to look for disturbances in the soil – tell-tale anomalies. You could hide a body, but not forever, and certainly not from Kev Cox. We would know at that stage whether there was anything significant to find.

And if there wasn't anything, I would feel like a fool.

A large gazebo had been erected on the left of the garden, providing shelter for the officers and crime scene technicians who weren't currently engaged in the search. The officers included not only Una Burt and Derwent, but Superintendent Godley too. The three of them were standing together, intent on their conversation. I'd have preferred to go back out on the street than stand under the canvas with them, but Liv had already headed that way.

'Any news so far?'

At the sound of her voice, the tight huddle broke apart.

208

'Not yet.' Godley looked past her to me. 'Good morning, Maeve.'

'Boss.' I hoped I sounded matter-of-fact instead of hurt. Derwent stared stonily into the middle distance while DCI Burt gave me a brisk, slightly awkward nod.

'This is your work, I gather.' Godley smiled. 'I shouldn't be surprised. You always find things other people miss.'

I was not going to allow myself to be charmed that easily. 'I would have missed it too if the neighbour hadn't told me about it.'

'But you were the one who persuaded her to talk.'

'The main problem was getting her to stop.' I turned to DCI Burt. 'Ma'am, is there anything you want me to do while I'm here?'

'You could brief us on what you know about Rachel Healy.'

I gave them a short rundown on her background and how she had disappeared. Godley listened intently, as if it was the first time he'd really paid attention to any of the details of her disappearance.

'It sounds as if there were suspects who should have been considered. The ex-boyfriend, for starters.'

Oh, I hadn't thought of that. I held the sarcasm back because Godley was, after all, many ranks senior to me. 'I believe the original investigation ruled Dan Forbes-Stanton out. Besides, he didn't strike me as the type.'

'Not every murderer looks the type,' Derwent said to the horizon.

'I'm aware of that,' I snapped, losing my hold on my temper for a split second. I went on more calmly. 'He was very quiet and direct and not at all upset by talking about their relationship or how it ended. If he'd killed her, I'd have expected him to be more edgy. I'd have expected him to talk a lot more than he did too.'

'Guilt does make people ramble.' Godley nodded. 'Fair enough. In the absence of any other reason to suspect him,

209

we'll assume he wasn't involved. But there must have been other suspects aside from Leo Stone.'

'Of course. Her friends were concerned about her. They were fairly certain she was in a relationship with someone else, but if she was she kept it quiet.' I folded my arms, shivering in the raw morning air. 'She was also using another phone, I think. I had a look at her phone records. I'd expected to find a record of multiple phone calls and messages to one number in the weeks before she died, but there was nothing.'

'So whoever she was seeing wanted to be untraceable.'

'Could have been a married man.' Derwent was now taking an interest in the mud at his feet.

'Could have been her killer,' I countered. 'We have to consider whether Kelly Lambert was involved in this. I can't imagine Rachel being in a relationship with Leo Stone, no matter how much she wanted to be degraded. But Kelly might be a different matter.'

'You liked him,' Derwent said, and I nodded.

'He has charm. Maybe too much of it. Anyway, we have no way of knowing who Rachel was involved with. If she had a separate phone for him, we don't know where it is now or what the number was.'

'But you still think it's worth looking for her here,' Una Burt said. I knew what she was doing: pinning this entire expensive search to me. *I* thought it was worth looking, so it was my responsibility.

'I do. In the first place, there's the blood. Then, to the best of our knowledge, Rachel disappeared from somewhere around King's Cross. That fits in with the other women; it's close to the major arterial road that Stone seems to have been using. In terms of timings, well, it's close to when Willa Howard disappeared. That made DCI Whitlock wary of Rachel, because he couldn't believe Leo Stone would strike twice in such a short space of time. I think it's possible, especially if something went wrong with Stone's plan. Maybe he killed her too soon, or she fought too much, or maybe it was Kelly who killed her instead of Leo. Whatever the reason, it didn't satisfy him. If that was her blood in the house, it suggests killing her was a messy business. We have no forensic evidence of where or how Sara Grey died, and we only have a tiny speck of Willa Howard's blood to tie her to this location. Rachel was different.'

'It's possible,' Godley said. 'But if we don't find her body—'

'—we can't charge either of them with anything. I know that.'

'So let's hope we find something,' Una Burt said. *For your sake* was heavily implied.

I'd always thought being a police officer was more exciting than a standard office job, but when it was boring it was truly dreary. I found it punishing to stand in the icy gloom of Leo Stone's garden, waiting for something to happen. Soon after Kev sent word that there might be something and they were going to start digging, Georgia Shaw arrived. She was carrying a cardboard tray with four coffees wedged in it: one each for Burt, Derwent and Godley.

'Oh, sorry. I didn't know you were going to be here.' I could see her weighing it in her mind: was it worth offering the fourth cup to me, since my star could be in the ascendant again? It would take more than a cup of coffee to win me over, I thought, and she must have reached the same conclusion because she took a sip from it instead, leaving a smudge of pink lipstick on the lid. Caffeine or bravado made her add: 'It must be strange knowing that no one really wants you to be here. No one from the families, I mean.'

'Rachel Healy's sister raised no objections, and Rachel is why I'm here.'

'Do you think she's been under there all along?'

'I hope not.'

211

She looked surprised for a moment, before she understood. 'Oh, well. Obviously we'd all prefer it if she was alive and well.'

'Obviously,' I agreed, and went in search of a hot drink of my own instead of a fight.

It was several long hours before Kev emerged from the tent at the other side of the garden and pushed his hood back as we all crowded around him.

'Well, we've found something.'

'A body?' Godley asked sharply.

'My best guess? More like three or four.'

Derwent gave a long, low whistle. I didn't have enough air in my lungs for that; I felt as if I'd been punched in the stomach.

'Why don't you know?' Una Burt asked.

'We haven't started taking them out yet so we can't see exactly what we've got, but you're looking at multiple victims.' Kev was pale, his usual cheerfulness subdued. 'You're going to need a forensic anthropologist to sort out the bones. They're in a right old mess. It's going to take a while to recover them, I'm afraid.'

'Take as long as you need,' Godley said.

Kev nodded, as if he wouldn't have done that anyway, and after he'd eaten a quick sandwich he disappeared into the tent again. The rest of us were silent, the mood gloomy rather than triumphant. Bodies were bad news, even if you were looking for them.

Dr Early arrived, ducking under the canvas with her usual air of being in a rush but sorry about it. After a short interval she reappeared and beckoned to us.

'Do you want to have a look?'

Godley strode across the garden and I followed along with the others. We all ended up clustered together in the mouth of the tent, jostling for a view of the muddy trench they had excavated.

212

'Stay behind this line.' Kev drew it on the ground with his toe. 'I don't want you lot hoofing all over the place.'

I was at the front, and tall enough to be able to peer into the trench without too much difficulty. What I saw would stay with me forever: a tangle of bones and cloth and hair smeared and sunk into soft black matter. The bodies weren't completely skeletonised but the bones were clearly visible – frail, arched ribcages, hollow eye sockets, a curved pelvis that was tilted at an angle. They had been tipped into the hole with little ceremony and no respect for how they fell. The remains of a gag wrapped around the lower half of one skull, a reminder that this had been a living woman once upon a time, a woman who had been scared, who had died in terror and torment and enforced silence.

I looked, and kept looking until I knew I had taken in all the details. Then I stepped aside to let Liv take my place. There was no sound apart from the shuffling of our feet on the soft ground. I wasn't the only one who was conscious of the weight of evil in that small space.

'What we've got,' Dr Early said, 'as far as I can tell, is four victims. By that, I mean I've found multiple bones and four skulls in various states of decay and damage. I'm not going to speculate on whether they are male or female, let alone who they might be or when they were dumped here or how they died. But what I can tell you is that they've been in the septic tank for a considerable time.'

'What does considerable mean?' Derwent asked. 'Years? Decades?'

Dr Early shrugged. 'We can examine the bodies, and Kev can get an analyst to look at the soil that surrounded them, but we may never know when they were placed here.'

'Could any of them be Rachel Healy?' Una Burt asked, handing Dr Early a copy of her photograph.

'I'd say it was unlikely, looking at the teeth. None of them has the gap.' She gestured with a gloved finger at her own mouth, indicating what she meant. 'Not that I'm an expert on forensic dentistry, but it's distinctive.'

'We're going to take our time about recovering the bodies, to give ourselves as good a chance as we can of gathering all the evidence,' Kev said. 'I know you'll want to tie it to a particular period because that will implicate the homeowner at that time.'

'Can you tell if the septic tank was still in use when the bodies were put in it?' I asked.

'It was empty,' Kev said. 'More or less. I think we can be pretty sure that the bodies were put in the tank after the house was connected to the sewage system. The council will be able to tell us when that happened. That should narrow down your list of suspects.'

'Oh, we know who was responsible for this.' Derwent looked around, challenging us. 'Or do we think it's a coincidence that we've found these bodies at Leo Stone's address?'

'Probably not.' Godley was looking grim. 'But I'd rather not take a chance on getting a conviction based on probability. With our luck, he'll have been in prison around the time the bodies were put in the tank, and his defence team will be able to suggest he wasn't free to commit the murders.'

'But there's no sign of Rachel Healy after all.' Georgia shoved her hands in her pockets and gave me a tight little smile. I knew what was coming and braced for it. 'You were right, Maeve, but you were wrong.'

'I've been thinking about that.' I turned to Una Burt and Godley, cutting Georgia out of my line of sight deliberately. 'I think I know where Rachel Healy might be.'

'What, again? We've been here before, haven't we?' Derwent's tone was designed to needle me and I fought the urge to snap back at him.

'Yes, we have. But this time, we have more information. Jill Ross told me that Leo moved the shed with the help of

214

his son. The bodies we located previously were dumped at the nature reserve where Kelly went with his school – a place where he was happy. Long Valley meant something to him.'

'So?' Derwent again. 'They searched every inch of the nature reserve and they didn't find her.' The muscles of his jaw flexed as he chewed a piece of gum; I caught a whiff of peppermint on the air.

'So we need to look at the other places that mean something to Kelly.' I shivered inside my thick coat: it was a cold day and I had been standing still too long, but that wasn't why. If I'd been determined to lock Kelly Lambert up, I couldn't have done a better job of pushing the investigation towards him. But there wasn't much choice about it. He'd failed to mention moving the shed, even if he hadn't understood why his father wanted to move it. Something would link him with one of the victims, if we looked for long enough, and if he was as guilty as he seemed to be. *The investigator should pursue all reasonable lines of enquiry* . . . 'We need to find out where Kelly's foster parents lived.'

It took a few phone calls to track down Colin and Pam Fields, and longer to explain to them why we needed to know where they had lived twenty years earlier.

'Kelly? He's not in trouble, is he, darling?' I could hear the receiver creaking in Pam's hand, protesting as she squeezed it. Colin had had a stroke so his speech was slurred to the point of being incomprehensible over the phone, and Pam had reluctantly taken his place. They sounded old and confused and I wished I had time to go and see them in person. They had retired to Cornwall, to a little village a long way from anywhere.

'It's a routine enquiry,' I lied.

'An enquiry,' she repeated. Then, louder, 'An *enquiry*.'

Colin Fields said something in the background and I strained to hear it but Pam had covered the mouthpiece at her end.

She sounded breathless when she came back to me, tension rather than exercise making her heart pound.

'Has this got something to do with Leo Stone?'

'It is connected, yes.'

'Of course it is. That man. Kelly should never have had anything to do with him. I warned him to stay away, but you know Kelly is such a decent person, he can't believe that other people aren't.'

The rumble in the background again, with a note of warning in it. Pam sighed. 'OK. All right. *All right*, Colin.'

'Mrs Fields, we need to conduct a brief search of the property because, as far as we know, no police officers have ever checked it over. We have two young women to look for and their families are desperate for any news at all. I'm sure you can understand how they feel.'

'Oh, I can.' Her voice sounded weaker. She'd never lost her South London accent despite moving around the country. 'We fostered twenty children over the years. It wasn't just Kel. We did our best to look after them and set them on the right track. Some of them came for years and some only stayed a couple of weeks, but I remember them all. There were two who died very young and three who lost contact with us completely, so you have to assume the worst, don't you? I think about them a lot. Wondering, you know. Out of all of them, there was only one we were glad to see the back of, and of course *he*—'

'Mrs Fields,' I said slightly desperately, as Una Burt made hurry-up motions at me, 'I don't mean to be rude but we do need to get on with the search.'

'Of course you do. I do ramble on.' At the other end of the line, Pam sighed. 'Kelly was with us for twelve years, from when he was six until he was eighteen. I'd have kept him longer but he wanted to go. He wanted to leave the place for someone else who needed it, he said. I'll never forget that. It broke my heart to see him go but it made me happy as well. He'd turned into such a fine young man.'

216

'Where exactly was this?' I was distracted by Una Burt, who was scribbling something on a piece of paper.

'We had a smallholding in Kent. Not much, really – enough for us to grow some of our food. I kept hens and we'd sell the eggs. It was nice for the kids to help out with the animals, if they were interested, and it helped us to make ends meet.'

'But you didn't stay there.'

'We was renting, darling, and the place was in a right old state. It was an old farm, you see, and the farmer had built another house for himself. The roof was leaking, the boiler was downright dangerous and none of the windows fitted. The farmer got the hump with us complaining all the time, was what it was. He didn't want to spend any money on it, you see. We was only paying a pittance anyway. He told us to sling our hooks and after we left I don't think he ever rented it out again.'

'Do you remember the address?'

'Middlebrook Down Farm. It was in the middle of nowhere, tell you the truth. We used to go into Faversham to shop but it wasn't what you'd call close.'

'We'll find it.' It would be in the fostering records if nowhere else, I thought.

Burt handed me the paper and I squinted at it, then felt my stomach drop. This was not going to go down well. 'Mrs Fields, the other thing I need to ask you is to keep our conversation to yourself. I know you probably want to let Kelly know that we're looking at the farm, but there's no point in alarming him.'

'I don't like secrets.' Pam's manner had become stiff again, wary of me and what I really wanted.

'I understand that, but Kelly feels a lot of loyalty to his dad. I don't want Leo Stone to know what we're doing, if at all possible, and I wouldn't want to put Kelly in a situation where he felt he had to tell him.'

Silence at the other end.

'I wouldn't want Kelly to get in trouble,' I said, shutting my eyes from sheer self-loathing.

'No. I wouldn't want that either.' The life had left her voice entirely. Whatever moment of understanding we'd shared had very definitely passed.

After I'd thanked her and hung up, Una Burt sniffed. 'She'll be on the phone to him already, more than likely.'

'She said she wouldn't contact him.'

'You know better than that.' Burt used the edge of her thumbnail to dig some food out from between her teeth. 'These people are all the same.'

'*What* people?'

'Do-gooders. They think they know better than the police and they certainly don't trust us.'

I wasn't altogether sure they should.

'Anyway,' Una Burt said, chewing the tiny fragment of food meditatively, 'it doesn't matter. We've got Lambert under surveillance, and Stone. If either of them tries to run, we'll pick them up.'

27

Three days. That was how long you could live without water.

Tessa blinked in the darkness, her eyes gritty under the lids. Her tongue felt swollen and stiff. Her lips were dry, the skin flaking away.

Three days.

She had water – of course she did, she was sitting within reach of the bottles.

But if she drank it, she would sleep. And Tessa wanted to stay awake now. If she slept, she might miss something. The chance of rescue. The chance to plead with her captor.

The chance to fight.

How long could you survive without sleep? Longer than without water, less than without food, Tessa thought, vague memories resurfacing of a cheerful guide on a walking safari in Kenya. *You need to stay hydrated. All animals need water more than anything else.*

Her new hiking boots had been giving her a blister and Paul had been in a mood, she remembered. The air around her had trembled with heat, with a dry, spicy smell rising from the grass where they trudged in single file. They had got up early to do the safari and Paul wasn't a morning person. Tessa could feel the heat of the sun across her shoulders, searing through the cotton of her shirt. She could see the guide's calves, teak-coloured and knotted with muscle, moving ahead of her quickly so she had to hurry to keep up.

We could have been beside the pool, Paul had hissed over her shoulder, and she had shrugged him off because you could be beside a pool anywhere, anytime, and this was a once-in-a-lifetime chance to experience being in the wild – this was a chance to feel *alive*. Except that her foot hurt her so much, but the pain wasn't just in her heel now; it was all the way around her ankle, as if something was digging in to her flesh, cutting off her circulation, tying her down . . .

Tessa came back to herself with a start.

She was so thirsty.

The water was spiked with something.

Or that was paranoia.

She was so thirsty.

Paranoia didn't really apply in this scenario. She had good reason to be scared.

Tessa slid her hands down under the blanket and worked a finger under the chain. The gap was definitely getting wider. No food, no water: she was shrinking. The smaller she was, the better her chance of getting free. And she was going to get free, somehow. She was not going to die in a dirty, stinking shed for no good reason.

So she wouldn't let herself drink yet. Soon, but not yet. She would count to ten thousand – twice – and then she would have one sip of water.

She closed her eyes.

One.

Two.

Three.

28

I would have liked to go straight to Middlebrook Down Farm once I had the address, but Kev Cox shook his head when I asked.

'Tomorrow at the earliest. Maybe the next day. We're not going to be finished at the Dagenham site for a while and we'll want to start at the address you've found early in the day, to get as much done as possible before nightfall. I think it'll be two days, to be honest with you.'

'You could send someone else.'

'Yes, I could, but I want to do it myself.' He said it pleasantly but in a tone of voice that told me he meant it, and wouldn't be moved.

I turned to Una Burt. 'What if Tessa Marsh is there?'

'I thought you were satisfied there was no connection with Leo Stone.'

'I've never thought there was a connection, but I don't want to take the risk. Leo was definitely with me at the time Tessa disappeared, but Kelly wasn't. We only have his word for how long he was waiting outside the office to talk to me.'

'I could ask for local officers to take a look, in case she's somewhere obvious.'

Kev grimaced, physically pained at the idea. 'Tomorrow. We'll go tomorrow.'

It felt too long to wait, but if Tessa had received the same treatment as the others, she would be dead. At least part of what was making me edgy was the desire to prove I was right after all, and I couldn't pretend, even to myself, that it counted as worthy motivation.

The following day, a small caravan of vehicles snaked down the M2, heading for Faversham and Middlebrook Down Farm. The old farmhouse was indeed empty, the farmer had confirmed from his home in Spain, where he'd retired to enjoy a decent climate. He was renting his land to a neighbouring farmer instead of farming it himself, so the farm buildings were all unoccupied.

'No one's been in there for a few years. I don't know what sort of state the place will be in,' I said to Liv, concentrating on staying at a steady speed as Derwent's car took a bend in the road far too fast in front of us, brake lights flaring and the back end swinging as he over-corrected.

'It makes it easier to search if it's falling down already.'

It wasn't quite falling down, but it wasn't far off it. The gate opened onto a single-lane track that led us down through orchards filled with rows of bare, twisted fruit trees, to a long, low farmhouse made of stone and red brick. Once it would have had a thatched roof but that was long gone. The corrugated metal that had replaced it was a patchwork of holes and moss. A straggle of outbuildings ran behind the house, the windows roughly boarded against the elements.

'How big is the area we're searching?' Liv asked.

'This part of the farm is on six acres. The whole farm is well over a hundred.'

'Shit.'

I grinned. 'Better hope we find something sooner rather than later or we're going to be here for a while.'

'Where are we going to start?'

'The farmhouse itself. Then the outbuildings. Then anything that could be a place to hide a body – if there's a well or a septic tank or something, that would be an obvious place to look. If we don't find anything and I can persuade Burt to keep looking, we might manage to get an aerial search – put a drone up and look for anomalies in how the earth is lying. We might get cadaver dogs to take a turn around the area. But the only reason we're here is because I have a hunch, really, and I'm not sure that would justify spending a lot of time and money looking for a body that might not be there.'

'You were right the last time.'

I nodded, thinking about the tangle of bones and clothes fragments and hair and soil that Kev had carefully extracted and delivered to Dr Early. Even now the pathologist and her colleagues would be going through the bones, sorting and numbering them, trying to find out who they were and how they had died.

'Come on.' Liv patted my arm. 'Let's get in there. Tuck your trousers into your boots because I bet you those buildings are full of rats and mice looking for somewhere warm to spend the winter.'

The farmhouse was icy and dimly lit, the walls bare stone inside as well as out. 'It's hard to imagine it was ever cosy,' I said, shining my torch around. 'But Kelly loved it here.'

'Maybe if the fire was lit . . .' Liv's voice trailed away. 'No. It's just grim.'

'And dirty.' I pressed a finger on the chimneypiece above the empty hearth and showed her my glove. 'I don't think anyone's been in here for a long time.'

A rattle on the stairs was Derwent coming down, bending to avoid banging his head on a low beam. 'No one's been upstairs either. Nothing but spiders and dust. This is a proper shithole, isn't it?'

'Houses get damp when there's no one living in them.'

'This isn't a house. It's a pig pen.'

'I'm sure it's not looking its best.' Why was it, I wondered, that I was so determined to defend Kelly Lambert's childhood home from criticism? Maybe it was just that I couldn't resist the opportunity to make Derwent frown and huff and strop off, banging the door behind him. I went up the stairs myself to look around at the small, low-ceiling bedrooms. There was a stunning view from the tiny windows, once you looked past the grime and the cobwebs: in spring the orchards would be snowy with blossom. When Kelly had lived here, the house had been full of other children – full of life, and love. A low beam that ran across one room had been irresistible: it was covered in graffiti scratched into the wood. I shone my torch along it, looking at the stick figures, the animals, names, dates, marvelling at the eternal human impulse to make a mark. I looked for Kelly's name and found it near the end, surrounded by stars and flourishes. It was between a neatly incised DAVID and a name that was almost scratched out. I peered at it, trying to decipher what it said. The first character began with what looked like a vertical downstroke leading into the start of a curve – an R or P, I thought, though it could have been a B. The rest of the name was obliterated, the wood chipped out to leave a dent in the ancient beam. I wondered if the damage was deliberate, or if the name matched one of the missing children Pam worried about.

A shout came from outside, sending a black scattering of crows to wheel around the treetops, squawking in alarm. It was the sort of shout that meant someone had found something worth seeing. I hurried back out across the cracked and weed-filled concrete to one of the more distant outbuildings where people were congregating, craning to see.

'What is it?'

Kev was standing at the door, stopping anyone from entering like the angel barring the entrance to Eden, although the angel wasn't usually portrayed as potbellied in a paper suit and holding a long-handled tool instead of a flaming sword.

'You can't come in, Maeve. Sorry.'

'What did you find?'

Derwent appeared behind Kev, his face pale. 'Give her some shoe covers and let her in, Kev. She won't do any harm.' He raised his voice. 'But none of the rest of you are coming in. Go and find something else of interest. And go carefully. This whole farm is a crime scene.'

Kev handed the shoe-covers over, pressing his lips together as if to hold back his disapproval. I put them on and padded past him, aware of the filthy looks I was getting from everyone else who hadn't made the cut. Derwent took my arm as I stepped into the darkness. The air was icy. It was like walking into a fridge.

'Watch yourself. The floor is uneven. There's no electricity, naturally. Kev is going to rig up a generator for us.'

'I can manage.' I shook him off.

'Fine.' He said it under his breath, making it absolutely clear that it wasn't fine, not at all.

'It's freezing in here.'

'Stone walls. They keep the place cold.'

I strained to see. As my eyes became more accustomed to the darkness, I could pick out tools hanging on racks. 'Is this a garage?'

'General DIY shed, I think. Garden stuff is on the left. Plumbing is straight in front of you.'

'A bath.' It was an old tin bath with a pipe leading from it to a drain. A hose was curled up beside it. Behind the hose there were five industrial-sized containers of bleach. I thought of Willa Howard, and the straw-like tangle he had made of her hair.

'Carpentry is over on that wall.' Derwent turned me around with a flourish. 'And in the middle of the room . . .'

'Is that a *bed*?'

'Sort of. I wouldn't fancy sleeping on it. There is a mattress, but—' He shone his torch over my shoulder and I jumped.

'Jesus Christ. Decomp?'

Three or four wavering, overlapping stains marked the mattress in different areas.

'Seems so. Can you smell it?'

'No.'

'Me neither but your nose is better than mine. I think it's pretty old. Kev got excited about the larva casings.' The beam of Derwent's torch swung around the base of the mattress, where hollow shells trembled in the draught from the door. 'You know what this is, don't you?'

'This is where he took them. Willa Howard and Sara Grey and whoever else he murdered.'

'After they were dead. Or he killed them here, I suppose. But I think he took them to Dagenham and killed them there, and then brought them here when he was ready to enjoy them.'

'Stop.'

'What? It's what he does. I don't get it, personally, but I assume there must be some sort of thrill in it or he wouldn't bother dragging them around. It explains the steel cupboard – a safe, leak-proof place to stash them. Dagenham was a useful stopping-off point, but this was where he wanted them.' Derwent's breath plumed towards me in the chill air. I stepped away from him onto nothingness, and swore as I stumbled.

'Careful.' His hand closed on my forearm, dragging me back to balance. 'I warned you.'

'So you did.' I switched on my own torch and shone it past him, over his shoulder. I had clenched my teeth to stop them from chattering and my jaw was aching. 'Carpentry tools, you said.'

'Yeah. They look in reasonable nick. I'd have expected them to be rusty. It's not just cold in here; it's damp too.'

I picked my way across the floor, concentrating on avoiding

the actual holes in the wood, and stopped in front of them. 'Look, they're not dusty. Someone has been here, and recently.'

'Someone,' Derwent repeated. 'Kelly.'

'When I met him . . .' I stopped, then tried again. 'When I met him he said something about having a workshop where he made his own furniture. And then he changed the subject straight away. He said he'd seen you outside the café. That's why I thought you might have taken the pictures of us together. But maybe he was lying. Trying to distract me.'

'Well. That's interesting. That he didn't want to talk about it, I mean. That he was prepared to lie.'

I took a deep breath. 'I'm sorry I believed him and not you.'

Derwent turned to look at me, but before he replied the door swung open and a block of white-grey morning light fell across the floor. 'Are you finished?' Kev asked.

'For now.' Derwent stalked towards the door, reaching for his phone. 'Do your stuff, Kev.'

I followed him outside, screwing up my eyes against the daylight. 'Who are you calling?'

'Burt. Godley. They'll want to know what we've found. And they'll want to tell the surveillance teams to prepare for an arrest. I don't want to arrest Kelly until we've found as much evidence as possible. No point in starting the clock ticking until we have to, as long as he doesn't run.'

'We haven't found a body, though.'

'Not yet,' Derwent said, and raised the phone to his ear.

We found her, in the end, or rather I did, in a building that had been a laundry something like a hundred years before. Now all that remained were two stone sinks and a battered copper vat with an enormous hole in the bottom and a lot of spiders. One corner of the room was filled with an ancient stone chimney breast but the fireplace at its base had been bricked up, quickly and messily, with yellow London bricks that matched nothing else on the farm. A word to Kev brought a man with a sledgehammer over his shoulder, and safety goggles, and a short way with demolition.

'Let's stop and have a look,' Kev said when the man had made a gap in the face of the loosely mortared bricks. He stepped forward and shone his torch through the opening. 'Ah.'

'Is that a good "ah" or a bad one?' Derwent demanded.

'It's a body.' He stepped back to let me see and I peered in with one hand over my mouth and nose to keep out the dust and the smell. She was lying on her side, her knees to her chest, the flesh falling off her bones where her withered skin had split. She was naked and her hair was so matted with filth I couldn't guess what colour it was but my gut told me it was Rachel who lay there, who had been entombed on this derelict farm and all but forgotten. I felt the sorrow of it – the waste of it – but at a distance, as if it was behind glass. I knew I couldn't allow emotion to distract me from the close concentration this scene required.

'Do you think it's her? Rachel Healy?' Derwent said it over my shoulder as he pressed forward to see for himself.

'Hard to tell,' Kev said. 'Bodies decay at different rates in different conditions. This one looks to be in a pretty good state, but it's cold here and dry and she was protected from the elements. She could have been here for years.' He shepherded us away from the fireplace. 'You're going to need to leave this to us now. There's a very good chance of recovering evidence from this body. The conditions mean she's well preserved and the area around her hasn't been disturbed since she was put in here. The bodies in the septic tank weren't in such good shape but this is exactly what we needed.'

'I'll call Dr Early,' I said.

'And I'll call the surveillance team on Kelly Lambert.' Derwent was also taking out his phone.

'You're going to get him arrested? Now?'

'No time like the present.'

228

'Don't you want to get more information about this crime scene? About the body?'

'The press are going to be all over this once they work out what we're doing here. This is the countryside: fuck all happens here. Someone is on the phone or on Facebook right now telling the world about the strange goings-on at the local derelict farm. You know that. I don't want to give Kelly time to prepare himself. He has no idea we know where he lived with his foster family, let alone that we've found all of this.'

'Why would he bring them here? This is where he was happy. It's the same with the nature reserve. And why was Rachel left here, hidden away? The other women were left in the open.' I shook my head, frustrated. 'None of this makes sense.'

'It doesn't make sense to me that you're trying to defend Kelly Lambert.'

'I'm not,' I protested. 'I want to make sure we're not making a mistake in arresting him now.'

'You like him,' Derwent said dismissively. 'That's why you're trying to explain the evidence away.'

'I don't *like* him. I don't want to rush this. Unless we think he's going to run, we shouldn't arrest him until we have as much information as we can.'

'There's a dead body in there. That's all the information I need. Remember his nickname? The White Knight?' Derwent stared down at me. 'It's the only thing that's been bothering me about Leo Stone. I believed he was involved, but whoever did this had to be personable. Trustworthy. He persuaded highly educated women to put themselves in his power. Leo Stone is neither handsome nor pleasant, but Kelly? Kelly fits the bill. I know you fit the demographic for his victims but I never thought you'd be taken in by him too.'

'I haven't been taken in by him,' I snapped, and Derwent took a step closer.

'You said it yourself: it's the places that were significant for *Kelly* that Leo used. But doesn't it make more sense that Kelly did it by himself? We thought Leo persuaded Kelly to help him move the shed to cover the septic tank, but maybe it was the other way round. Leo has never really fit the bill for our killer and that's why the evidence is far from compelling. If you ask me, that's why Godley is nervous about him getting off, and why the Greys are convinced he's innocent. They're right. He didn't do it. But Kelly Lambert did.' Derwent went back to his phone. 'I'm calling the boss. Let's see what he says.'

I knew what he would say already. Being able to surprise Kelly was more important than waiting for the results of the forensic investigation. Besides, there was enough evidence to consider charging him already. The custody time limit was less of an issue than the cost of keeping him under surveillance for the days or weeks it took for the lab to process the evidence. But I still felt there was something we were missing.

Derwent hung up and looked at me.

'That's it, then.'

'I suppose it is.' I walked away from him, irritated that he hadn't listened to me. Then again, Derwent had good instincts, and I usually trusted him to do the right thing. Which meant that I was wrong.

I went and found a low wall on the other side of the farmyard, staying out of the way of the SOCOs as they swarmed over the workshop. The farm was an enormous crime scene to assess, let alone process. It would be weeks before the work was completed, I suspected. And in the meantime, Kelly would be arrested, and charged, and remanded in custody. It was a small consolation that his father would be arrested too, as an accessory. He must have known what was happening. He had helped to cover the septic tank in Dagenham. I sat and thought about the four bodies we had uncovered there, and I shivered. Kelly was twenty-six. He had left his foster parents at eighteen. Had he started killing straight away? Was that why he had been so determined to leave his foster parents' care, dressing it up as consideration for others?

The phone in my pocket vibrated and I fumbled for it, my hands stiff from the cold. It was an unknown caller, the screen told me, and the number was withheld which wasn't all that unusual.

'Kerrigan.'

Silence. Then, 'Maeve.'

I knew his voice straight away; I would have known his voice anywhere. I found I was standing up without having consciously decided to get to my feet, and the main thought in my head was *not now* . . .

'Rob?'

There was a pause, and when he spoke again his voice was muffled, emotion thickening the words. 'I miss you.'

Shock had made me numb for a moment; anger brought back feeling with a rush. 'No. You don't get to do this. You don't get to call me and tell me you miss me. Not after all this time. Not after what you've done.'

'I know.' He sounded exhausted. 'I just . . . needed to hear your voice.'

On the other side of the yard, Derwent emerged from an outbuilding. He looked around, scanning the area. When his gaze got to me, he stopped and frowned.

'Why now?' I said into the phone.

'I can't tell you that.'

'Can't or don't want to?'

Derwent started to move towards me. I pivoted and jogged out of the yard, heading towards the car. Behind me, there was a shout.

'Kerrigan!'

'I don't know what you mean,' Rob said. 'I'd tell you if I could.'

'About your fiancée? Or is she your wife now? Did you manage to get around to the wedding or did you run out of time?' I unlocked the car and slid into the driver's seat. Derwent emerged from the yard at a run and skidded to a halt, looking for me. I slid down, not quite hiding behind the steering wheel.

'My fiancée,' Rob repeated.

'Is it a boy or a girl, Rob? Or did you find out? She must be due around now so you won't have long to wait.'

Derwent had spotted me. He steamed towards the car and I pressed the central locking button. He had to have heard the clunk but he tugged at the door handle anyway.

'Maeve, I didn't ring up for an argument. I rang because I miss you. A lot. I don't expect you to feel the same way—'

Derwent thumped his fist on the roof of the car, frustrated.

'I need to apologise. I need for you to forgive me for what I did. For hurting you, for running away.'

'And sleeping with your boss.'

He took a breath, as if he was going to say something, but the seconds stretched out in silence.

'Rob?'

'Please, Maeve. I need to hear that you don't hate me before I—' He broke off again.

'Before you what?'

'I can't tell you. I shouldn't be calling you.'

'Rob?'

'Look, I have to go.'

I closed my eyes so I didn't have to look at Derwent, who was glowering through the window. 'I do forgive you. I shouldn't. But I do. You did some stupid, stupid things, but that doesn't make you a bad person.'

'Some day, I'll explain.'

'Can't wait,' I said drily.

Derwent sat down on the bonnet of the car, making the suspension dip. He had his arms folded and his back was turned to me. Somehow, every line of it spoke volumes about how he felt.

'Are you all right? Are you happy?'

I laughed. 'I'm not sure about happy, but I'll live. What about you?'

'Same.' Another pause. 'I still love you, Maeve. I always will.'

Before I could reply, he had ended the call. I listened to the silence for a moment, then dropped the phone in my lap so I could start the car. The engine coughed into life.

Derwent didn't move.

I put my hand down on the horn and kept it there.

Nothing.

Well, he had been warned. I put the car in reverse and slipped back a few feet. Derwent rose smartly to his feet and turned to glare at me.

'Where are you going?'

Away from him before I had to cry, to be truthful, but instead of answering him I spun the wheel. I caught my lower lip between my teeth with such force that it was bruised for days afterwards, just to hold on to my composure, until I could turn away from Derwent's unflinching stare and drive across the rutted field that was our makeshift car park. Derwent got smaller and smaller in the rear-view mirror, but he was still watching me when I turned out of the gate, out of sight.

29

When the first link slipped over its neighbour, Tessa barely noticed. Her fingers were numb and she couldn't feel what she was touching. She had stopped caring. It was an endless task, a hopeless one, and she had given up a hundred times already. The only reason she went back to it, every time, was because there was nothing else to do. But it was futile. She couldn't hope to free herself. She couldn't—

A second link eased free, and she stopped. That was progress, for the first time. That was a start.

She tried again, scrabbling feverishly, praying, and after an eternity the third link came loose. Where there had been a knot, there was a loop. Not much of one, true, but something. Room to move. Some play in the chain that hadn't been there before.

An opportunity.

Hope, long abandoned, blossomed in her chest like a firework.

Stop, Tessa told herself, and breathed on her hands, rubbing her fingers back to life, working the sluggish blood into her fingertips. *Take your time. Don't panic. Don't rush it.*

If she rushed it, she could end up in a worse tangle than ever. *Patience.*

Except she had run out of that a long time ago.

Concentrate.

It was essential not to hurry but Tessa couldn't stop herself. What if the person who'd taken her chose this moment to come back? What if she had left it too long to make her escape? She didn't even realise she was sobbing and talking to herself, swearing, pushing herself on.

'Come on, Marshy. Come *on*. This is easy. You're just slow, that's all. You've got to speed up. *Come on.*'

It was a tangle of metal, an impossible cat's cradle, and then it wasn't: it was loops of chain that moved when she tugged at them, and shifted against her skin, and made space for her fingers to slide the loops down towards her heel. She eased them and forced them and pushed, careless of the damage she was doing to her skin, oblivious to everything except the terrible urgency to free herself and get out and *run* . . .

The chain slid over her foot and slithered away into the darkness. Tessa could barely believe it. She stood up too fast and fell, and stood again more carefully, her knees wobbling, her head spinning. She had been sitting down for days and now her legs cramped, the muscles weak. She rubbed her knuckles down her calves, pummelling them into life. Come on.

Come *on*.

When she had imagined making her escape, she had seen herself flinging open the door on daylight and sprinting as fast as she could for safety, for civilisation, her legs and arms pumping as she raced to freedom. The reality was not so heroic: an ungainly stagger, her hands outstretched as she felt for any suggestion of a door, a handle, a way out of this draughty shed . . . But of course the door would be locked, when she found it. Escape wouldn't be as easy as turning a handle. It couldn't be.

It was. Or at least, it was nearly that easy. There was a lock but it was loose, nailed into wood so weathered and dry that a couple of determined shoves dragged the nails free. The door juddered and swung back and she pitched through it, falling on her knees on a stony, muddy path. In front of her there were trees, tall ones. They were dark against a sky that was a few shades off black, light leaking into it from streetlights somewhere, a long way off. The trees tipped and swung, seesawing wildly, and she scrambled to her feet and ran towards them, towards cover. She didn't so much as chance a look back to see if anyone was watching her or what the hut had been like or even where she was. Like a wild animal her only thought was to get away, to hide, to find some kind of safety.

Tessa abandoned any thought of running almost immediately when she got under the shelter of the trees. The ground was treacherous, pitted with hollows and ridged with roots. She moved through it, her ears full of the sounds she was making: breaking branches, her ragged breathing, her heart pounding. Twigs whipped her face, invisible in the darkness, and unseen things seemed to clutch at her clothes. If she got lost, no one would ever find her, she thought. At least she would die on her own terms, outside, not trapped in the dusty horror of the dark shed. She would not go back there. Nothing would make her go back there.

There was no path so, blindly, Tessa tried to keep heading downhill. People wandered in circles, she knew, when they had nothing to guide them. But if she kept going downhill, she wouldn't double back on herself. It might have been untrue but it gave her the encouragement she needed to keep going.

Days in the shed had not prepared her for a hike over uneven ground. It was cold but she was soaked in sweat, her lips tasting of salt. She regretted not taking the water with her; that had been a mistake, even if it had been spiked with sleeping pills.

When she had gone as far as she could, she sank down at the base of a huge old tree. She put her head down on her knees and wept, drawing in huge lungfuls of the clean, cold

236

forest air. Somehow, after a time, despite the discomfort of her position and her thirst and the ache in her ankle, she shut her eyes and slept.

As Tessa came back to herself the sky was a definite shade of dark blue, and a tentative bird was hinting at the dawn in short, broken phrases. Another sound caught Tessa's attention, under the whisper and rattle of the leaves and bare branches. It was a sound so familiar that at first she couldn't connect it with what she had known in her life before. A rumble and swish, rising and falling, intermittent but regular.

A road.

A road with cars on it.

People.

Salvation.

Tessa stood up, aching all over as if she had been beaten soundly while she slept, and began to move towards the sound of the cars. Tears streaked her face. It was almost over. She was going to be all right.

Everything was going to be all right.

30

I filled a glass with water and downed it, standing up beside the sink. The kitchen light was off but there was just enough light in the sky for me to be able to see what I was doing. The main thing, I told myself, was to avoid making too much noise.

A snore floated on the air behind me and I held my breath in case it was a prelude to waking up. The clock on the wall ticked and I found myself counting along with it, until a second snore came, and a third. He had settled down into a steady rhythm, and I could relax.

It had been stupid to come here, I thought. Stupid to reach out for comfort instead of hiding away. Rob's phone call had knocked me sideways. Hearing his voice had been a shock after so long. I had wanted someone to put their arms around me and make me feel loved again, and I had known where to go for that. But that sort of attention didn't come for free. There was always a price to pay for it, even if I didn't know yet exactly how much it would cost me.

Meanwhile, yesterday's clothes didn't look as fresh as I would have liked. I checked the time. The train wouldn't be too busy yet – the commuter rush was still an hour or so off. There was no way on earth I was going to work as I was. I worked with a team of detectives; the thickest and least observant would notice that I hadn't been home. And the one I was really worried about was far from unobservant.

My phone buzzed on the counter, the vibration making it clatter though the sound was turned down. I snatched it up.

'Kerrigan.'

'Where are you?' Derwent's voice was loud and aggressive.

Shit. 'What's wrong?'

'Tessa Marsh has turned up.'

I felt it like a kick in my stomach. 'They found her?'

'She escaped.'

'*Escaped*? From where?'

'We haven't worked that out yet.'

'Doesn't she know?'

'Bit difficult to ask her. She's in a coma.'

'*What?*' I pinched the bridge of my nose, trying to ward off the headache that was threatening to build there. 'Start again. What happened?'

'She got out of wherever she was being held – somewhere in rural Sussex. She made her way to the nearest road, which happens to be a particularly fast stretch of the A21. For reasons known only to herself, the stupid tart stepped out in front of a lorry, presumably to flag him down. The driver didn't see her, which is a whole other shit show – he said he was checking his satnav. She must have tried to jump out of the way but he clipped her. When he stopped and went back, she was lying by the side of the road, out of it. She hasn't woken up yet.'

'Jesus. Poor Tessa.'

'Poor us, more like. If she hadn't got herself hurt she could actually have been some use. As it is, we've got nothing. They're going to use dogs to look for the path she took to the road. We don't even know which side she started from.'

'Right.'

'Sussex Police are handling the investigation along with DI Ownes. They're keeping it under wraps for the moment on the assumption that whoever took her doesn't know she's escaped. Burt wants us to go down there in case it was Kelly Lambert who took her in the first place.'

'It doesn't fit the MO for him to keep her alive,' I said.

'MOs change. Maybe he didn't have time to kill her. He had to hurry back to central London to get his own alibi sorted out, didn't he, once he'd taken care of his dad's? Maybe he got spooked by the police attention after that and didn't want to risk going back. She'd have died eventually. If it turns out he was connected with her disappearance, we need to know about it sooner rather than later.'

'So we're going to Sussex.'

'Basically, yes. Want a lift?'

Less than anything. 'Um, no. No, that's fine.'

'Have you still got the pool car from yesterday?'

'I dropped it back to the office.'

'So you do need a lift.'

'It's fine.'

'I'll swing by the flat and pick you up.'

There was no way round it. 'I'm not at the flat.'

Silence. Then, for the second time, he asked: 'Where are you?'

'Look, I've got to go.' I could hear creaking floorboards as someone moved around. Any second now, the kitchen light was going to go on. 'Give me the address and I'll make my own way there.'

With very bad grace, Derwent did, and hung up before I could thank him. The kitchen door creaked open. I took a deep breath before I turned around.

'Hi.'

'You're up early.' My father put the light on and padded across the kitchen, silent in his slippers. He filled the kettle and reached for the teapot. 'Staying for breakfast?'

'I have to go.'

'You'll have something before you leave.'

240

'I don't have time, Dad.'

'Your mother is worried about you.' He shook the tea in the canister, peering into it dubiously. 'Not that she'd say it to your face.'

'Why is she worried?'

'Ah, you know your mother.'

Indeed I did. Living in England for most of her adult life hadn't made her any less of a classic Irish mother. My parents had done their best to give me and my brother the childhood we would have had in Ireland, including intense involvement in every aspect of our lives. That hadn't changed as we got older – in fact, quite the reverse.

'She wishes I was settled down with a husband and children.'

'She wishes you were happy.' He concentrated on pouring not-quite-boiling water into the teapot and the cups to warm them. Tea-making was an art in my father's eyes; he could teach the Japanese a thing or two about the ceremony of it all, even in his dressing-gown in a South London kitchen at six in the morning.

'I am happy.'

'Are you?'

I'd said it without thinking. Now I probed the thought carefully, as if testing an aching tooth. 'I think so. I'm happier than I was.'

'I thought that fecker getting back in touch would have upset you.' Thin-lipped disapproval was the way my parents had reacted to the news that Rob had called me. I might have forgiven him; they certainly hadn't.

'It did upset me at the time but in another way it didn't.' I started to gather my things. 'It's nice to know he still cares. And it was good to say goodbye.'

'Was that what he wanted?'

'I have no idea what he wanted,' I said frankly, 'and I don't much care. It's not about him any more. It's about me. And

I don't want to waste any more time on him.' I leaned over and hugged my father. 'Thanks for letting me stay here last night.'

'It's your home. You can come here any time.' He patted my arm and I wondered if I would ever seem like a grown-up to him. Then I wondered if I would ever really seem like a grown-up to myself.

'I've got to go.'

'Take some food with you. You look half-starved.'

'Maybe next time.' I was halfway out of the door.

'Don't leave it too long to come back.'

'I won't.'

'And answer the phone when your mother calls you.'

'I always do if I can,' I lied.

'Hmph,' my father said, and turned his attention to the steaming kettle instead.

I came to the truck first; it was skewed across the carriageway, abandoned where the driver had managed to stop it. The road was coned off and the accident investigation was underway, with officers measuring and mapping what had happened. There was no visible damage to the truck, I thought, scanning it for blood or dents and spotting nothing. I had seen worse.

DI Ownes and Derwent were together at the roadside and I pulled in to the verge beside them. Derwent glowered at me. The inspector looked slight in her coat, the breeze lifting her short hair before flattening it against her head.

'Thanks for coming.'

'I'm so sorry it's not better news.'

Her face tightened for a second, as if she was fighting the urge to cry. 'Frustrating, isn't it?'

'In every way. How's she doing?'

'No change.' DI Ownes swallowed hard. 'It doesn't look good, from what they're saying.'

242

'Have you informed the family?'

'First thing this morning. But we're trying to keep a low profile and keep it out of the press. Once the accident investigation is over we'll clear away all the evidence that we were ever here. With any luck, our guy won't know about Tessa getting free for twenty-four hours or so.'

'If we can trace where she was held, we can set up surveillance,' Derwent said.

'I want to collect any forensic evidence first, but then we should pull back.' She pulled a face. 'Always a balancing act, isn't it?'

I looked around, scanning the dense woodland that stretched up on either side of the road. It was all too easy to imagine Tessa Marsh slithering down it in the dark, rushing from who knew what danger, throwing herself towards what she believed to be safety.

'Have you had any luck with finding where he kept her?'

'We're still looking. We've tracked back some of the way. It's hard going. She was covered in scratches – she must have fought her way through it.'

'Or he hurt her,' I said.

'No, they were all fresh injuries. The doctors said she was dehydrated and in need of a good meal but that was the extent of it. We think he must have left her with water and food or she would have been in a much worse state.'

'Was she sexually assaulted?'

'It seems not.' The phone hummed in her hand. 'Excuse me.' She half-turned to take the call, jamming her knuckle into the other ear. 'Really? How far? Are you sure?'

I looked at Derwent. 'He didn't hurt her, he didn't rape her and he left her with supplies to keep her alive.'

Derwent shrugged. 'Saving her for later.'

'Dead girls are his thing. If he wanted her dead, he could have let nature take its course.'

'Maybe he likes to do the killing.' Derwent stretched. 'Look, there are a million reasons why he might have wanted to treat Tessa differently.'

'If he was using her to provide his dad and himself with an alibi he should have done exactly the same with her as he did with the others.'

'In a perfect world, yeah, OK. But for whatever reason, he couldn't.'

'Or it wasn't him.'

'Where did you go last night?'

'What?' I should have been expecting it, but I wasn't; it was like a pit opening up in the ground in front of me.

'You heard.'

'It's none of your business.'

'They've found a hut.' DI Ownes came back, looking energised. 'The dog went crazy over it. If it's not where she was being held, it's a huge coincidence.'

'Fantastic,' I said, extra warmth in my voice because I was so glad to have an excuse to change the subject. 'How far do we have to go?'

'We're better off driving there, according to my DS. There's a single-track lane that goes quite near to it.'

'That would explain how he got her there,' Derwent said. 'Not much fun dragging a dead weight through these woods. I was wondering how he'd managed it.'

'You're right. I'll get someone to check for tyre marks. If we get a suspect we might be able to match the mud off his car.' DI Ownes pulled her keys out of her pocket. 'Come on. You can come with me. I don't want to block the lane with cars unnecessarily. I'm going to need space for the forensics teams and they take priority.'

I sat in the rear of DI Ownes' car and looked at the back of Derwent's head for the ten minutes it took us to find the correct road and creep along it. DI Ownes was justifiably worried about meeting any other vehicles and took it slowly, sitting bolt upright as close to the steering wheel as she could

244

get. Why did Derwent care about where I'd been? Except that I'd left him high and dry at the farm, which he was capable of resenting. And he was still angry that I'd disagreed with him about whether Kelly should be arrested or not.

I could tell him exactly where I had been the previous evening, and why I had gone there instead of anywhere else. I could tell him about the comfort of waking up in my childhood bedroom surrounded by familiar things. I could tell him that my mother had been only too glad to get the chance to fuss over me.

Then again, where was the fun in that?

'Here we are.' DI Ownes parked as her DS waved to us. He was a stocky man with an ancient waxed jacket over his suit as a concession to the countryside. The lace-up shoes he wore would have been a lot more suitable to a city street than hacking through the woods.

'The hut is down this track here, about a half mile in. You'd never come across it if you didn't know it was there.' He was sweating though it was a raw day, his face mottled red and white like a flitch of bacon.

'So no chance of someone happening to walk by and rescue her,' DI Ownes said.

'None at all. There's a gate about halfway along with a big "No Trespassers" sign on it. Even if you noticed the track, you'd never be curious enough to keep going.'

'What's the hut like?' Derwent asked.

'Filthy. Freezing. He did leave her some blankets and food. A bucket. Water. The basics. But he had her chained up.' The DS shook his head. 'Poor woman. She was here for almost a week. I'm not sure I'd last an hour in there.'

'Did you find anything useful? Anything that might lead us to the kidnapper?' I asked.

'We'll get the forensic team in as soon as we can. The main bit of good news is that someone parked a car on a lovely muddy bit of ground that's sheltered by the trees, right next

245

to the hut. We're working on the assumption it was the kidnapper – you wouldn't drive down the track unless you had to, and the marks are pretty fresh. Not much rain in the last week here, I gather, so we should get a decent set of casts from it.'

'Then all we need is a vehicle to match the impressions and we're in business. Let's go and have a look,' DI Ownes said, and set off down the track at a brisk pace. I recognised the hunter's instinct in her. She was close to solving a serious, high-profile case, which could only be good news for her career. Tessa Marsh had handed her a big break by escaping, it was true, but there was still an investigation to run and Ownes was on top of it.

The DS hadn't lied; it was a long walk to the hut. When we finally reached it, I stopped, struck by how dilapidated the structure was. It was barely holding together, the roof tacked on at a crazy angle, the walls leaning in.

'Who owns this?'

'I rang the council to check,' the DS said. 'This area was supposed to be cleared about thirty years ago but the locals objected. The council had sold the woodland to a private logging company and licensed them to cut the mature wood out, but some environmental activists got involved and scuppered the whole thing. The logging company didn't want the hassle and cost of a court case so they pulled out and sold the woods back to the council. The hut was abandoned. Now this area has a preservation order on it. No one's cutting down these trees any time soon.'

'So who would know about the hut?'

The DS shrugged. 'Locals? It looks as if it's the sort of place teenagers came to drink and get up to mischief at one time. There are a few old bottles and drinks cans around the back and a bit of graffiti, but none of it is recent.'

'But if you used to drink here this might occur to you as a place you could hide a kidnapped woman.'

'We're looking for someone who grew up around here or had connections around here,' DI Ownes agreed, her eyes bright. 'That'll help.'

Derwent made his way to the door, stepping carefully on the mats the DS had placed on the ground. He looked in without crossing the threshold.

'He wanted her to be all right, didn't he? Loads of food, loads of water. Enough to keep her here until Christmas, though I assume that wasn't the plan. And no ransom demand. No contact from the kidnapper at all.' He looked back at us. 'Are we sure the boyfriend's alibi is good?'

'It's fairly vague.' DI Ownes folded her arms, defensive even if she didn't realise she was reacting to Derwent's scrutiny that way. I knew the feeling well. 'But since her disappearance he's been distraught.'

'I saw the press conference,' I said. 'He looked sincere.'

'Your trouble is you still want to believe the best of people.' Derwent's voice was cutting and DI Ownes flinched.

'He doesn't mean you,' I said. 'That was meant for me.'

She frowned at me, at a loss, and I shrugged instead of explaining.

Derwent had stalked off anyway, heading around the back of the hut.

'Let's have a look at where she was kept.'

I followed DI Ownes and stood behind her in the doorway. There was something chilling about the set-up he'd left for Tessa: the serried ranks of water bottles and cereal bars and nothing but a pile of paper napkins for her to keep herself clean . . .

I frowned. 'Can I see one of those napkins?'

The DS picked one up and held it out on his gloved palm. 'What is it?'

'This logo.' It was a D in a circle. 'Do you recognise it?'

'No.' That told me DI Ownes had a healthier approach to feeding herself than I did, which wouldn't be difficult, admittedly . . .

'There's a company called Deliveration. They collect food from restaurants, takeaways, that kind of thing, and deliver it to your door. They're pretty popular.'

DI Ownes nodded. 'I've seen them.'

'Deliveries come with these napkins and branded wet wipes. It's all about delivering a good experience, not just a meal. That's the company ethos.'

'So?'

'So there must be millions of these napkins floating around. Anyone who's ever used Deliveration would have them. They give you stacks of them. But . . . Paul Bliss's best friend was wearing a Deliveration jacket when I was at Tessa's house.'

'Tenuous.' Derwent had come back without me noticing.

'I didn't say it wasn't. But it's somewhere to start.' I turned back to DI Ownes. 'The night before Tessa was kidnapped, she ate something that gave her food poisoning. Ask Paul where the food came from. Find out if it was a Deliveration order and, if so, who brought it to the house.'

31

The corridor outside the interview room was crowded and too hot for me. I drifted off for a minute, zoning out. God, but I was tired. As tired as Kelly Lambert, maybe, who was sitting a few feet away from me behind a wall, in the sixth hour of questioning, his lawyer writing notes as he fumbled for answers. I had watched a few minutes of it on the live stream that was playing in the meeting room. Kelly looked thin, jumpy, off balance.

He looked guilty.

Derwent's elbow caught me in the ribs and Una Burt's face came back into focus, her mouth moving. I forced myself to listen to what she was asking me.

'—not connected with other missing women after all?'

'The only connection is that it gave him the idea,' I said.

'This Oliver Jones.'

'Ollie. He's Paul Bliss's best friend.' I stood up a little straighter, blinking the exhaustion away as best I could. 'As soon as DI Ownes spoke to him he confessed everything.'

'His grandparents used to live about five minutes away from the woods,' Derwent explained. 'He spent his childhood running about there. That's how he knew about the hut.'

'Why did he want to kidnap Tessa?' Godley asked. 'Was he jealous?'

'Apparently not. Paul is a musician and Ollie calls himself his manager – he does various other jobs, including the food delivery stuff, and he arranges the odd club night here and there. He thought it was a golden opportunity to get some free publicity for Paul. "Get his face in front of the cameras" was the phrase he used.' I shrugged. 'He didn't tell Paul what he was planning because he thought it would be more credible. He brought around a takeaway the night before as a surprise. The big surprise was what was in Tessa's curry. He spiked her food so she was sick. He thought she'd skip school but she was too conscientious. He had to improvise.'

'I've got to hand it to him, he'd laid the groundwork,' Derwent said. 'It wasn't unusual for him to drop round with a meal for them. Paul Bliss never mentioned it to us when we asked him about it because it was so routine. No big deal.'

'According to Ollie, he was waiting outside the house when she came back from school. He told her he'd take her to the doctors. Instead he choked her from behind until she lost consciousness and put her in the boot of his car.'

'Risky,' Una Burt commented. 'He could have killed her.'

'He watched a video on YouTube about it,' I said. 'So it was perfectly safe.'

'Jesus.' Godley shook his head. 'The things people do.'

'How's the girl?' Burt asked, almost as an afterthought.

'Dying.' There were less brutal ways to put it but I knew Derwent was hiding how he really felt. I had seen him in the hospital, holding Tessa's mother's hand as she sobbed on his shoulder. So often it was what he did that gave him away rather than what he said.

'The family are donating her organs. They said it's what she would have wanted,' I said. 'And DI Ownes is going to charge Ollie Jones with everything she can think of. Kidnap, false imprisonment, manslaughter. The works.'

250

'Can they make manslaughter stick? He wasn't driving the truck,' Godley said.

'But she wouldn't have been there in the first place if Jones hadn't kidnapped her.' I shrugged. 'It's worth a try.'

'At least some good can come of it,' Burt said briskly. 'But what a waste.'

It was that, I thought, and more. I tried to be professional about how I did my job but I found it hard not to hate Ollie Jones for the casual, stupid way he had put Tessa in harm's way.

'It was a waste of our time,' Derwent said softly. 'You sent us on a wild goose chase.'

'The media had made the connection between Tessa and the other women who disappeared. We had to be seen to take action.' Una Burt glowered at Derwent, which had no discernible effect.

'Because the media thought we should? We're taking advice from them on how we investigate crimes now, are we? Letting them dictate our strategy?'

'Of course not.'

'You were more interested in how we looked than in what we were doing and whether it was of any value to our investigation.'

'If you had found Tessa Marsh alive it would have been worth it,' Godley pointed out.

'Yeah, but we didn't. We weren't even close.'

'Maeve worked out who kidnapped her.'

'Only when it was too late.'

I flinched and Derwent glanced at me. 'Not your fault, obviously. You did a good job.'

'Thanks.' *For nothing.* I took a deep breath. 'How are things going here?'

'Chris Pettifer is talking to Kelly Lambert.'

'He's a good interviewer.'

'He's not getting anywhere,' Godley said, his frustration obvious. 'Lambert's denying any involvement.'

'Is he talking?' Derwent asked.

'Oh, he's being very helpful, as far as he can be. But he can't tell us what he doesn't know. So he says.' From Burt's tone of voice she didn't believe a word of it.

'What about Leo?' I asked. 'What does he have to say about the shed and the septic tank?'

'He gave a no-comment interview.' Godley frowned. 'But we'll try again later.'

'He knows better than to say anything at all. Or at least his lawyer does,' Derwent said, and something in his tone made me look at him, only to find he was watching me. Waiting, I diagnosed, for me to blush at the very mention of Seth Taylor. *You make one passing reference to thinking someone is handsome . . .*

'Any progress on the post-mortems?' I asked.

'They're still working on the victims from the septic tank. We don't have IDs for them yet but they're cross-referencing the teeth with missing persons reports so with any luck we should get some names soon.'

'We haven't had much luck so far,' I commented.

'No, not a lot.' Godley smiled down at me. 'Except that it's lucky for us you're working on this. Without you, we wouldn't have located Rachel Healy or the unknown women in the septic tank.'

'Better than a cadaver dog any day.' Derwent dropped a heavy arm across my shoulders and my knees buckled a fraction; I hadn't been expecting it.

'You look tired, Maeve.' Godley's smile faded to concern.

'Up all night,' Derwent said before I could reply.

'Working?' Una Burt frowned. 'I didn't think anyone stayed late at the farm. I'd have given you some time off in lieu if I'd known.'

'It's fine,' I said, willing the colour to stay out of my face. I hated Derwent for putting me in this position; I was essentially lying about where I'd been and what I'd done. But I was damned if I was going to explain where I'd been. I'd rather crawl over broken glass than discuss my sex life, or lack of it, with the three senior officers in front of me. 'Please, don't worry.'

Burt had lost interest anyway. 'Well, you can take the rest of the day off.'

'That won't be possible, I'm afraid.' Derwent's voice was silky. 'We have Rachel Healy's post-mortem to go to later on.'

'It's fine,' I said again, sharper this time. 'I've got plenty to do until then.'

'And so do we.' Godley looked at Derwent. 'Josh. A word.'

Derwent followed him down the corridor and I watched him go. Troublemaking came as naturally to him as breathing, and I never, ever had the advantage.

Burt had already started to follow the others but she paused. 'You were right about Tessa. It was a dead end as far as this investigation was concerned. You still did a good job on it.'

'Thanks.' I was surprised at the compliment, and I was right to be wary, because there was a sting in the tail.

'DI Ownes let me know she was very impressed with you. If you ever want to leave this team, I'm sure she'd be happy to have you.'

'I don't want to leave the team.'

'If you ever did, I said.' Burt made a vague gesture. 'Sometime. You might change your mind.'

I might have no choice but to change my mind, she meant. I knew she didn't like me much, and I knew that Godley wouldn't necessarily intervene on my behalf. He would prioritise the team and our work over any individual. He'd done as much when he allowed Georgia to take my place in the investigation. Maybe DI Ownes wasn't such a bad option after all.

I went back to my desk feeling deeply discouraged, and occupied myself with dull admin for other cases to take my mind off Una Burt, the post-mortem and the seven dead women who seemed to be standing around behind me, waiting for me to find their killer.

Except that he was presumably down the hall, I reminded myself, thinking of Kelly Lambert and the slow, delicate way Chris Pettifer was filleting his story for lies. But why would he campaign to get his father out of prison if Leo was prepared to take the fall for the murders? Conscience kicking in? Family loyalty? Or it was all nothing to do with him, as he'd protested, and he was as innocent as his father's victims . . .

That was not a line of thought that would help anyone, I told myself. There was a part of me that still wanted Kelly to be innocent because I'd liked him and I didn't want to have fallen under his spell, like one of his victims. I'd found out the truth about him from a safe distance, not staring into his eyes as his kindness evaporated. *You fit the demographic*, Derwent had said with a barely concealed sneer, and he was right. I could have been one of the woman staring up sightlessly from their pit, if the circumstances had been a little different.

I forced myself to concentrate, and I was successful to the extent that I didn't notice Derwent coming back to the office. It was only when the phone on my desk rang that I looked up to see him staring at me. I glared back and picked up the receiver.

'Maeve Kerrigan.'

'This is Katy Lunn. I don't know if you remember—'

'I remember,' I said. 'Of course I do.'

'Oh, good. I'm sorry to bother you. It's just – well, Rachel's sister told us you'd found a body.'

I winced. I should have told her and Jenny Palmer. They had been waiting as long as Zoe. 'Yes, we have. We haven't formally identified her yet but we're working on the assumption that it's Rachel. I'm so sorry.'

'Oh.' It was a gasp, a half-sigh. That was the sound of hope dying, I thought. After a couple of moments, Katy had recovered enough to speak again. 'Well. That's that.'

'It's not official yet. If I can ask you to keep it to yourself for the time being—'

'I won't tell anyone. I don't want to tell anyone.' She sounded nettled.

'Thank you. I'm sure you wouldn't, but I had to say it anyway.'

'I suppose you do.' She fell silent but it was a silence that seemed weighted with something unsaid.

'Was there anything else I could help you with?'

'I – well. I suppose I have to come clean. I wasn't completely honest with you about Rachel's boyfriend when I said I didn't know who it was. But I wasn't sure. I mean, I'm still not sure. I didn't want to say anything if I wasn't sure.'

'I appreciate that.' I clicked my pen, fighting to keep the frustration out of my voice. 'But we can be discreet. We needn't mention you.'

'He wouldn't know who I was anyway.' Katy sighed. 'I suppose I didn't want to share it with you because it was the last secret I ever got to keep for Rachel. I was still hoping she might come back, some day, and I could ask her about it myself.'

'I understand.' I did, too, though I wanted to scream at her that it would have been a lot better for everyone if she'd *told* someone – anyone – when Rachel went missing, instead of waiting for her body to be discovered.

'I don't have any evidence,' Katy said, 'but I'm pretty sure she was sleeping with her boss.'

'Which one? She had two.'

'Oh. I don't know.'

Of course she didn't. 'Well, what makes you think that?'

'I heard her talking on the phone a couple of weeks before she died. She didn't know I was in the flat. I'd started a migraine at work so I'd gone home and put myself to bed. I'd been asleep but I woke up, and my head was still killing me. I knew there were painkillers in the kitchen so I went to

255

take some. Rachel's door wasn't closed properly and I heard her laughing. I was dopey from pain and still half-asleep. I couldn't work out what was going on – I thought she had someone in the room with her. I stopped for a second to listen.'

'What did you hear?'

'It sounded . . . intimate. I think he was doing the talking. Rachel was mainly laughing and – and sighing. You know.'

My love life might have been a cursed wasteland but I vaguely recalled that sort of phone call. I glanced up and discovered Derwent was still watching me. 'I know what you mean,' I said into the phone.

'When I realised what was going on, I went straight down to the kitchen. I was worried in case she thought I'd been eavesdropping on her. I took my painkillers and then I came back. As I passed her room I heard her say something like, "If I do that, will you give me a promotion?" And then she said, "I thought I was your favourite employee." And then . . . well, she said something about disciplinary proceedings.'

I could hear the embarrassment in her voice. 'Right. I understand.'

'What are you going to do about it?'

It hardly seemed important now that Rachel's body had been found, but I didn't want to put her off. 'I'll go back and talk to them and see what kind of reaction I get. I won't mention how the information came to us.'

'Thank you.'

'If anything else occurs to you, don't wait a few years to pass it on.'

'Yes. Sorry.'

'Better late than never.' I thanked her and hung up, and by the time the receiver was back in its place Derwent had wheeled his chair across to my desk.

'Well?'

I told him what Katy had told me and he looked sceptical.

'It's not proof of anything. She might have been role-playing with someone. The naughty secretary scenario is usually a winner.'

I raised one eyebrow. 'Is that so?'

'I've always found it does the trick,' Derwent said idly. 'What did you make of her bosses?'

'I wouldn't sleep with either of them.' I thought about Per Kemp and James Gallagher. 'Per was flirtatious. James was on his best behaviour. And he was the last one who saw her.'

'Can you imagine either of them whipping a woman for fun?'

I leaned back in my chair. 'What a question.'

'That's the point, though, isn't it? She was into being slapped around.'

'And choked.' I tapped my pen on the desk. 'I think James Gallagher is our man.'

'Why?'

'He gave me the creeps. And Per Kemp made a little joke about wanting to know what his partner had to say about Rachel. Gallagher was obviously uneasy about it. He was guilty about something. I thought it at the time, but I couldn't make any progress with getting him to talk. Anyway, we were looking for a serial killer, not a boyfriend.'

Derwent frowned. 'Yeah. And we know she was killed by Kelly Lambert, with or without his dad's help. Even if Gallagher was fucking her, it's irrelevant. I don't see how this helps us.'

'We don't *know* Kelly killed her. You think he did.'

He dropped his head into his hands and groaned. 'For fuck's sake, Kerrigan, give up on him. You found the body. It was on the farm where Lambert grew up. No one else could have put it there. No one else would have known about the farm, would they? No one else would have known it was a safe place to fuck dead girls.'

'Rachel was different,' I said. I was holding on to that

257

stubbornly, because it was true and because I didn't understand *why* she was different. 'You know as well as I do that this killer seemed attracted to women in peril. That's how he got the White Knight nickname. So what happened to Rachel that made her look appealing to the killer?'

'We'll never know.'

'James Gallagher said he let her out of his car and she walked away. He said he couldn't recall any drama.'

'But you think he was lying.'

'I wouldn't be surprised.' I bit my lip, thinking about it, then stopped biting it because it was still tender from the day before. 'James Gallagher could be the witness we've been waiting for.'

Derwent checked the time and stood up. 'Come on. Get your coat. Let's go and see what Mr Gallagher can tell us about how he gets his kicks.'

32

I liked to believe I could do anything Derwent could do, and do it in heels, but I had to admit he had the edge on me when it came to dealing with James Gallagher.

'How do you want to handle this?' I had asked in the car on the way to the Gallagher Kemp offices.

'He's a bully. Bullies don't like being challenged.'

'So you're going to challenge him.'

'That's what I was planning.' I could feel Derwent was watching me but I concentrated on the road. 'How was he with you when you interviewed him before?'

'I don't think he has a lot of time for women. He went out of his way to demonstrate I didn't intimidate him. And he said a couple of things that made it clear he wanted to put me in my place.'

'Did he, indeed.' That was all he said, and he said it quietly, but when I stopped at traffic lights and turned to look at him, he was scowling.

This time, we didn't wait in Gallagher Kemp's reception area. Derwent stalked straight through the door to the office as the receptionist flapped, and I followed meekly behind. James Gallagher was halfway through standing up when we walked into his room.

'Sit down.' Derwent moved around the desk so he could loom over Gallagher, who had subsided into his chair as if his legs had given way under him. I took a seat on the other side of the desk.

'What – what's this about?' Gallagher faltered.

'You didn't tell me the truth when I was here before,' I said. 'About your relationship with Rachel Healy.'

'I most certainly did.'

'Try again.'

Gallagher all but cringed as he looked up at Derwent. 'Try again? But I can't improve on the truth.'

'No. You can't. We know you were sleeping with her, Mr Gallagher.'

'But how? She didn't—' He broke off.

'Tell anyone?' I suggested. 'No. But she wasn't as discreet as you might have liked her to be. And you've just confirmed it was true.'

'What *is* the attraction?' Derwent sounded genuinely puzzled. 'Not shagging the pretty girl at work – I get that. It's the violence I don't understand. Whipping. Choking. Where's the appeal?'

'I – I don't—'

'Oh, but you do.' Derwent leaned down, getting in Gallagher's face. 'You hurt her because you enjoyed it, you sick little fuck.'

'You can't talk to me like that.'

'This isn't an official interview. There are no tape recorders. When we arrest you for perverting the course of justice and take you down to the station I'll have to mind my manners but here and now I can tell you what I think of you, and I think you're a lying prick.'

It was a bluff, I knew. The last thing we wanted was to arrest James Gallagher. Any lawyer would spot that we wouldn't want to undermine his credibility, especially if what he was telling us was now the truth. Proving he was a liar would be a gift to the defence in any trial where he was a witness.

But Gallagher wasn't a lawyer, and he was terrified, which was exactly what Derwent had intended.

'She wanted it.'

'Did she?'

'She begged me to do it.' He shook his head. 'You have to believe me, she was the one in charge. That's how it works. She said what she wanted and she told me when to stop. I did what she asked me to do. It looked as if I was in control but she was the one calling the shots.'

'You were her boss, though. So it wasn't a relationship of equals in the first place,' I said.

'That didn't matter. She didn't think of me as her boss.'

'But you were. She was dependent on you for her job. Her income.'

'I never thought about that.'

'You didn't have to.'

'I bet it started out as a harmless little fling and before you knew it you were in trouble.' Derwent got closer to Gallagher's face. 'Things went too far. You wanted a quiet midlife-crisis shag but it got too dark.'

'We shared similar interests. I don't think I need or want to say anything more than that.' Gallagher tried to take charge of the situation. 'If you keep badgering me like this, I'm going to call my lawyer.'

'Why haven't you called him already? What's stopping you?' Derwent grabbed Gallagher's phone off the desk and threw it into his lap. 'Oh, that's right. You don't want anyone to know what a horrible person you are. That's why you lied in the initial investigation. You put your reputation ahead of Rachel's safety. You put yourself first.'

'It was a difficult time in my life. I'd just got divorced. I – I wasn't making good decisions.'

'What happened the night Rachel disappeared?' I asked.

'I told you.'

'No. What *really* happened the night Rachel disappeared? They never found a trace of her on CCTV from the area where you said she left your car. They never found your car on the CCTV either. CCTV isn't fool-proof but King's Cross has a lot of it, so it's strange that no one caught you on camera. It's even stranger that we couldn't find any witnesses who saw Rachel there. You'd think that someone, somewhere, would have seen *something*. Unless you weren't there and your whole story was a lie.'

Gallagher leaned on the desk, bracing his forehead on his fist. 'I can't.'

'I think you'll find you can,' Derwent said, and the menace in his voice made even me shiver.

'What happened – I'm not proud of it. I'm not proud of what I did, or how I behaved afterwards. But there was nothing I could do. There was nothing anyone could have done after he took her.'

'Did you *see* him?' I demanded.

Gallagher nodded, his face working as if he was trying not to cry.

'And you didn't think that was important? You didn't think that was worth sharing with the police?'

'Once I'd started lying I didn't know how to stop.' Gallagher swallowed. 'Anyway, it was too late.'

Anger was a small, hard ball in the pit of my stomach. Derwent was pale, his mouth tight. I thought he was holding himself back.

'Tell us what happened,' I said levelly. 'From the beginning. And this time, don't leave anything out.'

'The first part of what I told you – that was true. I worked late that night and so did Rachel. She was waiting for me. She had been away and she said she'd missed me.'

'Where did you go after work?'

'I drove us to my house in Islington but we didn't go in.

We took the Tube down to Oxford Circus, to a little sushi restaurant I like.'

'Rachel didn't use her Oyster card that night.'

'No. No, I'd forgotten that. The terminals weren't working at that underground station so I had to buy us paper tickets.' He gave me a half-smile. 'You can check it if you like.'

'I certainly will. What happened then?'

'We ate.' He frowned, looking down at his hands. 'She kept asking if we could go. I ordered extra courses. Extra wine. I wanted to draw out the anticipation. I – I was looking forward to sleeping with her again. I mean, you've seen her picture. She was gorgeous.'

An image flashed before my eyes: a huddled, mummified corpse, her hair dusty, her skin peeling away from her bones.

'What happened then?'

'We drank a lot. More than usual. I only realised it when I stood up. Rachel was all over the place.' He grimaced. 'I had a rule that we didn't touch each other in public but I had to help her to walk in a straight line. We'd got return tickets so I took her back to the Tube station instead of getting a taxi. It's not a long journey back up to Islington.'

'What time was this?' Derwent asked.

'I don't know. Late. As I said, I'd had too much to drink. I wasn't paying too much attention to the time.'

'What happened then?'

'He picked us up on the Tube.' Gallagher shook his head. 'I was so stupid.'

'What did you do?' I asked.

'I couldn't keep my hands off Rachel. I pushed her against the glass partition and I stood in front of her where no one could see what we were doing. Or so I thought.' He swallowed. 'I groped her a bit, over her clothes. She was wearing jeans or trousers – something like that. They were tight. No knickers, I knew. So I felt her up a bit. She was laughing but she was trying to get me to stop too. I mean, we were in public. You know what it's like when you're pissed on the Tube and the rest of the carriage is stone-cold sober but you don't really give a fuck? It was like that.'

'I know I don't expect adults to behave that way on public transport,' Derwent snapped.

'Well. I regret it now. Anyway, I think that must have attracted his attention. I sort of remember seeing him in the carriage, watching, but there were loads of people in the carriage and he didn't stand out.'

'Did you see his face?'

'He had a scarf pulled up over his mouth and he was wearing a hoodie, so no, not really.'

'But he caught your attention.'

'Just because he was staring. I was thinking, yeah, mate, you wish you were me, don't you?' He gave a weak laugh. 'What a fucking idiot.'

'Did he follow you?'

'I think he must have left ahead of us and waited. I don't see how else he would have known where we were going. We got off the Tube and I hung back until the platform was empty before we started to walk out. I pushed her around a bit. Slapped her a couple of times.' He looked up at me and read something in my expression that made him defensive. 'She liked it. All of it. Doing it in public was a new thrill.'

'If you say so.'

'And you got off on humiliating her in public. You got a thrill out of letting everyone know you were going off to have sex with her,' Derwent sneered.

'I'm only human. And I was drunk. It was late.' He shrugged. 'If you think it's shocking, you need to get out more.'

I could imagine it as clearly as if I'd been there: the girl tottering on her high heels, evidently in thrall to the older man. The crisp sound of a hand hitting flesh, echoing over the rumble of the trains. The pair of them standing close together, Gallagher's hands revoltingly active on her body as the other passengers pretended not to notice, or stared, or occupied themselves with their own lives. The long journey up to the street, along tiled, echoing hallways, as she twisted in his grasp and protested and, eventually, submitted to him.

'You left the station.'

'It's a ten-minute walk to my house. We stopped a couple of times on the way. Dark corners. You know. I don't know how long it took us to get there, but more than ten minutes. He must have been watching the whole time. He was right behind us when we turned into my street.'

'Did you notice him?'

'Rachel glanced back and grabbed my arm. I – I shook her off. She wasn't supposed to touch me, you see. Because of the rules I'd laid out for her.'

'The rules,' Derwent repeated. Then, 'Go on.'

'I was pretty desperate to get into the house by then. Excited, I mean. Um.'

'I get the picture. You obviously didn't make it into the house.'

'No, we did. I went in to turn off the alarm and Rachel was following me in. He must have run up the steps behind her. I heard her cry out. By the time I turned around, he'd grabbed her.'

'What did you do?'

'I froze. I mean, I was just so shocked.'

'Did you get a better look at him?' I asked.

'No. He'd pulled the scarf up further, over his mouth and nose. I just saw his eyes. They were dark brown. Cold.' Gallagher shivered. 'I'll never forget them.'

'How old would you say he was?'

'Twenties. Something like that. The way he moved – he was fit. Not a big guy. Built like a runner more than a weight-lifter. You know. But he was strong.'

Derwent looked at me for the first time and I could read what he was thinking: *Kelly*.

'What happened then?'

'I offered him money. My watch. My car keys. He shook his head. He threw me some cable ties. Told me to tie myself up.'

'And you did.'

'I tried to leave them loose but he tightened them. There was nothing I could do. He had a knife and I knew he was prepared to use it. The things he said . . .' Gallagher's voice trailed away. 'I had nightmares, afterwards. He said he'd cut off my balls. He said I deserved it.'

'What was his voice like? Deep? High-pitched? Any accent?'

Gallagher shrugged. 'He sort of growled at us. I wouldn't recognise him if I heard him speaking normally, I don't think.'

'How did you get free once he was gone? Did you call for help?'

'I managed to get to my phone and I was able to press the button to redial the last number. It was Per – my business partner. He's always been someone I trusted. He came straight over.'

'And he didn't think it was remarkable that you had been tied up and left there?'

'I – I told him it was a practical joke. Nothing had been taken from the house. Nothing except Rachel.' He cleared his throat. 'I don't know what I said to him, but he just laughed at me and cut me free.'

'When he realised that Rachel was missing—' I began, and Gallagher raised a hand to stop me.

'It never came up. We never talked about it again. I don't know if Per had his suspicions about me and Rachel, but he must have decided he was better off not knowing. He knew I hadn't hurt her. And the business means a lot to both of us. A scandal was the last thing either of us needed.'

'Go back a bit. What was Rachel doing while you were being tied up?' I asked.

'She was going along with it.' He grimaced. 'The thing is

266

. . . I think she thought it was part of my plan. I'd told her things were going to get a little crazy that night. Taunted her, you know. Built it up. So I think she thought I'd set her up to be kidnapped. It was one of her fantasies.' A little anger edged his voice. 'I told you. She was into some weird shit. That was nothing to do with me. It was all her.'

'What happened in her fantasy, when she was kidnapped? Did she ever tell you?' I asked.

'She imagined the kidnapper raping her. Hurting her. She liked the idea of being powerless. In danger.' He licked his lips as if they were dry. 'She needed it to feel alive, she said.'

Derwent swore under his breath.

'So she didn't put up a fight,' I said.

'No. The opposite. She was crying but . . . it felt fake.' He rallied slightly. 'Part of me always thought that maybe she'd set it up herself while she was away. That me watching her being taken was part of the thrill for her. And, I don't know, maybe she'd decided to go away and stay away. I mean, isn't that possible? That it was a dramatic way of saying goodbye to her old life?'

'Dramatic and final,' I said drily. 'We found her body yesterday.'

'No. NO.' The howl came from his gut. There was no doubting his distress was real. 'Oh God, *no*.'

We let him sob for a minute or two. I stared out of the window, nauseated. She had deserved so much more than this money-obsessed shell of a man who had pretended he was strong. The whole thing had been an act. He was as fake as his receptionist's acrylic nails.

'You really persuaded yourself she was still alive,' Derwent said eventually. 'Quite the imagination you've got there.'

I roused myself to say, 'Well, if she was still alive then Mr Gallagher had nothing to reproach himself for.'

'Whereas in fact if he'd got off his arse and called 999 she might have had a chance to survive.'

'I should have told you everything. I'm sorry. I'm so sorry.'
Tears were standing in James Gallagher's eyes. He was broken,
barely held together by the designer suit. 'I don't expect you
to believe me, but I really loved Rachel. She was something
special. I'd have done anything for her.'

'Except risk your reputation,' I snapped.

'Or put up a fight against the man who took her and killed
her.' Derwent smiled, not pleasantly. 'Apart from that, you'd
have done anything at all.'

33

The body was stretched out on the stainless steel table, laid out for our inspection in the bright, pitiless overhead light.

'Well. Here we are again,' Dr Early said brightly, as if we weren't all standing around a naked corpse.

'Doc.' Derwent was staring at the table as if it had hypnotised him. With a visible effort he tore his eyes away from it. 'We've been keeping you busy.'

'You certainly have.'

'Any progress on identifying the bodies from the septic tank?' I asked, because I genuinely wanted to know and because I was putting off the moment when I had to turn my attention to Rachel Healy's remains.

'We've matched dental records on two of them to missing women – both sex workers, both drug addicts, both with extensive criminal records. They were reported missing eight years ago,' Una Burt said, from her position at the back of the room.

'Marginal women. Easy targets,' I said, and she nodded.

'Eight years ago, Leo Stone was between prison sentences. Kelly Lambert was eighteen,' Derwent said. 'He'd just left his foster family.'

'You think he went on a spree to celebrate.'

There must have been something challenging in the way I said it, because Derwent whipped around to face me, shoving his hands in his pockets, making himself look wider and more intimidating. I wondered if he even realised he was doing it. 'It's possible, isn't it? Maybe even likely. He's spent years waiting for his freedom and when he gets it he goes a bit wild, with the help of his dear old dad.'

'And then what? Leo goes back inside, Kelly abandons his desire to kill and goes back to being a nice guy for a while?'

'Until his dad gets out of prison.' Derwent shrugged. 'I don't know why you're trying to turn this into some big mystery. He might come across as a decent person but it's all part of the game.'

'That's enough.' Una Burt's voice cracked like a whip, and we both jumped. 'It certainly looks as if we need to focus on Kelly Lambert now but that doesn't put his father in the clear. Leo has been arrested, of course, and remanded in custody following the discovery of the bodies in the tank, but we will need to talk to him again in the light of the new evidence. So far he hasn't said anything. Liv is working on tracing next of kin for the women we've identified. She's talking to the officers who dealt with the original enquiries when they were reported missing. You should have a look at the files when you get back to the office, Maeve.'

And steep myself in more misery. Saying no wasn't an option, I knew, but I wished it was. Every victim came with a comet's tail of damage behind her, a trail of heartbroken friends and family. Dr Early had to think about how the women died. I had to know how they had lived too, and how they were missed.

'We're waiting for DNA results on the third woman from the septic tank but we're fairly sure we've identified her. Incidentally, I've also been able to identify a possible cause of death for her. She was strangled. Her hyoid bone was fractured. One is a mystery – she doesn't seem to match up

270

with any misper reports.' Above her mask, Dr Early's brows drew together; it really bothered her, I could tell, and I liked her for it. 'I can tell you what we know about her but it's not a lot. She was probably in her twenties, somewhere between five foot three and five foot five in height, bleached hair but the roots were dark. No dental work at all. No obvious injuries, distinguishing marks, chronic conditions. She was a heroin user, based on analysis of her hair. Other than that, she was too healthy to come to medical attention, or any other kind of attention since no one reported her gone.' The doctor sighed. 'I can't help thinking of her as a lost soul.'

'They all were,' I said. 'If we can work out where he found the others that might help.'

Dr Early nodded. 'I hate it when no one has reported them missing. It's not right that someone should vanish off the face of the earth without anyone noticing.'

'What about this one?' Derwent asked, gesturing at the table. 'Did you get started without us?'

'Rachel Healy.' Dr Early put a gloved hand on her leg in a proprietorial way. 'Why do you ask if I've started already?'

Derwent pointed wordlessly at the woman's chest, which was gaping open.

'I've done the preliminary inspection already, but I would point out, Inspector, that is not a Y incision on her chest and I'd thank you to give me a little more credit than that. My work is a lot neater.'

'Did he do that to her?' I knew Derwent well enough to know he was upset from his voice, though a stranger might have missed it: that careful, colourless way of speaking meant he was holding back his emotions. His hands were back in his pockets but I would have laid money they were balled into fists.

'He certainly did.' With a gloved finger she sketched the outlines of the horrific wound in the air above Rachel's chest. The injury was heart-shaped and ran from her throat down to the base of her sternum, covering the entire width of her chest. 'She was alive when he did this.'

Derwent shook his head. 'Bastard. That'll be where all the blood came from.'

'We couldn't see any of this when we saw the body in situ,' I explained to Una Burt. 'She was curled up and facing away from us.'

'How did he do it?' Burt asked.

'My best guess is that he used some sort of heavy cutting tool – something with a sharp edge. It would have been a gouging motion.' The doctor mimed it. 'As to why he did it, maybe he wanted to disguise what he'd done to her up to that point.'

'Disguise what?'

'Can you see this area here?' She pointed to the edge of the injury and I leaned in reluctantly, aware of Derwent doing the same on the other side of the table and Una Burt shuffling forward too. 'That's part of a bite mark. I think he lost control and he bit her, and all of these injuries were supposed to hide it.'

'Biting, gouging – this is a hell of a lot more violence than he used on the other women,' Derwent said. 'He didn't leave a mark on the others, did he?'

'Exactly. We couldn't be sure of the cause of death with Willa Howard and Sara Grey, because he'd done so little skeletal damage. I settled on asphyxiation in the end because it seemed the most likely cause of death but it was more because I'd excluded other methods of killing than anything else. This lady bled out.' Dr Early was hovering at the top end of the table, peering down at Rachel. 'As you can see, there's considerable damage to the face and the head as well. We took some X-rays to get a good look at the injuries and, in layman's terms, he beat her to a pulp. Multiple fractures, significant skin lacerations and this enormous wound to her chest which is probably hiding further damage.'

'So why did he hurt Rachel?' Burt asked.

'He lost control,' I said. 'She did something that upset him. She made him angry.'

'Maybe she fought him off,' Derwent suggested and Dr Early shook her head.

'She didn't have any defensive wounds. She was restrained at some point – see these marks?' Dr Early pointed at two areas above and below Rachel's elbows. 'She was tied to something. I don't know if she was tied up when he cut her, but if not her instinct would have been to grab at whatever blade or tool he used on her. That is, of course, if she was still conscious at the time.' Dr Early picked up a withered hand and turned it over, examining it closely. 'Nothing. Not even a broken nail.'

'So she didn't fight.' I looked at Derwent. 'Think about what Gallagher said about her, and her boyfriend. She liked being choked. She liked the idea of being kidnapped.'

'So you're saying she died happy?'

'No, of course that's not what I meant,' I snapped. What did I mean? The others were staring at me, waiting, while I struggled to breathe properly. The room seemed to be full of evil, and it was stifling. 'He likes women who are desperate. He likes to come to the rescue. He doesn't hurt them – that's important to him. He takes control of them, and the situation, and he kills them quickly. Then he takes them somewhere where he can enjoy being with them and there's no risk of being interrupted. He doesn't want to interact with them in any meaningful way. That interferes with how he sees them. In his head, he's rescuing them. Keeping them safe.'

'By killing them,' Derwent said, with a touch of sarcasm.

'I didn't say it made sense to a normal person. But the one thing that links all our victims, including Rachel, is that they were visibly upset.' I counted them off. 'Willa was arguing with her boyfriend in the pub and crying when she walked away. We don't know when he saw her and decided to target her but if he'd seen her in the pub or in the street she would have fitted his type. Sara had a flat tyre and had to walk home – she was obviously unsettled by it and felt unsafe, quite rightly as it turned out. She may have been distressed. We know she took a long route home. Rachel was getting slapped around by her lover on the underground. He came to the rescue. That's what excites him.'

'Or he can see they're an easy target because they're likely to be docile. They're not confident women. They're victims. Obedient. Compliant. You find a woman who's already off balance for whatever reason and she's not going to be on her guard. You can manipulate her more easily. Box her in. Take control.'

If you wanted to catch a wolf, you needed to think like a wolf. There were times, though, when I wondered if Derwent was a little too close to the wolves we hunted.

'Maybe it was both,' I said. 'But something made him flip with Rachel. Something she did went against his narrative. He lost control of himself. She made him angry.'

'More than just angry. The biting is a common feature of sex murders,' Dr Early said. 'I'll take particular care to check for any signs of sexual assault.'

'Right. She wasn't scared. She was excited. Maybe she thought it was role-play so she didn't follow the script he wanted. Maybe she tried to engage with him sexually. Whatever she did enraged him.'

'He hit her many times,' Dr Early said softly. 'I haven't been able to count the number of fractures in her face.'

'So his lovely, bloodless, controlled murder turned into a fiasco. He lost control,' I repeated. 'Control matters to him. He was ashamed of himself and what he'd done. He didn't want to be around her any more, unlike the others who he kept. He didn't want to display her once he was finished with her. He hid her away behind a wall and a couple of weeks later, way ahead of his usual schedule, he picked up

Willa Howard. This time, it followed the right script, and he was happy.'

'Poor kid,' Derwent said softly.

'Who, Willa?'

'All of them, really.'

'Let's get on with this,' Una Burt said from the back of the room and the pathologist flicked on the overhead microphone and began her recitation of the date, the time, who was present in the room, who was on the slab . . .

'I mean, I don't even have a vagina and it made me want to cross my legs.'

'Do we have to talk about this?'

It was as if I hadn't spoken.

'I never like that bit anyway.' Derwent shuddered theatrically. 'Feels all wrong to watch it. Intrusive. I know they can't feel anything but it's demeaning, the way the doc pulls them around.'

'A pelvic exam is a routine part of a post-mortem examination,' I said woodenly, trying to calculate how long the journey back to the office would take at this time of day. It all depended on traffic, and what route Derwent took. If he would only use a satnav, we could get where we needed to go a lot quicker. But DI 'The Knowledge' Derwent was far too good for that.

'Routine, yeah, but gross. Especially that one.' He made a retching noise and I wasn't altogether sure it was fake. Nor did I blame him. 'When the doctor went up there with the tongs I thought I was going to puke my guts up.'

'You always make such a big deal out of it if I feel sick at a post-mortem,' I protested.

'Most of them are fine. That one wasn't.'

'Good evidence, though.'

He flashed me a look for that, checking to see if I meant it. Good evidence for us. Bad evidence for Kelly Lambert. I had known he was in deep trouble the second the doctor

275

straightened up, triumph crinkling her eyes above the paper mask, and dropped a small object into the dish her assistant held out. It clattered with a dull sound, wood on metal.

'What the shit is that?' Derwent had demanded.

'It's a crucifix.' It was blackened, coated in degraded blood and tissue, and instantly recognisable to me as Kelly Lambert's work.

'It was pushed through her cervix. I saw the end of it poking out.' Dr Early had sounded pleased with herself for recovering it, and she had done well. It was one more thing to tie Kelly Lambert to the murders.

'What do you think it means?' Derwent wasn't going to let it drop, I could tell. Fifteen more minutes in the car, at least. More like twenty, probably. I abandoned the idea of stalling him.

'I don't know. He was angry with her. Maybe he felt he'd let himself down. She'd made him betray himself. His principles. His plan. Maybe he was trying to purify her.' I took a deep breath. 'Or it was none of those things. Maybe he wanted to hurt her and it came to hand.'

'So you're not on Team Kelly any more.'

'I never was,' I said, glaring at him. 'I was just doing my job.'

'Could have sworn you were smitten.'

'Absolutely not.'

'He's handsome.'

'If you want to get in touch with that side of your sexuality, don't let me stop you, but I think you could do better than Kelly Lambert.' I patted his hand. 'Don't sell yourself short.'

Derwent grinned, the creases deepening around his eyes. 'Come off it, Kerrigan. It upsets you that he turned out to be a wrong 'un.'

'No, what he did upsets me. He treated these women like they were worth nothing. They were useful to him. Beyond that, they had no purpose in life. No future.'

'Yeah, I wouldn't set him up on a date with anyone I liked.'

'I thought better of him, but I wasn't the only one. Whitlock liked him, and the Greys have practically adopted him.'

'I never spoke to him but he seemed harmless enough.'

'Exactly. Almost as if he went out of his way to seem unthreatening.' I shivered. 'Now that I think about it, I find myself wondering if that was deliberate. I should have been more guarded.'

'You had no reason to suspect him of anything.' Derwent could be generous as long as you were prepared to admit you were wrong.

'Apart from his background. I suppose you can't run away from your past and your family forever. Look at his dad – he's a thug. And his mother died when he was young. But Kelly had a chance to change how his life panned out. His foster family adored him. They gave him a good childhood. It didn't make any difference in the end.' I stared out of the window. A scattering of rain rattled against the glass. 'Maybe you can't help people. Maybe you should write them off at birth. Give them their CRO number along with their birth certificate and open a new file so it's ready the first time they're convicted.'

'This is cynical stuff. I'm surprised at you.'

'I *feel* cynical. I'm fed up with it.'

'Do you know what I think?' Derwent waited for encouragement to go on, which I did not provide. Undaunted, he steamed on. 'I think your trouble is you're too uptight. You've been working for too long without a break. You need a holiday. You need to dust off your bikini and get some sand between your toes. Read a book. Go for a swim.'

The very idea of lying on a beach made me feel edgy. 'I'm not going on holiday. I'm terrible at relaxing.'

'Fucking sightsee, then.' Derwent joined the end of a massive tailback and took the opportunity to look at me. 'You need a life, Kerrigan. You need a good meal, and a hobby—'

'Oh, come on.'

'—and you need to get out of your own head for a bit.

277

Drink, drugs, dancing – whatever lets you switch off. You'll burn out, otherwise.'

'I can cope.'

'Where did you spend last night?'

'Oh my God.' I let my head drop back against the seat. 'This again. It's none of your business. *Sir*.'

'Sir,' he repeated, and laughed without amusement. 'I know you want me to shut up when I get a "sir".'

'But somehow you never do.'

'I'm looking out for you. Let's be honest, you're pretty terrible at managing your private life.'

'It's called a private life because it's private.'

'You said it yourself. You're lonely.'

I had said that, in a moment of weakness that I regretted. 'I could get a dog.'

The response was instant. 'Not in my flat. No animals.'

'Not even a mouse?'

'No rodents, Kerrigan. No reptiles either.'

'A fish?'

'Only if it's in batter.'

'Thanks for the advice.'

'Do something about it, Maeve. Life is short. You only get one. You can't work yourself into the ground and pretend it makes you happy.'

'I said *OK*.' I was smiling but there was enough keep-talking-and-die in my face and my gritted teeth to make him go quiet, at last.

Or at least, I thought he had gone quiet. As it turned out, he was saving his parting shot for the parking garage at the office, where a handful of colleagues happened to be gathered: Chris Pettifer, Pete Belcott, Georgia, of course. I was walking towards them when Derwent called after me.

'I don't know who he was, Kerrigan, but he can't have been any good or you'd be walking around with a smile on your face.'

I didn't break my stride.

'Kerrigan, I'm talking to you.'

I pushed the button for the lift and the doors slid open immediately, because the power of prayer was a real thing. I pressed the floor I wanted and turned to see Derwent advancing on the lift. I held his gaze as my fingers trailed down the control panel to the door close button.

'What you need is a good f—'

The doors shut, hiding me from him and the smirking group of detectives who had turned to watch us. The best show in town, DI Derwent telling DS Kerrigan a thing or two. What a lad he was. As the lift juddered into life I checked my hair in the mirror, noting that my cheeks were hot with embarrassment and anger. *Deep breaths*. By the time I reached my floor, I was in control of myself again, for as long as it took for the doors to open. Derwent was standing there, smoothing his tie. He'd run up four flights to get there in time and he was barely out of breath.

'As I was saying. You need a good . . . fun evening out, Kerrigan.'

'That's not what you were saying.'

'I don't know what you mean.'

'You know exactly what I mean. That wasn't fair.'

He had the grace to look ashamed. 'I was trying to make you laugh.'

'Then tell me a joke or something. Don't embarrass me in front of our colleagues.'

'I'm sorry.' He sounded as if he meant it, for once.

'You should be.' I folded my arms. 'I went home last night. I spent the night with my parents, because Rob called me when we were at the farm. I needed a bit of looking after, and I got it. That's it. The whole story.'

'I knew it was him on the phone.' Derwent looked hurt. 'You could have told me where you were.'

'Why should I? It's still none of your business.'

'What did Rob say?'

'Also none of your business.'

'Come on, spill.'

'Really, why do you care?'

He shook his head, stubborn as ever. 'I want to know.'

'He said goodbye. He apologised for how he left, and he said goodbye. I don't know why he felt he needed to do that, but he did it, OK? And now it's over.'

Derwent took a step towards me and I held up a hand. 'Don't even think about trying to hug me.'

'OK, OK. Jesus, don't blame me.'

'Why would I?' I frowned at him, genuinely mystified. 'It's between me and Rob, or rather it was. Now it's finished.'

'And you're all right.' It wasn't quite a question.

'I'm fine.' I was, too. 'Now can we get back to work?'

He stood back and I started towards the office. 'Do you really want me to tell you a joke?'

'No, obviously not.'

'I've got some good ones.'

'I really doubt that.'

'A man walks into his bedroom carrying a sheep,' Derwent began, and I let the office door swing shut in his face.

34

I found Liv by the big noticeboard in the office, shuffling through a sheaf of printouts.

'Hey.'

She sketched a wave.

'Are you OK? You look pale,' I said, coming closer so I could peer at her.

'Not feeling great.' She let the words out between clenched teeth.

'Morning sickness?' I whispered and she shrugged, her expression halfway between hope and fear.

'Could be. Probably not though. I'm probably imagining things.' She glanced behind me and pulled herself together, turning back to the board to pin up a photograph.

'Who's this?' Derwent demanded, strolling across to join us. It was a picture of a hard-faced young woman, square-jawed and slim, her gaze direct and confident even though the photograph was a mugshot.

'Kitty Cliffe. Also known as victim one from the septic tank.' Liv pinned up another page beside her photograph. 'This is her criminal record. And this.' Another page went up. 'And this. And this.'

'Repeat offender,' I said. 'What sort of thing?'

'Shoplifting, assault, affray, assault PC, drug dealing, prostitution, more shoplifting . . .'

'I get the picture. Where did she start off?'

'She was from Nottingham. No contact with her family – she left when she was sixteen. Dropped out of school two years before that. There was an older boyfriend, her mum said, and he got her into prostitution. When the relationship ended, she decided to try her luck in London.'

'She survived for a decade.'

'Until she ran into the wrong client.' Derwent perched on the edge of a desk and folded his arms. 'I'd assume that's how he found her.'

'Not according to her probation officer. I've just been talking to him,' Liv said. 'She was trying to go straight.'

'That's what they all say.'

'No, really. She had a little girl who was taken into care at birth because Kitty had been using heroin throughout her pregnancy. She would have been two when Kitty disappeared. Kitty was determined to get her back, or at least to make sure she didn't lose any other kids.' Liv's chin crumpled. 'Sorry. All this makes me feel emotional.'

'I feel more sorry for the kid,' Derwent snapped. 'The ones that are born addicted to smack have a tough time of it.'

'Well, the little girl was adopted and according to the probation officer, she was doing perfectly well the last time he saw Kitty. Kitty had no direct contact with her daughter but the adoptive parents kept her informed, sent her letters and pictures – that kind of thing. And it made her determined to get better.'

'How determined, exactly?' I asked.

'She was doing her best. Some weeks were better than others. The probation officer said she was unlucky to get prison time the last time she was inside. She got nicked for possession with intent to supply – it was borderline but with her record the judge didn't want to give her the benefit of the

282

doubt. She went back inside for six months. When she came out, she went into a step-down facility.'

'And this time she was determined to change.' Derwent rolled his eyes. 'Exactly like the rest of them. Nothing like being surrounded by ex-cons to keep you on the straight and narrow.'

'The facility wasn't only for ex-prisoners – it was for women, but some of them were coming out of mental institutions or domestic violence refuges. The idea was to give them a secure place to live, help with job applications, clothes for job interviews, help with budgeting – basic life skills. It was the last place anyone remembers seeing her. When she disappeared, the staff weren't too worried. The kind of people who live there tend to have pretty chaotic lives. The rules in the hostel were strict to help counter that. There was a curfew, for instance, so if you weren't back in time, you were locked out for the night. When Kitty didn't turn up one evening, no one was surprised, although it was the first time she'd been late. They didn't report her missing until twenty-four hours had passed.'

'So he got a head start.' I stared at Kitty's face, trying to read personality into the tilt of her head. 'What do you think? Did he pick her up off the street like the others?'

'He was good at it by the time he came across Sara Grey. He picked a good location with no witnesses and no CCTV. He had practice,' Derwent said. 'I'd say yes.'

'Where was the hostel?' I asked Liv.

'Two streets away from the pub where Willa Howard was drinking the night she disappeared.'

'I knew he knew the area. You don't stumble across a pub like that. You have to know it's there.'

'If I had to guess, eight years ago he was cruising similar hostels looking for victims, because the next one was also straight out of prison when she disappeared.' Liv stuck the picture up further along the noticeboard. 'Barbara Dolan.'

Barbara had large, haunted eyes and high cheekbones. Her eyebrows were plucked into thin arches in the photograph, and it gave her an air of surprise.

'Barbara was from Aberdeen. It was her mother who reported her missing, but they didn't have what you'd call a close relationship – she hadn't seen her for several years. Barbara was an alcoholic and drug addict who we know was working at least some of the time as a prostitute eight years ago. She was twenty-three and officially homeless.'

'So where was she living?'

'She had a bed in a refuge in Hammersmith.'

'Hammersmith?' I looked at Derwent, who nodded.

'Not far from where Sara Grey was taken. He went back to the places he'd scored before. He knew these areas well.'

'When did Barbara disappear?' I asked.

'Six months after Kitty, give or take a few days. No one was exactly sure when she disappeared. The last time she signed out of the facility was five days before her mother raised the alarm but the staff weren't great about monitoring who was in and who was out. It was shut down not long after Barbara's disappearance. I'm still trying to track down the SIO on the case. I'd like to speak to anyone from the refuge who might be able to tell us about Barbara.'

'It might be worth finding out if Kelly Lambert volunteered at these refuges,' I said. 'He left his foster family to go and do some good in the world, they said. And, what a coincidence, to find suitable women to kill.'

'What about the third victim?' Derwent asked.

'Again, still waiting for an official confirmation, but this is who they think she was.' Liv shuffled through her papers and held up a picture. 'Evie Pascoe. She's the one who was strangled.'

The girl in the picture had brown hair, brown eyes and a round childish face above her school uniform. She was young, and pretty, and a world away from the other women who were stuck up on the noticeboard.

'Old picture?' I asked.

'Not that old. She was only nineteen. She fell in with the wrong crowd, by all accounts. The last time anyone heard from her she was living in a squat in King's Cross after dropping out of university.'

'When was that?'

'Six years ago.'

'He left quite a gap between victim two and victim three, then,' I said.

'She's a lot closer to the type he went for later. He started off with the prostitutes and drug addicts, but they were too easy. They weren't ultimately what he wanted. He wanted pretty middle-class girls. He wanted the girls who he couldn't have.'

I couldn't let Derwent get away with that. 'Kelly Lambert is handsome and pleasant. Why couldn't he have girls like Evie?'

'Fucked if I know. Maybe he felt insecure about his background or his level of education. He works with his hands. Maybe he was worried the nice girls would look down on him.'

'Or maybe he did get her.' Liv was reading the file. 'I haven't looked at this too closely yet, but one of Evie's friends said she had a boyfriend. No name but the description could match Kelly: dark hair, early twenties.'

'That's detailed. It could be anyone,' Derwent snapped.

'We don't have a name for the boyfriend, I take it.'

'Not as far as I can see.' She nudged the file towards me. 'You could have a look, though. Try to talk to that witness again.'

'Sure.' Six years later and the witness had been living in a squat at the time he made his statement: I'd be lucky to find him, and luckier if he remembered anything he hadn't mentioned about Evie or her boyfriend.

'And the fourth victim is unknown.' Derwent stood up. 'No one's looking for her, even now.'

'They're talking about doing a facial reconstruction,' Liv said. 'If there's the budget for it.'

'Hard to justify spending a lot to give her bones back to a family who don't care about her welfare.' Derwent rubbed the back of his neck as if it was aching.

'You don't know that they didn't care,' I said. 'She might have walked away from them. They might miss her terribly.'

'Well, if they do, they'll get little comfort from finding out she's dead.' He walked away, his shoulders hunched.

'Where are you going?' I called after him.

'They're interviewing Kelly Lambert downstairs. He hasn't been charged with this lot yet.' Derwent indicated the women on the noticeboard with a sweep of his arm.

'And what are you going to do? Watch the interview? We've got plenty to do up here.'

'Then you'd better get on with it.'

The door banged behind him. Liv gave me a quizzical look. 'Did you two have a row?'

'No, of course not. Well, not really.' I started leafing through Evie's file. 'That's not why he's in a bad mood, anyway.'

'Maybe it is.'

'He was the one at fault.'

'That usually makes him angrier,' Liv said, accurately.

'I'm going to take this back to my desk. Why don't you have a lie-down or something?'

'I'll be fine,' Liv said. A look of extreme concentration came over her face and she put down the papers she was holding before she hurried out of the room. I grinned, then sighed, and sat down at my desk. I had been trying very hard not to think about Rob, and his baby, and the way he'd sounded on the phone, but Liv had brought him back into the forefront of my mind. It was like brushing against an electric fence, a brief thrill of pain and shock. What had he wanted? To hear my voice. To be forgiven. All he had needed to do was ask. I had forgiven him, and meant it. There was a time that I would have needed more from him – a lot more – but much though I loved him, Rob was in the past now. I remembered what it was like to hurt for him, but the ache around my heart was gone. I sat and stared at the pages from the file, and read nothing, until I turned over a sheet and found Evie's photograph. She looked so innocent and trusting. The cruelty it must have taken to end her life took my breath away.

'Fucking get on with it,' I ordered myself, and started making notes. The witness who had mentioned Evie's boyfriend was one Klaus Maria Hummel, a German graduate student who was living in the squat over the summer to save money. He would be thirty now, I calculated, and there was every chance he was a respectable citizen somewhere or other. I started off with a basic open-source search and found him on the first page of results. Klaus was Dr Hummel now, and he taught in the physics department at the University of East Anglia. I found a phone number and listened to it ring, and ring, and ring, and just before I gave up there was a click.

'Hallo?'

'Is that Dr Hummel?'

'Speaking.' He sounded cheerful, until I explained who I was and what I wanted with him.

'Ah, Evie. Yes, that was a sad situation. Is there any news of her?'

'We've learned some new information that might help us work out what happened to her,' I said cagily. She hadn't been identified yet, and her family hadn't been notified, but it didn't take a genius to work out what I wasn't saying. For all I knew, Klaus Hummel might have been a genius. He certainly read between the lines.

'She is dead, then.'

'That hasn't been confirmed.'

'But there's a body.'

'I can't tell you anything else before we've spoken with her next of kin.'

'I understand.' He sounded downcast. 'She was so young. I always felt that we – the others in the house, you know – should have done more to protect her. Most of us were older.'

'How did she come to live in the squat with you?'

'She came with a friend – an artist, one of those very loud girls who dress to be seen. Evie was always in her shadow. She was like a little ghost. I hardly knew her. There were so many of us. Fifteen, sixteen people at times. The house had running water and a lot of rooms, so it was a good place to live. We kept it in good order. There were rules.' He stopped for a second and when he spoke again his accent was stronger, the emotion thickening his voice. 'She should have been safe with us.'

'Did you think someone else in the house was responsible for her disappearance?'

'No, no. There was no one like that.'

'I've been reading the statement you gave the police six years ago. You said she had a boyfriend.' I crossed my fingers in the silence after I spoke.

'Well, there was a guy. I don't know that he was her boyfriend. He was friendly with the artist girl and I saw him with Evie once, holding hands. They looked like they were boyfriend and girlfriend. But I don't know any more, I'm afraid.' The cautious scientist, wary of making assumptions.

'Do you remember his name?'

'No. I never knew it.'

'Or the artist's name?' I was pawing through the file, skimming for ideas. 'Sukey Cross? Could that have been her?'

'Yes, it was. Sukey.'

I tucked the phone under my chin and typed her name into the search engine. 'Shit.'

I said it under my breath but he heard. 'You've just found out that she's dead too.'

'I have.' I was staring at an obituary.

'Two years ago. Poor girl, she had leukaemia. She was talented, you know. I thought so even though I wasn't friendly with her. I saw it on Facebook and it brought back those long-ago days. And now you call me and it all comes back again.'

'Yes, I'm sorry.' I was equally sorry about the fact that Sukey was a dead end in my investigation.

'If I can help . . .' his voice trailed away.

'How well do you remember Evie's boyfriend? If I sent you a picture, would you be able to say if it was him?'

'Probably. I have a good memory for faces.'

That was something. 'This isn't an official ID. Would you be prepared to take part in a proper identification process if we need you to?'

'Of course. Anything that helps.' He gave me his email address and I sent him Kelly Lambert's mugshot. We made desultory small talk while the picture was finding its way to his computer: the weather, Norwich, what he was doing for Christmas.

'The message has come through,' Klaus Hummel said.

'And? Take your time,' I said, on edge. How long did it take to open a picture file?

He made a small exclamation, surprised. 'Ah. No. No, that's not him.'

'Are you sure?'

'Positive. It's definitely not him.'

So I wouldn't be able to connect Kelly Lambert to Evie Pascoe that easily. That didn't mean I wouldn't do it eventually. The more frustrated I felt – and frustration was knotting my muscles – the more determined I got.

'Thanks so much for your help.'

'Wait a second, though. I recognise him.'

289

'You do?' I said stupidly.

'Yes, of course. He was the boyfriend's brother.'

'His *brother*?'

'That's what I understood.' Hummel sounded puzzled at the shock in my voice. 'I might have been mistaken. My English wasn't so good at this time and I was sometimes wrong about what I understood. This man in the photograph was certainly a friend of Sukey. Another artist. I did not spend a lot of time with Sukey, though, so I can't be clear about it, you understand.'

'Do you remember anything else about him?'

'No. I'm sorry.'

'What about his brother? Evie's boyfriend? Can you describe him in any more detail?'

'No. They looked quite similar. The boyfriend was taller, I think, but that's all.' The shrug carried down the phone line. 'I wasn't particularly interested in them.'

I tried very hard to coax something more out of his memory but Hummel was adamant: that was all he knew. After I hung up, I sat for a moment and thought. Kelly had known Evie, even if he hadn't been her boyfriend. In fact, that might have been a key factor in turning her into a target for him. The killer's technique, after all, was to come to the rescue. A bad boyfriend might have tipped Kelly over the edge into violence.

But what if that boyfriend was his brother?

Liv paused by my desk. 'Why are you looking like that?'

'The witness recognised Kelly. He knew Evie when she was in the squat.' I looked up at her. 'Apparently Kelly's brother was her boyfriend.'

'Kelly has a brother?'

'So my witness said.'

'He was a foster kid, wasn't he? Maybe it was another kid who was fostered with him.'

'Maybe.' I picked up my phone while I searched back through my notes for the Fields' number, and winced when

290

Colin answered the phone. Pam wasn't there, I gathered from what he struggled to say.

'I just have one question. Someone mentioned that Kelly had a brother who he spent time with in London after he left the farm.'

'Yeah.' That was an easy word for him.

'Was that one of his foster brothers?'

He made a sound that I guessed was a no.

'An actual brother.'

'Yeah.'

'With the same mother.'

'Yeah.' His breathing was rapid and heading towards distress.

'With the same father?'

He gave a grunt that I interpreted as yes.

'I'm so sorry. I'll leave you in peace in a minute. Do you know his name?'

Colin said something but I couldn't begin to make a name out of it. I closed my eyes in frustration.

'Thank you so much, Mr Fields. If Pam comes back, could you get her to call this number?'

'Yeah.' He ended the call and I stood up. 'He had a brother. Could you let Pettifer know? He can ask Kelly about the brother. See if he denies it.'

'What about asking Leo?'

'Leo's not talking to us. Or anyone. He's going no-comment all the way.' I drummed my fingers on the desk. 'They're still searching Kelly's place, aren't they?'

Liv nodded. 'Taking it apart.'

'Get them to look for any reference to the brother. I'm going to go back and have another look at Leo's flat. The last time we searched it I didn't see any papers but there might be something we missed.' As I spoke I glanced out of the window. A woman stopped on the pavement opposite the office and checked her phone. Dark hair. Dark overcoat. She folded her arms and walked around in a tight little circle as the wind sent leaves skittering around her feet. 'You know what it's like when you don't know what you're looking for.'

'Like trying to find a black cat in a dark room on a foggy night,' Liv said.

'Just like that.'

A second woman was crossing the road, fair hair swishing as she checked left and right. She walked past the dark-haired woman without acknowledging her. The woman trailed after her, though, a couple of paces behind.

'And get Pettifer to ask Kelly about Evie. The witness said he knew her. Here, take my notes.' I hurried back to my desk and grabbed my things, throwing my notebook to Liv.

'OK, but what's the rush?'

'Just following something up.' I waved and ran before she could ask me anything more.

35

The two women weren't in sight when I emerged from the office. I crossed the road, dodging a black cab, and jogged to the corner. Fortunately for me, they hadn't gone far. They were standing together, one listening to the other. The blonde looked around as I came into view, and it wasn't my imagination that her face paled.

'Maeve.'

'Georgia.' I looked at the other woman. 'I'm sorry, I don't know your name. But I recognise you, don't I?'

'I don't know.' She snatched at the strap of her bag, ruining the effect of the blank look she was directing at me. I made her nervous, and that realisation made me all the more angry. No one could have guessed that from my tone, which was ice-cold.

'You were in the Court of Appeal the day Leo Stone was freed. You were sitting with the journalists. Afterwards, you were sitting in the corridor eavesdropping on my conversation with my colleagues.'

'It's a public place. If you choose to talk about an investigation somewhere public, you can't complain if someone listens.'

'That's right. And if I meet a witness in a public place, that's fair game too, isn't it? You're the journalist who wrote the article about my meeting with Kelly Lambert.'

'You're still calling him a witness? He's a murderer.' The dark-haired woman looked at Georgia. 'You were right.'

'Right about what, exactly?'

'Just that you're a bit too close to Lambert.' Georgia smoothed her hair, giving me a good look at her perfect manicure. 'It's unprofessional.'

'It's unprofessional to hang a colleague out to dry so you can take her place in an investigation.'

'I don't know what you're implying.'

'Then you must be very stupid. Unfortunately for you, I'm not.' I turned to the journalist. 'What's your name?'

'Holly Hawkins.'

'Do you work for the *Messenger*?'

'I'm freelance.' And young. And desperate for a story to make her name. I couldn't really blame her for doing her job. I got a decent grip on my temper and smiled.

'Well, Holly, I need to talk to Georgia. Would you mind leaving us alone?'

She thought about saying no, but in the end she tugged at her bag again, and nodded. 'I'll call you,' she said across me to Georgia, who looked sick. I waited until the journalist had walked away.

'When she calls you, don't answer. Block her number. This ends here and now.'

Georgia gave a little stuttering laugh. 'What does?'

'I know what you did. You took the pictures of me talking to Kelly Lambert because you knew you could turn it into an opportunity for yourself. You passed them on to Holly Hawkins because she could shop the story around for you, and she'd keep your name out of it. That's what happened, isn't it?'

'Why would I do that?'

'Because you got access to the investigation. You took my

place, remember? It was worth it to feed her a few stories when you got what you wanted in return.'

'I didn't exactly plan it. How could I? I didn't know you were going to do something stupid like meet Kelly Lambert.'

'Did you follow me out of the office that night?'

'No.'

'Then how did you know where we were?'

She made a big show of tucking a lock of hair back behind her ear. 'I was walking that way and I saw him stop to look in the window.'

'Him?'

'DI Derwent. He must have seen you in the café. Maybe he didn't recognise Kelly.' She sniffed. 'It wouldn't be the first time he only had eyes for you.'

I felt both hot and cold. Kelly hadn't been lying. He really had seen Derwent outside the door. 'What exactly did you see?'

'He stopped for a second and then he walked on. I wanted to know what had caught his attention. I realised you were with Kelly Lambert and I decided to hang around to see what you were doing with him.'

'Why did you care?'

'I don't know. I just – I just want to know how you do it.'

'Do what?'

'Work. Get people to trust you. Make people like you. People listen to you.' Her mouth tightened. 'Superintendent Godley listens to you. He doesn't know I exist.'

'That hasn't come overnight.' I stared down at her. 'I work hard. Too hard, probably. I try to understand people. And I've been lucky from time to time. There's no secret to it.'

'That's what you say.'

'It's the truth.' Anger was beginning to char the edges of my composure, in spite of my determination to stay calm. 'You're setting yourself up to compete with me as if there isn't room for both of us.'

'There isn't. I get the shit work to do. You're the one who gets all the interesting stuff.'

'Maybe that's how it looks to you, but—'

'You do what you want, when you want.'

I shook my head. 'You wouldn't still be on the team if I hadn't intervened with Una Burt on your behalf.'

'That's not true.'

'It absolutely is. You fucked up, and badly. You were going to get the blame for everything that happened last summer, and you know you deserved that blame. I felt sorry for you. I thought you had a lot to learn but you have potential.'

'Do you expect me to thank you?'

'Yes, I do. That's part of it, isn't it? You hate that you owe me one. You don't want to be grateful to me.'

'I remember what happened in the summer and it was at least as much your fault as mine.'

'Keep telling yourself that.' I leaned in. 'Remember, Georgia, I am you, plus a couple of years and a lot of caffeine, and I have very little patience for your games. I know what you're thinking before you do. You have a great opportunity to work on this team. So get on with the job.'

'Like you do.'

'Like I do.' I checked my watch. 'Now I have to go.'

'Where?'

'Daniel of Padua House.'

'Where's that?'

I was already halfway to the corner. 'Look it up.'

The front door was standing open when I got to the big, gloomy house. I stopped for a moment in the porch while I tried to see if there was anyone lurking in the hall. I was about to step across the threshold when I heard footsteps approaching from inside, quick and confident. A man came into view carrying a bin bag in each hand. There was something incongruous about the conscious drama of the robe he wore and the very mundane job he was doing. I searched my mind for his name.

'Brother Mark.'

'Yes?' He looked quizzical.

'Detective Sergeant Maeve Kerrigan.' I showed him my ID and he glanced at it, then back at me with recognition.

'You were here before when they searched Leo's flat. I should have known who you were.'

'No, not at all.' He looked slighter than I'd remembered, and the haunted saint look was gone, replaced with open friendliness. Presumably it helped that I wasn't standing at the head of a phalanx of investigators. 'Context always helps. I might not have recognised you without your robe.'

He looked down at himself and grinned. 'It probably seems strange to you that I wear it but I get a lot more respect when I'm robed up. Brother Mark is a lot more important than plain old Mark Peters.'

'There's a reason the police wear a uniform.'

He gave me a crooked grin. 'Plus you're armed.'

'That never hurts,' I agreed. I always carried my ASP extendable baton, in uniform or out of it. I slipped my hand into my coat pocket to check the comforting weight of it.

'What can I do for you?'

I explained why I was there and a worried look washed the smile out of his eyes.

'Do you have a warrant?'

'I don't need one. It's a Section 18 search.' He looked baffled and I relented: police jargon was not always the best way to get what you wanted. 'I'm looking for evidence of the offence he's in custody for. It's all signed off.'

'Do you want me to let you in to his flat?'

'If you have a spare key I can let myself in.'

'There's one in my office. Hold on.' He lifted the bags and carried them out past me. I heard them clattering into the bin by the gate as I walked into the hall, smelling that mixture of cooking and bleach that I'd found so off-putting before. It was overlaid now with the sour stench of the rubbish. Mark swept up the steps and back into the hall, closing the door carefully behind him. He turned and grinned.

'Don't tell anyone I left it open. I'm not supposed to, but it's easier when I'm doing the bins.'

'I won't say a word,' I promised. 'How long have you worked here?'

'Three years, nearly.'

'All on your own?'

'Mostly. It's not that easy to recruit people to work in a place like this. I've been on my own for the last year. But I get a stipend and a roof over my head and I'm able to help people who don't have a lot of support otherwise.' He looked a little embarrassed. 'I get a lot out of it. I don't know what I'd be doing if I wasn't here. I couldn't afford to live in London, anyway.'

'Do you keep a register of visitors?'

'I do.' He hesitated. 'Most of them don't get visitors. They're not allowed anyone except family and friends – no girlfriends or wives.'

'Or boyfriends,' I suggested.

'We don't allow – the trustees prefer – they don't—'

'I get the picture,' I said, to save him his actual blushes.

'It's a very conservative organisation. I don't actually approve of the rule against homosexuals. Part of my job is assessing potential residents. If I felt someone needed to be here I'd probably forget to go through those questions on the application form.' He went behind the desk and slid a battered A4 hardback notebook out of a stack. 'This is the register.'

I took it and leafed through, seeing that it was organised by date and in columns. Visitor's name, resident, relationship, time of arrival, time of departure. I ran my finger down the residents' column, searching for Leo's name.

'It was mainly his son who came. And his lawyer.'

I had just found Seth Taylor's name, the writing dark and small. It appeared again further down the page. In between, Kelly's signature was written with a flourish.

'No one else? No other family?'

'Not that I recall. But he hasn't been here for very long, of course. And I don't think he has much in the way of family.'

'He has another son, apparently.'

Mark stopped in the act of unlocking a cupboard. 'He's never mentioned that to me.'

'No, me neither. It came as quite a surprise.'

'Do you think it's important?'

I shrugged. 'Probably not. But you never know. Everything is potentially important in a murder investigation.'

'I'll take your word for it.' He went back to the cupboard, muttering to himself. 'Spare keys. Now, what number is Leo?'

I looked at the desk while I was waiting. It was neat, organised, devoid of personal belongings. It was a bleak kind of life he had, I thought, and a lonely one, but then who was I to criticise? I'd let work dominate my life for too long.

'Here you are.' He laid the keys on the desk and I scooped them up. 'Do you want me to take you up there?'

'I remember where it is. Thanks for these. I'll drop them back when I'm finished.'

'How long will you be?'

'As long as it takes.' I smiled, though, to take the sting out of it, and after a moment he smiled back.

I knew not to take the stairs too quickly; it was a long way up to Leo's flat. A couple of the doors stood open, the flats empty, waiting for suitable residents. It was a hell of a lot better than the refuges where Kelly Lambert's victims had been living, or the squat where Lambert had picked up Evie. There was privacy, and space, and Brother Mark kept things running smoothly. I could understand why Leo Stone had professed his conversion, for the sake of a decent roof over his head.

Up on the top floor I stopped for a second to catch my breath and pull on my blue gloves. The lock was loose, turning with the key when I slid it in. The door came open and I felt for a light switch, not wanting to go inside until I could see where I was walking. Something was bothering me, something I couldn't quite identify. The light came on and I looked at the hallway, seeing nothing out of the ordinary: no pictures, nothing personal, no signs of life. The flat was quiet, but it was a hush that wasn't absolute silence. I shut the door behind me and stood in the hall, listening. Water hissed in the pipes. A scrabble overhead made me jump, though I knew it was a pigeon landing on the roof.

No reason to be jumpy. No reason to wish I had brought Liv with me, or Derwent. He would have been barrelling into every room, scolding me for not having done a good enough job on the search when we'd been there before. But I had searched the place, and searched it well. If anyone had fucked up, it was him, not me.

I was arguing with an imaginary Derwent. Maybe I did need a holiday. Shaking my head, I took off my coat and jacket and hung them on the empty hooks by the door. I would start in the living room, I decided, and walked the length of the hall to the half-open door. The nape of my neck tingled as I went, my skin shrinking away from an imaginary touch. I checked behind me and glanced through every door I passed.

Nothing.

No reason for my senses to be on high alert.

Get on with it.

Bright electric light didn't do the décor any favours, I discovered in the living room. It wasn't a large room. The ceiling sloped and the window was a dormer that offered neither much light nor a decent view, a reminder that this was a converted attic space and I was a long way up. A stained couch was wedged under the sloping roof, opposite a cheap

TV. The floor was covered in institutional carpet, fibrous and indestructible, and it needed a good vacuuming. I lowered myself on to my elbows and toes, keeping everything else out of contact with the floor, and shone my torch under the sofa. A search was better than Pilates for testing core strength. There was nothing under the sofa except a sour-smelling carton from a take-away meal. Even Derwent wouldn't have missed evidence if it was under a piece of furniture, I reminded myself, and set about looking thoroughly – inside the sofa's cushions and along all its sides, checking the carpet tiles to see if any were loose, under and behind and on top of every item of furniture I could see.

By the time I'd finished in the living room I was sure as I could be that we hadn't missed anything. A creak from the hallway distracted me.

'Hello?'

No response.

'Brother Mark?'

Silence.

I stood where I was, listening. Old houses made odd noises, especially when they were subdivided. The radiator ticked behind me, the metal reacting to the hot water that filled it. The floorboards would be affected too, creaking as the pipes heated them. And that sound like breathing – that was my imagination.

I pulled the door open and stepped into the hall, because that was what I would do if I wasn't scared, and I had a job to do. It was dark. It was dark, I discovered, because the hall light – the light I had put on myself – was switched off. I shone my torch on the switch by the door, remembering how I had pushed down on it. Now it was switched the other way.

And opposite the switch, on the wall, hung my coat and jacket and bag, which contained my phone, my radio and my ASP, as remote and useful to me at that moment as the peak of Everest. All I had to do was walk the length of the flat to

301

reach them, past three open doors. It would take three seconds to do it. Two, if I hurried.

I hurried.

I was halfway along the hall when the bedroom door moved. With the sick inevitability of a nightmare the darkness inside the room coalesced into the shape of a man. He stepped towards me and I stumbled back against the wall, sliding along it fast, looking for a door before I recognised him and stopped.

'What are you doing here?'

Seth Taylor raised his eyebrows. 'I could ask you the same question.'

36

'Have you been here the whole time?'

'I got here about five minutes before you did.' He was looking faintly wounded at my tone which was, admittedly, on the aggressive side.

'Brother Mark didn't tell me you were here.'

'He didn't know.' Seth leaned against the wall, his hands in his pockets. 'The front door was open so I walked in.'

'The door to this flat was locked. That's why I had a key.'

'I carded it.'

'Where did you learn to do that?'

'A locksmith showed me how to do it.' He smiled. 'After he'd taken a hundred quid off me for opening my door when I locked myself out.'

'Why are you here?'

'I was picking up a few things for Leo.' He pushed the bedroom door open so I could see a bag on the floor. 'He needed his medication and some clothes.'

'Nice of you to do it.'

'He doesn't have anyone else now that Kelly's been arrested.' Seth shrugged. 'Anyway, you know how it is. The life of a defence lawyer is all glamour, twenty-four seven. If a client needs you, you go.'

'That's one reason why I wouldn't do your job.'

'There are lots of reasons why I wouldn't do yours.'

I ignored the challenge in his voice. If I argued with everyone I met who hated the police I'd never do anything else. Besides, I'd started it. 'Right. Well, speaking of doing jobs, I'd better get on with mine.'

'Which is what, exactly?'

'A second search in case I missed anything last time.'

'You have a warrant, I take it.'

'It's a Section 18 search so I don't need one, as you know. I don't break the rules, Mr Taylor.'

'Nor do I.'

I raised my eyebrows and gestured wordlessly at the flat, where he shouldn't have been. He bit his lip.

'OK. Fair point. I should have signed in.' He lowered his voice. 'I don't like Brother Mark much. He gives me the creeps.'

'Why? Because he likes dressing up as a monk?'

'I don't know what it is.' He moved restlessly. 'Look, are you here on your own?'

'Why?' That was the sort of question that always made me wary.

'I'll hang around if you want.'

'I don't want.'

'A place like this is full of criminals and most of them haven't seen a woman for a long time. The lock on that door is rubbish, as I proved. And you're here on your own.'

'You're never alone in the Met. I can get back-up straight away if I press the right button on my radio.'

'So where's your radio?'

It was in my bag, hanging up behind him. My turn to be caught out. 'It's close enough.'

'I'm staying anyway. I want to make sure you don't damage anything.'

'Fine.' Short of shoving him out of the door, I wasn't going to be able to persuade him to go anywhere. 'But if you must stay, stay out of my way.'

I stepped around him and put on the light in the bedroom. The single bed was unmade, the mattress stripped. It smelled of unwashed bodies. I pulled a face. 'Nice place he has here. I can see why you want to keep an eye on me.'

'It's hot, isn't it?' He took off his suit jacket and threw it on the bed. 'How long is this going to take?'

'I have no idea.'

He stood in the doorway and watched me working my way through the drawers in the bedside table. 'What are you looking for?'

'I don't know exactly. An address book, or a diary, or photographs, or letters.'

'Leo's not that organised.'

'Maybe not. You never know.'

I turned my attention to the chest of drawers that lurked behind the door. He moved so he could watch me lift everything out of the drawers and put them on the bed: socks, underwear, T-shirts, jeans, not much of anything and everything new but cheap.

'He doesn't have a lot of stuff. That has to help.'

'You'd think so.' I pulled the drawers out, one at a time, and checked them before I slotted them back into place.

'Can I give you a hand?'

'No.'

'I could put things away.'

I straightened. 'There's no need.'

'Are you always this defensive?'

'I'm not being defensive.'

His eyes glittered. 'What about now?'

'Now I might be,' I admitted.

'What are these letters or photographs supposed to prove, anyway?'

'You know I can't tell you that.' It occurred to me, though, that Seth might know something useful. 'Did Leo ever say anything about having another son?'

305

The surprise on his face was my answer. 'No. No, he didn't.'

'I found a witness who mentioned that Kelly had a brother. His foster parents confirmed it – well, sort of confirmed it,' I amended. 'We really need to trace him.'

'And this brother is Leo's son too? You're sure about that?'

'So it seems.' I sighed. 'I'm not sure of anything at the moment, including whether Kelly is guilty or not. If I can find the brother, I might find some answers.'

'What do you know about this guy?' Seth asked.

'Not much.'

'Do you have a name for him?'

'Not yet. And I can't tell you anything more than that.'

'Because we're on opposite sides.' There was something in the way he said it that made me look at him. He held my gaze for a moment longer than I might have expected.

When it came down to it, I didn't know Seth Taylor at all. I had taken him for granted – he was Leo Stone's solicitor, and therefore I needed to deal with him. But standing in the doorway of the small bedroom – blocking the doorway, to be accurate – he was just a man. A stranger. All that I knew about him was what he had allowed me to know, which wasn't a lot.

'Where are you from, Seth?'

'Why do you want to know?' he shot back.

'Making conversation.'

'I grew up in Dorset.'

'Really? I'd have picked you for a Londoner.'

'I've worked very hard to give that impression.' He flashed a grin at me. 'Country boy, through and through.'

'I suppose that explains the beard.'

'Don't tell me you don't like it.' He smoothed it with his fingertips. 'I think it's my finest achievement.'

'I don't know enough about you to argue the point.' I looked at him, trying to see past it. He was undeniably hand-some, with or without it. It was like Brother Mark's robe, I thought. It disguised and distracted from what lay beneath it.

And I was always inclined to look more closely at the things I wasn't supposed to notice.

'Believe me, it's the truth. This beard is my sole success.'

'I heard you were quite the high flyer.'

He looked pleased. 'Who said that?'

'I honestly can't remember. Someone at court.' I wadded the last clothes back into the drawer and shut it. 'So how come you took on Leo Stone?'

'I used to work for his old solicitor and I got to know him. I couldn't wait to get involved. There wasn't a lot of evidence against him, was there? His previous solicitor went through the motions. So did his brief. And then the jurors screwed the pooch comprehensively by admitting to looking up his previous. I briefed the best QC I know and got Leo out.'

'Until I ruined everything by finding some more bodies.'

He shrugged. 'We'll deal with that at trial. It's not over until it's over.'

'And you've got Kelly to blame.'

'I'm not going to disclose any details of our defence strategy, Sergeant Kerrigan, so don't even try.'

'I wouldn't dream of it.' I was checking the mattress, and under the mattress, and under the bed. 'Right. I'm as confident as I can be that there's nothing to find in here.'

'Which leaves the kitchen.'

'Which I searched before and I don't think I missed anything.' I considered it. 'But I could be wrong about that. And he could have moved something in there, I suppose.'

'Skip it.'

'I can't.'

'Let's get out of here.' Taylor yawned widely, showing off white even teeth. 'You don't want to be here any longer, do you?'

'Not much. But I'm still going to check the kitchen.'

I knew he would follow me to the kitchen and he did, taking up a position near the cooker while I began to check drawers and cupboards. The kitchen was altogether too small for someone else to be standing in it with me, and his eyes on my body were making me self-conscious.

'Hey, can I ask you a question?'

'Of course.'

'Did you ever read the letters that Leo sent to the Howards?'

'Nope.'

'Did you help him send them?'

That got a proper, 'No.' Taylor straightened up and glared at me.

'Sorry. I had to ask. So how did he get them out of prison?'

Taylor shrugged. 'A visitor? A guard? You know better than that, Maeve. Plenty of things go in and out of prison outside the official channels.'

'I'm not accusing you of anything. I'm just curious.'

'I'm not a rule breaker. I wouldn't risk it.'

He was breaking the rules by standing there in his client's flat, I thought, unsettled by the disconnect between what he said and what he did. That was a trick predators used, making you question what you'd seen with your own eyes. There was something about Taylor that felt a little off to me, something I couldn't quite pin down. He made me edgy and I couldn't seem to tell why. Maybe it was that my instincts were running ahead of what I knew about him.

I was alone with him and he knew I didn't have back-up.

I thought back to the first time I'd seen him, to the solicitous way he had guided Lambert out of court, taller than him, taking charge. He had been caring. Like a big brother.

What do you know about this guy?

Do you have a name for him?

'Tell me more about these letters,' Seth Taylor said to me, and I made my voice sound casual – as if I was a little distracted.

'They were illiterate and manipulative.'

'Leo's not a great writer,' Taylor said slowly. 'In fact, I think he missed out on a lot of education.'

'The problem wasn't really his spelling and grammar, to be fair. They were vile.' I knelt and popped off the footplate under the cupboards. 'All about Willa and what a stupid girl she was to let herself get killed.'

'Oh, Leo.' Seth shook his head. 'He shouldn't have said anything.'

'No, he shouldn't.'

'Did it upset the Howards?'

'Of course.' How could it not? I watched Seth out of the corner of my eye. Was he smiling at the Howards' distress? The beard made it hard to tell.

'I'll talk to him. But he doesn't always listen to me.'

'That must be frustrating.'

'Part of the job.'

I turned to leave the kitchen and he was blocking the door. 'Move.'

His eyes widened at my tone and he backed away. 'Sorry.'

I fought the desire to apologise in return. There was something wrong, something he was guarding from me. I couldn't work out why I felt on edge but I didn't trust him.

A rattle at the hall door made both of us jump. The door came open to reveal a slight, robed figure: Brother Mark. He was no one's idea of a knight in shining armour but I felt a flood of relief all the same. I'd had enough of being on my own with Seth Taylor.

'I didn't mean to interrupt.'

'Not at all. Come in,' I said a little too enthusiastically.

'I was checking that you were OK.' He frowned at Seth Taylor as he closed the door behind him. 'What are you doing here? How did you get in?'

'I managed to bypass your elaborate security arrangements somehow.' Heavy sarcasm. Taylor hadn't been joking about not liking the hostel's manager.

'You shouldn't be here.' Brother Mark stepped forward and the light fell on his face, which was pale and tight with anger.

'I'm getting some things for my client.'

'Then get them and get out.'

I had underestimated Mark, I thought, and I shouldn't have. He needed to be tough to deal with the residents of the hostel. With exaggerated care, Seth walked down the hall to the bedroom to finish packing the bag.

'Are you OK?'

Brother Mark was talking to me, I realised. 'Oh – yes. I'm fine.'

'Did you find what you were looking for?'

'Unfortunately not.'

He nodded and was about to say something when my phone purred into life. I apologised and turned away to answer it.

'Hi, Liv. What have you got?'

'I've been in touch with the shelters where the septic tank victims lived and they both said Kelly Lambert hadn't worked there at the time of the disappearances or afterwards. He'd have been too young – twenty-one is the minimum age for staff.'

'Well, it was worth a try.'

'Yeah, but I got them both to send over a full list of staff and volunteers so I could double-check and guess what? One guy worked in both places while Kitty Cliffe and Barbara Dolan were residents. He left right before Kitty disappeared and a couple of weeks before Barbara went missing. No one ever connected the two missing women so no one picked up on it.'

'Name?'

'Peter Lamb.'

'Lamb could be short for Lambert,' I said.

'That's what I thought. Fake names are always easier to remember when they're close to the real name. I haven't been able to trace him any further than that, I'm afraid.'

'Look, call the Fields again. See if you can get hold of Pam this time and ask her about Kelly's brother. And try to get hold of anyone who worked on Kitty or Barbara's disappearance. See if they remember talking to Peter Lamb.'

'Will do.'

She hung up and I looked down at the screen for a second, thinking about Peter Lamb fading into the background, out of sight. He'd left before the women disappeared, in both cases. That felt like too strong a coincidence to me. He'd found his target and then stepped into the shadows, to wait for the right moment when he could strike. Even the choice of name was a way of disguising himself, his true intentions. He would present himself as harmless, gentle, trustworthy. Kind.

'I think I've got everything.' Seth Taylor came out of Leo Stone's miserable bedroom, slinging the bag over his shoulder, and I looked up, and past him, to Mark Peters, and this time I saw him for what – and who – he was.

Seth Taylor was tall and the other man wasn't but he had two advantages: surprise and a weapon. His hand came up, holding a metal bar that had been hidden in the folds of his robe. It took a second before I recognised it was my own ASP. He swung it and hit Seth an inch under the knee. I heard the bone break. Seth crumpled and Mark hit him again, twice, across the shoulders and back, and it was all over, the work of a couple of seconds. Seth writhed, the tendons standing out in his neck as he howled his pain into the floorboards.

I found my voice and my courage at the same time. 'Stop.'

'Stay where you are or I'll smash his skull.'

I stopped where I was. I knew he meant it. His eyes were glittering. His knuckles shone white where he gripped the baton.

'Drop your phone.'

I let it fall out of my hand and it clattered to the floor.

'Kick it over here.'

I did as I was told, and Mark brought the ASP down on it so hard that the casing smashed along with the screen.

'Peter Lambert, I presume.' I swallowed, striving to sound calm. 'What's Mark? A middle name?'

He gave me a crooked smile that was a twisted parody of his brother's. 'I knew you'd work it out eventually.'

37

I took a step away from him, and another, and fetched up against the back of the hall. Nowhere to go. My heart was racing.

'What's your plan?'

Mark shrugged. 'Go. If you worked it out, someone else is going to do the same sooner or later. Better if I'm not around when that happens.'

'Go where?'

'I haven't decided.'

'You could hand yourself in. Stop running. Own up to what you did instead of letting your father and your brother take the fall.'

He laughed. 'That doesn't sound like a good idea to me.'

I took a step to my right, trying to make it look accidental. The contents of the kitchen drawers ran through my mind: there was at least one knife that might be sharp enough to wound. If I was quick, and if I took him by surprise—

'Go in there.' He jerked his head the other way, indicating the living room.

'No.'

'Do it or I'll kill him.' He lifted the baton and I knew he meant it.

'Isn't that the plan anyway?'

'That depends on what you do, doesn't it?'

He was lying, I thought, but I couldn't take the risk that I'd provoke him into killing Seth Taylor. I moved slowly, reluctantly, into the living room and he followed me. There was a difference in the way he held himself now, a swagger to his movements that hadn't been there before. He was full of confidence, the pious reserve discarded.

'You said yourself that someone else would work out what you did,' I tried. 'There's no reason to kill us. It won't solve any of your problems.'

'Oh, I don't know. It might confuse the police for a while if I make it look as if he killed you. Let's see. You fought him off bravely, because that's the sort of girl you are. He killed you but then succumbed to his injuries. Tragic. They'll be so busy weeping over you, they won't think of looking for me until I'm long gone.'

'They won't be fooled for a second.'

'You rate them too highly.'

I shook my head. 'I know my colleagues better than you do.'

'You think you know it all. You think you don't need help from anyone, don't you? No one's ever taught you how *weak* you are.'

'I thought you liked weak. Women in distress are your thing, aren't they?'

His tongue darted out to touch his upper lip, lizard-like. 'You don't understand it at all. I shouldn't be surprised. I take the ones who don't deserve to live. The ones who are stupid enough to let themselves be used. The ones who blunder into harm's way and let themselves get trapped and still think they can argue their way out of it. The ones who are exactly like you.'

'The truth is that you can only cope with women when they're dead,' I snapped. 'So who's weak now?'

'Wrong.' He shook his head, as if he had water in his ears.

'Most people would be revolted by corpses, but you prefer them, don't you? Even when they're rotting.'

313

'They're quiet.' His hands were working on the metal, the knuckles flaring white as he gripped it. 'They're so quiet. The only time I feel calm is when I'm with them.'

'Do you . . . touch them?'

'I *hold* them.'

Nice distinction. What he was saying, I thought, was that his interest in them wasn't sexual.

'What happened with Rachel Healy?'

There was no reaction to her name. Of course, he hadn't cared who any of them were or the lives they had led. He didn't care about their hopes, their dreams, their futures. He was interested in them dead, not alive.

'She was the one you walled up in a fireplace on the farm. The one you cut.'

His face went slack for a second and I saw it, the tiny tell that this was one subject he wasn't happy to talk about.

'You took her from her boyfriend's house. You followed them from the underground. He told us the whole story. It didn't go the way you wanted, did it? She didn't understand. She thought you were interested in her body.'

He smiled. 'I know what you're trying to do.'

'I'm curious about what happened. I've been trying to work it out for a while now.'

'You can't upset me.'

'Not the way she upset you, no.' I tilted my head sympathetically. 'It must have been awful for you. It all went so wrong. Maybe it was seeing them together – seeing him touch her. It put bad thoughts in your mind. You got distracted. Tempted. It wasn't how you wanted it to be, was it? But you couldn't help yourself. It must have felt like madness. You touched her, didn't you? You *bit* her.'

'I don't—'

'You've never really had a girlfriend, Mark, have you? There was Evie Pascoe, but you couldn't cope with her and what she wanted from you.'

314

'I thought she was different.' He swallowed, looking away from me. 'She was special. She understood about being quiet.'

'Rachel Healy brought out the animal in you. She made you become everything you hate. She made you hungry. She made you cruel. You wanted to use her, just like her boyfriend. You wanted to hurt her . . . and she liked it.'

He shut his eyes and shook his head. 'Stop talking about her.'

'You killed the others straight away, didn't you? That's part of the discipline of what you do. You took Rachel to your father's house instead and kept her alive because you wanted it to be different. You wanted to know what it would be like, didn't you? You wanted to be wanted. Rachel seemed to want you back, but then you punished her for it.'

'Shut up,' Mark shouted, and I flinched, but I wasn't finished.

'When you put the crucifix in her – the crucifix Kelly carved for you – was that to punish her? To purify her?'

'It was all I could find.' He had regained some composure. 'Don't let this little set-up with the robes fool you. I stopped believing in God when I was eight years old.'

'What happened?'

'My mother died. My father beat her to death.' His mouth twitched. 'The most precious time of my life was the time I spent with her when it was all over. I knew she loved me. Only me. Until the police turned up and ruined everything. They took her away from me and whatever I did, I could never get that feeling back again.'

Behind him, Seth Taylor dragged himself up the door frame, hand over hand. The effort made him tremble. I spoke louder, trying to drown out the sounds he made as he inched towards Mark.

'What about Kelly, Mark? Did you want him to be blamed? Was that why you left the bodies in the nature reserve?'

It didn't work. Mark glanced back at Seth, his expression pure contempt. 'What do you think you're doing?'

'Leave her alone.'

315

'Or what? You'll fight me? Please do try. I enjoyed it last time. But before we begin, you realise you have a broken leg, don't you? You've got no chance at all.' Mark swung the baton again, slamming it into Seth's broken leg. He fell onto the filthy living room carpet, his face the colour of putty, his eyes closed.

'Let's pretend for a minute that you could put up a fight.' Mark twirled the baton, pacing back and forth. He was enjoying this, I thought with a rush of anger that blew through the fog of fear in my mind. I took another step to the right as Mark muttered, 'Let's see what you're made of.'

'Leave him alone.' I was worried about Seth. His skin had a sheen of sweat over it and he was fighting for breath. I guessed he was in shock, and without treatment he could die.

'Shut up.' Mark pointed the baton at me without looking in my direction. 'This is between me and him.'

Seth groaned.

'Let's give you a choice. I won't hurt you any more. Not even a tap with this.' He put the baton under Seth's nose and pushed up, tipping the lawyer's head back so he could stare into his eyes. 'If you give me permission to kill her, I'll leave you as you are now. I won't touch a hair on your head. But if you don't . . . well, we've seen how good you are at fighting. You'll die too. Painfully.'

'Not much of a choice,' I said, and I barely recognised my own voice.

'It's a chance, isn't it? You could be lucky.' He was still crouching in front of Seth. 'You could gang up on me. Overpower me. Yeah, you can't stand and you can't really fight – come on, make a fist for me, tough guy. Oh, you can't. Never mind. You could still throw yourself at me and knock me over. Give the lady an opportunity to escape. Sacrifice yourself for her. It's what a real man would do. One with balls.' He tilted his head to one side. 'What do you say? Can I kill her? Will you let her die to save yourself?'

Taylor groaned. 'I can't . . .'

316

I took another step.

Mark ran the end of the ASP down the side of Seth's face. 'What's it going to be?'

'You . . . you want her. Not me. Kill her.'

'Seth,' I said, in spite of myself.

'I don't want to die.' He couldn't look at me. 'And he's going to kill you whatever I do.'

I moved then, making a break for the door. Mark was too close, too quick: he straightened and turned in the same moment, swinging the baton in a low arc. I was ready for it, though, and for him. I was counting on his instinctive reaction: to stop me, to fight me. Instead of trying to avoid it, I caught the baton and pulled, hard. I was watching for the moment his grip tightened on the metal and his balance changed from front foot to back as he leaned away to pull the baton out of my hands.

That was the moment I let go.

Mark fell back, staggering as he tried to keep his balance, his arms windmilling. I didn't waste any time watching him fall. I was through the door already, running for the end of the hall. I tugged at the door and couldn't get it open; Mark must have locked it behind him without me noticing. That explained why Seth had chosen the suicidal tactic of trying to attack Mark instead of escaping down the stairs. He had been trying to help me, and had paid the price.

I turned to the hooks and had enough time to pull my bag down before he thudded into the hall and came at me like a charging bull. I wanted my radio – I *needed* my radio – but I needed a weapon first. I swung it at him and heard his grunt of surprise as the weight of it hit him full in the face. But I knew it wouldn't stop him. He dragged the bag out of my hands and I let him have it, throwing my jacket in his face to slow him down for the fraction of a second I needed to dart through the nearest doorway and slam the door shut behind me. The good news: it was the bathroom and there

317

was a lock on the door. The bad news: the lock was a flimsy bolt, cheap and unlikely to stand up to any determined aggression. I slid it home anyway, and stood in the small, dank room for a moment, my chest heaving as I tried and failed to drag enough air into my lungs. A cursory look confirmed there was nothing I could use to barricade the door. I had minutes to work out an escape plan, if I was lucky.

I wasn't feeling particularly lucky.

'Open the door.' The words were barely muffled; the door was as dense as tissue paper. 'You might as well.'

I ignored him and climbed on to the seat of the lavatory. The window was stiff, the wood bloated with rainwater. I was in no mood to be gentle. I shoved it, hard, and cold air rushed at my face. I had done this before, I reminded myself as Mark hammered on the door. The sound changed as he switched to slamming the end of the baton into the wood again and again.

Time to go.

I swung myself up and through the window, sprawling on the roof and wriggling forward as I dragged my legs after me. I was almost out when something grabbed my ankle: a hand, the fingers strong as iron. I twisted onto my back and kicked with my free foot, aiming for Mark's face. More by luck than skill I caught him under the chin and he slipped off the seat. I almost went after him, dragged down by the sudden weight, until he let go of my ankle to brace himself against the wall. I scrambled backwards, scraping the skin off my palms although I didn't feel it then. As I'd expected, he jumped back up and grabbed the edge of the window frame to pull himself out. I got there in time to shove the skylight down and it smacked the top of his head with a satisfying thud.

'Fucking *bitch*.'

The words floated after me but I was already gone, slip-sliding on the slick lead that ran along the middle of the gully. On either side, a steep slope of slates reached higher than I could see and

I wasn't prepared to take a chance on what lay on the other side. I couldn't begin to visualise the layout of the old building, except that I had noticed one side mirrored the other.

So if I had come out of one window, there should be another on the other side.

It was just a matter of getting there.

Straight ahead of me stood a huge chimney stack. I slithered around it, one ear trained on sounds from behind me, where Mark was levering himself out of the window. He might not know the rooftop terrain either, I thought. Just because you lived in a building, that didn't mean you'd ever go out onto the roof . . . unless it was leaking and it was your job to maintain it.

I should assume he would know where he was going. I didn't.

Fine. At least I had a head start.

I scrambled out from behind the chimney and was greeted by a confusing vista of low walls, gables, chimney stacks and pipes. It had stopped raining but the roof was wet. The sky was the colour of a bruised apricot. This was the tallest building for miles and the view stretched away to green hills. I was more concerned by the realisation that we were, to all intents and purposes, invisible. No one would see me and call for help. I was on my own.

I ran for the other side of the roof and almost tripped over a parapet that framed a square flat window set into the roof. It was the roof light over the stairs, I realised. I skirted it carefully, wary of plunging through the glass. The hall was a long way down and the tiles hadn't looked particularly forgiving.

'You can't get away, you know. There's no way down from here unless you jump.'

I ignored him, concentrating on navigating a four-foot drop on the other side of the parapet. But I knew he was coming after me, and I knew he was taking his time, so he was probably telling the truth.

'No one knows you're up here. No one can see you. So there's no point in calling for help. No one will hear you and even if they do, they won't work out where the noise is coming from until it's too late.'

I had reached the chimney on the opposite side of the roof. I slithered past it, expecting to see the same arrangement as on the other side: a gully, a bathroom window. Instead, I almost pitched down a slope that ran right to the edge of the roof, between two gables. My foot skidded on the slates and I grabbed on to the chimney, the mortar crumbling as I clawed at it.

'Told you. Unless you can fly, there's no way out of this.' He was picking his way towards me, surefooted and confident. He had taken off his robe and now he looked like what he was: a compact and athletic man who was stronger and faster than me. 'Look, this isn't a bad place to die. The sky above you.' He made a vague gesture at it. 'It's peaceful.'

My foot slid again and I looked over my shoulder, assessing my chances. I couldn't go any further; there was no way I'd be able to slide across the sheer roof and reach any kind of safety, let alone clamber over the gables in search of a window that might not even exist. I waited Mark out, watching him get closer and closer. My hands were stinging now but I ignored it, and the ache in my shoulder muscles where they were taking the strain of supporting my weight, and the wind that cut through the thin cotton of my shirt and whipped my hair into my mouth, my eyes.

He jumped down from the higher wall and sauntered towards me. 'Come back from there.'

'No.'

'Then I'll have to come and get you.' He lifted the ASP. 'When I'm finished with you, your own mother won't recognise you.'

He was five steps away. Four. Three. I took a deep breath and swung myself around to the other side of the chimney stack, clinging on. It was square and broad, so much so that I could barely wrap my fingers around the corners with my arms at full stretch. The drop yawned behind me, the slates slimy under my feet.

I leaned my forehead against the brickwork and prayed. I had one advantage – height. In every other way I was out-matched. I'd lose in a fight, and badly. He was coming closer, edging forward.

'You're making me very angry.' His voice trembled. 'This is a waste of my time.'

I laughed shakily. 'I wouldn't want to inconvenience you.'

'Come *here*.' Rage made him reckless. He swung around the corner of the chimney stack and lashed at my hand, trying to dislodge my fingers. I moved my hand a second before the metal clattered against the brick.

Just a little bit further . . .

As if he heard me, he made a last wild attempt to dislodge my hand, leaning so far forward that I knew he had let go of the chimney on his side. I kicked at his foot and had the satisfaction of seeing it slide down the slope as if the sole of his shoe was greased. He screamed, and fell, and dropped the ASP. It skidded down the slope, hung for an instant on the edge of the gutter, then tumbled out of sight. By the time it clattered to the ground I was halfway across the roof, running for my life. I cleared the four-foot jump like a hurdler, hearing feet pounding behind me. It hadn't taken him anything like as long as I'd hoped to recover his balance, and that had been my one shot at getting away. There wasn't time for any diversions: I needed to take the straightest route to safety. I hopped up onto the parapet and leapt straight across the roof light, not allowing myself to think about falling short and what that would mean. My back heel clipped the edge of the glass and I heard it splinter but I made it to solid ground. I threw myself over the other side of the parapet, down the side of the second chimney, into the gully, and there, like a vision of hope, was the bathroom window, propped open, waiting for me to slide through it.

I almost made it.

38

I didn't even hear him behind me, or the take-off for the leap that sent him crashing into me. The impact knocked me off my feet, sending me sprawling against the steep side of the gully. He had landed on his back, between me and the window and instinct told me I couldn't risk trying to get past him; instinct sent me scrambling for the top of the sloping roof instead, clawing my way up the tiles towards whatever lay on the other side, because fear of the unknown didn't begin to compare to my fear of what I knew was about to happen. I got a hand to the ridge tiles before he dragged me back down, and I couldn't hold on, or get a purchase on the slates with the toes of my boots. *You've got to fight*, a voice inside my head admonished me. I felt nothing but weakness in my limbs: that was despair and it was no help.

I tried to elbow him in the face once I was close enough but he dodged away with contemptuous ease. In retaliation he grabbed a handful of my hair and slammed my face into the slates with sufficient force to stun me and bring tears to my eyes.

'Don't make this worse than it has to be.' He was panting from the effort of holding me down, though, and I took heart: he had no weapon now and he was tired from the chase across the roof too.

And I had more to lose than he did. I twisted and wriggled, and managed to turn to face him. I kneed him in the groin as hard as I could and he wasn't used to anyone fighting back like that. He wheezed with pain and surprise, and lifted his weight off me for an instant, then pinned me back against the roof. There was something intimate about it, as if what we were doing could be a twisted kind of romance. At that moment, I almost understood him. It was a moment with the shivery no-way-back certainty of falling in love. *So here it is at last. This is how it ends.*

'Why won't you give up?'

'I can't,' I said, because it was true.

He looked at me with something that was close to compassion. 'It won't work.'

I shook my head, but more because I couldn't allow myself to agree with him than because he was wrong. And if I had been cherishing any hope, it would have been snuffed out the next second, when he slid something out of his pocket and flicked it open. A blade gleamed: four inches long, maybe, and fine, but sharp enough. I grabbed his wrist with both of my hands and pushed with all my strength, twisting his hand back, my muscles trembling with the effort. He raised his left hand, and I braced for him to punch or slap me into submission, determined to hang on to his wrist no matter what. Instead he slid his forearm up under my chin, and leaned on it, and the pressure on my neck was intolerable, straight away. I let go of the knife hand because you could survive a stabbing, if you were lucky, but you couldn't survive without oxygen and I couldn't get any. I clawed at his arm, then reached for his eyes but I couldn't get close enough. He pulled his right arm back and I waited for the impact of the knife – they said it was like being punched hard, that you didn't even feel the blade or know how deep it had gone until it was too late . . .

He seemed to hesitate, then swayed sideways, and blood slid through my hair, seeping into my eyes. It took me a couple of endless seconds to work out that the blood wasn't mine. I had heard nothing at all, though I was pressed against him, but he was bleeding.

Later, I would be told the details: about the armed response crew running up the stairs, who'd seen my leap across the roof light and knew where we were, and where they needed to be, and how there was only room for one of them in the bathroom, and how he didn't have time to climb out of the window or shout a warning before he had to end Mark Peters' life, to save mine, with three shots fired in rapid succession. The first shot hit the right side of Mark's torso and punctured his lung, the second shot breached the brachial artery in his arm and was the source of much of the blood that drenched me, and the final, killing shot took off half of his neck.

But at that moment all I could hear was silence.

Mark fell to his knees, his eyes on mine, and then he sagged to the ground. His head lolled at an angle only the dead could achieve, his eyes staring blindly at the sky, his throat ripped apart. My knees gave way then, and I slid down the roof-slope, sitting in a miserable, shivering huddle beside the body while one firearms officer checked Mark for a pulse and another one tried to get some sort of answer out of me – was I all right, did I have any injuries, what was my name, could I squeeze his hand . . .

They let a HEMS team clamber through the window after a bit and I managed to talk to the doctor, my teeth chattering as she fired quick questions at me.

'You were lucky,' she said, in the end, after finding only cuts and bruises and the grazes on the palms of my hand that burned as if they were on fire. 'We'll test his blood to see if you need HIV PEP or any other treatment. You should make sure you're up to date for tetanus.'

I didn't feel as if I had been lucky, but I nodded, and I nodded again when she asked me if I wanted a sedative. Then she helped me to the window, where people were waiting to lift me down and help me through the bathroom, into the tiny hallway that was entirely full of emergency service personnel and even hotter than it had been before. They were treating Seth Taylor in the bedroom, I saw through the door, a cluster of boiler-suited medics working on him as he lay on the floor. I couldn't tell if he was alive; he was absolutely still, and they wouldn't give up on him until they had no choice but to admit he was gone.

'OK?' the doctor checked and I wanted to say no but I nodded again, fighting off the faintness that made my knees shake. I wanted to ask her about Seth Taylor, but only if it was good news. I didn't want to know if he was dying, or already dead.

It was cooler on the stairs but there were too many people here too: Una Burt who exclaimed sharply when she saw me, and Godley with a grey tinge to his skin, and a grim Chris Pettifer, and Liv whose face was a pale oval in the gloomy staircase, and a handful of uniformed officers who looked curious and embarrassed, and some paramedics shuffling their equipment out of the way, and armed response officers with their guns slung across their bodies, and it was one of those that had ended Mark's life, I thought. My eyes tracked down further, to Georgia Shaw, who had a hand to her mouth, her eyes round with shock, and I felt self-conscious for the first time – awkward, and ashamed.

I stopped on the top step.

'All right? Need a minute?' the doctor was still at my side, her eyes kind but professionally focused.

'I can't,' I whispered, meaning I can't walk down there, I can't walk past all of those people and talk to them, I can't find any more words today.

Footsteps on the stairs and a mild commotion as a man in a dark coat ran up two at a time, cutting through the crowd as if no one else existed, and of course they made room for him.

'Come on, princess. Let's get you out of here.' Derwent put

his arm around my waist, ducking under my arm so I could hold on to his shoulder.

I don't remember how I got down the stairs, even now. I have a suspicion that Derwent dragged me some of the way and carried me the rest of the time. I have a half-memory of Una Burt stepping forward, about to say something, and Derwent not slowing down. As we passed Georgia, I know he whistled a command to her, as if she was a dog. She followed at our heels, obediently, until he came to a halt on the first floor and propped me up against a wall.

'Why are you stopping? I thought we were leaving,' I said, trembling.

'We are, darling, but we have to get you cleaned up before you can show your pretty face in public.' Derwent was looking me up and down, frowning to himself. 'There are a hundred reporters outside this building and they'll put you on all the front pages if you go out looking like that.'

'There's b-blood in my hair, I think.'

'No shit.' He grinned at me and I managed a half-smile back, grateful that he was behaving as if all of this was completely normal. 'We need soap and water at the very least.'

'Her clothes,' Georgia said from behind Derwent.

'The shirt's finished. Trousers look OK from a distance.'

'Where's your jacket, Maeve?' Georgia asked.

'In the f-flat. I th-threw it at him.' I stopped, because I couldn't go on. I felt as if Mark's arm was still on my throat.

Derwent looked as if he was going to say something but gave a tiny shake of his head instead. 'Right. Georgia, we'll borrow your coat.'

'OK.' She started to take it off.

'Not yet.' Derwent took the time to give her a scornful look before he hammered on the nearest door with the heel of his hand. 'Police. Open up.'

'The building's been cleared.' Georgia pointed out. 'The flat's empty.'

'It's supposed to be empty. That doesn't mean it is,' Derwent said crushingly before he tried the door. It was unlocked and he swung in to check the rooms before he returned to Georgia. 'Stay out here. Don't let anyone in, and I mean anyone. Not the boss. Not God himself.'

Georgia frowned. 'Do you mean Godley, or actually, literally God?'

'Does it matter? I said anyone and I mean anyone.' He took my elbow and steered me through the door.

'Shouldn't I help Maeve? You could stay out here.'

'Yeah, I could.' Derwent shut the door in her face without another word, cutting off the noises from the house instantly, and we were alone. I could hear my heart beating. My breathing was ragged. He turned and looked at me. 'OK?'

'P-people keep asking me that and it always m-means they think you're not OK.' I folded my arms, hugging myself. My shirt was clammy and stiff where the blood had already dried.

'I think this place is unoccupied.' Derwent shook off his coat and his jacket and hung them up and I couldn't help recalling how I had done the same myself, and how it had almost cost me my life. The shivers turned into shakes and I shut my eyes.

'Don't go to sleep on me.' He caught hold of my arms and squeezed, his hands warm, waiting until I was able to look at him again. 'Did they give you something to calm you down?'

'Yeah.'

'Thought so. You're not usually this easy to manage.'

'Josh,' I said, and his face changed for an instant, so briefly I might have imagined it. Then he was gone, checking the flat again, this time for things rather than people.

'I've got a towel. Not sure how clean it is.' I heard water running, then silence. 'Bollocks.' He emerged from the bathroom, rolling his sleeves up. 'We'll be here until Christmas if you try to wash your hair in the shower. The water pressure is non-existent.'

I nodded, not really listening.

327

'Plan B.' He went into the kitchen and I heard him opening cupboards. When he returned, it was with washing-up liquid and a jug. 'The sink it is. Come on. At least the water is hot.'

'Washing-up liquid?'

'It'll get the blood out. It's all there was. Beggars can't be choosers.'

I trudged into the bathroom after him, and it was a relief of sorts to find it was nothing like Leo Stone's bathroom: different shape, large old-fashioned fittings, and even a different type of mould on the walls and ceiling.

Derwent was running the taps, filling the sink, but he was watching me in the small, brown-flecked mirror. I half-saw a figure from a nightmare reflected in the glass and couldn't recognise myself, but then he moved to block my view.

'Come on. I haven't got all day.'

I went to the sink and bent to wash my face. Blood spiralled through the water. Too late I remembered the dressings on my palms. 'I can't do my hair. My hands . . .'

'I've got you.' He moved to stand beside me and I crossed my arms on the edge of the sink so I could rest my head on them. He poured the water from the jug over my head and set about working the washing-up liquid through my hair. I hadn't expected him to be gentle, but he was, his thumbs slipping up the hollow at the back of my neck, his fingertips tracing the shape of my skull and the curve behind my ears, carefully, methodically. I shut my eyes and leaned against the solid, reassuring bulk of him for support. I felt numb, but tears slid out from under my eyelids all the same. The detergent was harsh but effective and it smelled of lemons, which was a hundred times better than the animal reek of blood.

It seemed like a long time before Derwent upended the jug over my head for the last time. 'There. You'll do.'

I took the rough, stiff towel he handed me, and pressed the water out of my hair as best I could.

'Can you tie it back?'

'Yeah.' I had an elastic on my wrist. I twisted the damp hair into a bun, the ordinary ritual of it soothing and familiar. Once it was up, my hair didn't look so obviously wet.

'That's better.' Derwent's eyes tracked downwards. 'We need to do something about that shirt.'

'You'll never get the blood out of it with washing-up liquid.'

'Not what I was thinking. Anyway, they'll want it for the investigation into the shooting.' He started to unknot his tie. 'Take it off.'

I could have left the bathroom in search of privacy, if I'd thought about it, but I was beyond caring. I undid the buttons, my fingers clumsy. *Don't think about Seth, and whether he lived or died.* I let the shirt fall to the floor and used the towel to wipe away the blood that had soaked through to my skin.

Derwent had stripped off his own shirt too. He was wearing a T-shirt-style vest underneath it. He pulled it off and handed it to me. 'Best I can do. It'll be too big, but . . .'

'It's fine.' I put it on, glad that it was just thick enough to hide my bloodsoaked bra. It was warm from his body heat and infinitely comforting. I knotted it at the base of my spine, pulling the cotton taut.

'That looks all right.' He tweaked one sleeve where it was rumpled, smoothing it over my arm.

'Are you finished yet?' Georgia stood in the doorway, her eyes darting between me and a bare-chested Derwent and the shirt that dangled from the hand that wasn't touching me.

'What do you want?' he snapped, stepping back a pace.

'I think we should go soon, if we can. Professional Standards are on their way.'

They would want to talk to me about Mark's death, and whether I could have done anything to avert it, and I couldn't imagine being able to talk about it yet.

'I'm ready,' I said.

Derwent glanced up from buttoning his shirt and shook his head. 'You still look like death warmed over. Georgia?'

She had her make-up bag with her, of course. She offered it to me and I held up my trembling, damaged hands. 'I can't.'

'Do it for her.' Derwent was concentrating on his tie and didn't see the look Georgia gave him, but she did as she was told, smoothing on foundation and concealer to hide the damage done by violence and my tears, and blusher that made me look less ashen.

'Mascara?'

I shook my head.

'You're lucky you don't need it. I look like a rabbit if I don't have any on.'

'Stop bonding and get on with it.' Derwent pushed past us and stood in the hall, shrugging his jacket on.

'Lipstick.'

'I can manage that.' I took it from her and smudged it on. The neutral pink managed to make me look more-or-less human.

'Perfect.' She held up her coat and I slipped my arms into it. The vest showed at the front, even when the coat was buttoned, but it would pass a cursory inspection. I went into the hall.

'Ready?' Derwent turned me around, inspecting me, and nodded. 'You'll do. Georgia, stay with her and keep moving. Don't stop for any reason. The car's parked on the other side of the main road, about fifty metres down on the left. If I get separated from you, take the keys, take her home.'

Georgia nodded.

He looked at me. 'Keep it together, Kerrigan. Almost there.'

'OK.'

'Take my phone. Pretend you've got a call if you need to.'

'Thanks.' I held on to it tightly.

'Let's go.'

I followed him out of the flat, aware of Georgia behind me. He moved at a fast pace, rattling down the last flight of stairs into the big hall. I didn't look left or right, concentrating on keeping up with him. The huge door was propped open

330

and he swept through it. The sky was wholly dark overhead now, the streetlights casting an orange glare that would disguise my pallor more effectively than the make-up had. I strode across the gravel and on to the pavement, and heard Derwent swear under his breath as he saw we had to go through the media cordon to get to the car.

'Why the fuck isn't the cordon further back?'

'They did it in a hurry.' Georgia came to stand beside him and I turned so my back was towards the cameras, as if the three of us had paused for a discussion about the case. 'We could wait until they move it.'

'No. I want to get her out of here.'

Obediently, I followed him to the side of the cordon, where a uniformed officer made a note on the scene log and let us through. I saw the car and made for it, my eyes on Derwent's broad shoulders.

'Josh!' A woman detached herself from the press pack and ran across to Derwent. She kissed him on the cheek. 'Where are you off to in such a hurry?'

'I'm working, Cin.' He said it with regret, as if all he wanted was to spend the evening talking to her. 'Sorry, I've got to go.'

'Cindy Yeboah.' She held out a manicured hand to me and I pointed at the phone I had clamped to my right ear and pulled an apologetic face.

'I know, I mustn't keep you.' She shook hands with Georgia instead. She had the kind of prettiness that was startling in person and worked well on screen: small, neat features, doe eyes, high cheekbones, immaculate make-up on flawless dark skin, sleek shoulder-length hair. The doe eyes missed nothing, I thought, as she looked back at me and frowned very slightly.

A droplet of water slid down from my temple to my jaw.

Her frown deepened.

Derwent moved in front of me and touched the journalist's arm, and it was so naturally done you might have thought it was casual. 'So how have you been?' He dropped his voice, murmuring, 'It's been a long time. Too long.'

I saw the exact moment she lost interest in me and focused on Derwent instead, and I took the opportunity to get away. Georgia unlocked the car with the keys Derwent had palmed her, and the two of us got in.

'Should we wait for him?'

'No. He'll be busy for a while if I know him.' I stared across at the two of them. He was standing close to her, leaning down to hear what she was saying. I couldn't see his face but I could see hers, and there was something unguarded about it. They were in a throng but they might as well have been alone.

'How does he do it?'

'He has a gift for making women feel special.' I tore myself away from them and looked at Georgia, who was raising her eyebrows. 'It doesn't work on me.'

'No. Obviously not.'

'Just drive,' I said, and propped my elbow on the car door so I could cover my eyes with one hand and shut out the world.

39

Georgia knew me well enough to stay quiet as she drove me home. I was the one who eventually spoke over the murmur of the satnav.

'How did they know I needed help?'

'It was a combination of things. You were really close – if you'd waited a bit longer to go to the hostel, you'd probably have found out the truth. Liv managed to get hold of the foster mother. She said Kelly had an older brother, Peter. He was actually with his birth mother when she died and it completely traumatised him. They took him in at one point, thinking that it would be better for him and Kelly to grow up together, but it didn't work out. He was violent and un-predictable. He broke a little girl's arm, but they thought it was an accident – gave him the benefit of the doubt. He stole from them, played up generally. They think he decapitated a few of their hens, though at the time they put it down to foxes. Then he tried to kill Kelly – properly went for him. That was the end of that. He got moved on. They said he was too damaged and too dangerous to be around other kids. Sounds as if he had a pretty grim time.'

'That fits. What happened next?'

'Liv got Pettifer to ask Kelly Lambert if it was true he had a brother, and he threw up right there in the interview room. He was absolutely terrified.'

'Did he know where his brother was?'

'No. He told us he was using the name Mark Peters now, but that didn't mean anything to any of us – no one connected it with Leo's address or Brother Mark. He said Peter had been working in homeless shelters when the first series of murders happened, and he'd wondered if he had anything to do with it but he didn't want to accuse him unfairly.'

'Fucking hell.'

'Also, he's terrified of him. I've never seen anyone react like that. He was shaking the whole time he was talking about him.'

'I'm not surprised.' I was thinking of the pleasure Mark had taken in torturing Seth, but Georgia put her hand on my arm. 'It must have been awful for you. You must have been so scared.'

'I was too busy running to feel scared,' I lied. Something in me rejected the idea of being anyone's hero. Blundering into danger was nothing to be proud of. 'What happened then? How did you make the connection to Brother Mark?'

'Derwent thought of checking the visitor records at Leo Stone's prison to see if he'd been there. We found Mark Peters visited a lot – more than anyone else apart from Stone's solicitor. But the prison said it wasn't suspicious because he was from Daniel of Padua House and the visits were to do with preparing Leo for his Catholic conversion.' Georgia shrugged. 'I said you'd been going to Daniel of Padua House the last time I saw you. And Derwent flipped.'

'I bet he was livid.'

She gave me a curious look. 'Upset, more like. He called your phone and it was off. He was really adamant that something was wrong. He was beside himself.'

'He doesn't like being left out.'

'He was worried about you.' She grinned. 'He used words I've never even heard before.'

'It was still good going to get the ARV crew to turn up.'

'That wasn't us. We made a request for the nearest response officers to go to Daniel of Padua House and check up on you and they told us there were ARVs on the way already.'

'Who called them?'

'Seth Taylor.'

I blinked. I had misjudged him. 'I wondered why Seth was in the bedroom when I came down from the roof. His phone must have been in his jacket.' I imagined him crawling down the hallway with his shattered leg and his other injuries, and the sheer courage it had taken to find a way of fighting back against Mark. Kill her, not me, he'd said, and I'd thought he was abandoning me, not trying to create a chance to save me. My throat tightened. 'Is he going to be OK?'

'HEMS took him to a trauma centre. I don't know which. Didn't you hear the helicopter lifting?'

I shook my head.

'It was while you were getting changed.' Georgia turned the car into my road and parked in front of the house. 'He had internal bleeding. They were worried about his liver.'

If another good man died because of me, I wasn't going to be able to bear it, I thought, undoing my seatbelt. 'Thanks for driving me.'

'I'm sorry I walked in on the two of you. I didn't mean to interrupt.'

It took me a second to work out what she was talking about. 'Oh – I was just getting changed. Derwent gave me his vest because my shirt was ruined. There was nothing to interrupt.'

'That's not how it looked.'

'Well, it's how it was.' I undid the buttons on her coat and shrugged it off. 'Shit, I don't have the keys.'

'Do these look right?' She held up a set. 'He gave them to me along with the car key.'

'Brilliant.' I reached out for them and she held them back.

'How come Derwent has keys to your flat?'

'It's his place. I'm renting it. I had to leave my last place in a hurry and he needed a tenant.'

'I bet he likes having you here.'

I took the keys and gave her a cold look in exchange. 'What are you implying?'

'Nothing.' She paused. 'I personally think it's better to have boundaries between work and my private life.'

'Then you haven't worked with Derwent very much. He doesn't really do boundaries. But he's been a good friend to me.' I couldn't begin to explain it to her – that there were times when our thoughts ran so closely I wasn't sure where I ended and he began. All the grief was worth it for those moments.

'Maybe that's why you don't mind.'

'Mind what?'

'The way he talks to you. The way he orders you around.' She shuddered delicately. 'I can't bear that kind of alpha male shit.'

'Don't fall for the image. Behind all the bluster and the snappiness, he's all heart.'

Georgia checked the time. 'I'd better get back to the scene.'

'Thanks for the lift.'

'No problem.'

I had stiffened up in the car and my muscles complained when I stood up. As I trudged up the path every scrape and bruise joined in the chorus of pain. I dragged myself up the stairs and into the bathroom. I wanted to put everything I was wearing in the bin but forensics would need some of it, and some of it wasn't even mine. I put most of my clothes in an evidence bag, and found myself burying my nose in the vest as I took it to the washing machine. It smelled of Derwent, familiar and reassuring, like the kind of hug only he could manage, and that only on life-or-death occasions.

The shower was almost too hot to bear when I stepped

under it but I was glad of it. I needed to get rid of every trace of Mark's blood, and the grime of the rooftop. I had peeled the dressings off my hands so I could wash my hair properly, using the most expensive specialist shampoo and conditioner I owned. It was hard, painful work, my skin stinging and my muscles aching. I let my thoughts drift as I scrubbed, following the path I could now see through the case. We should have found out about Mark sooner. I should have seen the significance of the erased name on the beam at the farm. I should have let Pam Fields talk about the children she'd fostered instead of cutting her off. I should have asked Leo's neighbour for a more detailed description of the son who helped move the shed. We should have found out more about the circumstances of Kelly's mother's death, the death that had put him on a different path from his brother's. It had been a detail, a single fact in an overgrown tangle of facts, but it had mattered, and we had discounted it, consciously or unconsciously, because there were women who merited the full force of a police investigation and others, like Kelly and Mark's mother – like Mark's first victims – who didn't. They seemed to be destined to die in one horrible way or another, no matter who tried to help them. But that was no excuse for not caring about the cruel acts that ended their lives.

Clean at last and wrapped in a towel, I ransacked the bathroom cabinets for the leave-in conditioner, mousse and curl cream that various hairdressers had persuaded me to buy over the years. I could only imagine how they would shriek with horror over the washing-up liquid. Derwent was such an awkward sod at times, and yet he was capable of being kinder than anyone I knew. It was just that the kindness was on his own terms. If he thought something was for your own good, he did it, whether it was a good idea or not, I thought, and wiped the steam off the bathroom mirror. No wonder Georgia had said he was controlling. He was far too involved with my life, unstoppable as water. At this stage he knew more about my recent relationship than either Rob or I did. He had insisted on knowing everything.

He had insisted.

I frowned, thinking about it. He had been worried about it. He had pestered me to talk to him about it.

I knew it was him on the phone.

What did Rob say?

I want to know.

Don't blame me.

Why would I blame him? What would I blame him for?

I stared at my reflection and found myself leaning on the sink for support.

What had he done?

I was sitting on the stairs when the doorbell rang, waiting. I opened the door and Derwent stepped into the hall.

'Sorry. It took me a while to get away.' He shut the door behind him and gave me a long, assessing look. 'You look better.'

'I couldn't look worse.'

'You sorted your hair out.' He reached out and caught a strand of it, pulling it down before he let the curl spring back. 'How are you doing?'

I shrugged. 'You know.'

'Yeah.' He took hold of my wrists, but gently, and turned my hands up to inspect them. 'Are they painful?'

I dragged myself out of his grasp and retreated to the rear of the hall, putting some distance between us. 'I'll be fine.'

'The DPS are going to catch up with you at some stage but I managed to persuade them to leave you alone for tonight. I thought you'd done enough for one day.'

'Thanks.'

'No problem. I'm glad you're all right.' He leaned on the wall, his eyes narrow with tiredness, the light finding the hollows in his cheeks, the curve of his lower lip. I tried to see him the

338

way other women saw him, the way someone like Cindy Yeboah or Georgia saw him. I looked at him as if I was seeing him for the first time, and maybe that was because I had never seen the real him at all.

He frowned. 'Why are you looking at me like that?'

'Like what?'

'Like I'm something you stepped in.'

I cleared my throat. 'I've been doing some thinking.'

'And?'

'And you lied to me.'

He tilted his head to one side, instantly irritated. 'This again. I told you, I didn't tip off anyone about your meeting with Kelly.'

'It's not about that. It's about Rob.'

He was good at hiding his feelings, in general, but for an instant he looked as guilty as sin and I knew I was right, which gave me no satisfaction whatsoever. 'What about him?'

'You deliberately misled me. You made up a story about him being engaged, and his fiancée being pregnant, and it wasn't true. Not one word of it. When he called me, he had no idea what I was talking about. He tried to hide it but he was baffled.'

Derwent was completely still, his face stony.

'I found his number in your phone.' I held it up. 'You know, you should change your PIN now and then. The call register was really interesting. He rang you the day before you told me he was with someone else. Funny how you didn't mention it. What makes it worse is that you lied to Liv too. She's my friend and you used her to make me believe what you were saying was true.'

'It wasn't like that.'

'Well, how was it? Because I can't see it as anything other than a betrayal. And it's exactly the kind of thing you would do. Don't pretend it isn't. You decided I needed to get over Rob. You decided to come up with a scenario that would be the end of it. You knew I'd never try to get in touch with him again if there was a wife and a baby to think about – if he had responsibilities that I thought mattered more than I did.'

'Yeah? So?' He stood away from the wall, pulling that trick he had of making himself look bigger and more intimidating. It was what I had expected. Derwent would never apologise even if he was indisputably in the wrong. 'You needed to get over him.'

'In my own time. Not when you decided I should.' I was so angry I was shaking. 'You went too far. You always do. You think it's caring but it's not. It's about power, and control, and to be quite honest with you it's more upsetting than being dumped was, because you *planned* it. He never meant to hurt me. You did, and you knew me well enough to know the best way to do it.'

'It was for your own good.'

'I thought I could trust you. I thought I could rely on you. I thought you'd never let me down.'

'I wouldn't.'

'You just did.' And I had persuaded myself we were friends. A shudder passed through me at the memory of his hands on me, of the casual intimacy that had let me undress in front of him and wear his clothes, of the tender way he had looked after me, of the things I had told him. I had learned to like him and come to trust him more than anyone else I knew, and I'd been wrong. I balled up the vest and threw it at him. It hit him in the chest and he caught it automatically. 'I think you should go.'

'Fine. But—' He cut himself off and shook his head. 'Never mind.'

'Say it.'

Slowly, reluctantly, he looked at me. 'It wasn't my idea. It was his.'

'Bullshit. He didn't have a clue about it when we spoke.'

'He didn't know what I was going to say. He told me to come up with something.'

'Why would he do that?'

'Because he's got a new job. He's doing something under-cover. I don't know what. If I had to guess, counter-terrorism.' Derwent rubbed his face. 'I shouldn't be telling you this. And he definitely shouldn't have called you up. It's against all the rules.'

'So he's doing something dangerous and he called me to say goodbye.'

'I suppose so.'

'And you made sure I didn't know.' But I wasn't sure I would have said anything different to Rob if I had known why he was calling. He was committing himself to doing something dangerous and I hoped he would be all right but I didn't feel the kind of clawing concern that I would expect if I was still in love with him. He was no longer mine to worry about.

No, what made me feel as if I was falling, as if I would never stop, was the fact that Derwent had lied to me.

'Maeve . . .'

'Get out,' I said, aware that it was irrational to be so angry with him, and all the more furious because of it. 'Get out.'

'So I'm getting the blame anyway.'

'It's what you deserve,' I snapped, without knowing if it was true or not.

The sound of the door slamming behind him must have woken half the street.

40

'Sergeant Kerrigan! Sergeant!'

I stopped on the steps of the hospital building, shading my eyes against the low winter sun. A slight figure was hurrying towards me, silhouetted against the light.

'Kelly, what are you doing here?'

'I wanted to see Seth Taylor. He's a patient here.'

'I know.'

Kelly stuck his hands in his jeans pockets, suddenly awkward. 'Oh, sorry. I didn't think – of course you knew he was here.'

'Only because I was visiting him today,' I said.

'How is he?'

He had been surprising, I thought, but I wasn't going to say that to Kelly. The tough, uncompromising lawyer was very different when he wasn't in a professional setting. He had been pleased to see me and hadn't tried to hide that. He had been off-hand about what he'd been through and rueful about the long recovery he would have from surgery to repair his shattered leg. He had been quick-witted, clever, and direct about wanting to see me again. Soon.

And mysteriously, I'd found myself not only agreeing, but looking forward to it. There was something about him that intrigued me. I couldn't believe I'd been scared of him in the flat. It seemed impossible, now that I knew where the real threat had lain. I hoped he hadn't noticed. I had misjudged him so badly. Guilt was making me be extra-nice to him now.

'He's doing fine,' I said, and hoped Kelly hadn't noticed the warmth in my cheeks. 'He'll be glad to see you. He's bored out of his mind. They've said he should be out of here in a few days but he won't be back at work for a while.'

'He deserves some time off.' Kelly swallowed. 'I wish it hadn't happened that way. For both of you. I know – I mean, I can imagine it must have been terrifying.'

'I've had better days,' I admitted. 'But I made it out in one piece.' *More or less.*

'Seth was a good friend to us. To my father. He went above and beyond for him. How Peter could—' Kelly clenched his jaw so hard that the skin blanched where the muscles were tight. 'He ruined everything I cared about, deliberately. And I had no idea. About any of it. I tried to keep away from him.'

'Peter must have been very envious of you.' The name sounded odd to me. I still thought of him as Brother Mark.

'He could have had exactly what I had. He had the same chances as me. He resented me for taking them and doing the best I could with what I had.'

'Some people can't be helped.'

'Like my father, you mean?'

'I wasn't thinking of him specifically,' I said carefully. 'But maybe it does apply to him.'

'Peter told me once that he killed our mother.' Kelly took a long, quavering breath. 'I don't know if he did or not. Peter said a lot of things to upset me and I was never sure if they were true or not. But Peter could make Leo do anything he wanted. And he was there when Mum died.'

'I went back and read the file on your mother's death. I spoke to the policewoman who was the first responder. She's never forgotten him, or your mum.'

343

Sandra West had given me a very vivid picture of the night Kelly's mother died, and the small boy who had bared his teeth at her and hissed when she tried to take him out of the room where the body lay. She still sounded disturbed, two decades on. I didn't think it was fair to pass the details on to Kelly.

'It might not have been Leo. All I can tell you is that your brother didn't point the finger at him at the time.' I gave a helpless half-shrug. 'He was only eight. He might not have wanted to lose his father as well as his mum. It's a lot to ask of a child.'

Kelly shook his head. 'He wasn't a loving sort of kid.'

You shock me.

He went on. 'You know I was taken into care before Mum died. That's why I wasn't there when she died.'

'I gathered that. Your mum was struggling, wasn't she?'

'Yeah, but that wasn't why they took me away. They'd have taken both of us, wouldn't they? But they took me and left him because he was the danger, not her. He tried to kill me loads of times.' He shivered. 'It wasn't sibling rivalry, if that's what you're thinking.'

'I wasn't. I mean, I should show you the scars my brother left on me, but I presume yours was in a different league.'

'He choked me until I blacked out. He tried to make me drink bleach. He shoved me down the stairs. The doctors thought Mum was abusing me when I kept having to go to hospital, but it was Peter. He hated me.'

'When he was on the farm with your foster parents—'

'He tried to kill me again.' Kelly nodded. 'They asked him to leave. And he loved it there, as much as he could love anything, so I think that really hurt him. I was terrified the whole time he was there but then I felt guilty that I was glad he was gone. He was the kind of person who couldn't help ruining things for himself and everyone else.'

'Why did you seek him out when you left the Fields' home?'

344

He ran a hand over his head, embarrassed. 'I don't know. The same reason I got in touch with Leo once he was released from prison, I suppose. They're family. I know I was lucky to pull my life together. I wanted to share the luck around.'

'You made your own luck. Don't waste any time worrying about your brother or what he did. It wasn't your fault.'

'I didn't know about it. About any of it. The women.' His skin had taken on a greenish tinge and I recalled what Georgia had said about him vomiting when his brother's name was mentioned. 'I would have done something. I would have stopped him. How he could do that . . . And how Leo could turn a blind eye to it.'

I had the feeling Kelly was the only person who was surprised at his father's ability to ignore what his older son was doing. He placed a low value on women's lives. I had been having nightmares – not about the flat, or the rooftop chase, but about the septic tank and the jumble of bones we had uncovered. Dr Early had been working to establish how exactly the women had suffered before they died, and what she had found out so far unsettled me to the point of wanting to sleep with a light on.

'Kelly,' I said slowly, and with some reluctance, 'you lied about knowing where Peter was, when we asked you. You visited your father at Daniel of Padua House. I saw your signature in the visitors' book. You must have known your brother was there.'

'Shit. *Shit*.' He walked around in a small circle, his hands clamped on the top of his head. 'I didn't think anyone had noticed. Am I going to be in trouble?'

I shrugged. 'I'd like to know why you didn't say anything.'

'I didn't know why they wanted to find him. I didn't know about you. Please, you have to believe me. If I'd known why they wanted to get hold of him, I'd have said where he was. Immediately. I'd have handed him over.'

'It's fine.' I thought of the neutral environment of the interview

345

room, and how he had been enduring an endless barrage of questions about his life. He couldn't have understood the significance of the question. And it hadn't cost me my life, after all.

Almost, but not quite.

'I want to know, really, if it was loyalty or something else that made you lie.'

'I thought he would get me locked up,' Kelly said simply. 'He always said he would. Like I told you, I was terrified of him. So was my father.'

'Can I give you some advice?'

He nodded, eyes puppy-dog round and trusting.

'Stop looking for reasons to excuse what your father did. He's not like you. You're not like him. Only he knows why he did what he did.'

'I would have stopped him.' Kelly was trembling.

'I'm sure you would.'

He tried to smile. 'I feel like I should apologise to you.'

'Please don't.'

'I'm going to see the Howards tomorrow, to apologise to them. I've already seen the Greys.'

'How was that?' I was genuinely curious about how the Greys would feel. They had been so convinced the real killer had yet to be found, and in a way they had been right. But they had also been devoted to the idea that Leo was innocent. All that anger had to go somewhere.

'They were so kind to me.' Kelly sniffed, blinking back tears. 'They want to invest in my business. Mr Grey is going to help me with it, he says. I don't know how they can be so generous.'

'They want something good to come of all this. It's the only comfort sometimes,' I said, thinking of Tessa Marsh's parents donating her organs.

Then, less charitably, I thought of the hungry look on Dr Grey's face when she talked about Kelly. I wanted to warn him to be wary; I had to remind myself he was an

346

adult, not a child. He brought out everyone's protective instincts, it seemed.

'Before you go . . .' He dug in his pocket. 'I made this for Seth. Do you think he'll like it?'

It was a bear, its head tilted at a sardonic angle. It looked simultaneously exactly like a bear and like Seth himself. I grinned.

'He'll love it.'

41

I walked down the corridor, my heels echoing on the tiled floor. The last thing I wanted was a conversation but the prison officer wasn't taking the hint.

'Ready for Christmas?'

'Sort of.'

'It's for the kids, really, isn't it. Got any kids?'

'No.'

'Plenty of time.' I didn't smile and he looked put out. He was mid-forties, with a beer belly and smudgy tattoos on both arms. 'Only making conversation. No offence.'

'None taken.' I went through the door he held open for me and found Derwent sitting on a chair in the corridor, his legs stretched out, his head tipped back as he stared at the ceiling. He didn't glance in my direction as I approached.

'I'm not late.'

'I know.'

'You must have been early.'

'Must have been.' He stood up and nodded to the guard, who was busily unlocking the door. 'Thanks, mate.'

'No problem.' The guard smiled at him, then allowed the smile to die as he turned to me. 'Knock when you're ready.'

'Thanks.'

348

I followed Derwent into the room, wondering how his back could be so expressive of hurt and self-justification when he had said nothing at all about it since the night I'd confronted him. He had been icily professional ever since, and I assumed he was waiting for me to apologise. He would be waiting a long time, I thought, but it was awkward now that members of the team had started to notice something was up.

'What *is* the problem between you and Derwent?' Liv had asked two days earlier. 'What did he do? Did he make a move on you?'

'Of course not. He wouldn't do that.'

Liv had nodded, her face carefully neutral in a way that told me she thought the exact opposite.

'It was about Rob.'

'This I have to hear,' Liv had said, and dragged me out for coffee (decaff for her) and a full debrief. At the end of it, she sighed.

'I mean, I can see why you're angry. I do understand you feel he betrayed your trust. I even feel betrayed and he only lied to me so he could convince you it was true.'

'Exactly. And don't forget he forced that trust between us in the first place. It's nothing to do with him and yet here he is, acting as a middle man between me and my ex.'

'Yeah, totally objectionable, but I don't understand why you're so angry with him. He's always been like this. He has no boundaries. You told me that yourself.'

'This is worse. He used what he'd found out about me to fool me. It's unforgivable. He's like those parasitic wasps that lay their eggs in other insects. He doesn't care how much damage he causes as long as he gets his own way.'

'Maeve.' Liv bit her lip, trying not to laugh. 'You do realise it's completely insane that you're more annoyed with him than you are with Rob? Rob was the one who walked out on you. Whatever he went to do, he left you high and dry. Josh overstepped the mark but he was trying to help.'

349

'No, that's what he wants you to think.'

Amusement was still uppermost on her face. 'Maybe you should think about why you're more upset about what Josh said than what Rob did.'

'I don't need to think about it,' I'd snapped, and I'd spent the intervening hours not thinking about it more than once every five minutes.

Now I forced it out of my mind; I needed to concentrate.

He was sitting with his back to us. The prison's interview room was small and bathed in the glare of two fluorescent lights. It was dark outside, turning the single window into a mirror, and I watched him watch us walk towards him. His solicitor stood up and nodded to me, his hand outstretched.

'David Finton.'

I smiled politely and shook his hand, noting that Leo had chosen someone older to replace Seth Taylor, a man his own age. I didn't know Finton, even by reputation, but his suit had seen better days and the collar of his shirt curled like a day-old sandwich. It wasn't an improvement on Taylor.

'Hello, Leo.' Derwent sat down in one chair and dropped his folder on the table with a clatter. Leo stared at him for a moment, then switched his attention to me.

'Detective Kerrigan.' He waited until I sat down opposite him, smoothing my narrow skirt over my knees. 'I wasn't expecting to see you.'

'We still have some questions we'd like you to answer.'

'Yeah, but like I said, I'm surprised they sent you.' He grinned, his eyes fixed on mine. Calmly, I set up the recording device and went through the expected preamble of date and time and where we were and who was present. It was the twenty-third of December, and out in the real world people were in a panic of present-buying and food-shopping and decorations as the clock wound down towards Christmas Day. But my world had shrunk to a room, a table, four chairs and three men, and I had all the time I needed. I leaned my clasped hands on my notebook and I looked back at Leo Stone without fear or aggression. I wanted him to want to help me.

I wanted him to trust me.

'Let's talk about your son, Peter Lambert, also known as Mark Peters, also known as Peter Lamb.'

'You killed him.'

I went on as if he hadn't spoken. 'I've been finding out more about Peter. He didn't have a very happy childhood, did he?'

He gave an irritable little flick with those ugly fingers. 'Suppose not.'

'Your first-born child.'

'I wasn't there most of the time. I was banged up.'

'You never mentioned him to us. Was that deliberate?'

'You should have found out about him. You shouldn't have needed me to tell you.'

'I've been reading up on what happened to his mother. He was there when she died.'

Leo nodded.

'When I talked to him, before he died, he said you were there too.'

The solicitor shifted in his chair but he knew what Leo was prepared to admit to and what he was going to deny, and so did I.

'I didn't hurt her.'

'You had a habit of hitting her, didn't you?' Derwent said.

'It happened. I wasn't proud of it.'

'Why did you hit her?'

'I drank too much and she was there.' He looked up at me quickly, as if he was hoping to catch me out. 'Does that shock you?'

'No. Did you kill her?'

'No.'

'Peter said you did.'

351

Four words but they made Leo fidget as if he had ants under his skin. 'He said a lot of things.'

'Was he lying?'

'Yes.'

'Funny,' I said calmly. 'If it was a lie, you should have been able to ignore it, shouldn't you? But according to you, he used it to control you. That's your excuse for helping him to kill.'

'I didn't *help* him.'

'You didn't stop him.'

'I couldn't.' Leo Stone smiled at me and his solicitor leaned over to whisper in his ear. I missed Seth Taylor acutely at that moment. It should have been him sitting there in a well-cut suit, the sharp brain focused on avoiding whatever traps I set for his client.

Leo cleared his throat. 'I'm not a murderer, you see. I'd never go after strangers. I didn't understand why Peter wanted to do it. He had all sorts of ideas about women and how they were supposed to behave. I tried to ignore him, to be honest with you.'

'You let him use your van.'

'I did.'

'And you let him store bodies in your house until he was able to move them to his workshop on the farm in Kent.'

'I didn't have anything to do with that. They were locked away. I never even knew they were there. I never had a key, did I?'

'Why didn't you tell the police about Peter once you were arrested for murdering Sara Grey and Willa Howard?' Derwent asked. 'You didn't have much to lose then. You were going to be locked up for life anyway.'

'Ah, but I knew I hadn't done it, you see. I knew I was innocent. I had a good chance of getting out on appeal, without the jury fucking up. The evidence was weak. Peter said as much. All I had to do was bide my time and he'd get me out again. But if I dropped him in it, we'd both be locked up forever. He'd tell them I'd killed his mum.' He smiled. 'I've always been a gambler. It was worth a try.'

'But you knew he was dangerous.'

'He wasn't going to kill anyone while I was locked up. Too risky for him.'

'And once you got out?' I asked.

Leo shrugged. 'You got there first, didn't you, pet? You were there when they shot him. I know that.'

I smelled blood again, as if I was still drenched in it. I asked the next question abruptly, trying to get away from my memories. 'Tell me about Rachel Healy.'

'Who's she?'

I opened my notebook and pulled out Rachel's picture, sliding it across the table.

'That one.' The dark eyes were hooded. 'That was a right old mess.'

'When we searched your flat you told me about Daniel of Padua – do you remember that? About how he was martyred. They let him bleed to death.'

He shifted, uncomfortable.

'Was that how Rachel died?'

'I wasn't there. I only saw her after he cut her. He wanted her to die slowly. He wanted to hurt her. Not like the others.'

'He hurt the first ones,' I said levelly. 'The ones from the septic tank. The ones you helped him to hide.'

'Did he?'

'When we found them, one was still wearing the gag he used to silence her while he tortured her.'

Leo grinned at me. 'Then she shouldn't have screamed so much, should she?'

Beside me, Derwent shifted in his chair so his knee pressed against mine: solidarity, or a warning not to lose my temper.

'Did Rachel scream?'

'I don't fucking know, do I? She died. It must have taken a while. She probably didn't enjoy it. Made a mess.'

353

'Did you clean it up?'

'I did my best,' he growled.

'Did you want Peter to be caught?'

'Yes. I did. What he did was sick. He was sick in the head and no one could help him. He was never going to stop. I was scared of him. Everyone was.'

I remembered the man I'd seen on my first visit to Daniel of Padua House, and the look of pure fear on his face as Brother Mark spoke to him. The things we see and don't understand . . .

'Tell me about the letters you sent to Willa Howard's parents.'

Leo leaned back in his chair. 'What about them?'

'Did Peter help you send the letters?'

'No, that was Kelly.'

It surprised me and he saw it. 'Not expecting that, were you? You know, everyone loves Kelly. Always did. He was a beautiful little kid. He was a good boy. You could almost think he was nothing to do with me.' Leo grinned. 'But he's mine, all right.'

'Was it his idea?'

'At first. He wanted me to get them on our side. Having the Greys as supporters helped a lot with the campaign. The Howards were harder to crack.' Leo dug for something between two of his teeth, his thumbnail scraping at the stained enamel. 'Different tactic, wasn't it?'

'Torturing them?'

He shrugged. 'Had to have a bit of fun now and then, didn't I?'

'Did Kelly know the kind of thing you were saying in the letters?'

'That was all me. Kel didn't know anything about it.'

That was something, I thought, but I was flustered and I hoped it didn't show. I'd thought I knew everything, or could guess it, but now I was groping my way in the dark again.

354

Leo leaned across the table again. 'Didn't you ever wonder what Peter knew about Kelly that kept him in line?'

I hadn't.

'Evie Pascoe.'

'What about her?' Derwent snapped.

'Do you know who she was?'

'She was Peter's girlfriend and she disappeared. We found her body in the septic tank behind your house.'

'Guess who had an alibi for that.' Leo's dark eyes were fixed on mine, his smile teasing the corners of his mouth.

'You?'

'Oh, I did. Definitely. I was in prison.' Leo grinned. 'No, Peter did. He was somewhere up north when she disappeared. So tell me something, missy. Who put Evie in the septic tank?'

'Why don't you tell me?'

'I don't know. Not for sure. But I know one thing. Kelly does whatever Peter tells him to, just like me. He might not look like me or talk like me but underneath it all, he's the same.'

I was cold with horror. Kelly had vomited when they asked him about his brother, and shook from fear, and we had all assumed he was scared of what his brother would do when we found him – not of what his brother would *say*.

'Did you think Kelly was the good one and Peter was the bad one?' Leo laughed. 'That would be too easy, wouldn't it? No, it was never that simple. What Peter said was that Kelly always wanted Evie. He didn't like that she preferred Peter, but she did. He was older and serious. Quiet, like. Kelly was more outgoing but that didn't do it for her. And it drove him mad.'

He wanted the girls who he couldn't have, Derwent had said, and I had argued with him about it.

They say kids are a blesing I think they brake your hart

'But you'll never prove it now. Too long ago. All I can tell you is hearsay.'

355

That grin again.

'So Kelly's all right, isn't he?'

After the interview I dragged myself back to the security desk, thoroughly depressed, and gathered up my belongings.

'Nothing we can do about Lambert.' Derwent was filing his belongings into his pockets. 'Assuming it's true and not Leo's way of fucking with us.'

'With me,' I said. 'That was designed to get a reaction from me.'

Derwent shrugged. 'Could have been. Could have been the truth too.'

I stayed silent until we were walking out of the prison.

'The stuff he said about Kelly – I'll pass it on to whoever's looking after her case but I can't see them being able to take it further. He won't be charged, will he?'

'Unlikely.'

'No justice for Evie Pascoe.' I thought I sounded matter-of-fact, but Derwent glanced around at me with that quick compassion that always disarmed me.

'You did the best you could. All the way through. Whatever happened, none of it was your fault.'

'Peter Lambert died because I couldn't wait half an hour to talk to his foster mother.'

'Peter Lambert died because he was trying to kill you. Even the IPCC said it was good shooting.' Derwent stopped and took hold of my arm, turning me to face him. 'You don't need to feel guilty about him, if you do. Remember what he did.'

'I do remember it. I think about the women, often.' I was shivering. 'What if there were others? Why would he stop, because his father was in prison? What if he changed his MO? Or went back to the kind of women no one misses? Sex workers or immigrants or homeless kids? What if there's another body dump somewhere and we just haven't found it yet? Maybe he would have confessed, if we'd arrested him.'

'Let it go.' Derwent shook me, but gently. 'You didn't let anyone down.'

'Thanks,' I mumbled. I couldn't look at him. 'I thought you were angry with me.'

'I was.' He was silent for a moment. 'I thought you were completely out of order. I didn't want to admit I was in the wrong. But I thought about it and I can see why you mind.'

'Can you?'

'Yes, of course. It's a compliment to me, really,' he said, moving backwards in the direction of his car. 'You were shocked I lied to you. That shows you trust me.'

'Trusted you. Not any more.'

'Oh, you'll be wary for a while. But you know I have your best interests at heart.'

'I know nothing of the kind,' I snapped.

'You'll thank me one day.'

'For interfering and lying to me? I think not.' I squared my shoulders, because what I had to say needed to be said. 'You did the wrong thing, even if it was for the right reason. And you need to stay out of my personal affairs. It's not appropriate for you to be so involved in my life.'

He looked wounded. 'I thought we were friends.'

'We are. But from now on, if I want you to be involved in my personal life, I'll ask you for help.' *Stand your ground, Maeve.* 'Otherwise, you stay out of it. We don't talk about it. You don't ask about it.'

'Fine.' He sat into the driver's seat and concentrated on adjusting the mirror.

'Promise me.'

A sigh. 'OK. I promise. Your life is your own business. And when you *obviously* need my help, I'll wait for you to ask.'

'Now we're getting somewhere.'

He started the engine. 'I want you to be happy, you know.'

'I know. But it's not up to you to make me happy.'

For a moment I thought he was going to say something

357

else, but he nodded instead, and shut the car door, and drove away as I stepped back to avoid the spray of gravel and rainwater thrown up by the tyres.

There was a message on my phone when I got around to looking at it, and I tapped to open it. A photograph appeared on the screen: a stranger with familiar eyes. I called the sender back.

'Hey.' I could hear the smile in his voice, and it made me smile too.

'I can't believe you got rid of the beard.'

'You said it was a deal-breaker.'

'Well, it tickled.'

'So it's gone,' Seth said easily, as if it wasn't a big deal to make a dramatic change like that after precisely three dates, all of which had taken place in his flat because he was still more or less housebound. 'Are you OK to come over?'

'I'll be there in an hour.'

'I'll cook.'

'I'm not hungry,' I said, and he laughed, and hung up.

I walked back to the car and threw my things into the boot, and with every step the gloom lifted a little more. There was more to life than work. The past was one thing; the future was another.

An hour, I'd said.

I made it in fifty minutes.

Acknowledgements

Thanks as ever to the tremendous team at HarperCollins, especially wonder-editor Julia Wisdom and Kathryn Cheshire, and the eagle-eyed copy-editing of Anne O'Brien.

Thanks to all at United Agents, truly a great collection of people, and in particular my brilliant agent Ariella Feiner and her assistant Molly Jamieson.

Huge thanks to my readers for waiting *fairly* patiently for this book. Most of the threats of violence were aimed at my characters, which I appreciate.

This book simply would not exist without the love and support of my family: James, Edward, Patrick, Frank and Alison, Kerry, Michael and Bridget and many others who lent their time, their advice and their practical kindness through difficult days. I'd particularly like to thank John Cummins, a true gentleman and friend.

In London, I had the benefit of tireless support and friendship, particularly but not solely from Claire Graham, Alison Gleeson and Sarah Law.

Katy Lunn and Jenny Palmer Eriksson lent me their names for characters in this book. The ones I invented aren't as remarkable as these two very special women.

In all the places, virtual and real, where the crime-writing community gathers, I found good advice, great loyalty and the darkest jokes known to man. They always know the right thing to say, especially if that thing involves creative swearing.

I'm always awed by the time and effort put in by bloggers and book fans; it's all appreciated. I'd like to single out Rick O'Shea for running his phenomenal book club, and many book events, with tireless enthusiasm and engagement.

Finally, but most importantly, I'd like to thank Sinéad Crowley and Liz Nugent, who are the very best of people. I speak to them almost every day but somehow never get to say how much I appreciate them, so this book is dedicated to them, with love.